GW00393935

A
Second Chance

Marcia Whitaker

To Marie,
Congrats my friend!
An American
author to a British
author. To success
Marcia W.

Cover design and photography by David Whitaker
https://DaveWhitakerPhotography.smugmug.com

Visit my website at www.MarciaWhitaker.com or
Through Facebook at https://www.facebook.com/MarciaWhitakerAuthor
Email at MarciaWhitakerAuthor@gmail.com

PUBLISHER'S NOTE

For my husband, David G., and boys, Seth and Tyler

Thank you. Without your support, encouragement, and patience, I would have never achieved my dream.

L.B.

IN MEMORY OF

My cousin, Eileen, who lost her battle with brain cancer on 6/28/16.
Heaven has another angel.

ACKNOWLEDGMENTS

I would like to thank the following for their tireless input without whose help this book would never have been completed.

Thank you for your patience and guidance, your use of the editor's red pen...

Samantha Stroh Bailey and Erin Foster, my wonderful editors, extraordinaire. Your suggestions were exactly what I needed at a time when giving up sounded more plausible.

With deepest love to my husband, Dave, who was instrumental with his nonstop encouragement to me in the writing of this book. He read every page twice and was my greatest critic.

Huge thanks to my Betas -

Courtney Kelly. What can I say? Courtney was instrumental in the final beta read of "A Second Chance." Without her guidance and fact checking, I'm not sure the book would have gone to print.

To my sister-in-law, Mary Rumsey and sister, Sandi Flagler, who all gave me my first read.

To the Peregrine Pointe Betas -

Sheila Bowling, Jo Tranter, Kathy Haycock and Ember Lambert. Thank you from the bottom of my heart.

To the management at the Buckhorn Exchange. Bill Dutton, thanks for letting me use your name, even though I took liberty in changing it slightly. And Christopher Murray, thanks for the enlightening chat and beverage.

And lastly, The George Noory Coast to Coast AM Show for sparking my interest and giving me the idea.

If I've forgotten anyone, just know I am forever grateful.

Prologue

August 11, 2017

Julian

The hair stood up on the back of my neck, again. It was the same inexplicable sensation I felt whenever Amber was near.

A framed photo of the sweetest girl I'd ever known sat in its rightful place on the corner of my desk. As I entered my office on the ninth floor of the Denver Medical Center, a burning persistence flowed through my veins. Unable to keep her out of my thoughts—especially today—where she continued to invade my mind, body, and soul.

I'd been at the hospital since four in the morning. My feet were beginning to ache, my back hurt and my head throbbed, but nothing some ibuprofen couldn't cure. Unfortunately, I agreed to guide a tour for the new class of first-year college students this afternoon, prolonging the day.

I rounded my desk and settled into my chair, reflecting on the fact that today was my thirty-fifth birthday. Coincidentally, my first date with Amber happened on this day nineteen years ago, setting into motion a relationship few have ever known. (Suffice it to say, I'm still discovering sand in my butt crack all this time later.)

It sounded cliché, but it was love at first sight. She was beautiful, witty, intelligent, sexy and kind, not to mention, caring...Christ, she was caring. With a quiet grace about her, she'd become the love of my life. At the time, we were teenagers but experienced more than most people twice our age. I laughed to myself—my age *now* was twice our age then.

I loved staring at her and memorized every curve. I had no idea a girl could have such a perfect body. Then and now, just thinking of her aroused me. She amazed me in every sense of the word.

We shared our hopes and dreams for the future. But our future never happened.

Amber died in my arms on August 2, 1999. I hoped I would never have to go through the horrendous pain I felt that day ever again. Sometimes I wondered how I got through it. I still found it hard to believe she was gone. *Forever.*

Understanding her fate, she selflessly told me to move on with my life. At the time, I didn't know how to do that without her. For all intents and purposes, I still don't.

I missed her long, golden blond hair cascading in soft curls down her back. I missed her stunning, arctic blue eyes, both haunting and beautiful at the same time. They looked deep into your soul, as though she saw every immortal reflection. I missed her fiery spirit when she stood up to me. I chuckled at the thought.

Because I promised her I'd work toward becoming a successful neurosurgeon, dammit, I was determined to follow through and make her proud.

Amber whispered to me in her affectionate way, sweet and unassuming, *Julian, you must promise me you will realize your dream of becoming the doctor you've always envisioned, and know that I'll always love you.*

It was her unyielding strength that pushed me to succeed beyond all barriers in my way.

"I will always love you, too," I echoed her sentiment.

Her last words have confounded me for eighteen years. She lay limp in my arms, struggling to push the sound from her tender, soft lips—something about seeing me again and my destiny. Even though an effort for her to speak, she also mumbled something about the number eighteen. Everything came out a breathy slur, difficult to understand. Holding her in a tight embrace with tears streaming down my face, I reassured her; I would most definitely see her again. She smiled and then gently slipped away.

Why would she be so concerned with my destiny while she fought for her next breath? Christ, this was so completely like Amber—always thinking of others to the end.

Eighteen years had passed since her death. I treasured those memories of her beautiful smile when I stared at the photograph of her on my desk. With her head propped in the palms of her hands, she lay on her belly in the tall grass. Her elevated bare feet locked together at the ankle behind her. An innocent smile touched her lips—the way I would always remember her. It was my favorite photograph showing off her intense, electric blue eyes. I captured her forever on film that day on one of our many visits to Windsong Lake.

I ignored the disturbance outside my door and leaned back in my chair staring at the name plate on my desk: DR. JULIAN H. CAHILL, NEUROSURGEON. Then it occurred to me; that's how I got to where I was today. I did it for her. I did it *all* for her. I placed all my efforts into my studies. Between the four years of undergraduate work, four years of medical school, and seven years of residency, it should've been obvious. If it wasn't, passing the Medical Licensing Exam and becoming board-certified made it so.

In my inbox from the week before, I'd received an email from the AMA board of trustees naming me the recipient of an American Medical Association's award—the highest honor in my field. All my hard work and perseverance had finally paid off. The awards banquet wasn't for another month, but because of my busy schedule, there'd be little time to focus on a written speech. Though, I'd pull it off. I always had in the past.

I let out a satisfying breath. "Please tell me I've made you proud, Amber Lynn Scott."

In retrospect, I always knew when she was near—both in life and death. I closed my eyes and tipped my head back against my chair recalling a day years ago when the connection with her was the strongest I'd felt since her death. It happened during my second year of residency. I'd been working the evening shift when two siblings were brought in after a car accident. Sadly, the teenage boy died, but his younger sister—a little blond girl—suffered a head injury...

"Hi, I'm Dr. Cahill." I leaned over the gurney and looked into her bloodied blue eyes.

In her small, frightened, ten-year-old voice she asked, "Where's my brother?"

"He's in the next room," I told her. I would let her parents break the sad news to her.

She lifted her hand to her head and winced in pain. "It hurts right there." She pointed to the area above her right ear.

"Okay, let me take a look." I put my hand on her forehead and the hair lifted on the back of my neck. The same electrical jolt felt whenever I believed Amber was near. Yes, she was here to comfort this child. Caring...even in death.

AFTER THE STUDENT TOUR, I was heading to Castle Pines and joining my parents for a birthday celebration. Being Friday, I had the weekend to recoup. *Maybe I could hit the gym before dinner.*

My colleague pushed this tour on me last minute after he agreed to swap with one of my assigned conferences the following week. Given that I already had another engagement today, this session was a major inconvenience.

Celebrating my birthday always left a bitter taste in my mouth but my parents insisted. I looked forward to my visits, even though it meant I'd be bombarded with questions regarding my relationship status. Christ, I hated those questions; mostly because I wanted the answers to them myself. Still, it was exasperating.

Castle Pines, an affluent suburb, used to be my childhood hometown before relocating to the Denver area, closer to the hospital.

The ever-growing village sat in the foothills of the Colorado Rocky Mountains—a place I spent many days hiking to clear my head of the demands of life. It offered the quiet security of a gated community along with the feel of an upscale metropolitan area and, of course, it brought back pleasant memories of Amber and me. Her family moved in next door three weeks before the start of our junior year of high school. I couldn't take my eyes off her. And as luck would have it, she felt the same way about me.

I remembered how grief-stricken the Scott family was following Amber's death. Considering how unbearable the pain was for me; I couldn't imagine their heartache and misery.

Since I'd be in the neighborhood, I contemplated the thought of swinging by to see Lyle and Elizabeth. I made a point of visiting them whenever I was in the area, but my trips to Castle Pines were too infrequent to keep me in the loop of everyday happenings. I thanked my parents for their lengthy updates via email.

I jerked my head back to the buzz of my phone vibrating on the surface of my desk. By the sound, I knew it was an incoming text.

Sarah: Happy Birthday, sexy! Haven't seen you in a while. Are you ignoring me? Want to get together tonight?

I loosened my tie, stretched my neck, and grabbed hold of a pen lying on top of some paperwork. Flustered, I began tapping it on my desk. Each tap sounded like a ticking-time-bomb going off in my head.

Rubbing my temples with one hand, I typed out a response with the other.

Me: Thank you. Busy tonight, maybe tomorrow. I'll let you know.

She responded immediately.

Sarah: Is something wrong?

I stared at her text. Was something wrong? According to Sarah Andrews, we'd been a couple for two months. But she wanted something I was unable to give her—a commitment. Not because she wasn't my type—blue eyes, blond hair, nice ass, and great in bed, but I didn't love her. That fear of loss I went through with Amber gripped me, preventing me from finding any solid enjoyment with Sarah or any other woman. Not for lack of trying. No one ever measured up to Amber and it pissed me off. I was sabotaging my relationships and couldn't move forward. It wasn't like I didn't have the opportunity; females were appearing out of the woodwork, falling all over me.

Sarah was different though. She was beautiful, kind, soft-spoken, and awkwardly clumsy which was how we met. She'd fallen out of a chair and hit her head, knocking herself unconscious. I'd been the neurosurgeon on duty when she was brought in by ambulance with a deep gash to her head.

Ever since, I've teased her mercilessly about her lack of coordination, never wasting a moment demonstrating how to sit properly in a chair. She looked beautiful when she scowled at me. But…she wasn't Amber.

Amber was the only girl who made my heart pound. She sent electricity through me with her touch. I never felt those feelings with other women. Could Sarah stir those feelings in me again?

Besides, completing my medical degree had always been at the top of my priority list and, without a doubt, my education took up the bulk of my time.

I answered her text.

Me: Just busy. I'll call.

My phone buzzed again.

Sarah: Okay, later.

"DR. JULIAN CAHILL, please come to the front desk of the Neurology Unit." The public address system buzzed as I dropped my phone into my shirt pocket. The new freshmen class had arrived for their tour.

The wheels of my leather chair squealed when I pushed back away from my desk and stood up. I shook my head and stole another quick glimpse of Amber's photo, which, in turn, reminded me of the bright multicolored ring on my right hand. I promised her I'd never take it off and ultimately, never have.

With a heavy sigh, I kissed my index finger, lowered it to the photograph, and brushed it across her lips, silently wishing I had one more day with her. A cold shiver gripped me as I proceeded out the door of my office and strolled down the hall to the main desk.

Admittedly, I'd always wanted my own practice outside the sterile, pungent odor of the hospital, but the head of human resources offered me a salary I couldn't refuse in exchange for three years of employment. Soon, I would relocate my office elsewhere, away from this smell of death and tapioca pudding. But this wouldn't happen for another year or so. And who knew where my life would be then. Still, I continued to look forward to fewer demands of my time.

"Hi, Dr. Cahill, the incomin' Neurology class is here and waitin' fir their tour," announced head nurse Hayes.

Her Alabama roots were still prominent in her accent despite the fact she'd worked the main desk of the neurology floor for twenty years. She's been the most highly skilled nurse on the staff for years.

"Thank you, Maribelle."

I turned my head and introduced myself. "Welcome to Denver Medical Center. My name is Dr. Julian Cahill, and I'm one of the neurosurgeons on staff here."

With a circular swing of my arm, I motioned for the group to follow me. I walked to the end of the west corridor and stopped outside the Neurological Rehabilitation Unit. I turned my tall frame around and grinned, noticing a nervous and fidgeting group, consisting of twelve males and three females. My thoughts transported me back to my tour of this very hospital seventeen years ago. I experienced as much enthusiastic allure then as I did today. I loved my work and immersed myself in it. Maybe it was a means to an end with a hope to help forget the past. However, as hard as I tried, it didn't happen.

"This unit is a fifteen-bed inpatient rehab unit specializing in patients with neurological injury, surgery, or illness," I explained. "Right now, it is at capacity."

There were a couple of raised hands from the group. In detail, I answered each question even as the unit buzzed with activity while patients wrestled through a regimen of rehab tasks.

I carried on with the tour, walking to the East corridor. "This is the Neuroscience and Stroke Unit. It is a thirty-bed unit which provides care to individuals with neurological symptoms associated with stroke, neurological disease, and post-surgical observation."

Granting them full access to each unit, and answering all questions aimed at me, I paused, remembering when I brought Amber here for her treatments. She was physically weak, yet so emotionally tough. I held her hand while the doctors pumped the toxic medicine into her veins. I think she knew her fate, how futile her treatments became, and only did them for my benefit. I never let on that I knew. Even the familiar smell of antiseptic still lingered in the stale air, invading my nostrils.

Forty-five minutes later, all fifteen students had a better idea of what the field of neurology held in store for them. They looked overwhelmed—a deer in the headlights kind of overwhelmed.

After briefing them with a detailed handout—with an explanation of each unit—I thanked them for their interest and wished them luck with their future endeavors.

Traditionally, before concluding my tours, I insisted the group introduce themselves, yet I hesitated, knowing my parents were expecting me within the hour. Nonetheless, today would not be different. Despite the delay, I turned my gaze to the gentleman on the left, indicating to start with a nod of my head.

"I'm Michael Silvera from Littleton, Colorado."

"My name is Alexis Erikson, and I'm from Salt Lake City, Utah."

One by one, they proclaimed their names and hometowns until reaching the last girl on the right. Why hadn't I noticed her before? I nearly lost my balance and stumbled backward at the sight in front of me. My eyes made contact with hers as she opened her mouth to speak and hastily closed it again. She sucked in a deep, shaky gasp. Despite being unable to utter a syllable, she stared at me with her bright blue eyes. A color so hauntingly familiar, I felt as though she was peering into the depths of my soul.

My body trembled while I struggled for my next breath. A burst of electricity between us left me dazed.

Her long, golden blond hair cascaded down her back, a familiar beauty that completely entranced me. I felt weak, my knees buckling. My breath caught in my throat as my eyes did a double take. I wanted to touch her, just to make sure I wasn't dreaming. She could've been my sweet Amber's clone.

"Destiny Bradshaw from Boulder, Colorado," she said, sighing with relief when she finally found the strength to finish.

What the hell just happened here?

PART 1

Chapter One

Nineteen Years Earlier - 1998

Amber

Whoa! My sister caught sight of me staring at the gorgeous guy shooting hoops next door when I bent down to grab another box from the trunk of the car.

The evil glare of Robin's deep-set, hazel eyes followed my gaze. "You know, he's probably a conceited ass," she huffed. "You're a beautiful, strong-willed and confident girl, Amber. You've never taken crap from anyone and could date whoever you wanted—so why him?" Her focus moved back and forth between him and me.

I grabbed her arm and turned her to face me. "Why not him? You're basing your opinion on your own insecurities. You don't even know him. How can you make assumptions like that?"

She ran a hand through her wavy, shoulder-length, caramel-colored hair. "Jeez, Amber, we've just moved across the country, and you're already drooling over some jock, not to mention he's obviously our next door neighbor. I can't believe you're even entertaining the idea of approaching him. Haven't you learned from what happened to me?" She shook her head, lifted a box labeled "living room" from the back seat and headed for the house in a snit.

Here we go again.

It wasn't that long ago when I comforted my older sister over her latest failed relationship. Robin was inconsolable. She learned firsthand how hurtful high school athletes could be after one nearly broke her in two. Inevitably, this made her skeptical of all of them. Since then, she has tried to convince me they were all total scumbags. It all started then. She dated Halfmoon High School football quarterback, Johnny Rhodes, for two years before she found him cheating on her with one of the varsity cheerleaders. She has continued to approach every athlete with an unwavering disgust ever since. Later, when he came groveling back to her, she wanted nothing to do with him, effectively shooting him down like a clay pigeon at a skeet shooting competition.

Get out of my life! The answer is no! I don't want you back…ever! He never had a chance. I admired her tenacity, but on the other hand, we were polar opposites.

I drew in a deep breath and released it. "Well, if you haven't noticed, I'm a sixteen-year-old girl, who's just enjoying the glorious view in front of me."

Staring at him had me hoping it would lead to something more. I wished Robin would move on and get over her past loss, which kept dragging her down like a pair of knee socks with worn-out elastic. It always came up anytime I so much as glanced at a nice looking guy. Did I even have a chance with her constant interference?

"Robin, what happened to you could've happened to anyone. It wasn't just because he was a good-looking athlete. Get over it already." I let out an exasperated sigh and followed her to the house with a boxful of pots and pans. "How do you even know he's into sports?"

"Oh c'mon. You can see him playing basketball, right? He's gorgeous, and he's obviously working out for some reason." She set the box down on the dark cherry hardwood floor of the living room and walked back to the open door. She crossed her arms over her chest and tapped her foot on the stone floor of the foyer. "Cripes, just look at him." She pointed her index finger in his direction. "He must have every girl in the high school drooling over him; hell, probably some of the guys too." She burst out in laughter.

Shaking my head at her ridiculous assumption, I thought about her words. What if he was gay? No, I refused to even consider that a possibility. I made a tsking sound with my tongue at her and carried the box of rattling cookware to the kitchen. The clanging of the pots and pans within heightened my frustration with Robin. "Very funny!" I yelled. "You're entitled to your opinion!"

Our tiffs were always about guys. It became a ritual for her, always looking out for my best interests, even though her disapproval of him wouldn't make a difference to me. It never had with any others.

I threw my hands in the air. "I give up." I needed to get away before I said something I'd regret.

Taking two steps at a time, I made my way upstairs to my bedroom at the end of the hall. The smell of fresh paint instantly invaded my nostrils when I walked through the door to a heap of clothes on the floor. Wrinkled dresses, blouses, and slacks laid there in a pile in the center of my room, waiting for hangers. So, I promptly began organizing my enormous walk-in closet.

After the last piece of my wardrobe was put away, I paced endlessly, wearing a circular pattern in the golden-colored carpet thinking about my last boyfriend, Danny Bochner. Absentmindedly, I touched my lips. Danny was a good kisser. We dated for two months and did everything together. One such memory came to mind. We'd attended a Red Hot Chili Peppers concert and it poured that night, creating a mud bath, soaking us to the bone. Mud covered the ground everywhere, so we dove into it. I never laughed so hard in my life. Though, our parents weren't so happy when they came to pick us up. Yes…Danny was fun. When he started pressuring me to have sex, I dumped him. I was on the pill (only to regulate my period,) so it wasn't a case of getting pregnant. I couldn't imagine losing my virginity to someone I didn't love. Danny screwed that all to hell and he regretted it. All that happened right before my family moved across the country from upstate New York to here in Castle Pines, Colorado.

Did I make a big mistake with Danny? Maybe I shouldn't have been so impulsive. No, that wasn't who I was. Jeez, now I'm arguing with myself.

The window of my bedroom faced out at the front of our house where, once again, my eyes led me to the mysterious guy still shooting baskets next door. I settled my focus on him once more. What a remarkable physique. I couldn't pry my eyes away. With broad shoulders, and slicked-back, golden blond hair with a slight wave to it—long enough to touch his shoulders—he radiated pure masculinity. He was no Danny. At a little under six feet, Danny's crew cut, jet-black hair, and thin frame were no match for this guy.

I wanted to run my hand down his six-pack abs, as he trounced around the chalk-drawn basketball court, making every shot he attempted. From my distance, I couldn't see his face, so the color of his eyes eluded me, but I'd been close enough to know he was worth a second glimpse. At five-foot-nine-inches, and taller than average for a sixteen-year-old girl, I could see I'd be gazing upward into his eyes. My draw to him on some ethereal level was beyond anything I could comprehend. No…he was no Danny.

I headed back downstairs and outside to grab the last box from the car as I shot a glimpse around the aspen tree-lined street of our neighborhood.

Thick fluffy clouds floated by in the cobalt blue sky on this breezy August day. A lawn mower roared from across the street and filled the air with the scent of freshly mowed grass. Mr. Lawnmower Man waved to me. I waved back.

The neighborhood had curb appeal as well. Separating us from the neighbor to the left were two very tall pine trees—a height I'd never seen before. A few dead branches on one suggested it might be struggling for life. On the right, between the good-looking guy's house and ours, one lone maple tree stood poised and proud, waving its waxy green leaves in the warm breeze. It reminded me of the colorful maple trees of the northeast. Suddenly, I couldn't wait for autumn.

From the back seat of the car, I clutched the last box labeled "kitchen," turned and met Mr. Great Looking's eyes staring back at me. My breath caught in my throat, and my body tingled all over. Could he be attracted to someone like me—blond, blue-eyed and slender? I also considered myself somewhat intelligent. Some guys felt put off by that. I refused to act dumb in front of any guy, so I hoped he'd be okay with it.

He thrust out his chest and smiled. I gave him a little wave and nearly fainted when he waved back. A thousand fluttering butterflies instantly materialized in the pit of my stomach.

Say something. Ask him his name.

I couldn't move my lips. The inability to speak was foreign to me, but today my throat seized up. I was mute, too afraid to ask. His beauty flabbergasted me. I must have looked like a bumbling idiot. Why was I drawn to him? What were his interests? His age? How would I approach him? I had so many questions in my head but uttering any of them seemed an impossibility. *Way to not act dumb, Amber. Jeez.*

Embarrassed, I trudged up the sidewalk and made a beeline to the house. Before going inside, my eyes took one final glance at him on the other side of the hedgerow. Would my new found track skills land me over that barrier in one fell swoop? It appeared the right height for me to scale without too much difficulty and dive into his arms. I chuckled. I could stretch my legs, but graceful coordination was not part of my repertoire. I imagined falling flat on my face. Being most vigilant of my accident-proneness, I'd regret the attempt and so would he. I shook my head of my wayward thoughts and went inside, cursing myself all the while. Now he probably thought I wasn't interested. Nothing could be further from the truth.

"Bring that box in here, honey," Mom called from the kitchen. She was putting the utensils away into the silverware and cutlery drawers.

"Sure, Mom. I'm so happy to be here. Driving across the country in four days was exhausting. Except, I miss my friends, already." I couldn't hide the melancholy in my voice.

"You've never had a problem making new friends. You're outgoing and very likable. You'll be okay." Standing at the sink wringing out a sponge, she started wiping down the counter. "Have you seen your bedroom?"

If she was trying to cheer me up, it worked.

"Yep. Love it."

My mom and I shared similar looks—blue eyes and blond hair. Because of a childhood accident, of which I'd never heard the actual story, she harbored a scar over her left eye. Even with this tiny flaw, my mom was still beautiful, inside and out, and the best storyteller I'd ever known. When Robin and I were younger, we favored her bedtime stories to any of those from a book.

"You sure?"

"Uh huh. When do you start your new job at Walgreens?"

"Next week."

"Are you the head pharmacist there?"

"Yes. Why do you ask?"

"No reason," I said. "There's a guy playing basketball next door I wouldn't mind meeting. Did you see him?"

She began scrubbing the fridge and turned to me with her level stare. "No, I've been in the kitchen all afternoon. Why don't you go introduce yourself?"

Tracing my fingertips along the edge of the dark granite countertop, I looked at her and shrugged my shoulders. "I'm too nervous." Just the mention of him made my stomach quiver.

"What?" she exclaimed, running a hand through her pixie hairdo. "Why?"

"I don't know. For some reason, he intimidates me."

"Oh honey, that doesn't sound like you." She pulled her oval glasses down and looked at me over the rims.

"I know, I can't explain it."

"What about Danny?" she asked.

My mom was a soft shoulder to lean on when it came to those delicate issues where Robin and I were concerned, but I steered away from her advice in the "boyfriend" department.

I folded my arms, turned my head away from her and quickly changed the subject. "Did you see the view of the Rocky Mountains?"

"It's beautiful, isn't it?" she said, eyeing me skeptically. I could tell she knew what I was doing. She had that look I knew so well…narrowed eyes, scrunched face. But she never goaded me for more information than I was willing to give. I loved that about her. She would often test the waters but recognized when I wasn't ready to talk. She knew I would gladly share when I was ready, and I knew she would always be there for me.

"Daddy will be happy to see us when he comes home from work." I desperately missed my dad after he left New York the week before to start his job here. I checked the time on my watch. It was nearly four o'clock.

"Yes, he certainly will," Mom added. "He called and said he'd be here around five thirty."

HERE I WAS IN CASTLE PINES, Colorado, just three weeks away from starting eleventh grade in a school where I didn't know anyone. I would be lying if I said I wasn't scared.

I found myself standing in the living room, void of furniture, boxes covering the floor, and staring out the window. My eyes caught the beauty of the lone maple tree in the front yard. Nothing compared to the kaleidoscope of colors represented by maple trees in the fall.

I chewed the inside of my cheek repeatedly when my thoughts drifted back to school. What would my friends be like? Who would I sit with at lunch? What would I wear? Would I like my teachers? Would they like me? My head was reeling, and my palms began to sweat. I rolled my neck and shoulders around trying to get the kink out. It couldn't be that bad, could it? After all, the student body at Castle Rock High School exceeded my old school, Halfmoon High by nearly three hundred, making me certain that the circle of friends would be limitless.

But, I was a secure and grounded teenager who felt comfortable with the life she had in her old town. I had friends and popularity in my former school. The last thing I wanted to do was to uproot myself and move lock, stock, and barrel away from all that was familiar to me. What laid ahead for me here? I grimaced and shook my head.

"Man, this house is huge," Robin said, abruptly appearing in the room. From where?

"Yeah, I know. Did you see the size of our bedrooms?" A spontaneous giggle erupted from my lips. "I've already put my clothes away."

"Yeah, I wish my friends from back home could see this." She frowned, no doubt realizing the uncertainty of that.

"I guess we're moving up in the world!" Mom yelled from the kitchen.

Robin rolled her eyes. "For you, maybe."

MY DAD WALKED IN THE DOOR promptly at five thirty.

"Daddy!" I was the first to leap to my feet and greet him with a hug and kiss, followed by Robin.

"It's awesome seeing my beautiful daughters. You all made it," he said as he emerged from the kitchen into the living room, wrapping his muscular arms around us.

With thick, sandy-brown hair and dark, sapphire blue eyes, Lyle Scott was a quiet, reserved man. To him, a peaceful evening at home watching sports was always preferable to a night out with a loud crowd.

Releasing Robin and me, he scooped my mom into his arms and gave her a tight bear-hug.

"Hi. We've missed you," she said. They kissed chastely.

My forty-something parents had the kind of love between them that I hoped to have someday.

"Missed you too, Lizzy," he said.

My mom managed to scrape something up for dinner, and the four of us sat around the island eating, chatting and laughing the evening away. We told my dad about our long drive here while he filled us in on his new job. I felt a paradisiacal calm when he was home…all was right with the world.

Later that night, Robin and I sat on my bed chatting until midnight, exchanging views on guys, school, movies, and the latest clothing fads. She was a tad shorter than me, but I was a smidgen more curvaceous. I thought she was attractive—a bona fide beautiful—but she would often disagree. When the phone rang with guys asking her out—that was proof enough. I couldn't have played catch-up if I tried. She used to tell me in her unconvincingly way how I was more beautiful because I had blond hair. I rolled my eyes.

Before deciding to call it a night, she tried once again, to warn me away from the boy next door, but I wanted nothing to do with it.

I grinned at her. "You know your freckles glow when you scowl."

"Ha, ha. Very funny." She scrunched her face at me, got up from the bed and made the trek across the hall to her room.

In the quiet of the night, I slipped under the blankets of an air mattress on the floor of my bedroom. I stared at the four walls until drifting off in the late night, dreaming of a blond-haired hot male.

I AWOKE ABRUPTLY WITH A TREMOR. From outside, a loud rumbling made my windows rattle. Stretching my tired body from under the warmth of my blankets, I sat up to investigate the irritating disturbance. I padded to the window and noticed the truck with our furniture had arrived.

I glanced at the clock. "Ten! I've never slept that late."

I sprang into action, deciding on a quick shower. I dragged on a pair of blue jean shorts and white T-shirt embroidered with *Halfmoon High School* in forest green across the front, reminiscent of my old school. I pulled my hair back into a ponytail and stared at myself in the mirror. I never felt like I had self-esteem issues, but the girl glaring back at me stubbornly disagreed. I brushed my teeth and headed downstairs to help out, eager to have my real bed to sleep in again.

From a truck that looked larger than our house, two muscular men carried the TV cabinet into the house. Two others unloaded the sofa and dining room table and set them on the lawn.

Ah, finally somewhere to sit down.

My dad had already left for work while my mom was making a ruckus in the kitchen. Robin and I were browsing through boxes of knick-knacks in the living room when the doorbell rang.

"I'll get it! Our first visitor!" Robin screamed a decibel too loud for this early on a Friday morning...well, at least for me. Wearing a pink lacy tank top and boy shorts, she bounded toward the door. With my excitement mirroring hers, I glanced over as she pulled it open. In front of her was the most incredibly sexy guy I ever saw. It was him— Mr. Gorgeous, Hot Guy, Mr. Good-Looking—all rolled into one ravishingly handsome male. I took a step and froze, raising my hand to my mouth to stifle a gasp. Robin and I stared. He looked to be over six feet tall. Standing in our foyer, he was more beautiful up-close, in the flesh. Our jaws, hanging so low, would be scraping against the surface of the floor before long. Mr. Divine's probably second-guessing his decision to come over.

"Hi, I'm Julian Cahill. Welcome to the neighborhood," he said in a smoky, seductive, caramel-laced voice.

He speaks.

Julian Cahill, Amber Cahill. I tested out his name with mine. Okay, I didn't know him, but on some rudimental level, I wanted to marry this guy. Call it love at first sight. I shook my head. *What are you thinking, Amber?*

He turned and pointed in the direction of his house. "My family lives next door, and I was wondering if you needed any help moving heavy boxes."

My heart started to pound. *Help us?* Robin and I glanced at each other, undoubtedly looking to see if we shared the same feelings and erupted in giggles. Like a couple of idiots, we were so tongue-tied, that any effort to utter the slightest syllable was outright nonexistent. Mute again, I thought to myself. Jeez.

"Hi, Julian, I'm Elizabeth Scott." My mom rushed into the room from the kitchen—coming to save-the-day.

Oh, thank God.

She narrowed her eyes at Robin and me.

"Come in, dear. How lovely of you to lend a hand." She shook his hand. "This is Robin, and over there is Amber." She pointed to each of us.

Julian nodded politely and stepped into the living room. Our eyes met, causing an instantaneous electrical current to run between us. My hands began to feel clammy and my breath caught in my throat. I couldn't believe this beautiful guy was in our house…Looking at *moi.*

"Hi—Julian," Robin and I stuttered in unison. We both looked at each other wide-eyed. And like the teenagers that we were, burst into giggles, again.

He smiled, and I caught a glimpse of his beautiful blue eyes before he cast them to the floor. Yes, standing ten feet from me was a divinely, exquisite male, and I had cotton mouth.

My eyes prowled his body from head to toe. Wearing a V-neck white T-shirt and black shorts, Julian's muscular arms flexed by his side. His soulful, azure blue eyes, filled with a soft expression when they connected with mine. He had full lips and a strong, rounded jaw. My thoughts wandered, wondering what it would be like to kiss those lips. We had the same golden blond hair, too. He was the most gorgeous guy on the planet, possibly the entire universe.

Back straight, eyes forward, I made my way across the room, putting one foot in front of the other (praying I didn't trip) to greet him.

"It's nice to meet you," I squeaked, extending my sweaty palm to him. My voice cracked from the dryness in my mouth. He had that freshly-showered, musky, masculine scent. Oh, he smelled good.

"Likewise," he said, taking my proffered hand.

I felt nervous, my heart pounding outside my chest.

Robin met him with a firm handshake. "Saw you shooting hoops yesterday. Do you play for Castle Rock High?"

How did she regain her equilibrium so quickly? I couldn't believe she just asked him that. I suspected she was trying to prove a point to me. *Please say no, Julian.*

"Nice to meet you, Robin. I used to play basketball, but not anymore. School work and my job have taken priority. How 'bout you?"

Yes!

"Well if cheerleading counts as a sport, then yes, I used to do that at our former school."

"Yep, I think we can count that." He turned to me. "How about you, Amber? Do you play any sports?"

Oh my God. He's asking me a question. Voice, don't fail me now.

He shook my hand, looking at me with a gleam in his eyes as if he was trying to communicate something without words.

I cleared my throat. "I—I was also a cheerleader." My voice stammered.

"Cool, where did you move from?"

"New York," I responded quickly.

He jerked his head back. "Really...the city that doesn't sleep? I've always wanted to visit New York City."

"No, we lived in upstate New York," I said, finally finding my firm voice. "It was more of a suburban setting where we lived, much like here, but without the beauty." My smile was brazen wondering if he picked up on the double entendre.

He blushed. "What brought you here?"

He got it.

"My dad transferred to Denver for his job."

"Cool."

Robin butted in. "We vacationed here many times, and our parents fell in love with the area. I want to attend the University of Colorado next year. So, here we are," she said, not stumbling over a single word. How did she do that?

"Awesome, you'll love it here. I'm interested in CU, too," Julian said.

"That's great," Robin said and excused herself to join my mom as they continued to unpack the floor-to-ceiling boxes labeled "Living room." Her dismissal had me concluding that her "jocks are ass" issues seeped into her psyche once again. But I saw the look on her face when she laid eyes on him.

Can't fool me, sis.

Julian and I were left standing face to face in bumbling—albeit, thrilling, small-talk.

I caught him looking at my chest. Was he checking out my boobs? Was Robin right about him?

"Is that the name of your old high school?" he asked.

Phew, the sirens silenced in my head. Though, I felt a tiny bit disappointed. I hoped he was checking me out, too.

"Yes," I said, fidgeting with my thumbs. I clasped my shaking hands together behind my back to hide any further visibly awkward finger moments.

"I'd love to hear about your life growing up in New York sometime," he said.

I moved closer to him, closing the distance between us. "Love to."

Looking at me with a warm smile, Julian seemed so relaxed and confident, unlike me, resembling a puddle of goo. I smiled back. Could he be interested in *me*?

"I'd love to hear about your life growing up, too," I said, staring—hopefully undetected—at his perfectly chiseled body. My fingers ached to touch him.

"Born and raised in Castle Pines, Colorado." A proud smile spread across his face.

I melted at the sight.

Sliding his hands into his pockets and shifting from foot to foot, he asked where he could start helping. From across the room, my mom thanked him for the offer and motioned to start carrying boxes upstairs.

A few moments later, the movers appeared in the living room with my bed frame in tow.

"Follow us," I told them.

Julian and I grabbed a few boxes and directed the men up the stairs to my bedroom. We dropped the boxes on the floor while the burly men placed my ivory bed frame in the empty space along one wall. They left and returned moments later with my matching dresser, vanity, and nightstand, placing them where I directed.

"Would you like me to open this?" Julian asked, placing a box on the floor.

"Um...sure," I said, not knowing its contents. *This could get awkward.*

I watched, relieved when he tore open a box full of DVDs.

"In the closet. I'll go through that box later," I said and placed the small box I was carrying on the floor. "How old are you?" I blushed.

What a dumb question. Of course, he's much older than you. I mean, look at him.

"Sixteen. How old are you?"

My mouth dropped wide open. "Holy crap, we're the same age! I turned sixteen last May. Are you going into the eleventh grade?"

"Yep," he replied, looking like he just won the lottery.

"So am I." I couldn't believe the incredible luck just bestowed upon me. Glancing at his sculpted body, I couldn't believe he was only sixteen. "You must work out hard."

"Well, I make an effort to exercise every day," he said in a nonchalant tone. "I'm a bit of a health nut and like to stay active." He glanced awkwardly at me as his mouth turned up at the corner.

Nice.

As the afternoon wore on, Julian talked about his life with his dad and stepmom, Nancy. He said it wasn't always easy with her, but the close relationship with his father balanced it out. He shared stories of the places they visited and things they did. There was such a love and devotion in his voice. It made me smile.

We hauled the rest of the boxes from the living room upstairs while comparing stories of high school and our lives growing up in the east versus the west. Before I knew it, a competition ensued.

"But we have the best seafood." I widened my stance and planted my hands on my hips.

"We have the Rocky Mountains," he retorted.

"Fall foliage."

"No humidity. And sorry, but we have fall foliage here, too." His comebacks always topped mine.

I narrowed my eyes at him. "I'll give you that one. Umm, we have countless days of rain. Okay, that's not a positive one, but it was the best I could come up with quickly." I burst into giggles.

"Shall I go on? My list is endless."

"Okay, okay. You win."

"Besides," he said, looking at me with a corny expression that flittered across his handsome features, "it's a moot point because you live here now."

I bit my lip, trying not to giggle. "That is true."

Emptying a small box of jewelry that sat on my bedroom floor, I placed them in my vanity drawer. I turned and examined the layout of my furniture. I wanted something different. "I'm not sure I like my dresser against that wall. Will you help me move it over there?" I pointed to the adjacent wall.

He made a quick scan of my body, moving his eyes from head to toe. "Sure, you look somewhat muscular. Can you lift the other end, Amber?" He pinched the bridge of his nose, waiting for my reaction. I wasn't sure, but I thought I saw him smirking.

Creep!

"What are you implying? Admittedly, I'm not as strapping as you, but I can hold my own," I stated proudly and shook my head.

Lifting one end of the dresser, we moved it slow and steady.

Having demonstrated my strength, I stuck my tongue out at him.

He chuckled. "Cute…and so ladylike, too."

"Yup, that's me." I snorted.

We slid my bed closer to the window. Yes, from this spot, I could stare out the window…at him.

"You mentioned a job. Where do you work?" I asked as he watched me pad across the room and sit on the floor to empty another box. I didn't want him to see my legs shaking, either.

"I work in a body shop, restoring old cars for my friend, Chad. Did you have a job back in New York?"

"Yep, I had an after-school job as a swim instructor at one of the local fitness centers. I loved it. I taught three, four and five-year-olds the fundamentals of water safety and how to blow bubbles. Some of them already knew how to swim, so I just refined their technique."

"So, you're a decent swimmer yourself?"

"Yep, want to race me someday?" I tore my eyes from the box of trinkets and winked at him.

"Nah, I suck at swimming." He started swinging his foot back and forth, looking embarrassed.

You don't look like you could possibly suck at anything.

Over the course of the afternoon, I learned Julian was at the top of his class in academic rank.

The similarities between us were astounding. When I shared that I was second in my old school, we had a good laugh. I pouted when I mentioned the depressing thought that maybe my rank would drop at Castle Rock with more competition.

He rolled his neck and cleared his throat. "I really wouldn't worry about it."

"Are you dating anyone?" The words were out of my mouth before I could halt them. I couldn't believe I just asked him that.

His swinging foot suddenly went still. "Not really."

Huh?

"Oh, okay." My scalp prickled.

"What I mean is that I'm not dating anyone steady."

Oh.

Why did I feel uneasy now? Enough of that topic.

Julian lowered his head and said, "I have to head home."

Crap, me and my big mouth. It was evident he didn't want to talk about his past relationships, and now he wanted to leave. I tightened my lips together and scolded myself. My heart sank.

"My folks are taking me out to The Rusty Hammer for my birthday dinner," he added.

His Birthday? My mouth dropped open for the umpteenth time. "Is it your birthday today?" I squealed leaping to my feet, grateful he wasn't leaving because of me.

See, you were overreacting.

Julian turned a shade of scarlet. "Well, it's tomorrow actually, but we're celebrating tonight. It's not a big deal."

"Oh my God, Happy Birthday, Julian!" Bravery struck me when I found myself embracing him in a quick hug, taking him by surprise. I pushed away before he had a chance to respond. "The eleventh of August, huh? My mom's birthday was a week ago. You're both Leos."

"Thank you, Amber." He smiled and playfully touched my arm. "I love your name…a pretty name for a pretty girl."

"Aw, thank you." I blushed and tilted my head to the side giving him a genuine, honest-to-goodness, Amber-Scott-smile.

His breath hitched, looking dumbstruck. *Ah yes, my charms were working on him.*

"You're very welcome. I'll have to wish your mom a belated happy birthday on my way out."

"She'd love that."

I tore a piece of paper from my notebook, wrote my phone number on it and handed it to him. "Here, give me a call and maybe we can get together tomorrow or some other time…if you'd like." He took the paper, folded it and slipped it in his pocket.

Please call me.

"Okay, sounds like a plan."

I walked him down the stairs to the door. "Have a great birthday dinner and eat an extra slice of cake for me." I innocently brushed against him. "See you later."

His lips parted. "Thanks, I will."

My mom emerged from the kitchen. "Thank you, Julian, for all your help today."

"You're welcome. And happy belated birthday to you, Mrs. Scott."

"Well, thank you dear, and please call me Elizabeth."

Julian nodded, turned and left.

While I watched him hike across the front yard, past the maple tree and scale the hedgerow to his house, he spun around and gave me his ginormous smile. I gulped in shock. He turned the tables on me. I narrowed my eyes at him, and he chuckled. I smiled, rotating around in time to see Robin rolling her eyes.

"You're going to be sorry, Amber." Her tone was a warning. I ignored her.

My mood was not going to be affected by another one of her lectures. I arched my neck and went back upstairs. I was not in any frame of mind to hear her preach to me about any misguided advice. I continued unpacking as my thoughts drifted to Julian. He was extraordinary. Yes, amazingly gorgeous. I couldn't stop smiling. He summoned feelings in me I'd never felt before.

I continually fought the urge to touch him, run my nimble fingers through his silky golden hair and wrap my arms around his waist. Did he feel the same way about me? Perhaps he didn't. No, I dismissed that idea. My intuition told me different.

Still, I couldn't wait to see him again and glared at the phone, anticipating its ring. I looked forward to tomorrow. I felt confident and incredibly thrilled. My shoulders immediately relaxed. All the earlier knots in my stomach vanished. I was going to be okay.

Even though I'd only known Julian for less than a day, I wanted to buy him a combination thank you and birthday gift.

BACK HOME FROM THE NEAREST Walgreens drugstore in Castle Rock—a short five-mile trip from our house—where I bought the perfect present, some wrapping paper, and roll of tape. Since I only had my permit, Mom went along for the ride. It also gave her an opportunity to check out her future place of employment in the world of pharmaceuticals.

Before I escaped up the stairs to my room, she narrowed her eyes at me with concern. "Don't you think you're jumping in a little too fast, sweetheart?"

"I feel like I've known him forever, Mom. Besides, this is just a small thank you gift." I held it up for her.

With a gentle smile on her face, she nodded in agreement at my unusual purchase.

Chapter Two

Any attempt at sleep eluded me as the hope of a first date with Julian today made me restless.

I dragged my pajama clad body out of bed and began scrutinizing the setup of my room. It screamed "neat freak." In my head, everything had a place and needed to be there. The paisley-colored duvet cover of my bed matched the pillow shams, and my five stuffed animals faced forward, leaning against my four decorative pillows. Framed photos of my friends and me lined the surface of my dresser, and vanilla scented candles sat on my bed stand.

Robin appeared, and leaned against the door jamb as I finished unpacking a box of books, placing them on my desk.

"Hey, Sis, can you help me set up my bedroom? Love what you've done here."

"Sure, for my favorite sister…anything."

She rolled her eyes at me. "I'm your only sibling, silly."

"Then you're my favorite." I grinned and blew air kisses at her.

I dressed quickly and followed her across the hall to her room.

Our favorite pastime as little girls always found us playing dress-up with our mom and dad's old clothes, pretending to be a married couple, sometimes enlisting the help of the neighborhood boys to play the father.

We sat on the beige carpeted floor of Robin's bedroom and started going through cardboard tubes filled with posters of different rock bands. Robin found one of the Goo Goo Dolls. She climbed on her bed and hung the poster on the wall above the dark cherry headboard.

"I love Johnny Rzeznik. His raspy voice sends shivers down my spine. He's a total babe and such a hot guitarist," she said, fanning herself.

"I agree, especially the guitar riffs in the song, "Iris.""

She jumped down from the bed, wrapped her arm around me and simultaneously we burst into the song.

"You have such an excellent voice, Amber. You should consider joining a vocal group at school."

"Aw, thanks, Sis. Actually, I've thought about that."

"I'm serious," she said unrolling a poster of Metallica and pinning it to the wall between the two windows overlooking the backyard. "You'll be the envy of the entire school with that voice."

"Thanks again." I smiled with a brief nod. "Speaking of school, any final decisions where you want to go to college?"

"No, but I'm giving serious consideration to the University of Colorado in Denver or possibly Aspen University."

I admitted the thought of her leaving for school gave me the chills. She was my rock and my best friend. I needed her like I needed to breathe.

"I want to commute." She fixed her eyes on me through a lazy squint. "I'll miss you too much if I go away. Someone has to take care of you."

She practically read my mind, except the part about taking care of me. *Honestly.*

"I'm worried about you. I saw how you were ogling over Julian yesterday. Just be careful." She pressed her lips into a fine line. "I can give you a list of reasons why you should steer clear of him."

And just like that, the topic of conversation took a 180-degree turn.

I opened my mouth and closed it again, at a loss for words. She was frustrating, to say the least. "Are we rehashing this same old argument again? I thought we were talking about colleges."

She scooted across the room and sat down on a teal-colored, wingback chair. It was the prettiest shade of teal, but in her new room of green and beige, it didn't seem to fit the color scheme. She pulled her legs up, draping them over the chair's arm. "We were, but now we're discussing Julian."

Crap. Robin did this so well. "Look, I understand your concern, but I think I can take care of myself. Stop being a mother hen. And quit being so pessimistic."

She strummed her fingers on the arm of the chair and shook her head in annoyance. "I'm not pessimistic; I'm just a realist."

I rolled my eyes at her. "I like Julian, and I think he likes me, too, so you need to trust me to go with my gut on this."

I wasn't a pushover, and the thought of anyone walking all over me made my stomach churn.

She arched her brow at me. "So, tell me, what's he really like? He's seriously good-looking. I'm a little jealous."

I wanted to smack her. "You? Jealous of a gorgeous guy?" Had she changed her point of view in the last fraction of a millisecond? "Well, I have to agree, but his personality is even hotter. Like me, he's going into eleventh grade and is at the top of the class academically, so he's quite the brainiac, too."

"Wow, I wouldn't have expected that—intelligent *and* good-looking? Yum, a delicious combination." She swung her legs around, planting them on the floor, then grabbed a box and carried it to her closet.

Still seated on the floor, I leaned back on my arms and fanned my legs out in front of me. "You do realize you're being a hypocrite now, don't you?"

"If I can give you my two cents, I'll give you a break, okay?" Her tone had changed to something more serious. "But only until he does something to break your heart."

"Thank you, but I don't need you coming in to save-the-day. Besides, you make it sound like that'll happen."

Poking her head from the closet, she eyed me skeptically. "I don't know. I certainly hope not."

I sighed and stood, then meandered over to her bed. There, sitting on her pillow was a ratty old teddy bear I think she'd had since she was born. She wouldn't part with it. I felt sorry for the man who would someday marry her because he'd certainly play second fiddle to that damned stuffed bear. "When are you going to get rid of this?" I faced him toward her. "Jeez, he's falling apart."

"I love my one-eyed Teddy." She ran over and snagged him from my grip, embracing him with a tight hug.

Give me a break.

We spent the next couple of hours chatting and rearranging her bedroom to her liking.

"There, I like this. Thanks, Ambie." Robin grinned.

"You're very welcome, Robbie." We giggled.

JULIAN PHONED a little before noon.

"Hi, I'm glad you called," I said sweetly, my insides jumping with joy.

He cleared his throat and asked if I'd like to go out to lunch with him. "H-how's one thirty sound?"

"I'd love to. Where do you have in mind?" My awkward, squeaky voice reared its ugly head.

"We're going to my favorite restaurant. My dad will be driving us. I don't have my license yet, but hopefully next week after I take my driver's test."

"Cool."

"Did you finish unpacking?"

"Yes." I was practically mute again. I couldn't think of anything else to say.

"Okay, s-see you l-later," he muttered, as if nerves wracked within him, too.

I hung up with a ridiculous grin on my face.

I bounded up the stairs to my bedroom and sitting on my dresser, Julian's wrapped birthday present caught my eye. I hope he'd see the humor in it. It wasn't like me to go out and buy a present for some guy I'd met the day before, but somehow this felt right.

I showered and hunted down something to wear. From my dresser drawer, I pulled a pair of white capris and dragged them on. I slipped into a pretty pink loose fitting top, and my white thong sandals.

I brushed out my long hair, letting it flow down my back. I applied mascara to my eyes, gloss to my lips then stepped back from the mirror. I thought I looked pretty. Would Julian think so?

Anxiously, I made my way downstairs anticipating his arrival. When the doorbell rang moments later, my heart rate kicked up a notch.

The expression on Julian's face when I opened the door was nothing short of perfect. His mouth hung open like a baby waiting for the next spoonful.

"Whoa," he muttered with eyes roaming my body from head to toe. His hungry gaze made me feel cherished.

Wearing a pair of khaki shorts and white T-shirt, he looked like he just leaped from the pages of an *Urban Outfitters* catalog. Blazing warmth spread over my already overheated body. My breath left me in a rush.

Oh. My. God. He was so hot and sexy and beautiful.

I tilted my head to the side, practically drooling, and sighed. "You look good." His face went crimson.

I tried to look unaffected but was about to faint from swooning at the guy standing before me. His hair looked the same as it did the day before—wild and untamed. I liked it. How could someone be so hot? And he wanted to date me. How did I get so fortunate?

"Thank you, and you look nice yourself, actually quite pretty, Amber."

"Thank you, too." I blushed. *Damn.*

"Are you ready to go?" he asked politely.

"Yep, let me grab my purse and a sweater."

"Have fun, you two." Mom appeared from the dining room.

"We will," I said.

Julian opened the rear door of his dad's BMW for me, and I scooted across the seat, giving him room to slide in beside me. As hard as it was, I tried to stay calm. I took a deep breath and exhaled. He rubbed his hands down his shorts, as if to dry the sweat pouring from his palms. I know…mine were clammy as well. For whatever reason, that small gesture made me relax.

"I'm nervous, too," I said, trying to ease the butterflies swooping around in my stomach. "Hey, how was your birthday dinner last night?"

Julian puffed out a long breath. "Awesome, though, I'm officially sixteen today."

"Beat 'cha there."

"That you did. You told me your birthday was in May, but what day?"

"The fifth."

He looked like he was mulling something over in his head. Perhaps he was making a mental note, committing the date to his memory bank. Nope, my birthday would not be forgotten.

Julian's dad turned and smiled. "Hi, Amber, I'm Logan Cahill. It's nice to meet you. Julian tells me your family just moved from upstate New York." He reached over and shook my hand.

"Yes, we did. It's great to meet you as well, Mr. Cahill." I smiled.

I saw Julian's muscular, chiseled looks came from his dad. Logan was also a tall, well-built, handsome man. That was where the similarities ended. He sported light brown hair, slicked back away from his face with dark, blue eyes. Wearing a thick mustache with a touch of gray, he reminded me of a young Tom Selleck.

As he pulled out of the driveway, his eyes caught mine staring at him in the rearview mirror. I quickly looked away. Awkward moment alert.

I didn't know what the future held for me, but if it included Julian Cahill, I certainly hoped he looked as distinguished as his dad. I shook off my wayward thoughts. *Get a grip, Amber. You're getting way ahead of yourself.*

Julian's dad headed east along Castle Pines Parkway and took the entrance to Interstate 25 North toward the city of Denver.

Logan glanced at me from the rearview mirror. "I've been to Upstate New York a few times on business. What town did you live in?"

"We were from Halfmoon."

"Oh yes, I know that area. What does your dad do?"

"He's an engineer, I mean chemical engineer."

Mr. Cahill squinted his eyes and ran his fingers through his mustache. "Who did he work for?"

"A company called, Malta Silicone," I said.

"Really? Well, it's a small world, because that's where I did business."

"Wow, I'll have to mention that to him." I didn't know why, but I liked Mr. Cahill right away. Like Julian, he seemed like a quiet, soft-spoken, inscrutable man…the kind who protected their secrets well. But what did I know? I just met him.

"What's your dad's name?"

"Lyle Scott."

"Hmm, doesn't ring a bell to me."

"What do you do, Mr. Cahill?"

"I'm co-owner of Cahill Software, located right here in Denver. My company tests the engineering software used on computers around the world."

Wow! "Impressive." I could tell this was where Julian got his intelligence. "I'll have to call you if we have computer issues, then." I grinned.

"Absolutely." Logan chuckled.

After a comfortable silence, I turned to Julian. "Why is this place your favorite restaurant?"

"Other than the fact that it has great food, I know the owner."

"Oh?"

"Yup, you'll see."

THE NICKEL BISTRO, located along Broadway Boulevard, exuded an upscale feeling, reminding me of my neighborhood back in New York. The street buzzed with people out for a stroll, ducking into small shops along the way.

Sandstone brick and marble made up most of the building's outer structure, looking cozy and delightful. Of the many visits by my family over the years, I'd never seen this part of the city. We stayed closer to the mountains.

"I'll be so happy when I get my license and not have to be carpooled around by my parents," Julian said, opening the thick, wooden door of the restaurant, ushering me in.

"Your father is very nice. I like him."

"Yep. We get along great."

'60s rock-and-roll music was the welcoming theme as we entered *The Nickel*. The Beatles, "I Want to Hold Your Hand," boomed from a jukebox beside us. The bartender was preoccupied but still managed to greet us with a quick wave.

"Hey, Julian." His voice resonated from across the room to where we were standing.

"Hi, Mr. Nickels."

"Is he the owner?" I asked, glancing at an older man. He looked to be in his fifties, heavyset and wore a handlebar mustache.

"Yep, that's him."

"Cool."

The gentle touch of Julian's hand on my elbow made me shiver as the hostess escorted us through the café to a private booth in the far corner of the restaurant. The friendly, appealing atmosphere calmed me. Shiny oak floors and a stylish bar nestled along one wall made of dark, cherry wood gave the restaurant a feeling of warmth. The aroma of rich cuisine filled my nose.

A window overlooking an elegantly manicured courtyard, dotted with beautiful flowers, drew my attention to the foreground outdoors, while snowcapped mountains encompassed the distant landscape. A man and woman nuzzled together inside a white marble gazebo surrounded by a garden of colorful symmetry. I stared open-mouthed trying to imagine what Julian did to reserve this seating arrangement in such a short span of time. It was the best location in the house.

As if reading my mind, he explained, "I had a job mowing Mr. Nickels' lawn a year ago. He'd do anything for me and vice versa."

"This place is fabulous, Julian. However, the irony of the name isn't lost on me. Do I sense you might be a tiny bit strapped for cash?" I giggled.

Julian chuckled deviously. "Very funny. Edmund *Nickels* is the owner," he said, emphasizing his last name.

"Oh, so the name has nothing to do with the cost of a meal here?"

"No." He laughed.

As we sat down in the booth across from each other, my thoughts led me to my gift for him. Grabbing my purse, I reached in and pulled out the small present. "I bought you a gift. Happy birthday."

His face lit up with complete shock as I slid it across the table. He jerked his head backward examining the small package. Without taking his eyes off me, he slowly unwrapped the gift with his deft fingers. *How I would love those fingers on me.*

"It's a roll of Life Savers! Awesome! Thank you so much, Amber. This is very thoughtful." His eyebrows squished together, looking at me as if asking for an explanation.

"It's because you are a life saver, Julian, in more ways than you know. I didn't know how I was going to face a new year in a new school, but with you around, I'm sure I'll be fine." I was bound and determined to make him understand what his friendship meant to me.

Julian shrugged his shoulders and frowned. Had I said something wrong?

"What would you like to eat?" he asked, handing me a menu. He'd completely ignored my kind words. Maybe he felt uncomfortable receiving compliments.

Moments later, an attractive waitress with a high-pitched, shrill voice—staring a little too long at Julian—appeared at our table.

"What would you like to drink?" she screeched.

It was one of those instances where the voice didn't match the face. I think Julian picked up on it too, when we both peeked at each other above the menu and grinned.

"I'll have an ice water with lemon, and…" Julian pointed his chin, prompting me to go ahead and order.

"I'll have a cranberry seltzer if you have it," I said.

"Alright," Miss Shrill Voice said as she sashayed her ass in Julian's face and walked away. I giggled, watching him roll his eyes.

He looked up at me, his eyebrows deliberately raised. "That's a high-maintenance drink if I've ever heard of one."

I straightened my back and mock-buffed my fingernails on the front of my shirt. "Well, I'm a high-maintenance girl."

He cocked his head to the side. "Well, maybe I'll maintain you."

"Don't make promises you can't keep." I snorted dismissively.

He chuckled.

A few minutes later Miss Shrill Voice arrived with our drinks. "Are you ready to order?" she asked.

I decided on something light and tasty to calm the nerves in my stomach. "The shrimp salad for me, please," I said and took a refreshing sip of my cranberry seltzer. *Oh, this is crisp and delicious.*

After Julian ordered a hamburger, Miss Shrill Voice turned and made her way across the room, disappearing into the kitchen.

"Are you ready to order?" Julian mimicked her in a high shrieking voice.

With my mouth full of delicious ice-cold liquid, a giggle erupted from my belly, and sticky, red cranberry drink spurted through my nose all over the table. "Oh my God. My nose is burning. I'm so sorry." I couldn't stop laughing. "You nailed her voice perfectly," I chortled. Could this have been any more embarrassing? *Way to go, Amber. That should impress him.*

Julian broke out in hysterical laughter that echoed throughout the room. "Are you okay?" He grabbed a handful of napkins from the adjacent booth, gave one to me and used the rest to blot up the nostril soup from our table. My sides hurt from laughing. He was too funny.

"It stings, but I'm fine."

After regaining our composure, he asked if I liked to hike. "I know some great trails around here."

"Sure, I love hiking." I beamed. "I've been all through the Adirondack Mountains back in New York, and my family did some light hiking when we visited here."

Julian took a sip of his water and pointed out the window to the distant rocky slopes. "I'd love to take you up into those mountains someday."

"I'd love that. I also love biking. In fact, guess what?"

"What? Or do you want me to guess? We could be here all night then."

He had a great sense of humor. I tilted my head to the side and twirled my hair around my index finger. "Well, I can even ride a unicycle. How about that?"

He looked at me, eyes shining. "Impressive. I've never tried it."

"I perfected it by holding on and circling our car."

"Very ingenious."

"Well, I don't have a high IQ for no reason."

"Duly noted. I'll keep it in mind next time I need help with quantum physics."

"Smart ass." He always had an answer for everything.

Engaged in deep conversation, laughing and sharing childhood stories, we both jumped in unison to a loud crash. A waitress dropped an entire tray of drinks a few feet from our table. Broken glass scattered across the floor, narrowly missing my bare sandaled feet. She apologized, blushing as her puny eyes shifted to Julian. Great, another gawker. Of course, I was reminded of my own ogling of him the day before.

"Julian, is that you?" Batting her eyelashes at him, she completely ignored me. She had long, straight, auburn hair and piercing, dark, whiskey brown eyes. She'd be quite attractive if it weren't for the black lipstick and matching nail polish. Who was she, and how did she know Julian?

My eyes focused on the gothic owl tattoo on her right forearm as Julian asked, "Hey, how are you, Mitzi?" With a sideways smile on his face, he introduced me to his friend. "This is Amber Scott. She just moved here from New York."

With a quick, repugnant glance toward me, she mumbled, "Hey," then returned her cold stare back to Julian.

Wow, what's up with her? No doubt disappointed she couldn't be me, sitting here with the most beautiful guy in Colorado?

"Amber, this is Mitzi Carlisle. She's in our class at Castle Rock." Julian's voice was somehow different. I could tell he didn't care for this girl, and, quite frankly, neither did I.

"Pleasure to meet you, Mitzi," I said with as much fake enthusiasm as I could muster. My first impressions of people were more accurate than I wanted to admit, and I'd convinced myself I had her pegged. I instantly disliked her and couldn't place a finger on why. The thought that I'd see her in school made me gag. Something about her didn't seem right to me. I mulled it over in my head but dismissed it.

Noticing Julian's lack of interest in her, Mitzi scurried off in a huff, almost like she was expecting something more from him. Instead, he returned his attention to me. She left behind a smattering of spilled drinks and broken glass shortly before Miss Shrill Voice arrived with our food, sidestepping the debris on the floor.

Moments later, a cleaning crew appeared and begrudgingly cleaned the mess.

"What's Mitzi's problem, Julian?" I asked.

"She's not worth an explanation, Amber. Please, let's talk about something else, okay?" Tension outlined his face. It seemed she had irritated a few people with Julian being one of them. Maybe they dated in the past, and it ended badly. Yeah, for her maybe. I didn't want to even entertain that as a possibility.

Even so, the exchange between them remained interesting, but I agreed to drop it and start in on my lunch. My stomach continued to flip-flop, and I couldn't control the spasm of my bouncing left knee. I dug into the salad anyway. It tasted delicious.

"Have you dated many girls before?" I blurted out. "Never mind, I'm just babbling. Of course, you have." *Just look at you.*

Julian's eyes went wide, and he started frantically rubbing his hands down his legs.

Jeez, what did I say?

He raised his burger to his mouth, took a bite, chewed and swallowed. "I've never had more than a couple of dates with anyone," he finally said.

My heart sank and posture sagged. I'd reached my quota with him then. Was I wasting my time? With my days numbered, I resolved to ignore the sensitive subject and just have a great time. Deep in the recesses of my brain, I cringed. Robin was right. And I hated the fact that she was right.

We talked and ate and talked some more. It was the best shrimp salad I'd ever had. My hunger had returned, eating every last bite until it was gone.

After finishing my lunch, I faked an excuse to use the ladies' room but instead asked the hostess to surprise Julian with a birthday cupcake and lit candle. When she obliged, I decided to use the restroom after all.

Reapplying some lip gloss to my lips and brushing out my hair, my mind began to wander. Would Julian ask me out again? I just didn't know.

A woman with platinum blond hair washing her hands, nodded to me as I stared stone-faced in the mirror.

"You're a beautiful young lady," she said. "I'm not sure what you're pondering, but don't let your beauty deceive you, honey."

"Thank you." I blushed, confused by her words. That would go down in history as one of the strangest statements I've ever heard.

Once I returned to our private table nestled in the corner of the café, Julian gestured for me to sit next to him.

"Gladly," I said, smiling to myself, banishing the peculiar conversation with "Restroom Woman" from my mind.

I scooted into the booth, intentionally skimming against him and pressed my hips into his. I felt brazen, and he moaned softly, confirming my decision to be bold. Julian noticed my eyes focused on the lovers outside the window.

He stuffed a french fry in his mouth and offered me one. I shook my head. "Since you're new to the city, I'd like to show you around the Denver area and take you to some of my favorite spots," he said.

Well, that sounded like more than two dates. Was our relationship going to go beyond today? I hoped so. Julian was way out of my league, and the thought that he'd continue to see me felt like an impossible dream. Maybe, just maybe there lay hope for me.

"I'd love that!" I exclaimed, clapping my hands together. I still needed pinching when I stared at Julian's beautiful face, wondering what I did to get so lucky. I noticed his attention riveted on me as well. There was still so much I wanted to know about him. Though, he didn't seem to be the type to disclose it all. Did I want to open myself up to a world of pain? For now, I was happy and kept my questioning to the simplest subjects.

"So where are these favorite spots?"

"After we finish eating, I'll take you to my all-time number one favorite place."

I batted my eyelashes at him. "Sounds great."

"You look very nice today," he said. "I'll confess that I was watching you move in while I was shooting hoops. I couldn't take my eyes off you." He flushed and ran his hand through his hair.

Really? I watched wide-eyed, unable to comprehend what I'd just heard. How did I not notice this? My heart skipped a beat. Right now I would give anything to run my hands through that hair. "Thank you. I thought you were too wound up in your game to notice us."

"Seriously? Why do you think I was playing for so long?" He sat back and straightened his shirt.

"Damned if I know." I feigned innocence and giggled.

I couldn't keep my eyes off you, either.

"I noticed you were watching me, too." He chuckled arrogantly, looking a bit too over-confident. "I'm right, aren't I?"

Smug ass. He was right though. "Yes," I said softly, taking a long, pleasurable sip of my drink. I liked him…a lot.

"See, I'm a very observant person." He said with a rightfulness and superiority.

He was so sexy.

"Touché, but you can't fool me, Julian Cahill. There's not a single man on earth who is observant, so what gives?" I raised an eyebrow at him.

He pouted. "Okay, let's just say I saw you blink in my direction once or twice. Enough said."

I laughed. God, he was too funny.

While deep in conversation, I gave a silent cue to the hostess. Shortly thereafter, a uniformed crew arrived at our table singing "Happy Birthday." The priceless image of Julian's gaping jaw made me laugh when they placed the candlelit cupcake in front of him. His face sported the illustrious ten shades of red.

He straightened himself, looking macho and tough, sucked in an extra deep breath and then gently blew the flickering light of the candle out until all that was left were scented fumes rising from the wick. I clapped, and the crew followed.

"Thank you, Amber. That's very sweet of you." He blushed. I think I actually saw his ears turn red. "When the heck did you do this?"

"Oh, c'mon Julian, don't you know the old going-to-the-bathroom trick?" I felt proud I'd pulled it off.

We dove into the scrumptious chocolate cupcake with creamy vanilla icing swirled on top.

"Chocolate is my weakness, you know?" I smiled.

"Is that so?"

"Yup, I'm a chocoholic." I giggled while swirling the tasty treat around in my mouth.

Below the table, he placed his hand over mine and softly caressed my knuckles with his fingers as we continued our conversation. The butterflies in my belly surfaced again. He was touching me.

"What kind of things do you like to do?" He asked.

"Other than hiking, I love to sing and play my guitar."

His eyes lit up. "I play guitar, too."

"Seriously? We'll have to play together sometime."

"By all means." He used his index finger to wipe a smidgeon of chocolate from the corner of my mouth.

My heart skipped a beat. How was I going to form a coherent thought after that? I started twirling my finger in my hair again. "Um, as I said earlier, I'd love to go hiking in the Rocky Mountains. I fell in love with the beauty of the Rockies years ago when my family explored a few of the easier trails."

He smiled, as Miss Shrill Voice was back at our table asking if we needed drink refills. I think she needed another refill of Julian. We shook our heads, so she placed the check on the table and left.

I loved hiking but combined with the fact I'd be doing it with Julian gave me hope I wouldn't be cast aside like the rest of his dates.

Julian glanced at his watch. "Holy shit, it's four o'clock!" He looked up at me. "We've been sitting here for almost three hours."

"Well, it doesn't feel like it. I've had a fantastic time. Thank you." I started fiddling with my napkin, wrapping it around my index finger.

"The pleasure was all mine, Amber. Would you like to take a walk? I'm getting restless and tired of sitting. I could talk with you all day."

I dropped the napkin on the table and scooted out of the booth. Where was he taking me? "Of course, I'd love to. Let's try to walk off some of these calories before we need to head home."

Julian finished his water, paid the check, and we left.

WALKING THROUGH the heart of Denver, Julian pointed out

various landmarks along the way and offered a full account of each when our hands inadvertently brushed against each other, shooting tingles through my body. At that moment, he grabbed my hand and linked our fingers together. He wasn't shy and had a take-charge kind of personality. I liked that. I sensed him contemplating his next move as he lifted my hand to his lips and gave my knuckles a soft, sensuous kiss, igniting my body to the core. Was I dreaming?

Blood pumped through my veins as my heart responded with a pounding beat. I was beyond excited. For now, conversation ceased and was replaced by a nervous energy between us. I think Julian felt it too, but appeared so calm and collected. How could he sustain such remarkable composure when all I felt was a tickling down in the depths of my belly? Perhaps, he'd done this before? I didn't care. I was happy.

The sun skimmed the horizon in the brilliantly-colored sky, rich with warm vermilion reds and tangerine oranges. People bustled up and down the sidewalk going about their afternoon errands, perusing the stores with clear intentions.

We walked along when Julian tugged at my hand, abruptly stopping me. "This is Clint's Barber Shop. When I was a little kid, my dad and I used to drive up here to get our hair cut. Before leaving, I would make him wait while I stood and stared at the barber shop pole. It mesmerized me, like the twisting red, white, and blue stripes spun around endlessly. This brings back great memories, Amber." Julian stood and stared, as if remembering a magical moment with his father.

Lost in thought, he looked off into the distance at something, "I'd like to take you to my favorite place. You up for it?" It sounded somewhat suggestive.

"Sure." I pulled him closer to me. He gave my fingers a firm squeeze. This day couldn't get any better—that much I knew. I secretly prayed Robin was wrong about him. This felt different from my relationship with Danny. More mature.

He turned and smiled at me. I melted when I got a glimpse of those gorgeous blue eyes staring back at me. I returned a mega smile back. He ran his thumb across my knuckles. "You're awfully quiet, what are you thinking about?"

"I was just thinking about you and how great a time I'm having." I smiled. "Thank you for that."

"I'm having the time of my life, too." He smiled back.

Julian never let go of my hand as he led me inside a gated park. We headed toward a sign that said: Windsong Lake.

Pointing at a spot on a distant tree, my eyes lit up. "Look, Julian, there's a mountain bluebird."

"How did you know that?" He raised an eyebrow.

"I studied birds at my 4-H group in my younger years. At the time I thought about becoming an ornithologist. The mountain bluebirds also have a distinctive turquoise color. The Bluebirds in upstate New York are more of a royal blue but just as rare and beautiful."

"I'm impressed by your furry, feathered friend's familiarity." He laughed aloud.

"Very amusing. I'll have to remember that one." On brave impulse, I innocently nudged him with my shoulder. He really did have a great sense of humor. "We made bluebird boxes and always had a backyard full of them. You know, they have to be strategically placed to attract the birds."

"Nope, I can honestly say I know very little about birds," he said, making me feel warmed by the fact that I taught him something.

Walking along a narrow dirt path through some tall grass, Julian released my hand and scoped out a private area where we sat in the warm sand along a rock-laden shore. Hidden by massive boulders on each side of us, a rush of adrenaline spiked through my veins in anticipation of what was happening around me. Completely secluded from peeping eyes, my heart began thumping so vigorously, I wondered if he heard it. As if he read my mind, Julian took me by surprise and planted a soft kiss on my lips. I mirrored his actions, pulling him toward me, my hands on the clean-shaven smooth skin of his cheeks. He shifted his weight, pushing me to my back, placing his strong hands on each side of my face and caught my mouth again, deepening the kiss with passion.

Stunned by his swift movements, I moaned against his lips as his invading tongue became intertwined with mine. Danny was a good kisser, but Julian had me seeing stars. There was no comparison between the two.

He wrapped me in his arms, lying alongside me. I grabbed his hair—that luscious hair—and threaded my fingers through the softness of it...*finally*. I pulled him to me, kissing him harder. He groaned a sexy sound that made my insides quiver to the core. I wanted to touch him all over. I burned with desire for him, his masculine scent spurring me on. What was happening? These emotions felt foreign to me. He needed me; I needed him.

Julian quickly released me and looked down into my eyes with an apologetic stare. "I'm sorry, Amber. I don't know what came over me."

"Julian, I wouldn't do anything I didn't want to. Please don't be sorry."

"I—" He trailed off with a blank stare.

"What is it, Julian?" Oh no, here it comes—his goodbye to me because I didn't measure up to his standards, just like all the others. I felt like a complete ass. Robin was right. *Spit it out, dammit!*

He stayed quiet.

I braced myself for the blow about to be imparted on me. "Talk to me, Julian. I didn't do anything wrong, did I?"

Stroking my face with the tips of his fingers, he broke the silence with his soft and emotion-filled voice, "I really like you. You're...different than the other girls here."

"Different? How am I different from them?"

"I don't know. You're not all about the...'oh Julian, pick me' kind of crap. You're more down to earth, I guess." He smirked.

I giggle-snorted, relief flooding my body as I let out the breath I didn't realize I was holding. Though, his words confused me: *Pick me?* What did that mean? And he said it with such a derogatory tone. I ignored it, because it didn't matter. He just said he really liked me. And the feeling was mutual.

"You are the most stunning girl I've ever met. I find you sexy and irresistible," he said, tilting his head to the side, emotion spilling from him.

I had a sappy grin on my face. "Julian, I'm speechless. That was the sweetest, kindest, most thoughtful thing anyone has ever said to me."

Something wonderful that I can't explain is drawing me to you as well.

"You're such an enigma. Look, let's not overthink this, okay?" I said, quietly.

"Enigma, huh?" A hint of a smile befell his lips.

"Yes, enigma." *You're mysterious.*

I cracked a smile, and he shook his head.

Later, the sun played hide-and-seek with the clouds until it set below the horizon as we settled ourselves into each other's arms. We sat in silence just staring at the approaching sunset. Dusk settled around us as the sky became a beautiful splash of chestnut browns and mahogany reds, interwoven within the deep blue palette behind. The waves of the lake crashed in uneven inflection along the shore, creating a soothing harmonic symphony.

We switched positions while I laid my head on him, listening to the beating of his heart and feeling the rising and lowering of his chest as he breathed.

"You know, I remember when I was around fourteen, I used to take walks into the woods behind our New York house. I found a private spot where I'd lay on the ground and look to the sky through the leaves of the trees. I'd close my eyes and try to imagine myself drifting in a magical world of vivid colors. Weird, huh?"

Julian gazed at me through glossed-over eyes. "No, not weird at all. I've done the same thing right here in this spot."

My jaw dropped. "No way. Really?"

"Yep."

We stayed silent. Life was perfect. He made me so happy.

Chapter Three

Julian and I'd been together for nine dates in sixteen days. The happiness I felt turned my mind to mush, unable to decipher my left from my right. But the end of August crept closer and closer with the start of school looming heavy over me.

He'd just dropped me off after our date at the movies. I felt giddy with delight that not only had I lasted beyond the Julian Cahill, *I've-never-had-more-than-a-couple-of-dates-with-anyone*, disclosure, but we'd actually discussed a future together.

I exited the car and slammed the door shut. I rounded the rear to the driver's side, bent down through the window and gave Julian a soft kiss on the lips. I then left a trail of kisses from his ear to his jaw line. "See you tonight," I whispered, brushing my lips against his ear.

Julian sucked in a shaky breath. "Can't wait."

I turned, leaving him wide-eyed and breathless. Through the hedgerow, past the maple tree, along a newly worn path between our houses, I danced all the way home. I couldn't wipe the grin from my face.

After countless late night phone conversations, I felt I knew him better, too, but did I? If asked to describe him, I'd say soft-spoken and humble about summed it up—an enigma. He didn't talk much about his former girlfriends and would change the subject whenever I brought them up. I still wondered about his "oh Julian, pick me" comment on our first date. It didn't seem to be an issue, so I vowed to ignore it.

In fact, Robin admitted she'd been mistaken about her first

impression of him. *Finally*. Now maybe we could put that argument to sleep.

True to his word, Julian took me hiking in the Rocky Mountains. We hiked a three-mile trail to Emerald Lake. At over 10,000 feet, we began at the trailhead of Bear Lake that led us to magnificent views of the most beautiful lake I'd ever seen.

When I thought of that day, my heart skipped a beat…

I stood along the rocky shore, staring at the mirror image of the mountains on the surface of the glassy lake when Julian came from behind and scooped me into his arms—my back to his front. I didn't say anything but could feel his excitement pressing into my back. I wanted to wiggle my butt into him but didn't feel gutsy enough. Instead, I remained still in the confines of his strong arms snaked around me.

He pressed his nose into my hair and trailed kisses down around my throat. I craned my neck to give him easier access, resting it on his shoulder. He smelled heavenly. He whirled me around, pressed his palms lightly against my cheeks and lowered his lips to mine with a sweet tenderness. I moaned softly and closed my eyes to savor the experience.

"God, you turn me on," Julian whispered in hushed, excitable tones.

"Hmm."

NANCY CAHILL, JULIAN'S STEPMOM greeted me at the door when I arrived for dinner. Julian had eaten with my family a handful of times, but tonight, I'd be eating with his. I admitted I felt nervous about meeting his stepmom. When he talked about her, there'd be an emotional void, leading me to believe they had a nonexistent relationship. Sadness filled my heart.

"Welcome." She scowled, standing stiffly with her nose turned up as she held the door open for me. Her large, smoky black eyes and big hair dwarfed her small frame. She nearly frightened me.

Julian called her Nancy and she didn't seem to mind.

"Nice to meet you, Mrs. Cahill." I stiffened but mustered up enough civility to respond politely.

"Come in, please."

I noticed Julian chatting with his dad in the living room when I walked in. You could see the love and respect between them. When his eyes met mine, that adoration instantly flip-flopped to me. My skin flushed.

"Hi." My voice sounded breathy. His beauty derailed me.

"Hey." He grabbed my hands, pulled me into him, and gave me a quick kiss. "How would you like to go to my family's camp tomorrow?"

"Sure, if it's okay with both our parents."

"Let's plan on it," he whispered. I closed my eyes, relishing the heat from his breath in my ear.

I turned to his stepmom as she placed a large, flat dish on the table. "Mrs. Cahill, your house is beautiful."

The gorgeous interior of the house had an earthy, crisp, lemony scent. The warm cream-colored walls of the living room displayed a collage of photographs showing Julian at various stages of his life. If possible, he might've been more adorable as a young boy, with wavy blond hair framing his cute little face. My curiosity got the better of me as to why there weren't any of Logan and Nancy, not even a single wedding picture.

Facing the fireplace, a pale chestnut over-stuffed sofa, love seat, and recliner sat around a large square coffee table in the center of the room. A beautiful bouquet of flowers in an opulent, blue painted vase decorated the mantel. The room looked perfect for sit-downs and comfortable conversations. Nancy may have lacked personality, but she did have great decorating tastes.

"Thank you. Please find a seat at the table. We'll be eating shortly." Her stern look told me one thing—don't cross me.

I sat next to Julian at the wide, polished, walnut table while Logan and Nancy took seats opposite us. Nancy prepared a simple ziti casserole, salad, and creamed broccoli. It may have been simple but tasted delicious.

The dinner conversation immediately turned to me and my life before moving to Colorado. I felt uncomfortable talking about myself, always being a foot-in-the-mouth ordeal. Sometimes I felt as though I had no filter, and Nancy certainly didn't help matters by intimidating me. My body became hyper-aware of my surroundings. But I made it through with a respectable amount of social graces that would have made my parents proud.

From the kitchen, the phone rang. *Ah, saved by the bell.* Nancy excused herself, stood from the table, and in short strides, picked up the call.

Logan ignored her and restarted the discussion. "You mentioned what your dad does, but how about your mom? What does she do?"

"She's a pharmacist at Walgreens in Castle Rock," I said.

"Wonderful. How about you? Did you have a job before moving here?"

"I was a swim instructor for young children at one of the local fitness centers."

Moments later, Nancy returned with a scowl. "Caroline Parker has gone into labor. I'm sorry, but I need to deliver another baby. Please excuse me."

I wasn't positive, but I thought I saw Logan flinch. "Okay, Nance," he said half-heartedly.

For whatever reason, I relaxed after Nancy left. In fact, the demeanor around the table changed. A pained look marred Logan's face while Julian's shoulders noticeably softened. Weird.

Logan continued the conversation. "What are your plans for the weekend, Julian? Are you working at the shop?"

"Nope, weekend off. I'd like to borrow the car and take Amber to the camp tomorrow."

I tried to gauge the reaction on Logan's face when Julian divulged his plans. I wasn't sure, but I thought his lips twitched.

"Okay, I *trust* that you'll drive carefully."

I felt my face flush. Logan appeared suspicious, looking for the tiniest slip in Julian's expression, but luckily self-confidence and vigilance won out.

"Thanks, Dad."

After dinner, I helped Julian with the dishes, chatting idly. "So what does Nancy do for a living?"

"She's an OBGYN at Denver Medical Center."

"How often does she get calls like that?" I asked thinking about how unusual a career choice it was for someone so cold and distant.

"All the time."

"Wow, I don't know if I could work a profession like that."

He shrugged his shoulders. "It's the life of a doctor."

THE FOLLOWING MORNING, I had trouble restraining my excitement at the prospect that Julian would be taking me to his camp today. I cherished these occasions when we could spend the day together. According to the map, Shadow Mountain Lake would be a lengthy, two hour drive.

When he wasn't home doing chores, his time was spent working for his friend, Chad, owner of Watson's Body Shop.

I searched for something comfortable to wear and decided on a pair of cream-colored shorts with a loose teal-colored tank top.

After digging my tote bag from my closet, I packed a swimsuit, towel, suntan lotion, reading material, and some light snacks for our day at the lake.

"Are you ready to go, babe?" Julian asked warmly, greeting me at the door. His presence always sent a warm tingle throughout my body. He intoxicated me.

"Heck, yes."

With his new license in hand, Julian opened the front passenger door to his dad's car, and I climbed in. He darted around and clambered into the driver's seat. As I suspected, Julian passed his driving test on the first try the week before with flying colors.

"Nice car. What is this?" I asked, running my hand across the soft leather seat.

"It's a BMW 840ci coupe." He winked at me. "One of BMW's top of the line. My dad asked for my opinion, and between the two of us, we opted for this make and model." He turned the key, and the engine roared to life. "Nice, eh?"

When Julian spoke of his dad, a warm glow sparkled in his eyes and vice versa. I saw how Logan worshiped the ground Julian walked on—as it should be. But sadness filled my heart seeing the disheartening rapport Julian had with his stepmom. Even Logan expressed very little affection toward Nancy. Definitely peculiar. But I noticed an abiding respect amongst them all.

Easing the car out of the driveway and heading toward Castle Pines Parkway, Julian began describing his 1969 fire-red, Chevrolet Camaro Z28. In more detail than I needed, he talked about the labor intensive restoration process. It'd clearly become his pride and joy, making me feel a twinge of jealousy. I mentioned how I knew very little about cars, but that didn't stop him from explaining where each and every nut and bolt went. I imagine he felt the same on our first date when I went on about my knowledge of birds.

"Chevrolet originally built the Z-28 for the Trans Am racing series." He playfully grinned and continued. "It has a unique hi-performance 302 cubic inch V-8 engine, which Chevrolet advertised as 290 horsepower to avoid high insurance rates for owners. In reality, it actually tested at over 400 horsepower."

I rolled my eyes—*men and their cars*. Julian's passion, or dare I say, obsession, for his Camaro and cars, in general, was astounding.

"It's going to be another month or so before she'll be road ready," he said, showering me with his huge boyish smile. "But, she's all mine, and I can't wait to take you for a ride."

"I can't wait, either." I reached over and grasped his arm. "You really know your cars, don't you?"

"My dad got me into them when I was very young. He once told me a story from when I was two years old. It was after dark as we followed a car with a familiar back end when I said, 'Look, Daddy, there's a Corvette.'"

"So cute, not to mention that you knew the make and model by the time you turned two."

"Apparently."

I glimpsed at Julian. He looked deliciously sexy in his light blue, button-down shirt paired with some beige cargo shorts.

As we pulled onto Highway 70 on our way to his family's camp, he caught my eyes fixed on him.

"Don't think I can't see you staring, Amber." He tapped the wheel with his fingertips in time to the music coming from the car's sound system, playing a Led Zeppelin tune.

"I can't help it. You're so seriously handsome to look at."

"Said the most beautiful girl in the USA," he replied with a sheepish grin. Reaching over, he rested his hand on my thigh, his thumb caressing it with soothing circles.

"Keep your eyes on the road. You know how concerned my mom felt about me riding with a newly licensed driver." I placed my hand on top of his. "Eyes forward, babe."

Before long, the surface of the road shifted from smooth to very rugged. The tires of the car thrummed loudly, pulsing rhythmically over every crack in the road. Julian reached over and cranked the volume of the radio up, and together we started singing the end of Zeppelin's "Stairway to Heaven."

"You've got a great voice, Amber."

"Thanks." I blushed, but didn't want to talk about my voice and turned the music down a tad. "Can I ask you a personal question?"

"Of course, anything. You know that."

"Well, Nancy looks much older than your dad. Is she?"

"Yeah, she's six years older than him."

Wow, six years. That's quite an age difference. I don't think I could date someone that much older than me. "How did they meet?"

Pushing a few buttons, Julian adjusted his side mirror then glanced briefly at me before returning his eyes to the road. "They met through my dad's older sister, my Aunt Jenny. Nancy delivered my cousin, Becky and I'd been told she delivered me, too."

"Then where is your biological mom?"

He frowned. "My dad told me she died when I was a baby, so I never knew her."

Holy cow, died? A lump formed in my throat. He'd never really had a stable mother figure in his life. His and Nancy's relationship seemed strained most of the time, which part of me could understand. I mean, she wasn't all that warm and fuzzy to me either. I couldn't imagine life without my mom.

"Oh, I'm sorry, Julian. Has your dad ever talked about her?"

Staring straight ahead, a pained expression crossed his face. "No, he doesn't convey much information about that time in his life. I'm not sure what kind of relationship they had."

His mom died. Wouldn't he want to know about her?

"Do you ask?" Jeez, I would want to know everything. "Aren't you the least bit intrigued?"

"Of course." He scrunched his face at me. "I see the kind of relationship you have with your mom and can't help but feel envious. You know…wondering what my mom was like." His eyes returned to the road. Deep sorrow spilled from his voice making me question my decision to bring up the subject. "Wouldn't you?"

"Yes, of course I would. Have you ever insisted he tell you about her?"

"Yeah, but he doesn't seem to want to discuss it with me, so I don't push the issue. Maybe her death was too horrific for him. I don't know. It's not worth digging up painful memories. She died, I never knew her…so it's kind of a moot point. I trust that my dad would tell me anything worth sharing."

A moot point? What? I couldn't believe he just said that. Why wouldn't he demand information from his dad? It made me angry that Logan never shared the details of Julian's mom with him. What kind of father did that? "I just wondered, Julian. Sorry for being so intrusive."

I wanted to take him in my arms, so I reached over and placed my hand on his thigh. I could tell by his smile; this seemingly innocent touch meant the world to him.

He lowered his hand to rest on mine. "Don't be. You know you can ask me anything."

"Have you ever seen pictures of her?"

He shook his head.

Wow, he didn't even know what she looked like. Maybe I should do some digging and see what I could come up with myself. Or maybe I should just leave well enough alone.

"What is her name?"

"I don't know. My dad told me he'd tell me one day, but it was too soon." A blank stare crossed his face. "A couple of years ago, I asked to go to see her grave. He looked terrified at the thought. I told him it was okay. So, I dropped it."

"You're a stronger person than I would be." I'd want to know everything and wouldn't stop until I had it.

Understanding his silent pained look, I chose to end the questioning. I wanted to ask him about his dad's marriage to Nancy but decided against it. Anyway, it was none of my business.

Instead, I turned my focus to the wide open scenic highway. Colorado blue columbine wildflowers and aspen trees interlaced through the pine forest, while snow-capped mountains embraced the distance landscape. I inhaled the woodlands piney scent.

We arrived at the Cahill camp shortly before noon to blue skies and balmy temperatures.

AFTER A FULL DAY of swimming, boating on the catamaran and tour of his family's cabin—where we had sex for the first time—we decided to sit by the pier and relax. I watched, mesmerized as the catamaran seesawed up and down with the waves. The soothing sound of the whitecaps racing toward the shore hissed and crashed along the water's edge. It reminded me of the times Julian took me to Windsong Lake to sit in our favorite spot.

We dragged our books from my tote bag and began reading quietly on a lounge chair, my back to his front. He caressed my knuckles with his thumb's delicate touch. The soft whisper of a breeze caught the sail of a boat in the distance, propelling it across the lake. While Julian perused through the latest medical journal, I drifted off thinking about our first time making love…

"Welcome to Chez Cahill cabin," Julian announced. "After you, madear." He motioned for me to walk through the door into his camp.

"With pleasure, sir," I muttered. While he held the door open for me, I closed the distance between us and brushed my hips along his thigh. He eyed me with a sharp inhale. "Wow, this place is cool."

"Shall I give you a tour?"

"I'd be disappointed if you didn't."

The Cahill cabin, a rustic log dwelling nestled in the woods of the mountain-fed lake, had all the amenities of home. Knotty pine covered the walls throughout, with wooden floors polished to a warm honey-gold, and open ceilings with exposed rafters. My eyes zoomed to the seamless windows in the living room with breathtaking views of the surrounding area. French doors led out to a raised deck overlooking the bright blue freshwater lake.

Julian led me into one of the bedrooms, took my hand, and gently pulled me over to the bed. "This is my room." His eyes connected with mine. "Amber...um...do you want to have sex with me?" He looked down at the floor and cleared his throat. "I hope you feel like I do."

Sex? Was I ready? Were we ready? We'd grown so close over the past three weeks, but was that enough? Deep, deep down, I knew this was what I wanted. But now, faced with the reality of doing it, could I go through with it? I couldn't do it with Danny. Could I do it with Julian? Did I love him?

Julian shook out his hands and looked restless and nervous. "I'm sorry, we don't have to. I just thought we were ready. Your silence is speaking volumes."

Had he done this before? I didn't know. My insides trembled, and I found my voice. "Yes, Julian, but I've never done this before. I'm—I'm a virgin, so this is a huge step for me. I really want to do this, but I'm scared." I closed my eyes and took a deep calming breath.

A long silence followed. Was he upset about me being a virgin? Maybe all his other sex partners were more experienced. If that's the case, then he'll surely be disappointed with me.

Looking deep in thought, Julian finally spoke, breaking the

deafening lull that filled the room, "We'll go easy and take it slow. I'm scared, too."

As I stood beside him at the end of the bed, he reached up, put his hand under my chin and lifted it, meeting his scorching eyes. He groaned and kissed me...softly.

I moaned back. My fingers twisted in his beautiful, silky hair, returning the kiss.

Julian's other hand splayed behind my back, drawing our bodies together, hugging me tightly against his muscular chest. I felt his excitement against my belly. Moving his hands to each side of my face, he kissed me as if it would be his last kiss. An instant arousal overwhelmed me. Our tongues tangled together with urgency. Gasping for air, we pulled apart, panting.

"Can I remove your top?" he asked, breathing heavily.

"Yes," I said, my voice quiet.

As I raised my arms, Julian took the bottom hem of my tank top and, inch by inch, pulled it up over my head. He dropped it on the floor at my feet. To my surprise, he skillfully unclasped my bra and at a leisurely pace, lowered it down my arms while leaving a trail of kisses from the crease of my neck down to my breasts. I heard my bra fall to the floor. Now naked from the waist up, my body felt ultra-sensitive to his touch.

His fingertips grazed my breasts. "God, your skin is soft."

I blushed.

He whispered in my ear, "Wow." Then examined me with his head tilted to one side. "Beautiful, just beautiful."

I took a deep breath and exhaled gently. "I'm feeling self-conscious."

Lifting his finger to his mouth, he said, "Shhh, don't be. You have no idea how gorgeous you are." He appeared so much more experienced than me. Had he done this before? Did I care if he had? I willed myself to relax.

My heavy breathing increased, nearly passing out with desire, thinking about what this entailed. I was treading in new territory. A tickling deep in my belly had me feeling weak and shaky. The sensation swept through me as if I was floating in a sea of happy pills.

"Now I'd like to remove your shorts. Is that okay?"

Julian's respect of my feelings made me want him even more. If he'd wanted to rip my clothes off with animalistic abandon, I wouldn't have objected.

"Yes." I shivered. *Get it done already.* My insides screamed for relief. His nimble fingers skimmed my belly down to my shorts. He unbuttoned them and lowered the zipper. Grasping the top, he gently dragged them off while his hands grazed over my behind and down my legs. He let them drop to the floor where they pooled at my feet. My body shook as I stepped out of them. While balancing on one foot, I used the other to kick them across the floor.

Thank goodness I wore my pink lace panties. A sudden awareness grabbed me. I stood there, nearly naked, while he was fully dressed. I blushed again. Shit!

Julian lifted his hands and briefly caressed my breasts again, tugging on the nipples and sending tingles down to the core of my clit. I tossed my head back, exhaling sharply, savoring his touch.

"Your breasts are perfect," he said. "You are beautiful."

Standing face to face, gazing into his stunning blue eyes, I leaned in and kissed him on the lips, barely touching him. I felt him smile against my mouth. "You're too sweet."

Slowly and methodically, he removed my panties, skimming his fingers down my legs. After tugging off his shirt, he pulled me into him, pressing his bare chest against mine. He let out a low sensual moan as the tips of his fingers trailed down my back with a gentle caress. My whole body responded with a tremble.

I looked at his partially naked body, and understanding my anticipation, he nodded his head. Recklessly, I undid the button of his shorts. Before I pulled them down, he stopped me and reached into his pocket and retrieved a condom.

Hmm, a bit of a foregone conclusion.

I looked into his eyes. "Thank you for being responsible—but put it away—I'm on the Pill. Before you jump to conclusions, I've been on it since the age of fourteen to regulate my period."

Okay was all he said, but I saw his relief in his slow smile.

I tugged at the top of his shorts, pulling them down, feeling every ripple as my hands slid along his long, muscular legs. Oh my, was there anything about this guy that wasn't sculpted and perfect? Even his bare feet were sexy.

I revealed his boxer briefs. Raising my head to meet his eyes, I put my thumbs in the elastic waistband and pushed them down. Both of us stood naked, gazing into each other's eyes with a desire and longing. Julian softly kissed my lips, scarcely touching me. I wanted him so bad.

He made quick work of the bedding, promptly pulling back the blankets, and gently laid me down with my head on his pillow. I felt the bed shift as he sat astride me.

Our eyes locked together and he asked, "Are you sure you want to do this?" He looked beautifully gorgeous above me.

"Yes," I sounded breathy.

Lowering himself onto his elbows, he positioned himself at my opening and effortlessly eased himself part way inside me. He groaned loudly. "God, this feels good."

I was really doing this…with this beautiful guy.

"Ouch! Be careful. It's a little painful."

"Sorry. Do you want to stop?"

Julian pulled out and when I gave him the silent, keep-going nod, he gradually pushed back in until I felt a "pop" as he ripped through my virginity.

"Ouch, that hurt, but it is getting easier," I said, but the soreness had not yet subsided. "Go slower. I have to get used to this. I'm not quite there yet."

"Okay, if this is too much then we can stop." I noticed regret in his eyes, always thinking of me. I loved that.

"No, I want to do this. Keep going. It's getting better."

Julian continued his descent on me moving in further and further with each gentle thrust of his body. Slowly, with each plunge, the pain lessened. As he rubbed against that sensitive spot, my body started to respond.

Little by little, he finally reached the end of me. I felt every inch of him, our connection deep, and the feeling full and tight. I moaned in pleasure.

He stopped and wiggled his hips in a circular motion. "I'm so close, Amber. I want to make this last," he groaned.

"Keep going, Julian, please."

Julian started to move with a purpose. He didn't stop.

My mind drifted, and suddenly I was riding a roller coaster, cresting at the top of the track. From my breasts down to my toes, the feeling felt powerful; I'd lost all cognizant thought. I was falling…fast.

"You are perfect. This is perfect," he said through guttural sounds as he started moving faster, kissing me with deep passionate licks.

The friction began to drive me over the edge as he rubbed against that sensitive area. My whole body fell into his rhythm. I started thrusting up and down, in and out, meeting him with each movement. My fingers dug into his backside, leaving marks in their path. Our naked bodies locked together, slippery from sweat. My body felt tense and rigid, my legs shook uncontrollably. My eyes rolled back into their sockets, and I started to fall, fall, fall around and around him as this incredible feeling overtook my body.

"Oh my God!" I came forcefully. As my orgasm ripped through my body, Julian followed suit. His eyes squeezed shut, and with his face buried in my neck, he came long and hard.

"Uhh." He collapsed his body onto mine, pressing his full weight into me.

Once we regained whatever composure we had left, we lay side-by-side wrapped together in each other's arms, both well-sated.

Julian raised his head and glanced at me with an enormous smile. "That's the most amazing thing I've ever felt in my entire life, and I want to do it a thousand more times with you. Please say you will."

"Hmm…" I agreed, nodding frantically. Words fell short in my overly sensitized state. We both laughed. No doubt he'd done this before. His experience showed. I hope he wasn't disappointed with me.

"You are easy on the eyes, Julian." I reached up and traced my index finger across his lips.

"Do you need glasses, Amber?" A perplexed look crossed his face.

"Um… have you looked in the mirror lately?"

"Sorry, it was quick. I couldn't hold it back." He apologized.

And just like that, he changed the track of the conversation. "You won't hear any complaints from me," I mumbled. But I didn't have the heart to tell Julian how very sore I was.

Looking visibly hesitant to share his next thought, he glanced at me with a bewildered stare. "I don't know what you're doing to me, but I'm falling hard for you. These last three weeks have been the best of my life."

"Back atcha, Julian." I was on cloud nine, flying somewhere over the Rocky Mountains.

Yes, I loved him.

"HEY, SLEEPYHEAD, WAKE UP." Julian's voice sounded like warm caramel.

I yawned. "What time is it?"

"Nearly six. We should get going home. You've been asleep for a while." He nuzzled my neck, whispering in my ear, "You were smiling. What were you dreaming about?"

With a bashful grin, I stretched my arms and legs as we stood from the lounge chair. "Nice try, but I don't kiss and tell, so I'll just thank you for a perfect day, babe."

I squealed when his hands reached around and tickled my belly. "Best day of my life and they'll only get better."

He spun me around and his lips locked on mine, kissing me sweetly.

We pulled apart, breathless. "Yes, they will." I nodded.

Chapter Four

School—the one word capable of completely unraveling me—became the source of all my apprehension. Feeling the September morning sun on my face succeeded in calming my wavering nerves.

Julian ducked down and climbed into the back seat of Robin's car ahead of me, my eyes privy to his perfectly chiseled ass staring me in the face. I suddenly felt brazen, bent over, and kissed it.

"Amber!" Robin scolded me with a tsking sound as she opened the driver's door.

Robin bought an old, beat-up, baby blue 1985 Honda Civic the week before, with her own money. She loved it and offered to drive Julian and me to school until his car was road ready.

"I can't help it. It's so beautiful," I said as Julian shuffled across the seat. He turned, lifted his arm and pulled me against him.

"Whatever floats your boat, sis," she chuckled, and my ever exuberant sister slipped into the driver's seat.

"I'm a basket case," I said, reflecting back on the previous ten first-day-of-school-jitters. "Why does the first day of school always make me feel queasy?"

Julian reached over and held my hand, giving me soft reassuring squeezes. "You're not alone. I'm feeling it, too."

I decided on a more conservative look with a pair of black cropped pants and a blue fitted top for the first day, hoping I'd fit in. As always, Julian looked sexy in his khaki shorts and simple deep blue T-shirt.

As Robin eased the car out of the driveway and headed south on Meadows Boulevard toward the high school, I thought about the last three glorious weeks of the summer with Julian. There was still so much I didn't know about him, but when I turned to study his face, a minuscule hint of a smile kissed his lips. What was he thinking? I could only guess.

"Thank you for the last three weeks. They've been the best of my life."

"Mine, too," he replied.

I took his hand and linked our fingers together.

NESTLED IN THE FOOTHILLS of the Rocky Mountains, Castle Rock High School's red and brown brick exterior paled in comparison to the white, snow-capped beauty behind it.

Pulling into the parking lot ten minutes later, Robin entered the area assigned for seniors and parked the car. "Okay, we're here."

Hand-in-hand, with nervous energy, Julian and I stepped through the front entrance of the school. My mind drifted, thanking the good Lord he'd brought me here the week before to walk through my schedule, showing me where each of my classrooms would be. As it just so happened, we shared the same homeroom.

As we headed down the blue locker-lined halls of the freshly painted school, an over-eager brunette stopped Julian, practically falling into his arms.

"Are we on for tonight, Julian?" she asked, leaning into him while noticeably batting her eyelashes.

What the hell? Were they dating?

Arching back, Julian reached around my waist and pulled me closer to him, as if shielding himself from her. "Um, not tonight," he said, kissing my hair and smacking his lips together. If there was any doubt who he was dating before this encounter, it should be clear now. Suddenly, I felt proprietary and uncomfortable. I squeezed him tighter against me.

With a snooty laugh, the girl looked at me, then turned back to *my man,* "O—kay."

"Bianca, I'd like to introduce you to my girlfriend, Amber Scott. Amber just moved here from New York." Gesturing with his hand between us, he continued, "Amber, this is Bianca Pantilla."

"Uh…nice to meet you, Amber." Her voice was deep and raspy. She glared at me with her piercing, big brown eyes. Was she jealous? Of course, she was. Why did I care?

"Nice meeting you, too, Bianca. Being new here, it's always nice meeting Julian's friends," I said with as much sincerity as I could, given the cool stare aimed back at me. Was I reading too much into this girl?

It reminded me of the sneering look by the waitress in the restaurant. What was her name? Mitzi, I think. She made me feel uncomfortable as well.

"See you later." Julian grabbed my hand, knocking me off kilter, and pulled me in the direction of our homeroom. He left Bianca looking dazed and confused. I noticed a tension in the air between them.

I tugged him back to look at me. "Why did she ask if you were on for tonight?"

"Uh…a bunch of us were getting together, that's all."

I saw his face twitch as we toddled along another twenty steps, met by the onslaught of another group of females—six of them—hanging all over him. Undoubtedly, they all saw what I'd been gawking at since I set eyes on him three weeks ago. With all of them chatting at once, my mind swiftly shut down. Was this what he meant by the "pick me" comment? Through all the monotony, I did observe occasional eyelash fluttering. It felt like a competition. Any moment, I swore I'd be hearing Don Pardo's voice coming through the PA system announcing the winner of a date with Julian Cahill. Jeez.

After the usual first day pleasantries, we finally reached our homeroom, stopped by some of his male friends along the way, as well. Brad, Nate, and Darius were some of the names I remembered hearing Julian say as he proudly introduced me as his girlfriend. I couldn't get my head around this. Julian couldn't have been more popular.

As we sat at our desks in homeroom, I turned my attention to the unpleasant snickers from around the room by some of the girls. Some regarded me shrewdly, while others acted gracious and sociable. Receiving the evil eye was not something I aspired to, though. I was well-liked and respected in my old school and had plenty of friends, so this was very unusual. Besides, I didn't even know what my transgressions were. I felt confused, on the verge of tears, like I drew the short straw today.

What's the deal with Julian and other girls? I felt as though I'd intruded in on some private conspiracy into his personal life with the girls from hell. I understood the desire to be around a gorgeous guy, but this was ridiculous. Did he ever tire of the over-flirtatiousness thrown in his direction at every turn? I'd just had it thrown in my face for the last fifteen minutes and wanted to dig a deep hole and crawl in.

I closed my eyes and pictured myself back at Julian's camp, the first time we had sex. I wanted to return to the ecstasy of that day again.

These were his friends though, and I should show some semblance of respect. Maybe I'd have a better outcome tomorrow. On one level, I had hope; but on another, my head drowned in doubt.

"Okay, Julian, you are one idolized son of a bitch," I said, reacting to the rioting emotions within me as we moved down the hall to our first class after the bell rang.

He shrugged, looking apologetic and uncomfortable. "I'm sorry."

"I'll get over it," I uttered with as much bravery as I could, even though my insides knotted up. "See you later."

Before going our separate ways, Julian turned to me with a pathetic pouty face. "I'll miss you."

I smiled and melted at his endearing words. He made me feel better. "I'll miss you, too."

Thanks to my thorough tour of the school by the best boyfriend ever, I found my chemistry classroom quickly. Microscopes, beakers and Bunsen burners filled the space around me. Our teacher, Mr. Lynch had written his name on the chalkboard.

Instantly, I found an empty seat at the front of the room. Before placing my backpack on the seatback of my chair, I retrieved a notebook and pencil from the inner pocket.

I sat quietly next to a guy with jet black hair, wearing a pair of black framed glasses. A backward baseball cap sat on his large head. He turned to me with a devious grin.

"Heard you were Julian's flavor-of-the-week" His voice sounded low and gravelly.

"Huh?" Before he could respond, the waitress I met on my first date with Julian walked in, scanned the room, and immediately sat in the seat on the other side of me. What was her name?

Changing tactics, I turned my attention to her. "Mitzi, right? I'm Amber Scott. Do you remember me from The Nickel Bistro when I was with Julian Cahill?" I asked as nicely as I could muster, even though I remembered my aversion toward her.

She peeled off her jacket and draped it across her chair. Once again, my eyes focused on the gothic owl tattoo on her forearm. Upon closer inspection, I noticed the eyes were hollowed out. Very creepy.

"What are you staring at, bitch?" Her arrogant words told me she wasn't all that thrilled to see me again, either.

"What is your problem, Mitzi? Did I do something to you?"

"None of your effing business," she hissed at me.

"Well, it *is* my effing business when you give me that attitude." I turned away from her and wondered how I was going to make it through the rest of the class.

"You think you can hold on to Cahill just because you're playing the pretty bitch card? You're wrong. You'll be next." She gave me an indignant shoulder shrug and turned her back to me. I barely knew this girl, and was already visualizing duct tape over her mouth.

"My relationship with Julian has nothing to do with looks." *Did it?* My mind flitted back to the words of the "Bathroom Woman," *You're a beautiful young lady, I'm not sure what you're pondering, but don't let your beauty deceive you, honey.*

I turned back to Joe Baseball Cap when he tapped me on the shoulder. "After Julian's finished with you, would you like to go out with me sometime?"

When Julian was finished with me? "Umm, no, I don't think so." Although he wasn't bad looking under that cap.

Wow, my first class, my first day in a new school and I encounter this? *I was Julian's "flavor-of-the-week"?*

My heart sank. So many of the girls here hated me. What did Julian have to do with this? What had I done?

Except for Joe Baseball Cap's odd comment and Mitzi purposely knocking into me while I was peering into a microscope, the rest of the class went without incident.

Minutes later, the bell rang. I rose from my chair to move on to my next class. Walking down the hall, I felt a tap on my shoulder. I stiffened as my defenses went up. I fully expected another tongue-lashing for what, I didn't know. I turned and saw an attractive girl with short, dark blond hair with bangs and big, chestnut brown eyes. Her freckles stood out against her sunburned face. She wore blue jeans and a denim jacket over a white top with casual buckle strap ankle boots.

"Hi, I'm Shelby Quade. You're new here, aren't you? Amber is your name, right?" she asked sweetly.

My whole body relaxed at her kindness, finally changing the hostile tone of the day in a more positive direction. "Yes, but apparently I'm not very well-liked by some of the other girls. What is the problem? I can't figure out what I've done." Tears threatened before I finished.

"It's not you, Amber, it's them. Just ignore it. Hey, are you the girl who's dating Julian Cahill?"

"Yes, why?"

"No reason. It's just all over school that he has a steady girl now, that's all."

"Okay. Is that unusual?" I prompted.

"Well, kind of. Haven't you talked with him about this?"

"Talked about what?" I shook my head to clear the confusion within it.

"Oh, this is none of my business, Amber. I'll see you later." She quickly turned and disappeared into the crowd.

Damn. *What the hell is going on here?*

Suddenly Robin's—*you'll be sorry*—statement rang loudly in my head. I had to think long and hard about my relationship with Julian. I just had the best three weeks of my life, but now everything was unraveling. I'd invested less than a month of my life with him. Would it be easy to make a clean break? The thought made me flinch. I couldn't see myself without him. I loved him.

I turned and headed to my next class, wondering how the news of our relationship traveled so quickly. Was I Julian's first steady girl? I found that tidbit impossible to believe. His words from our first date sounded again in my head. *I've never had more than a couple of dates with anyone*. Why?

He was the most gorgeous guy I'd ever seen. The ambush of females in the hallway this morning was clear indication that he could have any one of them, although he made it obvious that I belonged to him. Why me? Which ones did he date? Therein laid the question.

DAY ONE OF SCHOOL stood as one of the worst days of my life. Robin quickly grasped onto my scowl as Julian and I climbed into the back seat of her car. He wrapped his arm around me, and I leaned my weary head on his shoulder.

"I had a great day!" Robin exclaimed. "What's the problem with you, Amber?" She narrowed her eyes at me with an I-told-you-so look.

"I'm not in the mood to discuss it right now," I said, looking at Julian out of the corner of my eye. An unreadable gaze shifted across his face.

Robin sported a silent brooding look, no doubt recognizing my sullen mood. I knew what that meant. She'd pursue it later. She knew me better than anyone.

"What's wrong?" I felt Julian tense as he asked the question.

My shoulders slumped forward. "I said I don't want to talk about it now."

"Okay." He backed off, fear etched in his sharp features.

I didn't want him feeling guilty about the way the girls treated me at school. I couldn't bear for him to think this was any fault of his, but I did need to ask him about the "flavor-of-the-week" comment.

Silence filled the car for the rest of the ride home. I watched as Robin began tapping her thumb on the steering wheel. I could read her thoughts. I'd hear about at home. I spun my head to Julian in time to see him grimace, subtly shaking his head. I turned away and stared out the window, wondering how I was going to handle this situation. I didn't feel like discussing my day with anyone.

We arrived home minutes later and Julian recognized my unspoken thoughts to be left alone. Looking shaken and nervous, he asked if he could see me later on.

"Of course," I said. "Just give me time to unwind, okay?"

"Sure," he said, his sad face emerging. He bent down, gave me a sweet kiss on the lips, and headed home.

Robin dragged me by the arm, knocking me off balance, as we passed through the door of our house. Immediately she spun me around. "Okay, spill it, Amber. What has he done? I told you I wasn't going to interfere unless he did something that warranted it. I don't like what I just saw in the car, so start talking."

I lowered my head into my palms and sulked.

"Talk to me. I'm not going to let this go until you tell me what happened. Did you catch him with another girl?" she accused.

I lifted my head and looked her straight in the eyes. "Not exactly, it—it isn't his reaction toward the other girls that concerns me; it's their reaction toward me."

With her mouth wide open, she stared at me with a look that would fatally burn you if you got too close.

"I knew it, Amber. I told you. Why is it that great-looking guys come with so much fucking baggage?" She threw her hands in the air. "You can't trust the jocks, especially the good-looking ones, and Julian falls into a category all his own: a seriously, unbelievably, great-looking category. I'll admit it; he's definitely H – O – T."

At least she was on board with every other girl in the school.

"Stop it, Robin! I mean it. It wasn't like that!"

"Then how was it?" She probed, her brows creased. "How is this different?"

I began to cry. How did I go from feeling on top of the world to the depths of despair in twenty-four hours? I trudged to the living room, plunked down on the sofa and buried my head in my hands.

I could sense Robin's close proximity, her eyes watching me intently. I hoped for some sympathy, let alone a little comfort, but something told me that wasn't going to be the case.

"What happened, sis?" Her voice softened. "Talk to me, please."

Wiping the tears from my cheeks with the back of my hand, I shivered and felt drained. I decided she might have some supportive insight on this and help me see a different perspective.

So, I looked up and began talking.

Chapter Five

Robin stood stock-still with a don't-mess-with-me scowl on her face. The proverbial toe-tapping of her shoe on the hardwood floor ticked in my head like a bomb ready to detonate.

"Well, start talking, Amber," she demanded, arms crossed at her chest.

I hesitated briefly, unsure of where to begin. She willed me with her penetrating stare, so I proceeded.

"Robin, Julian is obviously popular with the girls." My earlier tears continued to fall like little rain droplets down my face. "They flirted right in his face. I felt invisible, like they didn't see me standing there next to him wrapped in his arms, basically feeling like an intruder. Throughout the entire day, I'd been on the receiving end of some pretty unpleasant remarks and stares. One of the nicer girls even alluded to the fact that Julian's never had a steady girl before."

Robin moved to the sofa and sat next to me. "Holy crap, it's worse than I thought." She wrapped her arm around my shoulder, her face tense and filled with emotion. This was typical of her—flaring nostrils one minute, offering an understanding nod the next.

I clasped the side of my aching head as a surge of splitting pain pounded within. "I can't gauge how Julian feels about all this, either. I thought he looked uncomfortable with all the attention but maybe that's because I was there? I don't know."

Danny's and my relationship was never this complicated. We'd been known as a really cool couple.

She stroked her hand down my arm, effectively making my chills disappear. "Oh, Amber, I'm so sorry you had to go through something like this on your first day in our new school. I love you, and it hurts me to hear you talk like this. I don't want you to go through what I went through." She paused and looked as though she was mulling something over in her head. "Listen, Julian is a gorgeous guy, and you have to expect that he will attract the attention of a *lot* of girls. That's the unfortunate reality of it."

I nodded. Was I overreacting? Maybe so, but my instincts told me differently.

"Until now, there hadn't been much competition, which I can't explain. Being the newcomer, those girls regard you as a threat, but you're the lucky one who has him, not them. I'm sure that's how they all feel. Give it time. Once they get to know you, they'll see how wonderful and kind you are." She reached across the end table, snagged a tissue from the box and handed it to me. "And...," she paused and looked me in the eyes, "if they continue to be a problem, well then, they'll have to answer to me." She let out an unladylike snort.

I wiped my nose. "I hope you're right." Robin always found a way of making me feel better. She could drive me crazy with her over-protectiveness, and I knew it stemmed from her break-up with "Football Johnny," but she was borderline obsessed with my happiness. "By the way, what exactly happened the day you caught Johnny?"

Robin removed her arm from my shoulder and repositioned herself to face me. "I've never shared this with anyone. Promise me you'll keep it to yourself."

"Promise." I made an X across my heart.

"It was after cheerleading practice. I was heading to the girl's locker room to change. As I rounded the corner of the hallway, I heard the entire football team chanting, Johnny, Johnny, Johnny. My initial thought was that he'd done something great during practice. But when they saw me, they stopped abruptly and scurried like timid mice in every direction. I opened the door to the girl's locker room to find Johnny locking lips with that bitch, Roxanne Davies." Robin buried her face in her hands. "I told him to go to hell, grabbed my backpack and left. I was humiliated."

I leaned in and wrapped my arms around her. "I'm sorry, sis. I really don't think Julian would do that to me." I tried to reassure her.

She pondered her next thought. "Well, in the three weeks you two have been dating, I've seen how much he cares for you and how happy he makes you. He appears to be an honest, great guy." She stopped and looked away from me. "Damn is he gorgeous," she said under her breath then turned to me as if trying to gauge my reaction.

I rolled my eyes and agreed with my I-know-what-you-mean nod.

She went on, "That combination doesn't come along very often, so when it does, take full advantage, Amber. You're a lucky girl. I'm kind of jealous, too. I wish my boyfriends treated me the same way Julian treats you."

I reared my evil chuckle at her. "How ironic, though…weren't you the one encouraging me to stay away from him not too long ago?"

"If you say so." She waved her hand in dismissal.

Yes, the unpleasant memory of Robin's glowering look at Julian during our first week of dating popped unwelcome into my head. Every time he came over, she eyed him with contempt, waiting with bated breath to read him the riot act for breaking my heart. It made me uneasy. I couldn't imagine how he felt. He never let on, but undoubtedly, won her over.

"It isn't a happily-ever-after yet," she huffed. "I'm just trying to offer an encouraging perspective. I'm not one hundred percent on board with him. Something doesn't sit well with me, but I hope I'm wrong." She trailed off… "I'm not saying it will work, but sometimes you need others to point out the obvious."

"I suppose," I sighed.

We hugged. I loved her more than life itself. We were eleven months apart, but she had wisdom beyond her years. What would I do without her?

I headed to the kitchen, greeting my dad with a kiss on the cheek as he walked in the door. Mom stood at the stove tossing spicy Chinese chicken and broccoli in a large wok. A ginger and garlic aroma filled the air making my mouth water.

"Hey, Daddy, how was your day?"

My dad and I grew closer to each other when we bonded over

college hockey. As a child, he'd take me to all the home games of his alma mater. As we sat amongst the frenzied fans, he'd patiently explain the rules, even when it appeared to annoy those around us. In time, not only had I learned the game, but knew the names of all the players. It was a special time in my life and his.

"Well, I'm still learning the ropes in this job, so I guess we'll call it hectic and demanding," he said, looking questionably at me. "You look upset. Did something happen at school, pumpkin?"

He placed his briefcase on the kitchen counter, opened it, and pulled out a thick manila folder.

I wiped my eyes with the back of my hand and sat on one of the bar stools. "Yeah, but I can handle it, Dad. New student syndrome, I suppose." I didn't want to chat about school. It was a sore subject for me, so I used my distraction technique and changed the subject. "Mr. Cahill told me he did some work for Malta Silicone. I thought since you used to work there that maybe you might've met him."

"Really? That's quite a coincidence," Mom interrupted, tossing the food around in the wok.

"Yes, it is. What's his first name?" Dad asked.

"Logan. Logan Cahill. Do you remember him?" I asked. *What would be the chances of that?*

My dad tugged off his suit jacket and draped it over the back of the bar stool. "The name doesn't ring a bell, but his face may."

"He reminded me of Tom Selleck," I snickered.

My dad chuckled. "Is that so? I'm sure we'll meet them soon enough. Are you seeing Julian this evening?" he asked as he sat down on the bar stool next to me.

"I don't know. I hope so."

"Your mom and I agree that you're to do your homework beforehand."

"That's right, honey. Homework first." Mom said sternly.

"I will. I will. I'm going to go start it right now."

I hopped down from the stool and headed upstairs to my bedroom, closed the door, and sauntered to the window. I stared out at Julian's house, embracing the peace and quiet, thinking about what Robin said. Was she right? Was time what I needed?

A PATTERN DEVELOPED for the following two weeks of school. Wake up, go to school, encounter torment, go home, and try unsuccessfully to inveigle information from Julian, go to bed. I gave it time, except the harassment continued. I never gave up hope, but the bottom line…it got worse. I resigned myself to my new reality. There were enough girls who treated me respectfully, so it wasn't a complete wash.

Even though I prayed for a different outcome into the second week, it became abundantly clear that my life wasn't going to be any better. I still had issues with Mitzi and Bianca. They were downright nasty. Most of the others resigned themselves to the fact that Julian and I were a couple. But that didn't stop the occasional snotty glare or foul language directed at me when I walked by them. I even contemplated the thought of breaking up with Julian, but the voice in my head screamed, *No!*

There were some good times as well. When we'd arrive in the morning, I always looked forward to walking hand-in-hand down the hall with my guy. I tightened my grip each time a girl trembled and swooned at him, no doubt catching a glimpse of Mr. Gorgeous. By the time we reached homeroom, Julian's numb hand drooped heavily by his side. I laughed, watching him shake his arm out, trying desperately to regain feeling. It became shamefully apparent that he was well-liked by girls. On the other hand, I'd been perceived as a hindrance, a thorn in their side.

Another bright spot in my otherwise hideous life was chatting with Shelby every morning in homeroom. Shelby dated Brad Wyss, Castle Rock's quarterback and also one of Julian's best friends. She and I became the best of friends from day one, sharing everything. Shelby had been a breath of fresh air next to the other girls in the school. I cherished her friendship. Because of her, it wasn't a chore to drag myself out of bed every morning. I was eternally grateful she approached me on the first day.

I pushed up from my warm bed on this Wednesday morning and headed to the bathroom. My rioting emotions prevented me from another good night's sleep. After my shower, I dragged on a pair of comfortable black Capris and yellow T-shirt, hoping for an optimistic outcome to my day. Based on the previous two weeks, I didn't feel confident.

Julian and I cuddled together in the back seat of Robin's car on the way to school. A light drizzle fell and the overcast grayness matched my mood.

"Just wanted to let you know Shelby's coming to my house this weekend, so if you wanted to hang with Brad…" I stopped, almost feeling like I needed his permission.

"Okay," he said, looking deep in thought.

"Are you sure?"

"Uh-huh."

I sensed something was wrong. I opened my mouth, but closed it, deciding on silence for the rest of the ride. I caught Robin's intermittent glance in the rearview mirror, disapproval etched in her beady eyes.

SHELBY MET ME IN HOMEROOM before the first bell.

"I let Julian know you were visiting this weekend?" I told her.

"Great. I told Brad, too. It's a "girls only" weekend." We both giggled and walked together to our first class.

"See ya, girl," she said.

"Later, Shelb."

For obvious reasons, chemistry class became my least favorite of the day. "Good morning, Mr. Lynch," I said, walking through the door. I reached my seat and fixed my book bag to the chair back.

"Good morning, Amber," he said.

I lugged my textbook from my backpack, grabbed a pencil and sat down.

"Oh look, there's Miss Pretty Bitch." Mitzi walked in, instantly wreaking havoc on my morning. My body cringed, reminding me why I hated this class so much. Even though, there were other available chairs within the room, she always took the empty seat next to me. She'd done that since the first day of school, as if to intimidate me. It worked.

I tried to ignore her.

"What's the matter, Pretty Bitch? Cat got your tongue?" She turned and whacked the palm of her hand into my head.

I whipped around and stood, foaming at the mouth. "That's it! Keep your filthy paws off me, you pathetic excuse for a human being!" I wanted to wipe that shit-eating-grin off her face but restrained myself. My nostrils flared and I pushed her, making her fall to the floor. I'd reached my breaking point.

She grunted, got up and lunged at me. I sidestepped her and all hell broke loose. I heard the distinct chant of classmates surround me. "Girl fight!"

"Ladies!" Mr. Lynch yelled above the commotion of voices within the room. "Both of you, stop! Now! Mitzi, you over there and Amber, you there!" He pointed to a different seating arrangement for the both of us.

I felt my face flush. I couldn't have been any more humiliated.

Amidst the racket, I gritted my teeth and hauled my body across the room to a desk far from the despicable, Mitzi Carlisle.

With a pounding heart and quivering muscles, I felt so outraged I wasn't sure what happened from that point on. I wanted out of this classroom. How could my life get any worse?

I ambled along silently to my next class, stopping at my locker. I dialed in the combination, opened the door and leaped backward, "Ack, what the hell is that?"

"What's that awful smell?" A passerby said, plugging her nose.

From the bottom of my locker, the stench of a dead animal invaded my nostrils. I covered my nose and quickly slammed the door shut. My eyes darted to the left and right, looking for the culprit as my pulse quickened. Nobody stood out from the hurried mob trying to make it to their next class before the bell rang.

My body convulsed and my legs wobbled. Who did this and how did they get the combination to my locker? I suspected one of the many girls who'd been giving me the evil eye for the past week. A myriad of emotions instantly overwhelmed me. Anger, fear, sadness, unease…you name it; I felt them all.

My lips began to tremble. I wanted to cry. Which one of them hated me enough to do this? Mitzi had just clobbered me in the head.

Was it her?

I tracked down a custodian and had the repulsive rodent removed from my locker, along with changing the combination.

I felt on edge through the rest of my day, constantly looking over my shoulder, hearing the echo of footsteps following me. I held my books tightly against my chest, walking from class to class. Everything startled me. *What the hell?* I tried unsuccessfully to shrug it off.

I STOOD IN MY BEDROOM staring out the window, wondering when my life became a living hell. Julian popped into my thoughts. It all started with him. Would it eventually get better? That was the million dollar question.

Robin popped her head in the door. "Everything okay, sis?"

I turned and she saw my pout.

"What happened?" She frowned.

I told her about my encounter with Mitzi.

"That girl is going to answer to me." She gritted her teeth, walked in and sat on my bed.

"Someone put a dead rat in my locker."

"What the hell?" She glared at me with cold, hard eyes. "A dead animal?"

"Yes, I had the cleaning crew disinfect my locker and change the combination." I joined her on the bed and plopped my head down on my pillow, burying my face.

"Look at me," she begged.

I turned over and met her face, skin stretched into a snarl.

Her eyes widened. "Did you tell principal Dodds?" She got up and started pacing the room in circles.

"I'm sure the custodian told him."

She stopped, bent down and held my head in her hands. "You don't know who did it?"

"No, but I sensed whoever it was, stayed close to me all day."

"Amber, you need to tell Dodds."

I took a deep breath. "I know." I exhaled. "I just felt a little overwhelmed today. I'm afraid to go back to that god-awful school. It's been something different every day."

"Oh, Amber. You need to break up with…"

"No! Stop. That's not going to happen."

"Fine," she said with a scathing tone. She turned in a huff and left.

I rose from my bed and strayed back to the window. Oh, the warmth of the late afternoon sunlight falling on my face felt good. I gazed out at the cloudless, deep blue sky thinking about nothing at all…except Julian, of course. My mind always drifted to him. Was breaking up the answer? Maybe Robin had a point. I'd been miserable since school started. But everything was fine prior to that. Was I just the bullied new student or did it go deeper?

I finally calmed and decided to call him.

"Hi," I said, barely whispering. "How are you?"

He sighed heavily. "I'm okay but worried about you. Want to come over?"

"Yeah, but I have to finish my homework first."

"Okay, can't wait to see you."

I smiled at his words. He couldn't wait to see me. Well, the feeling was mutual, but we needed to talk.

JULIAN HUGGED ME TIGHT. "What was the matter with you after school? I was so scared I did something wrong." He brushed his soft lips against my cheek.

It felt like he was trying to distract me from the issue at hand. I didn't fall for his scheme. We traipsed down the hall to the living room and stood by the sofa. I wasn't ready to sit down yet.

"It's the same story every day, on repeat, Julian. I – I don't know what more to say that I haven't already told you."

He took my hands and sighed. "What happened?"

We stood there eye-to-eye…silently imploring the other to speak.

Always being me, I started in. "The girls, Julian, they are major league unfriendly toward me. Mostly Mitzi Carlisle." My body shook when I relayed this morning's chemistry class incident. "Can you shed some light on this?"

Julian shuffled backward, creating space between the two of us.

"What did Mr. Lynch do?"

"What do you think he did?" My voice oozed discontentment. As always, I wasn't getting anywhere. "Did you know someone put a dead rat in my locker?" I sounded pissed. "Is this the way it will always be around you? I have a hard time sharing. In case you didn't know, I'm a tad jealous." I'm sure my face matched the red shirt he was wearing.

Julian paled as he wiped the sweat from his forehead. "You don't have to worry about sharing me. I'm all yours, Amber. Do you know who put the rat in your locker?"

Way to change the subject, Cahill. No way was he going to distract me with his flippant attitude. I needed to get to the bottom of this. "NO!" I screamed. "I thought maybe you could enlighten me."

He repeatedly raked his hands through his hair and wouldn't look me in the eye. "How the hell would I know?"

My arms thrashed around like a maniac on PCP. I couldn't control them, and right now, I was downright furious. "Last week some guy asked if I was your 'flavor-of-the-week.' What the hell did that mean?"

His eyes darted to mine and his hands shot up in a defensive gesture. "I have no idea." He dismissed it with a snort. "Who told you that?"

I started pacing around the room, unable to stay still any longer. In turn, I bashed my hip against the corner of a desk. "Ouch. Shit!" I rubbed at the sore spot. "Well, that's going to leave a mark."

"Are you okay?" he asked.

"Yes. Don't try to change the subject, Julian."

"Christ, Amber. I'm just asking if you're all right." He frowned and flopped down on the couch.

"I'm fine." I went on. "Some guy wearing a baseball cap backward said it. What difference does it make who? Oh, and he asked me out on a date. Maybe I should take him up on it."

Julian's shoulders tensed as he took a deep breath and let it out slowly. He crossed his arms and cast his blue eyes to the floor. I could tell he was withholding information from me.

"Julian, this past month has been the best of my life, but there are some things I don't know about you. Talk to me…please."

A lump swelled in my throat. What was I getting myself into? I really liked him but felt overwhelmed. He kept dark secrets, I knew that, but maybe now wasn't the time for prying it out of him.

Well, to hell with that!

I stopped pacing and looked him in the eye. "How many of those girls have you dated?" I blurted out.

"A few."

A few? I took a deep breath and held it in. Finally, some new information. I exhaled slowly and kept going; asking the one question I knew had a painfully obvious answer. "How many is a few, Julian?" After the words tumbled from my mouth, I regretted them. Did I really want to know? Would it make a difference?

"I don't know. Why are we talking about this?"

"Because I'm just trying to figure out what I'm up against. Is this the way you're approached by girls all the time? This whole scene is freaking me out."

With widening eyes, Julian took a deep, shaky breath and remained silent. Shit. We'd gotten nowhere.

"Talk to me, Julian. Why do they all seem to dislike me? What's going on?" Then it hit me like a wrecking ball. I squeezed my eyes shut and asked the one question I needed to know but was afraid to hear the answer. "How many have you had sex with?"

He rubbed the back of his neck and lifted his head, meeting my eyes. "A few," he said, his shoulders sagging. "What do you want me to say?"

Well, "a few" appeared to be a popular answer. "Is there a definitive number?" I asked, being blunt.

"I don't know." He buried his face in his hands.

Crap! How could he not know how many? Unless...I shuddered. There had to be a lot. I wanted to cry. My bottom lip quivered. "Am I just another notch in your bedpost?"

"Shit, no!" he grimaced. "How can you think that?" He pulled me down to sit next to him and wrapped me in his arms. "It doesn't matter how many, Amber. You're the last for me. There will never be anyone else. Once they get to know you, I'm sure they'll all come around. Please, don't leave me."

I shook. I didn't know how I felt about this news. Did this change how I felt about him? Did I still love him? Yes, I did.

"I'm not leaving you, okay?" At least I got something out of him. My head nearly exploded and my legs felt like jelly. I decided to put the events of the day behind me and move forward. Julian started opening up, but I didn't want to push my luck. "I'm hungry. Shall we eat? My mom is making pork chops or would you prefer eating here."

His shoulders relaxed. He got up, pulling me with him and dragged me into the kitchen. "I prefer here. Do you know how to cook?"

As a young child, I used to love standing by the stove watching my mom cook and learned some basics. I even perfected a dish or two I'd considered edible. "Well, I wouldn't label myself a gourmet chef yet, but I do know how to cook a tasty hamburger."

"Sounds perfect," he said.

By the time I'd cooked two Cajun spiced hamburgers and oven sweet potato fries, Julian had produced two side salads.

I watched as he continually licked his lips while cutting up the veggies. He looked adorable.

"Hungry?" I asked, grinning at him.

"Starving," he groaned, breathing in deeply to catch the scent of the burgers.

"Me too. Let's eat."

We sat cross-legged next to each other on the living room floor, while enjoying our meal and watched a video of him as a little one-year-old baby. We laughed at the cute toddler, attempting to read an upside down book.

"Amber, this is good. You can make this for me anytime."

I finished my food and moved subtly, snaking my arms around his waist and squeezing him into me. I laid my head against his chest and inhaled his masculine scent, my earlier hissy fit forgotten. He had an uncanny way of making me forget my anger.

Swallowing his last bite, Julian pulled my head away from him, lifted my chin, and planted a soft kiss on my lips, igniting my libido. "Are you okay?"

"Yes. Thank you for opening up to me," I whispered against his mouth.

"Okay." Julian said the words, but I wasn't sure he felt them and then quickly changed the subject.

"My folks are at a charity dinner tonight and not expected home until late." He winked. "Would you like to fool around?"

"Oh?" I paused. "What do you have in mind?" I giggled.

Julian stood, pulled me up by my hands, and swept me off my feet. Cradling me in his arms, he carried me upstairs to his bedroom and threw me onto his bed. I squealed with laughter, landing on my back.

I loved his bedroom décor—very masculine and straightforward. A Moroccan rug covered the floor at the base of his bed surrounded by pastel blues throughout the cozy room.

"I'm going to have my way with you right here, right now. How about that?" He laughed.

"I like that idea."

I looked up into Julian's beautiful, steely blue eyes. Outside of school, I experienced a totally different guy. He seemed more relaxed…that was until I brought up the subject of girls. Then a closed off and distant Julian appeared. I resolved that one day he would tell me. I needed to take baby steps with him.

"Alrighty then."

In a mock maneuver, Julian pounced on top of his queen sized four-poster bed in an attempt to startle me, landing on his hands and knees, straddling my body. He hovered above me, his broad smile priceless and locked his focus with my eyes.

I reached up, grabbed his hair, and pulled him down to me, kissing him with passion and eagerness. Our tongues tangled, deepening the kiss. With sheer quickness, I moved, flipping him off me and straddled him as he fell to his back, feigning weakness. I bent down and planted a trail of kisses along his neck. "Time to remove this," I declared, lifting his shirt by the hem. Julian arched his back and helped by raising his arms.

Tugging his shirt over his head, I tossed it to the floor and pushed him back down. I leaned over and planted kisses from the base of his neck down to the beginning of his chest hair. Placing my hands around his muscular biceps, I held him down and started fluttering my tongue back and forth across the tip of his aroused nipple. He groaned deeply. A riotous excitement sparked my libido as my body responded.

"Ah, you've hit a hot spot to my dick, Amber." He chuckled, squirming uncontrollably.

Still writhing at my ruthless invasion of his nipples, moving from his left to right, he made a half-ass, unsuccessful attempt to push me off him.

"Damn, you're strong."

"You'd do well to remember that too, Julian." I giggled and continued to pursue his nipples, licking and sucking.

He wasn't fooling me, though. I knew he could easily buck me off if he wanted to. While thinking those words, Julian flipped me onto my back and held my hands beside my head.

"You'd do well to remember my strength, too." His laugh was deep and throaty and his lips attacked mine again, kissing me like it was his last. Breathless, we invaded each other's mouths, our tongues entwined.

Through my shorts I felt his excitement as he pushed his erection against me, up and down, rubbing right where I needed it. I savored the feeling, cherishing his experience. He stopped, released my hands, and reached down to remove my shorts and panties with an enthusiasm I'd not seen before. Then, with the quickness of a cheetah on the Serengeti, he removed his shorts and boxers.

"That was fast." I giggled.

"I'm glad you're impressed." He smirked.

Throwing the clothes aside, he chuckled and lifted the hem of my shirt up over my breasts and started sucking on my nipples. They hardened and puckered as he pulled on the tips with his teeth. I fought for a breath and tried to buck him off to no avail. He grabbed my hands again and held them down on each side of my shoulders and started his fierce onslaught of my breasts again.

Fighting for breath, he continued his torment of my breasts. "My turn now," he exhaled.

I squirmed wildly. "Ah, Julian, you're driving me crazy. You win."

"That's the point here, Amber." I felt him grin against my nipples.

Letting go of my hands, Julian positioned himself against my wet sex and eased himself inside me very gently. He didn't stop until he was all the way in.

"Uhh, you're extremely tight, Amber. Am I hurting you at all?"

Julian always cared how I felt and that meant more to me than anything. I considered myself a lucky girl.

"No, not anymore. It feels unbelievable. Keep moving, please," I wheezed.

"Good, let me know if you want to stop."

"Okay."

He growled a low, husky sound, pressing into me while I moved my hips in time with his. I didn't have any sphere of reference, but the sex we shared was amazing.

"Christ, Amber, this is good. You're so snug. We're meant for each other, like a lock and key."

"Yes."

Julian pulled out slowly, and then with a swift movement, started licking my nipples again, pulling and sucking them with his mouth.

Desperate for a release, I surrendered to him. Oh my, this felt heavenly. I writhed and twisted, unable to stay still. Once again, he eased into me, pulled out, and rammed into me hard. I heard his harsh breathing in equal time to my panting.

"Argh, oh, that feels good," I moaned.

"Shit, Amber, I'm gonna come."

"Don't stop, please, Julian," I hissed through my teeth, nearing my climax.

Julian moved, dropping his weight on top of me and rammed into me again and again and again. I dug my fingers into his backside dropping them down to his butt. I felt his slick chest against my pounding heart. His mouth invaded mine again, kissing me with animalistic fervor. Our tongues twisted around each others. A frantic passion consumed us. He slammed into me at a wild pace. Faster. Faster. My body tensed, my legs shook uncontrollably, my eyes rolled back into their sockets, and I screamed while an orgasm ripped through my whole body over and over and over.

I wrapped my legs around his back and pulled him into me, wiggling for some more needed friction while my core continued to convulse. Tingling throughout my body overtook my senses, and an unbridled smile spread across my face. I loved this guy. I loved him so much.

"Oh my God, Julian," I panted, gulping precious air into my lungs.

I released my leg grip from his back. He steadied his weight onto his hands and looked down over me. Through clenched teeth and closed eyes, he continued to ram into me hissing and groaning. The muscles of his body tensed and shuddered, as he emptied himself inside me, finding his own release. He cursed and dropped down, bearing his weight on top of me.

"Ah," he groaned.

Julian's collapsed body pressed into mine. His weight pushed me into the mattress, and he rested his head in the crook of my neck, planting kisses behind my ear.

As our breathing eased, we changed positions, laying in each other's arms with my head on his chest, listening to the pounding of his heart calm to a normal rhythm.

I tickled the tips of my fingers through the hair on his chest. "That was wonderful. I like make-up sex."

"Me too," he whispered. "I love it when you come. You squeeze me so tight and I can feel you pulsating around me. You have such an adorable look on your face."

"So do you."

Running his fingertips up and down my arms, I detected a quizzical look on his face.

"What's the matter?"

"I've noticed a mark on your back left shoulder blade. What is it?"

"It's a birthmark."

"Do you realize it's in the shape of a heart?"

"Yes, I've been told that before and have seen it in the mirror."

"It's cool." He brushed his hand over the mark and pressed a soft kiss to it.

A shiver ran through me at his contact. "I've grown rather fond of it myself."

BACK AT MY HOUSE BEFORE Julian's parents made their way home, I couldn't wrap my head around the way I felt about him. Even in spite of his evasiveness.

I walked in the door to Robin sprawled out on the sofa, snacking on chips and salsa, watching TV. She glanced at me with that know-it-all look in her eyes.

"What's up, Amber?" She raised her eyebrows at me. "You look like the cat-who-ate-the-canary."

"Nothing," I lied.

"Oh please, I know the walk-of-shame when I see it." She grinned wickedly.

My eyes widened as a horrified expression crossed my face. Was it that obvious?

"Please don't tell Mom or Dad, please, please, please."

"I won't if you tell me all about it."

"With all due respect, Robin, this is blackmail in its lowest form." I traipsed into the room and sat on the edge of the chair across from her.

"I don't care what it is, just spill it," she demanded with a devious chuckle.

I trusted her with my deepest, darkest secrets and could rest assured they would go no further than us. We had that mutual sisterly bond between us.

"Okay, I—I think I love him…"

Before I could say another word, she cut me off. "What? You couldn't possibly know what love is, Amber."

"Do you want to hear what I have to say or not?" I snapped.

She dipped another chip and raised it to her lips. "Sorry, go on," she implored and put the chip in her mouth.

"We have this connection. It's like he's the other half of my soul and vice versa." I shivered when I said the words.

"Yeah, yeah, yeah, tell me about the sex." She leaned her head toward me and laughed.

I didn't want to share the intimate details of my private love life to anyone, not even my sister. I felt like it'd betray Julian. I'd never asked her about her extracurricular love life. Why couldn't she extend me the same privacy? I exhaled and decided to exercise some discretion, and dialed it down… a few thousand notches. "It hurt the first time, but now it's all right," I said nonchalantly, hoping to drop the subject.

She swallowed and her eyes went wide. "Holy crap. You mean you've done it more than once?"

"Um, yes, a few times."

"I had no idea. I thought you said you loved him based on this one encounter. Please tell me that you're being careful."

I nodded. I swear she didn't blink.

"Oh, my little sister is no longer a virgin." She stood and moved to hug me.

"Right and keep it to yourself, sis."

"I will. I promise."

And with that, she closed the bag of chips, turned, and walked into the kitchen. I heard the fridge open, and my shoulders slumped. I sighed, feeling relieved for now, but knew Robin, and that she'd *never* drop it.

Chapter Six

Shelby arrived at my house at three in the afternoon for our much needed girl-time weekend.

We bounded up the stairs to my bedroom, closed the door and plopped down on my queen-sized bed.

I laid on my belly, hugging my pillow as she leaned back against the headboard.

Wasting no time diving into the nitty-gritty, she began, "So tell me, what is going on in school?"

"I wish I knew. Many of the girls hate me." I frowned. "I don't know what I've done, either."

"Really? I've seen Mitzi." She paused and shifted onto her side, resting her head in the palm of her hand. "She's a nasty piece of work. Just ignore her."

"I'm trying, but she just gets in my face."

"Who else is harassing you?"

"Mostly just Mitzi and Bianca." I rolled onto my back and stared up at the ceiling. "What do you know about Julian before I moved here?"

"Um, nothing personal, only that he was popular with the girls." She shrugged her shoulders and stopped, looking as if she was pondering something. "In fact, very popular," she finally said. "It's weird, but I never saw him with the same girl twice."

An earlier conversation with Julian popped in my head. *I've never had more than a couple of dates with anyone.* I began to wonder how many of the girls he'd actually dated. I never got an actual number. Maybe I should have pursued it further.

Shelby's insight into the life of the enigmatic Julian Cahill was sketchy—only aware that he was popular with the girls—she'd never been interested in dating him.

"I guess I always thought it was odd he never had a steady girlfriend because…well, you know…he's so hot," she said with a twisted smile.

I giggled. "So you think so, too?"

"Uh, yeah. Probably the hottest guy in the school."

"Hey, he's mine," I chuckled. "Brad's not so bad himself."

A moment later, when she didn't respond, I looked at her. She appeared to be somewhere else. A blank, slack expression filled her face.

"Earth to Shelby. You have it bad."

"Yep. I love him and he loves me, too."

I sat up and reached over to my nightstand and plucked a framed photo of Julian and me and handed it to her.

"Wait, what's that mark on your left shoulder blade?" she asked, snatching the picture frame from my hand.

"Birthmark," I told her, stretching my head around to look at it.

"It's in the shape of a heart. How cool."

"Yeah. I've seen it. Julian mentioned it, too."

Shelby studied the framed picture. "You two make a great-looking couple. Jeez, check out all that blond hair." She looked up and asked the one question only my sister dared to ask. "How's he in bed?"

My mouth fell open and I playfully swatted her.

"Well…?" she implored me.

I hid my face in my hands. "He's fucking great," I said, peeking through my fingers.

"Amber Scott!" she barked with laughter. "Do you kiss him with that mouth?"

I nodded. "Well, how's Brad?"

Fanning her face, she smiled.

I absolutely loved her with all my heart. She was exactly what I needed in my now tumultuous life. My spirits had finally lifted.

THE FOLLOWING WEEK my good mood was crushed when the phone rang. Standing in the foyer with the door open, I took a deep breath of the chilly October evening air, hoping to hear Julian's voice on the other end.

"Hello?"

"Bitch. You'll get yours."

"What? Who is this?" I asked, and then the line went dead. The voice on the other end sounded muffled, unrecognizable. A knot formed in my stomach and my anxiety level shot up. It'd been the third one of those calls in the last three days, always with the same message.

"Who was that?" Mom perked up from the sofa.

"Another call from—"

"That's it!" she interrupted. "I've had enough of this. I'm calling the police and having those calls traced. What did they say this time?"

"Same as every other time." I sighed, dropping my head to my chest, remembering a time when my life was simple and uncomplicated. How did I get from there to here? Shaken to my core, I felt exhausted. Somebody out there was taking great pleasures in dragging me through an agonizing hell.

I suspected it was either Mitzi Carlisle or Bianca Pantilla going out of their way to make my life miserable. I'd guess the mysterious person on the other end of those threatening phone calls was one of them. But which one, I didn't know. And now, to make matters worse, I felt as though I was being followed, hearing the ire of heavy footsteps through the halls of the school. Even cars drove slowly by our house after dark.

Mom stood and disappeared to the kitchen. Moments later I heard her talking on the phone. I couldn't make out what she said, but concluded she'd dialed 911. I dragged my feet upstairs to my bedroom and began my homework.

I had a target on my back and didn't know why. Wheedling any information out of Julian was like running a marathon—all 26.2 miles of it. He admitted he'd had sex before me, but wouldn't divulge with how many girls. "A few" was always his response. Maybe I should get a final tally.

The phone rang again. My shoulders tensed at the mere thought of another one of those phone calls. This time Julian's voice echoed in my ear.

"Hey, what are you doing?"

I let out the breath I hadn't realized I was holding. "Sitting on my bed. I just received another one of those phone calls."

"I'm sorry, Amber."

"It's not your fault, besides my mom dialed 911 to put a stop to them." It always came down to him apologizing for my harassment. Why?

"Good."

"What are you doing?" I asked, chewing the nail of my index finger down to the quick.

"Thinking about you. Want to go for a ride in the Camaro?"

"Sure, but it's nearly nine o'clock."

"We won't be long. I just need to get out of the house."

"Okay. Can I drive?" I asked sweetly.

"Um..."

"Never mind, only kidding." *I just wanted to hear your reaction.*

Julian completed the restoration work on his '69 Chevy Camaro. On occasion, he'd let me drive the beast, as he called it. Of course, he had to teach me how to drive a stick shift. I scowled at the memory. *Let the clutch out and give it gas at the same time...Be careful...Don't roll back...You're going to hit the car behind us...Stop!...Give it more gas...Do you want me to drive?* To him, it probably seemed like I was a hopeless case, but eventually, I perfected it. Even so, he preferred driving.

Almost out the door, I stopped at my mom's voice coming from the kitchen. "Where are you going at this late hour, Amber?"

"Julian's. I won't be long."

"No. Tell Julian you'll see him in the morning." She looked me in the eye with her don't-cross-me stare. "You two are spending too much time together."

"Please. I'll just be fifteen minutes."

Sitting on the sofa, Dad spoke up from behind the evening paper. "Your mother said no, Amber. It's a school night. Have you finished your homework?"

"Yes." *Damn!* I sagged against the door and lowered my head.

Pressing my lips together in a firm line, I told them I'd need to call and let him know.

"Make it quick," he snapped.

"Okay." I scowled but knew better than to test my parents' limits.

I stormed back up to my bedroom in a huff, angry at the fact that I'd been forbidden to see Julian. I grabbed my phone, dialed his number and plopped down on my bed. As the phone starting ringing, the rattle of a trash can scoffing across the sidewalk outside made me jump. A neighborhood dog began howling in the distance. I leaped up and made a beeline to the window. Glancing down toward Julian's house, I froze and my scalp prickled. I felt the beat of my heart triple, nearly exploding with fear. Squinting my eyes, I noticed two hooded figures sneaking around, peeking into the windows of Julian's house. Who were they?

Bouncing up and down on my toes, my body quivered, urging Julian to hurry up and answer the damned phone.

He picked up on the fourth ring. "Hello."

Nearly hyperventilating, I held myself tightly, wrapping my arms around my belly. "Finally! Julian, it's me. There are two people outside your house prowling around. Are you alone?" My words came out briskly, my breathing erratic.

"Yeah. Where?"

"Our house side. Are your doors locked?"

"I think so."

"I'm scared, Julian. Can you sneak over here? Quickly. You're not safe there." I felt unease in my gut, my legs buckling. "Go out your back door. I'll meet you at ours. Be careful."

"Okay." His voice cracked. "I'll be there as soon as I can."

Adrenaline spiked in my veins as I raced down the stairs to the back door of the house, filling my parents in on the whole ordeal. My dad leaped up from the couch and met me in the kitchen, while Mom made another 911 call.

My father ran out the door ahead of me at the same time I heard a loud bang and jerked backward. It sounded like a muffled gunshot. *Julian!*

"Be careful, Daddy." Panic rose in my throat.

"I will. Wait here, Amber." My dad sucked in lungfuls of air.

"Julian!" I yelled. I held my breath, waiting for his response. None came. My body started shaking uncontrollably. I would never forgive myself if anything happened to him.

Mom joined me at the door, wrapping her arms around me. "It'll be okay, honey."

Minutes later, my dad appeared from behind the garage with Julian alongside him. *Oh, thank God!* I held the door open as they dashed inside. I pulled it shut and locked it. I turned, took Julian into my arms and hugged him tightly.

"Sorry, Amber, I stumbled over the trash can," Julian said, out of breath.

I quickly skimmed my eyes up and down his body. "Are you okay?"

"Yes." He swept a hand across his forehead wiping away the sweat.

"Come in and sit down, Julian." Mom said. "Are you sure you're okay?"

"Yes. Thank you, Mrs. Scott."

OFFICERS BEN KEILLOR AND JOHN ZEBB told us they did a full scan of the surrounding area and found nothing unusual.

My mom invited them in, and we all moved to the living room.

"Amber Scott?" Officer Keillor scowled at me. Perhaps he thought I lied.

"Yes," I said nervously.

"What did you see, Miss Scott?" Keillor asked, dragging his fingers through his dark brown mustache. He had dark protruding eyes and wrinkled skin. I guessed his age to be around sixty.

I went on to describe the scene from the moment I dialed Julian's phone number.

"What time was it when you looked out your window?" Keillor went on.

"Nine o'clock," I said, absentmindedly looking at the clock.

"Could you see if they were male or female?"

"No, Officer. They had hoodies pulled up over their heads." I cleared my throat and frowned. Being targeted was bad enough; now Julian was on the receiving end of it, too.

"Did you hear any conversation?"

"No, I'm sorry, I didn't."

After what felt like thirty minutes of grilling me then Julian, the officers wrote down everything we told them. We all stood and walked them to the door. Before they left, Officer Zebb, a tall, husky man, suggested Julian stay with us until his parents returned home.

"Absolutely." My dad nodded, shook hands with the men and they left. He turned and pulled me into his arms. "Well, that was an interesting chain of events."

Julian scrubbed a hand across his reddened face, no doubt feeling a twinge of embarrassment mixed with regret. "I'm sorry for the trouble I've caused, Mr. Scott."

"No trouble at all."

My mom gave him an understanding nod. "Anytime we can help, Julian."

My dad patted Julian on the back and turned toward the upstairs. "Well, if I'm no longer needed, I'm retiring for the night. Stay safe, Julian."

"I will. Thank you for everything, Mr. Scott."

Just then, a cold shiver spread through my body at the possibility that I might've met the culprits face-to-face if my parents hadn't stopped me from leaving the house.

"What time are your parents expected home, Julian?" Mom looked at him; concern drenched in her words.

"They told me around midnight."

"You can sleep here, honey. It's nearly ten thirty and a school night."

What? Julian sleep here? Yes! I couldn't believe what my mom suggested. *He could sleep in my bed with me.* I screamed at her in my head. *Keep dreaming, Amber.*

"Thanks for the offer, Mrs. Scott. I'm usually up late studying anyway. I'll wait for my parents."

"Amber, you need to get to bed." She scolded me like I was five years old. How embarrassing. I'd have been grounded for life if she only knew what Julian and I were up to the night before.

Sneaking around had become a mission, a very delectable mission. We couldn't get enough of each other, but searching for a safe place to make out without being caught became a major undertaking. We laughed each time we succeeded.

"Mom, please let me stay up with Julian until his parents get home."

She let out a deep breath. "Okay, but no complaints tomorrow morning about being too tired."

"Promise." I made an X on my chest with my forefinger. "Cross my heart, Mom."

She narrowed her eyes at me and made her way up the stairs. Seconds later I heard her bedroom door close.

I grabbed Julian's hands and tugged him into my arms. "It looks like you're the one who's being targeted now."

He snickered. "I don't think so, Amber."

We plopped down on the sofa and simultaneously puffed out a deep breath, exhausted from the evening's events.

I stared into Julian's eyes, wondering what he was thinking. "Can you believe what's going on?"

He squirmed uncomfortably. "No, but if I find out, they're going to wish they stalked someone else." Julian held me close and remained silent except for his soft breathing against my neck.

Would we ever find out who it was? A shiver swept through me with everything going on in my life. The dead rat in my locker, the ominous phone calls, the feeling of being followed everywhere and now this.

I snuggled closer to Julian.

THE NEXT MORNING, through heavy lidded eyes, an exhaustion drenched my body but I didn't dare tell my parents. I'd be on the receiving end of enough verbal lashings in school; I didn't need it at home, too.

Walking down the hallway to homeroom, I spotted a flyer hanging on the wall. It mentioned a talent competition in the school auditorium at the beginning of November. I grabbed Julian's arm and drew his attention to it, "Do you want to compete with me? We can play our guitars, and I'll sing."

"Sounds like fun. Do you have a song in mind?" he asked.

"Well, my mom is really into The Moody Blues. She plays their CDs all the time. How about 'Nights in White Satin?' It's an easy one to play."

"Great idea. It shouldn't take too long for us to polish it up."

MY PARENTS ENFORCED their door-stays-open policy when Julian was in my bedroom. Sometimes we needed the quiet while doing our homework together. On this particular afternoon, we set school work aside and decided to practice our song for the talent show.

While rummaging through my closet looking for the music score to our song, Julian sat on my bed, strumming his guitar. I abruptly paused when I heard him softly singing the lyrics to the song.

Stunned silent, I quietly listened. His voice wafted toward me like caramel sliding down the throat. Noticing the words—those words—the L-word. He sang them with such emotion. This guy of mine melted my heart.

Without contemplating my next move, I scrambled to my feet, exited the closet and engulfed him in my arms.

"Oh my God, Julian, that was beautiful! Let's make this song a duet." I let out an appreciative sigh.

"Are you sure? I think you have a voice better suited for this song."

"Seriously? You've got to be kidding."

After harassing him for the next five minutes to sing with me, he reluctantly agreed. We ran through the song over and over until feeling satisfied with our arrangement, harmonizing perfectly.

Exhausted, we called it a day. We both had our homework to finish and wanted to avoid another late night. We'd had so many of them lately.

Julian got up off my bed, grabbed me, and planted a kiss on my lips, making me melt. Together we walked down the stairs toward the door. Sashaying over to him, I pulled him into me for a hug. I always had a hard time saying goodbye.

"By the way, Amber, my car is back in the shop. Do you think we could bum a ride to school with Robin in the morning? My car won't be ready until tomorrow afternoon."

"I'm sure it won't be a problem."

Staring at him as he made his way across the worn path, past the maple tree to his house, I never got bored watching his perfectly shaped, muscular ass. He exaggerated his strut with a cute swagger, for my eyes only. I thanked God every day he lived next door.

I YAWNED NON-STOP on the way to school the next morning, my late nights taking their toll on me. A bright spot in my otherwise sleepy morning was gazing at the splash of glistening gold and burnt orange colors of the aspens trees swaying in the breeze.

Julian raised an eyebrow at me. "Tired?"

"Enough of the witty commentary." I nudged him in the side, but still couldn't hide my fatigue.

My morning passed slowly, catching myself dozing in history class. I looked forward to the afternoon classes I shared with Julian. He made me feel safe.

Quickly, I made a stop at my locker and then headed off to my math class at the other end of the school, the longest walk between classes for me. I didn't mind because I'd be seeing Julian.

Without warning, my body slammed hard against the lockers after rounding the corner outside the library.

"Hey, bitch."

I turned and spotted Bianca peering into my eyes. Ah yes, how could I forget the tall, leggy brunette, with piercing dark brown eyes and big boobs, who practically fell over Julian in the hallway on the first day of school? She reeked of tobacco. I had a hunch she smoked like a chimney. Her biting words weren't the first ones she'd directed at me, and I knew they wouldn't be the last, but touching was going too far.

"Don't you dare push me again," I hissed at her.

Rolling her eyes, she turned and huffed off.

"Yeah, you keep rolling those eyes, Bianca, and maybe you'll find a brain back there," I stated proudly, amazed at my ability to be humorous at a time when I could've just crawled under a rock and disappeared.

She gave me the finger. What was it about those two girls?

"Your IQ, I assume?" I yelled at her. My humor knew no bounds.

On the way home from school, I cuddled up with Julian in the back seat of Robin's car, thinking of my day. Except for being on the receiving end of Bianca's vengeance, and the strong feeling of being followed, I rated the day a success. I ignored it.

Alongside me, Julian's silence spoke volumes when I told Robin about Bianca. Darkness crossed his face.

"She pushed you?" Robin squawked.

"Yeah, can you believe that?" My frustration grew as Julian appeared to ignore our conversation, remaining quiet. Sometimes, I couldn't figure out where he was coming from. Did he doubt me?

As we pulled into the driveway, I turned to him. "Want to get together at my house tonight?"

He exited the car, turned and opened his mouth, then stopped short. "Um...okay." he finally mumbled.

"Good."

"I've got to pick up my car first. I'll be over later," he said, his frustration apparent, exhaling heavily. He turned and headed home.

"There is something he's not telling you, Amber." Robin eyed me; distrust etched on her face as she placed her backpack on the table when we walked in the door.

"I know."

"You know?" she asked, her voice incredulous.

"Yes, but I can't figure it out. Every time I talk about those girls, he seems to tune me out. I'm going to get to the bottom of it tonight. Trust me."

"Good. You need to find out what his issues are before your relationship goes any further." She stormed off in a huff.

I headed up to my bedroom, plopped my body onto my bed, and buried my face into the palm of my hands. My emotional state had been to hell and back since dating Julian. I loved him, but not at the expense of my happiness.

I slowly recovered my composure before Julian arrived for dinner, making my way downstairs as the doorbell rang.

"Hi, Mr. Scott, thank you for inviting me to dinner this evening."

"You are certainly welcome anytime," my dad said.

Mom prepared her famous homemade meatloaf, seasoned red potatoes, and glazed carrots. The table conversation ebbed and flowed with Julian sharing stories of his childhood with everyone.

After dinner, Julian and I headed into the den to do homework.

"We need to talk about some issues that are bothering me," I said, closing the door. Julian plopped down on the loveseat and let out a loud sigh.

Suddenly a cold, harsh atmosphere descended upon the room as he looked up at me. Shit, he looked angry. Well, so was I.

"Amber, why is this whole fucking situation such a concern to you? As I've asked before, what do you want me to say?" Julian ran his hands through his hair. He got right to the point, clearly frustrated with this issue.

I stood in front of him, hands on my hips, dumbfounded by his lack of concern. He tried to ignore the problem again. As tears welled up in my eyes, I couldn't figure out why he was so angry. I hadn't even asked him anything yet, and he'd gone all defensive on me. At this point, I didn't feel like being doubted and frankly wanted nothing more than for him to leave. I'd had enough. I knew I wasn't going to get anywhere tonight, so there was no point in trying.

"Why don't we call it a night, okay?" I huffed, turning my back to him and headed for the door. "I've got a lot of homework, and my head is reeling from your shitty lack of concern."

"Amber, please don't. I don't see what the problem is here. Please stop making an issue out of this." He grimaced. "Fuck!"

He muttered something under his breath that I couldn't make out, but thought I heard him say, "*Girls.*"

I whipped my head around. "What did you say? I'm effing pissed at you!" My voice escalated. "For starters, you could begin by acknowledging my feelings. Defend me for cripes sake!" I slammed my hands on my hips. "I told you I don't like sharing and you keep shutting me down every time I mention this. Look, I don't want to fight anymore, so let's take a break from each other this evening. I'd like you to go home."

I opened the door and gestured for him to leave.

With a low growl, he stood up. "I'll talk to Mitzi and Bianca tomorrow, okay? We'll get this sorted out."

I couldn't believe what I'd just heard. I didn't want him anywhere near those bitches. He just didn't understand. Would we ever get past this? "Are you kidding me?" My voice scaled new heights. "You're going to talk to them?" I screamed. "Forget it, please just go."

"Christ, Amber, I...," he trailed off.

He came toward me and made an attempt to pull me into his arms, but I sidestepped him and moved away.

"Don't. I need some space right now. I'll see you in the morning," I sniffled, wiping a falling tear from my cheek with the back of my hand.

"Don't do this," he said, glaring at me in agony.

"If you care about me, then you'll leave. I can't deal with your shit right now. Please, just go, okay? Unless you feel like spilling it, I'll see you in the morning."

He looked down. "Yes, maybe I should go."

Fear instantly gripped me. Did he want to break up? *No, that's not what I meant.*

Saying nothing more, Julian turned, headed to the door and left. Feeling deflated, I wanted to stop him but knew I'd regret it. This was it. My body went limp. My heart sank.

After he left, I bolted upstairs to my room, kicked the door closed, and found myself sobbing into my pillow. The thought of losing him made me ill. I raised my head and locked my eyes onto the framed photo of us, sitting on my nightstand, a happier time, I thought. I grabbed it and heaved it across the room and began shaking uncontrollably.

A soft knock on my door pulled me back into the now.

"Come in," I said, bawling.

"What happened?" Robin crossed the room and sat on the bed

beside me. "I heard you yelling."

"I don't know. Julian's so detached from it all. I just want him to acknowledge it, that's all, but I think we might've broken up!" I cried.

"Why, what did he say?"

"He got all defensive." I frowned. "It's almost like I'm imagining this whole ludicrous situation. I never thought it would come to this. Never!" I howled. "I love him so much, but I don't know if we're going to get past this. This might be the end."

"I can't tell you what to do, but I will say that he's got some serious issues that he's not telling you. It's probably wise that you end it right now." Her voice sounded sad. "If you need a shoulder to cry on, mine is here, Ambie."

"Thanks, Robbie. Love you, Sis."

AFTER A RESTLESS NIGHT and very little sleep, I still felt raw from my argument with Julian. He made an attempt to apologize after I called him to explain my decision to ride to school with Robin instead of him.

"I'll see you at school." I sounded grumpy and agitated.

My sister and I arrived at school with a few minutes to spare before the first bell rang. I wore my chic jeans with a slit above each knee coupled with a simple white T-shirt, ready to take on the day, despite the uneasy feeling that encompassed me.

I knew I'd see Julian in homeroom and wondered what to say to him. Would he even talk to me after the way I'd treated him the night before? Would things be awkward between us? He sounded completely wrecked on the phone earlier this morning; leaving no doubt he had no intention of breaking up with me. Would he finally decide to discuss this with me later or continue to shut me out? It turned into a make or break situation for me, with it being up to him.

I turned the dial of my combination lock, opened my locker, and grabbed my chemistry textbook for my first class when I felt it. Without warning, my body crashed against the wall with a revolting thud as a piercing, and jagged pain shot through me.

I heard the first-period bell ring when my head collided hard against the lockers. A deep groan left my body as I struggled for my next breath. I lost my balance and found myself sprawled on all fours, dizzy and disoriented. It vaguely registered that I had a metallic taste in my mouth. Unable to defend myself, I slipped into a protective fetal position. Once I regained my strength of will, I looked up in time to see Bianca and Mitzi hovering, coming at me with hurling fists and pelting boots.

So much was happening at once, I hadn't realized the excruciating pain on the right side of my stomach was blood bubbling up through a wound. My white top, now soaked with my blood, clung to my skin. I thrashed around screaming in pain.

A bona fide panic gripped me, my heart beating out of my chest. I couldn't breathe. *Somebody help me!* I tried to scream, but no sound came from my lips.

I finally found my voice. "You stabbed me!" I wheezed. "I'm bleeding. Somebody help me, help me." But my words were barely audible.

"Who the fuck do you think you are, bitch?" Mitzi shrieked, kicking me again and again, knocking the wind out of me. I groaned. "You think you can have Julian to yourself and tell him who he can and cannot date? He belongs to all of us. I told you you'd get yours."

I didn't have a chance with two of them against one of me. My body stung with pain and horror. I tried to scream, but getting the wind knocked out of me inhibited that tiny accomplishment.

The shouts and screams coming from all around faded in and out, which brought a minuscule bit of relief due to the fact I'd been unable to carry out that feat by myself.

Out of nowhere, while trying to fight the stabbing pain and dizziness, I heard the roar of a familiar voice.

"Holy fucking hell!" Julian's voice resonated through the halls. "Someone call an ambulance! What's this shit, you goddamn bitches?"

"Amber!" I heard the faint voice of Shelby. She clutched my head in her lap, mumbling something unintelligible.

Before I could register what was happening, Mitzi and Bianca crashed into the lockers across the hallway. I heard screams coming from every direction, but my head felt so thick, I couldn't make out any words. Julian burned with rage…I saw that. Through all the pain, it dawned on me that he was here to save me. Maybe now he would believe me.

A puddle of my blood soaked the floor in front of me. My body began shaking uncontrollably. I felt woozy and faint.

Suddenly, chaos and mayhem surrounded me as Principal Dodds made his way to the scene. "What is going on here?" Investigating the sight around him, he started barking orders. "Call an ambulance!" I heard him holler as the room began to spin.

Before I had a moment to focus on what just transpired, I felt Julian's gentle arms cradle me. "Stay awake, Amber. Don't you dare go to sleep. Please, stay awake." His voice trembled. "Shit." At the speed of a jet moving at Mach two, he removed his shirt and pressed it against the stab wound on my belly.

"Amber. You'll be okay," Shelby cried.

"Julian, Bianca stabbed me." I reached down to the spot on my stomach.

I noticed his eyes flash with torment and indescribable pain. "Shhh, don't touch it, Amber," he choked out the words.

While Principal Dodds asked me simple questions, I saw school personnel escort Mitzi and Bianca down the hall toward his office. "Get Amber an ambulance—now!" he bellowed again.

"One is on its way, Joe."

"Ouch, my side is burning in pain, Julian. I don't feel good."

"I'm so sorry, Amber. I had no idea they'd do that to you. I'm so, so sorry. Please believe me," he pleaded, his eyes glossed over with tears.

I wanted to wipe them away, but my rioting pain repressed that simple gesture. His expression turned to torture and fear.

"Please stay with me. Don't you dare go to sleep," Julian demanded again.

I felt light-headed, and the room lights dimmed. With a blinding headache and stinging pain in my side, Nurse Hassler appeared moments before the EMTs rushed down the hall with a stretcher. After a quick examination, the medical team covered my wound with bandages, then lifted my body onto the gurney and whisked me away.

Dazed and groggy, I was vaguely aware that Julian was holding my hand. The ceiling lights went in and out of focus as I made a vain attempt to keep my eyelids open, but lost the battle, and everything went dark.

Chapter Seven

My body burned with pain. The gloomy stares of my mom, dad, and Robin greeted me when I managed to open my eyes.

Mom caressed my forehead. "Hi, honey, how are you feeling?" Her soft words washed over me.

"Hey." My voice sounded weak. "My side hurts, and my head aches." Inspecting the site where the pain was emanating from, I lifted my hand to feel a bandage covering my stomach and winced.

"I got stabbed, Mom." I started trembling at the thought. "It hurts...bad."

"Yes, you were stabbed. Your doctor had to surgically close your wound. You've been asleep for a few hours."

"Hey, pumpkin. Are you cold?" Daddy whispered, obviously noticing my uncontrollable shaking.

"Yes, could I have another blanket?"

"I'll get one for you dear," an attractive red-headed nurse said and traipsed off out of the room.

"Amber, you need to get better." Robin caressed my arm. "When I heard you were hurt, I drove here as fast as I could."

Tears spilled from my eyes when I looked around. Attached to my left index finger was a clothespin like clip with a wire attached on one end, running to a machine over my head. To the right, a heartbeat appeared on the front of a monitor beeping a regular rhythm. A bag fastened to a pole above my head dispensed a clear liquid into an IV affixed to my arm. The distinct smell of sterile gauze and iodine filled my nostrils. Slowly, it dawned on me I was in the hospital when the pretty red-headed nurse, wearing black-rimmed glasses, re-entered my room with a heated blanket and placed it over my shivering body.

"Is that better, Amber?" she asked. Her name tag read L. Torres, RN. "Are you in any pain?"

"Yes, that's better, thank you. My stomach and head both hurt. Could I have a painkiller?"

"I'll get something for you."

When she exited the room, I quietly inquired, "Where's Julian?"

"He was here earlier but said he'd be back later, honey," Mom said, concern written across her face.

"He saved me, Mom. He saved me." I cringed in pain.

"We know, sweetheart. Shh, calm down."

"When can I go home?"

"The doctor will be in later to examine your wound and give us a better idea then, but I'm sure you'll be staying the night."

I replayed Mitzi's words, mulling them around in my head. *You think you can have Julian to yourself and tell him who he can and cannot date? He belongs to all of us.* What did that mean? Was he part of some cult?

I started weeping...long, heaping tears of angst. "I was so scared they were going to kill me." With the attack fresh in my mind, I gripped the bed railing when a burning pain shot through my side. "They tried to kill me and would have succeeded if Julian hadn't saved me."

"We heard, sweetheart. Shh, you're safe now. Stay calm and go back to sleep." My dad caressed my arm, lifted it, and leaned his cheek into the palm of my hand. It felt prickly and rough, but I didn't care. I loved my daddy.

A FAINT KNOCK ON THE DOOR of my stark, white hospital room at five thirty in the afternoon startled me from a light doze. Julian strolled in and sat in the chair next to my bed. He tucked a fuzzy brown teddy bear with a bright yellow ribbon tied around its neck into the crook of my arm. On the stand beside my bed, he placed a delicate glass vase with a single long-stemmed yellow rose.

"Hi. Thank you. I love it." I turned and inhaled the sweet fragrance of the rose.

"Hey," he whispered.

"We're going down to the cafeteria to grab a bite to eat, sweetheart. We'll leave you two alone." Mom said.

"I love you guys," I called out, grimacing in pain as my mom, dad, and Robin left.

"We'll be back," Robin called back.

"Okay."

Julian moved to sit on my bed. His tortured expression spoke volumes. "I'm so sorry this happened to you."

"You looked angry," I murmured. "I'm scared, Julian."

"Oh, believe me, Amber, I was way more than angry." His eyes filled with torment. "I still am. I despise them but don't want to discuss that right now and get you all agitated." Julian bent down and kissed me on the lips. "We'll talk later, okay?" Very tenderly he brushed the hair away from my face. "How long are you going to be here?"

"I'm not sure. Although, my mom thought I'll be here overnight. Hopefully, I'll be able to go home tomorrow."

"I'm so, so sorry." He frowned and shook his head in disbelief.

"This isn't your fault." I tried to placate him.

"Yes, it is."

"Why do you say that?"

"Not now. We'll discuss it some other time. I'm sure you need to rest."

"Yeah." Frankly, I felt too exhausted to argue. He said he'd discuss it with me later. I believed him.

OFFICERS KEILLOR AND ZEBB stood at the base of my hospital bed and began questioning me about the events of this morning. My mom, Robin, and Julian stood quietly, listening to my description of the incidents as they unfolded while my dad paced back and forth, running his hand through his hair. My heart sank. I didn't want to relive that whole torturous ordeal, especially in front of my parents.

"Miss Scott. We won't take up much of your time." Officer John

Zebb said. "We need to ask you a few questions."

"Okay."

Julian moved to the chair, and my mom positioned herself on the bed and stroked my forearm. Robin remained standing, staring blankly into space, pain imprinted in her wary expression.

Officer Ben Keillor continued, "Do you know who stabbed you?"

"Yes. Bianca Pantilla and Mitzi Carlisle."

"Both of them stabbed you?" He looked pointedly at me.

"Bianca stabbed me, but Mitzi punched and kicked me."

"Do you know why Miss Pantilla stabbed you?"

I told them I didn't know but suspected it had something to do with jealousy. Out of the corner of my eye, I saw Julian flinch. What did he have to do with this? Thank God I was too tired and sore to delve into it with him.

"Did you see the weapon used?" Officer Keillor continued with his cold, intimidating stare.

"No, it happened so fast." I squeezed my eyes shut and quivered at the thought of that knife pummeling into me. "Mitzi Carlisle kicked me with the toe of her boot." I cringed when I relayed the jolt I felt when her foot repeatedly plunged into my ribs.

"I think she's said enough," my dad said, dismissing the officers. My stomach knotted up, and my body continued to spasm. He stroked my forehead with the back of his hand until my body calmed.

"I think we have enough for now." Zebb cut in. "Thank you, Miss Scott. We'll be in touch."

As they turned to leave, I took a huge, deep breath in an attempt to relax and released it slowly.

Julian stood and took my hand. "I'm going to let you rest, Amber. I'll see you tomorrow."

I nodded, because, frankly, I wanted nothing more than to be left alone. I had nothing left inside me. "Bye," I said, forcing a smile as he turned and left. I sensed our relationship had turned a corner, the breakthrough we needed. Was it a positive one, though?

Robin squeezed my hand, bent over and hugged me. "Oh, Amber, I can't believe this happened to you. I'm so sorry I wasn't able to protect you."

I flinched. "The bitches attacked me out of the blue. It happened right before the first bell. I never saw it coming."

"Fuck them," she hissed, releasing her hold on me.

"Watch your language, Robin," Mom reprimanded. "Don't stoop to their level."

My dad narrowed his eyes at her. "It's time for Robin and me to head home."

"Okay," I said. "I'll see you tomorrow."

THE EARLY MORNING SUN filtered through the blinds of my window when my eyes glanced at the clock on the wall. It said six in the morning. Mom slept soundly on a cot next to my bed.

Taking register of my body, I decided that my belly and ribs still smarted, not the kind of intensity of the day before but I had to move cautiously. My headache had subsided slightly but still throbbed sporadically, so more pain medication was in order for that today.

"Mom," I spoke with a hushed voiced. Her eyes flashed opened.

"Is everything alright?" she asked.

"I wanted to thank you for staying with me. And to say I'm so sorry this happened."

"Oh, honey," she frowned. "I wouldn't be anywhere else. Why are you sorry? It wasn't your fault."

"I never told you, but those girls had been taunting me at school since the first day."

She sat up with an abrupt pause. "What? Why didn't you tell me?"

"I didn't want you to worry because I didn't want you to feel sorry for moving."

"Oh, Amber, sweetheart." Her lips trembled as she looked at me with a pained stare. "What precipitated all of this?"

"That's what I don't know. New student syndrome, maybe?"

"Well, you don't have to worry because you're not going back to that school." She got up off the cot and sat down on the bed beside me. She repeatedly brushed her hand across my forehead.

How did I feel about that disclosure? Did I want to start over in another school? It could be the same torment all over again. I couldn't bear that.

"I'll be okay, Mom. Plus, I have some pretty good friends. I don't want to go to another school. Please let me stay at Castle Rock."

"We'll discuss this later. First and foremost, you need to get better." As she rose from the bed and headed to the en suite bathroom to freshen up, my dad strolled in.

"How are you feeling today, pumpkin?"

"Better, Daddy. I want to go home. Where's Robin?"

"She went to school." He moved to the chair and sat down. "Have you seen the doctor?"

"Not yet, but the nurse told me he'd be around this morning." As I said the words, a tall man with dark, wavy hair, wearing a white doctor's coat, approached my bed. He introduced himself as Dr. John Manzo.

"Hello, Amber, Mr. Scott." My dad nodded, and they shook hands. "Let's take a peek at your wound," he said as my mom appeared from the bathroom. He turned to my parents and asked for some privacy.

"We'll be back, soon, honey."

AFTER CAREFUL EXAMINATION by the nice doctor, I was given my release instructions by the staff. X-rays confirmed bruised ribs, but no broken bones. Additionally, I'd been prescribed pain medicine for a mild concussion.

After Dr. Manzo left, Nurse L. Torres helped me walk to the bathroom. My legs wobbled, but I was able to wash my face and brush my teeth. Oh, that felt good.

"Let's get you back to bed before you fall, Amber," she said.

With a bent back and hunched shoulders, I retook fifteen tentative steps back to my bed, making it without any mishap along the way. As painful as it was, it felt good to be vertical again.

"What does the 'L' stand for?" I asked as she pulled the blanket over me.

"Lynn," she said with a smile.

"Wow, that's my middle name."

She nodded and patted my hand. "It's a lovely name, isn't it?"

Moments later Shelby peeked in the door. "Hey, you up for a visitor?"

"Absolutely. C'mon in and sit. My parents should be back soon."

She sat in the chair next to my bed and grabbed my hand. "How are you doing?" her soft words washed over me.

"I'm sore but alive, Shelb. I can go home today."

"Thank God."

I winced in pain trying to turn to my side for a better view of her.

"Don't move, girlfriend. I'll shuffle this chair around." The feet scraped against the floor like fingernails on a chalkboard as she moved it to a better position. "There, how's that?"

"Better."

"Oh, Amber. You wouldn't believe what Julian did after they wheeled you out of the school."

"Really? What?" I tried desperately to remember my last moments with him before I passed out. All that came to mind was him holding my hand.

"He was completely wrecked. He just stood still; shoulders slumped in outright despair. Dodds brought him another shirt to wear."

Yes, I remembered he took his shirt off to press against my wound.

"He dragged it over his head when some girl I didn't know—I think it was Lesley Potter—approached him. He lashed out at her, telling her to get the hell away from him." Shelby paused and shifted in the chair. "I was afraid he'd do something he'd regret. It was a good thing Mitzi and Bianca weren't there, or I'm sure they wouldn't be breathing another breath. I mean it, Amber. He looked outraged."

I couldn't pry my eyes off her. "Go on," I pleaded.

"He saw me and asked if I'd help him find Robin. I told him I would."

My eyes misted. Oh, my sweet boyfriend. Right then I wanted to give him a hug. I missed him.

"Oh Amber, I'm telling you this because he sounded so broken—totally and utterly crippled."

A lump formed in my throat. Julian thought this was his fault. I couldn't wait to talk with him.

MY HOSPITAL DISCHARGE came just after three in the afternoon. I'd been instructed to stay home from school for the next two weeks. My mom agreed to take time off from work to stay with me.

We stopped at her pharmacy on the way home to fill the pain prescription. Overall, I was happy to be alive. I'd been told the knife's blade narrowly missed the celiac artery in my stomach. Another centimeter to the right and I might've bled to death. My body started shaking again.

"Shh, sweetheart. We're almost home." Mom caressed my arm with her free hand while driving with the other.

I SHUFFLED TO THE SOFA of the living room and sat very gingerly, wincing in pain. Mom walked beside me, in case I fell. I didn't. I laid my head on her lap as she massaged my forehead with her gentle hands.

"Thank you, Mommy, for staying with me and taking such good care of me. I love you so much."

"I love you too, honey," she said. "I just want to make sure you're alright. You're still my little girl, you know?"

I felt a warm-fuzzy at her words. Sometimes I missed those days when I was a kid. She always made everything better.

"What does Julian have to do with all of this?" she asked in carefully spaced words. Her hand stilled on my head.

I twisted my neck to see her expression. Beads of sweat formed on her upper lip. "Why do you ask?"

"Because you were well-liked before you started dating him, honey."

I rolled to my back. "I don't think this has anything to do with him, except jealousy." What was she implying?

"Amber, this is something more than jealousy." She narrowed her brows and pursed her lips. "I'm concerned for your safety."

"What are you getting at, Mom?"

She shook her head, drew in a breath, and then released it. "I—I think you should see less of Julian, that's all."

My heart lurched into my throat. *No. No. No.* I couldn't bear to be without him. "Let me talk to him first." My entire body tensed. I decided to use my distraction technique with her before she demanded I stop seeing him altogether. "Tell me a story, Mom."

She cleared her throat and sighed heavily. "I know you're trying to change the subject, so we'll let it go for now." She paused. "I don't want you to get all riled up."

"Okay." I nodded. I loved my mom. I marveled at how easily she'd read my mind.

"It's been a long time since I've told you a story."

"Tell me how you got that scar above your eye."

"Are you sure you want to hear that story after what happened to you yesterday?"

Did I? Was this story so gruesome I would have nightmares? I'd been having enough of them with my own misery; I didn't need them with hers. "Yes," I said.

"Well, it's unpleasant."

"I've been waiting for this story since I've been old enough to remember, Mom." I couldn't believe I was finally going to hear it. Very carefully I pulled my knees to my chest and curled up in her lap.

She took a deep breath. "Well, when I was around nine or ten years old, my older brother—your uncle Jack—bought one of those remote controlled helicopters with money he earned from his paper route. It was a kit that required a great deal of modeling and building. He spent several painstaking hours assembling the chopper, finally finishing it. It took him days to learn how to navigate it without crashing. Jack had that never-give-up type of personality. It took the patience of a saint to control and maneuver high above the ground. He flew the helicopter up and down with the finesse and skill of a professional pilot. I never had the coordination Jack had to manipulate it, but at least he let me practice." She paused and glanced down at me. "You sure you want to hear this?"

"Yes," I said, while she continued caressing my forehead, pushing the hair away from my face.

"Well, one day he was flying it around the backyard when he lost control, and it plummeted to the ground. One of the rotor blades broke off. Jack stormed into the house, upset with his own negligence. He tried to come up with a quick fix, and the only replacement he could think of was a paring knife blade. Unbeknownst to my mom, Jack managed to remove the handle and devise a way to attach the knife blade to the spinning shaft. He thought he was so crafty and asked me to come out and watch it fly. So I did. It lifted off the ground and immediately started spinning erratically; flying at eye level very close to me, when out of nowhere the knife came loose and caught me square above the eye, right there." She pointed to her scar and grimaced as if it had just happened. "I screamed, and Jack panicked. Blood was everywhere. Jack kept yelling, *'I'm sorry, Lizzy, I'm so sorry.'* An ambulance rushed me to the hospital with a knife blade protruding from my eye. It was surgically removed and took a year to heal before my vision was completely restored."

"Wow, so what happened to Uncle Jack?" I looked up at her with a bewildered stare.

"My mom and dad were angry and destroyed the helicopter. Uncle Jack learned a valuable lesson that day."

"Thanks for finally sharing that story with me, Mom."

"How are you doing?"

"Hmm."

All the same, being home would give me the time to think about my life in the last two months. It'd been anything but normal. Up to the present time, I'd moved clear across the country, started dating the most gorgeous guy in the universe, lost my virginity and, lastly, been bullied, stabbed and beaten to a pulp at school. I hadn't had this much happen to me in all my previous sixteen and a half years. I couldn't wait to see what my seventeenth year had in store for me. Jeez.

Mom stood and disappeared into the kitchen as I nodded off into a light slumber.

An hour later, Robin stormed in the door, waking me. "Amber, your stabbing is all everybody's talking about at school. I'm so glad you're home." She sat and folded me in her arms.

"I don't want to relive that attack, sis," I said.

"I still can't believe it happened," Robin retorted. "Psychos."

Mom reappeared in the room. "Feeling any better?"

"I'm going to call Julian and let him know that I'm home, okay, Mom?"

"Honey, you should rest. Make it quick."

Robin handed me the phone and disappeared upstairs. I hurriedly dialed Julian's number. He answered on the first ring.

"Hi, I'm home," I said sweetly.

"How are you doing?"

"Other than the stab wound, I have a mild concussion."

He said nothing, but I sensed the grief and torment in his deep sigh. "I'll discuss this with you tomorrow, but you need to rest tonight."

"Okay, I'll see you tomorrow."

My mom propped a pillow under my head, pulled a blanket over me and headed to the kitchen to start supper while I nodded off.

THE CLOCK ON THE MANTEL said eight in the evening when I woke from my doze. I felt pain everywhere. My head throbbed, my ribs ached, and the pain radiating from the knife wound felt like my insides were being ripped out. I squirmed uncomfortably, trying to push myself up.

"Hey, sweetheart. What do you need?" Mom asked from the chair across the room.

"Pain medicine, Mom. Please."

I downed two painkillers with a glass of water and plopped my head back down on the pillow. My lip trembled as a sob erupted from my throat. My body shook every time I thought about yesterday. I couldn't believe Mitzi and Bianca tried to kill me. My instincts told me they were bad news from the start. Why didn't I listen to my gut? It was my own fault for not mentioning it to my parents. Surely they would have put an end to the threats.

I stared at the ceiling, thinking about Julian and drifted off again.

THE DOORBELL RANG startling me out of my sleep. Morning

light streaked through the windows, realizing I'd slept all night on the sofa. Glancing at the door when Mom opened it, a ridiculous grin spread across my face seeing Julian standing there.

"Come in, Julian. Amber is on the sofa. She needs her rest, so please make it quick." She didn't look any too pleased. I scrunched my face at her. What I had to say couldn't be said quickly.

"I will, Mrs. Scott." With his head hung low, he approached me.

"Hi," I whispered.

"Hey."

"I'm glad you're here. I missed you, but we need to talk."

I saw my mom raise her eyebrows at me, sensing her displeasure again. I narrowed my eyes at her as she vanished into the kitchen.

"I know. I missed you, too."

I rose from the couch, trying desperately to keep myself from tearing my stitches open. Very gingerly, I took Julian's hand, dragged him into the den and closed the door. I greeted him with a kiss. Pain and agony filled his face.

"Start talking," I said, slowly curling my arms around his waist.

Very carefully Julian locked his arms around mine and rocked me for several minutes. He stayed silent. We hugged. He buried his face in my hair and inhaled deeply. This is what I needed. He felt so good. I breathed in his intoxicating scent.

I placed my hand on his chest and pushed away enough to look into his glossed over eyes. I lifted my arm to caress his cheek with the back of my hand, wincing when my ribs protested.

"None of that, Julian Cahill, you're going to make me cry, too." I pouted. Clutching his hand, I signaled to move to the loveseat and sit. I folded my left arm around his neck as he lowered me gently to the soft cushion.

I raised my head to look into his eyes. "Talk to me, Julian, please."

He shuffled back, dismissing me. "You should be lying down."

"I don't want to lie down. I want to see your face." I could tell he was trying to postpone the inevitable. Well, no way. I eyed him skeptically. "For the fourth time, talk to me."

He sat next to me, brushing his fingers through my hair. "What do you want to know?"

"Well, for starters, why the sudden mood shift?"

A long pause followed, the silence in the room almost deafening as Julian looked through me with a blank stare. Worry and dread flitted across his face.

"Julian, no matter what you tell me, it won't make a difference in the way I feel about you."

He grimaced. "Those are some pretty powerful words. You haven't even heard me out yet."

"It doesn't matter. I can't imagine my life without you."

He finally started talking. "Amber, as I've told you, I've never had any lasting relationships until I met you. You've completely derailed me. I've never felt about anyone else the way I feel about you. I've had a hard time getting my head around it. These feelings are unfamiliar to me."

"What does this have to do with Mitzi and Bianca? Mitzi told me you belonged to them. What does *that* mean?" My tone was harsher than I intended. "Why would she say stuff like that?" I urged him to continue.

Julian took my trembling hands and pulled them to his lap. I felt an anxious queasiness building deep in my belly. I knew he was out of my league but didn't think it would end like this.

He shifted his position, tucking one leg under the other and looked into my eyes. "Well…I've dated many girls, Amber…a lot. I know you said you were very jealous, so I hope what I say, won't scare you away. Please tell me that you'll hear me out before making any rash decisions about our relationship."

"I will. I promise," I stuttered, thinking the worst. "So, your point is…" I nervously implored him, not knowing where he was going with this. "How much is considered a lot?"

Pausing and shaking his head, he said, "I don't know…probably close to twenty."

Whoa, what was he saying? Did he date Mitzi and Bianca? Were they on the list of "a lot?"

"I don't get it, Julian. Did you date *them*?" I started to shiver. My body began to sting with pain. Was he going to tell me the truth?

"Yes," he said, dropping his chin to his chest.

My shoulders tensed and a lump formed in my throat. How could I date someone who would stoop so low as to date a couple of psychopaths? My heart sank. He'd dated Mitzi and Bianca, the bitches who stabbed me.

Clutching my hands, Julian continued, "Hear me out, please." He let out a moan. "You look like a deer in the headlights."

I nodded, and fell speechless.

"Before you came into my life, Amber, I embraced and welcomed the attention I drew from all the girls, which, as you've seen, is quite a bit." He rolled his eyes. "What guy wouldn't? When you receive the kind of attention I got, you run with it. I was quite the player and dated a lot of them, having sex with a few." His face flushed.

"Were Mitzi and Bianca on the sex list?" It was bad enough that he'd dated them. Could I handle the fact that he'd had sex with them, too? I shut my eyes tight, bracing for the truth. When I reopened them, Julian was shaking his head. *Oh, thank God!*

"They were pressuring me to, but that's when you came into my life," he said, scrunching his face.

What? I couldn't believe what I was hearing. If I hadn't come along, he might've had sex with those fucking whores? I cringed at the thought.

"Talk to me. Please," he begged.

"They tried to kill me over you," I said through gritted teeth, my words barely audible.

"I know. I know. I'm so, so sorry." He flinched. "I didn't want any long term relationships because I couldn't deal with the bullshit that came with them. No commitments, no responsibilities. I had the best of both worlds. Free to come and go as I pleased. They all knew how I felt. Supposedly, I didn't handle it appropriately, but none of them cared—at least that's what I thought."

"You were an asshole, Julian. Call it what it was."

His neck flopped downward, and he whimpered, "Yes, I was." He hesitated, lifted his head and focused his deep blue eyes on mine. "A poor choice, I realize now. Most of them were only one date. At times, I was dating a different girl each week. Some girls were a little more possessive than others, but I made it clear that nobody owned me. But

I didn't take into consideration the repercussions of all that until I met you. I promise I will never do anything like that again. Please don't leave me."

"How many did you have sex with? Tell me the truth." I had to hear a number and to know what I was up against.

He shook his head and stared down at his hands. "I would say about six or seven."

Holy crap! He was only sixteen. I did say I wouldn't break up with him no matter what. But this was horrible. Could I forgive him? I wasn't sure I could.

"And you might've had sex with Mitzi and Bianca if I hadn't come along? How could you?"

"Remember, they were pressuring me. It was only one date with them, but they continued their pursuit of me, as you witnessed."

"Because you didn't make it clear that sex was off the table!" I snapped at him. I couldn't believe he'd dated those witches and to think he may have had sex with them was unbearable. Could I ever forgive him for that?

Frowning, Julian watched me as he went on, as if to make sure I wasn't going to bolt. "I wasn't exclusive to anybody, and they all accepted that. If they didn't, then there wouldn't be a second or subsequent date. That's how it always was until you lured me in with your goddamn magic spell. I don't want anyone else, now or ever, Amber."

No words came to me. I sat and stared into his steely blue eyes. Suddenly the *"flavor-of-the-week"* comment became abundantly clear. He was a goddamn player and dated Mitzi and Bianca. Alarms should've been going off in my head, but, surprisingly, they weren't. Would this matter to me? Could I get beyond this? I knew there was something about him, but this went way beyond that. I felt stunned by his admission, which must have looked apparent on my face.

"If you're completely disgusted with me, I'll show myself to the door." He punched his fists against his thighs.

Everything became crystal clear to me. I knew what I needed to say and began. "Julian, that was quite a confession...," I paused, "Thank you for finally fessing up, but I don't know why you felt you couldn't tell me this sooner. Are you being truthful about not dating anymore?"

"Yes. There will never be anyone else for me." He looked guarded, but visibly relaxed.

"Good. Now, let me get a few things off my chest." I took his hands and pulled them to my lap. "First...if you *ever* knowingly do anything like this again, I swear I will never, *ever* speak to you again. Got it?" I admonished him with a blank stare.

He swallowed hard and nodded.

"Second...this was only partially your fault. The other half lies with Mitzi and Bianca because I think they would have tried to kill me either way. But you should've told me sooner, and I'm pissed that you didn't. Thank God they've been arrested. And thank God I'm alive. My parents pressed charges. I hope they throw the book at them."

"Don't try to sugar-coat it, Amber. It was entirely my fault. If I'd told you the truth from the beginning, they could've been stopped."

"Possibly," I said. I wasn't going to disagree.

"I thought you'd break up with me if I told you I'd dated Mitzi and Bianca. I couldn't take the chance of losing you. If I'd known for one minute they'd try to kill you..." He dropped his head into his hands, "Christ!" Letting out a deep, shaky breath, Julian placed his arms around me. "I promise I'll never put you through that again, Amber."

"Okay."

Was all this forgivable? He sounded genuinely sorry. Should I give him a second chance?

Scarcely touching me, he turned my body to face him. He raised my chin with one hand while placing his other on the side of my face. He looked deeply into my eyes, bent down and touched his warm lips to mine, giving me the sweetest of kisses.

I groaned in pain, wrapping my arms around him, feeling his rigid muscles and gently pulled him against me. I didn't want this moment to end. After a while, he released his grip and in a haze of emotions, said the words I never thought I'd ever hear.

"I love you, Amber Scott, with all my heart and soul," he said, wrapping me in his arms.

My boyfriend said he loved me. At that moment, I knew Julian was the guy I wanted to spend the rest of my life with.

I decided to forgive him, mostly because, (for lack of a better description,) his "extracurricular activities" happened before I moved here. He'd been faithful to me since. *That* was something I could live with. Despite my parents' opinion about keeping my options open, I wanted him…only him. No one knew the kind of relationship we had.

With tears streaming down my face, I looked deep into his blue eyes and choked out, "With all that being said, my feelings for you have not changed. I love you, too, Julian Cahill," echoing his sentiments. My heart tightened for him.

"For as long as I'm breathing, it will only be you. I love you so much. I can't explain it, but I knew you were the one who would change my life forever." His voice was deep, measured, forceful and with perfect enunciation. It resonated over me.

"Ditto, Julian." I stopped. "Magic spell, eh?" I grinned.

"No, I said goddamn magic spell." He laughed.

This wasn't the end; it was a new beginning. "I love you, Julian."

He was committing himself to me. He was mine. Only mine. Forever mine.

Chapter Eight

I stood at my window gazing out at the mottled sky glistening off the leaves of the large maple tree. The colors had changed from pea green to a lemon yellow and gold or as Julian called it…Amber. Many of them had already fallen to the ground—an indication that November was just around the corner.

My life changed drastically in the month following the stabbing. My relationship with Julian turned a corner. There were no more secrets. He made it very clear that he was exclusive to me and only me. I hadn't realized I'd never seen that side of him.

Mitzi and Bianca had wreaked havoc on our lives. They'd been expelled from school permanently, and my parents immersed themselves in the disciplinary procedures of both of them. The trial would take months, but until then, they would sit in a juvenile detention center. Hurray for me.

My stitches were removed to reveal a two-inch scar along the right side of my belly. Still tender to the touch, I remained on the road to recovery.

I'd convinced my parents to let me stay in Castle Rock High School and looked forward to it now. Surprisingly, everyone wanted to be my friend. Surfacing from every nook and cranny, where were they a month ago?

I moved to my bed and lay on my back, staring up at the ceiling, while my mind drifted to that first day back…

I stood in front of my locker, when a momentary twinge of pain shot through my belly. I looked around noticing the area was spotless with no trace of my blood anywhere. I began trembling.

"Hey, you okay?"

"Thank God you're here," I told Julian. "I don't know if I could have done this without you."

THE PHONE RANG, startling me out of my thoughts. Julian's name popped up on the caller ID.

"Hey, babe."

"What's up?" I asked.

"Meet me at the maple tree." I could sense his grin. What did he have up his sleeve?

"Okay, be right out."

I grabbed my sweater and hustled out the door in a flash. Standing along the worn dirt path, in front of the maple tree was Julian. My eyes darted to the small screwdriver in his hand.

I gazed at him, puzzled. "What's going on?"

"I had an idea." His smile was infectious.

"I'm all ears."

"We're going to carve a heart and our initials into this tree. Every time we pass by, we have to touch the heart. That way we know we'll always be connected…here." He placed his hand over his own heart.

I stood there, stupefied with wonder and love. "I love this. I love you."

He demonstrated how to use the screwdriver then handed it to me. "Here, put your initials right there." He pointed to a section of the tree at my eye-level.

"With pleasure, babe."

Julian retrieved a jackknife from the front pocket of his jeans, and the two of us began carving our initials into the fresh bark of the tree.

Fifteen minutes later I finished. "There. 'A' and 'S.' " I stood back to admire my handiwork.

"Nice job. I like the curlicue of the 'S,' " Julian said and bent down to kiss me.

I watched as he finished the 'C' for Cahill. "I never realized what your initials spelled out until now. Wow. 'J' and 'C.' That's freaky."

Julian carved the heart between our initials, and then backed up to appraise his creation. "I like it. What do you think?"

"It's perfect...," I linked my arm with his at the elbow, "like you."

"No matter what, you can't forget to touch the heart each time you pass by. No excuses."

"Okay," I said. "Same goes for you."

He grinned. "Absolutely. With pleasure."

BACKSTAGE BUZZED WITH THE SOUNDS of everyone putting the final touches on their performances. Tonight's talent competition had my body wracked with nerves.

It was a cool, crisp, early November night, leaving only a blanket of stars to give light. Endless hours of homework and Julian's utter tenacity that we commit to practicing our song every night made it a long stressful week. He drove me crazy. Being a bit of a perfectionist, he left nothing to chance. I'd scowl at him, but he just brushed it off with a snide chuckle. Gah! God, I loved him...everything about him.

Shelby sat at the piano playing for the crowd, singing her interpretation of the song, "Imagine," by John Lennon. I peeked through the burgundy velvet curtains of the auditorium, looking for my mom, dad, and Robin, spotting them immediately, seated in the front row.

I'd decided on a flirty, amber-colored dress which fit like a glove around my figure with cute black flats. I pinned my hair up on one side and weaved some baby's breath through it while the remainder was left flowing down my back. Julian looked as sexy and gorgeous as ever with his hair slicked back, disheveled, just the way it was the first time I met him. He wore a pair of black linen trousers with a black button-down, and a tie that matched the color of my dress. We shopped together for our clothes. Actually, he chose my dress, saying it reminded him of me.

"Psst, Amber, come here. Let's go over the song one more time before we go on."

"Julian, if I go over this song one more time, I'm going to puke," I huffed, good-naturedly, of course. "Are your parents here?"

"Nope, I don't think so," he said with a sorrowful tone to his voice.

"Why aren't they here?"

"No idea."

Why wouldn't his parents show up on a very special night for him? I'd noticed Nancy's reluctance in wanting to be a part of his everyday life but supposed it was because she wasn't his biological mom. That still wasn't a reason not to be here and support him tonight. I always thought she gave the impression she cared for him. And then it registered that maybe she was delivering another baby. I remembered Julian mentioning how she received those kinds of calls all the time. Though, there was no excuse for his dad's absence. Their relationship was strong, Julian idolized him. What was more important than being here for his son? I felt utterly heartbroken.

As I glanced at the program, I saw that we were scheduled to perform next. The butterflies in my belly surfaced again, and I began pacing back and forth behind the curtain. As always, Julian looked calm and cool as a cucumber, sitting on a metal folding chair, softly playing his guitar.

Finishing her performance, Shelby stood from the piano and took a bow as the voice of Principal, Joe Dodds, piped through the PA system, "Can we hear your appreciation for junior, Shelby Quade, and her beautiful rendition of "Imagine" by the late John Lennon?"

After the applause died down, Dodds approached the microphone again. "Up next is a couple who have been in the headlines lately..." He stopped when another deafening round of applause echoed throughout the auditorium, making my nerves prickle tenfold.

The news story that followed after the stabbing incident at school made the local headlines. Julian and I became a couple of celebrities in the weeks that followed, making us both uneasy being in the limelight.

Dodds went on, "Let's hear a round of applause for juniors, Julian Cahill, and new to Castle Rock High School this year, Amber Scott."

With our guitars in tow, we headed for center stage, passing Shelby going in the opposite direction. I whispered to her, "That was beautiful." Julian nodded in agreement.

"Thank you, guys. Good luck," she whispered back.

Appearing from behind the curtain, we stumbled back at the ear-piercing reception which hung in the air like a cymbal crash.

"Wow," I mouthed to Julian.

He smiled affectionately at me.

We pulled two empty stools together, plugged our guitars into the amplifiers, adjusted the microphones, and sat down. I couldn't control my trembling legs.

Catching sight of the packed house, we waited for the applause to die down. Proud smiles stretched across the faces of my family when I looked at them. My dad winked at me. I gave him a small, inconspicuous nod back.

Julian tapped on the microphone, testing its liveliness. Pulling it to his mouth, he spoke into it, "Good evening, everyone. Amber would like to thank all of you who sent get-well cards. They were very much appreciated."

I had the best boyfriend ever. Another round of applause ensued.

"Tonight we are going to play our rendition of "Nights in White Satin" by The Moody Blues. We hope you enjoy it."

He gestured to me with raised eyebrows and a nod of his head, looking for my ready sign to begin. I rubbed my sweaty palms down my dress and nodded back.

"Three, two, one," he mouthed as we strummed the first riffs.

We were in sync, not missing a beat as we began to sing in harmony. My nerves instantly dissipated. Everything was right with the world at this moment. I was with the guy I loved, singing with every bit of emotion I could elicit into the song.

One verse down, alone in our private universe, we pressed on; singing as though no one else existed. Julian's smooth and soft as silk voice hummed inside my head like he was living and breathing them.

We launched into the chorus, our gazes locking onto each other.

He closed his eyes and tipped his head back.

The love I felt for him at this moment was unmistakable. One more verse down. I willed myself to keep singing. I must finish without succumbing to the emotion building inside of me and fall into a limp rag right here on stage.

I pushed forward, finally ending the song with a flourish, immediately followed by the deafening roar of a standing ovation.

I took a deep, satisfied breath and looked toward my family. Smiles of joy crossed the faces of all three of them.

Julian leaned over and kissed me on the cheek and whispered softly in my ear, "You sounded beautiful."

"Thank you. So did you." I sat motionless, reduced to a puddle of tears. The applause went on and on as we stood, took our bows, and turned to exit the stage.

Principal Dodds made his way to the microphone again. "Let's hear it again for Amber Scott and Julian Cahill."

The clapping intensified again. Barely off stage, we turned and took another bow, then departed through the backstage curtains.

We made our way out to the crowded auditorium to watch the remaining acts, finding two seats together on the aisle. My legs resembled jelly. With our performance over, pride filled our hearts, excited that we pulled it off.

After the three final acts and announcement of the winner, the show came to a close. Since Julian's parents weren't here, we found mine in the crowd.

My mom was a blubbering mess. "That was gorgeous, you two, congratulations. I knew you'd win," she said, sniffling, "One of my favorite songs."

"Thank you, Mom."

"Yes, thank you, Mrs. Scott." Julian smiled.

"Told ya your voice would be the envy of the school, Amber," Robin said. "Loved it."

"Thanks, sis." Once again, she was right. "Hey, Mom, Dad; Julian and I are going to grab a bite to eat, so I'll be home later, okay?"

"Sure, have a good time, you two," Mom said.

"WHERE SHALL WE DISPLAY this trophy, Julian?" I gave him a lopsided smile and innocent kiss on the lips after climbing into his shiny red Camaro. It was a long night, but we were giddy with delight after winning the competition. He started the engine and headed out.

"You keep it. You sounded incredible and deserve every bit of the praise. I want you to have it as a reminder of your hard work," he said.

"I'm not going to take all the credit. I couldn't have done it without you. You were equally brilliant, probably more so."

Julian brushed off my compliment with a shoulder shrug. His humbleness knew no bounds.

I examined the trophy, running my fingers across the inscription on the plaque. *Castle Rock High School Talent Competition, First Place.* It portrayed a person standing and singing into a microphone.

"I know a way you can share it with me," he said with a wicked grin. "I'd like to get you out of that gorgeous dress and have my way with you. What do you say?"

"I say, yes please, but where?"

"Hotel room?"

"Well, since my parents won't be expecting me home right away, I'm good. How about you?"

"I'm good, too," he responded bitterly.

My thoughts drifted to his parents and their decision not to attend the competition. And *now* they missed his winning performance.

THE MOUNTAIN VIEW INN, located on the outskirts of Denver, stood amongst a backdrop of Aspen trees. We pulled into the crowded parking lot and found a space. Julian opened my door, reached for my hand, and helped me out. Before I realized what was happening, he grabbed me around the waist, pulled me tightly against him, and planted a deep kiss on my lips. Our tongues invaded each other's mouths, twisting with soft touches. Running my fingers through his hair, I pulled him harder against me. I couldn't get enough of him. My chest pounded, frantic to have him, heart and soul.

Breathless and panting, Julian released me. "Let's get inside before I rip you out of this dress in the parking lot."

I giggled a cheery sound while the two of us danced across the pavement, reveling in the crunch of the brittle leaves beneath our feet.

We strolled inside the lobby of the luxury Inn and approached the concierge desk. Shiny tile floors and a baroque charm surrounded the entrance area, with a wide sweeping staircase straight ahead.

After Julian filled out the necessary paperwork, he received the keys to room number 203. I blushed, fidgeting with my fingers, knowing the look on our faces was undoubtedly giving us away.

Climbing the staircase, I asked, "Do you think the second floor is reserved for mindless sex?"

"I can't speak for anyone else, but I can assure you, that will be the case with us," he said, grabbing my hand.

We moved along to the end of the hall, fingers linked together, and opened the door to a classic hotel room, characteristic of all the customary amenities. Gold colored drapes hung in the window and a matching comforter covered the king sized bed with two tiny chocolate mints on the pillows.

Julian lifted me into his arms and carried me into the room. I clasped my fingers behind his neck, tugged my dress up around my waist and swung my legs roughly around him as he kicked the door shut. He caged me against the wall and had his lips on mine with urgency. With reckless movements, we were devouring each other. I felt his excitement against my sex. I was needy for some friction. He pushed against me through our clothing, as if reading my mind.

"Christ, you look sexy in this dress, but I'm desperate to get you out of it," he said, showing me his smoldering look.

"What are you waiting for?"

Losing myself in his passion, I let him carry me to the bed and lower me to my feet. After he switched on the bedside light, we disrobed, ripping our clothes off and tossing them aside. Breathing heavily, I tasted his mouth on mine again. We were all hands and mouths and lips. I wanted him so bad.

After removing our clothes, he discarded the bedding to the floor. He gently lowered me onto the cool sheets. Against my heated body, this felt good. Making his movements deliberate, he pushed my legs apart, and before I could protest, his tongue was at my breasts, arousing me.

"Oh God, Julian." I quivered from the sudden sensation at my nipples. I couldn't keep still from his persistent licks. I felt his smile against me.

He groaned. "Your breasts are beautiful. I want to make you come just by my soft touch of them." He pulled on the tips with his teeth.

I arched my back. He was good at this. At that moment I thought maybe it wasn't so horrible that he had experience. No, I didn't want to think about his former sex partners.

Julian used his tongue to flitter rapidly back and forth across the very tip of my nipple. He drove me wild, with gentle bites, sucking and pulling. My breath hitched as he repeated his torture over and over. My legs began trembling, my fingers gripping the sheets. I felt that familiar feeling build inside me. I wasn't sure how much more of this I could endure, but he continued his gentle licks, going back and forth between both of my breasts.

My breathing turned irregular and erratic. "I'm so close."

Unable to hold it back, I climaxed all around him. I yelled out his name when I lost focus of my surroundings. I had no idea that I could climax from just his touch of my nipples. It felt incredible.

Julian positioned himself over me and lowered himself to his forearms. Without losing eye contact, he eased into me. He didn't stop until I felt every inch of him.

"Oh God. You're so ready for me. I can't get enough of this. Shit, I'm going to come so fast."

He stilled and buried his face in the curve of my neck while placing sweet kisses along the outline of my jaw and around to my earlobe.

"Julian, please. I can't take it anymore."

"I want to make it last." Hissing through his teeth, "Ah crap, I can't." I knew he was close.

Through our harsh panting breaths, he began moving faster and more deliberately. My legs started trembling again; my body warm and tingly. I was at the edge of a precipice, falling into the abyss as another orgasm ripped through my core, shredding me. Julian shuddered violently as we both found our release together.

"Uhh," he groaned and collapsed on top of me. I ran my fingers through his hair, caressing him softly.

Once our breathing slowed, he raised his head and stroked my lower lip with his thumb.

"You are perfect. I can't get enough of you. I think of having sex with you every minute of every day. I love you so much, it's painful," he said with a silly love-struck gaze.

"Back atcha, babe. You know how much I love you, too."

I couldn't believe the good fortune bestowed upon me. Julian Cahill loved me. I repeated it over and over. I still had a hard time getting my head around it. Why me?

We ended up cuddling, my back to his front and a few deep breaths later, I fell asleep.

> Julian is calling out my name, but I can't see him. Everything is dark. Where is he? I try to answer him, but no words come from my mouth. I want to go to him. I try, but I can't move. Why can't I move? "Help me, help me." My breathing is heavy and labored. My heart is pounding. I'm calling his name, "Julian! Julian!" But there's no sound coming from me. I try to sit up, but I can't. I struggle hard, my body jerks and finally, my arms move. There he is. I grab his beautiful face and tell him, "I'm right here. I'm Amber. I'm right here, Julian."

"Amber, Amber, wake up."

"What?" I said groggily.

"I think you were having a nightmare. Wake up."

I opened my eyes, shaking, face-to-face with him.

Looking at me, he frowned. "You were grabbing my face and kept repeating that you were Amber and were right here. What the heck were you dreaming about?"

"Oh God, I had a horrible dream. You were calling out my name, but I couldn't see you. It was dark and cold. No matter what I did, I couldn't get to you. It was horrifying." I cleared my throat and gulped for air.

He wrapped his arms around my shoulders and pulled me tight to his chest until my body calmed. "Shh, I'm right here. We fell asleep.

It's midnight. We'd better start thinking about going home."

"You're right. My parents are probably wondering where I am."

Julian decided on a quick shower while I slipped my dress over my head. As he headed to the bathroom, my eyes focused on his beautiful naked butt and muscular outline. Just looking at him, I felt the beat of my racing heart and the sound of my heavy breathing. He was so freaking hot. I sighed loudly.

"What?"

"Nothing. Just enjoying the view."

He wiggled his butt at me and disappeared into the bathroom, gloating all the way.

I shook my head. "I'm thirsty, Julian. I need a cold glass of water. I'm going to go hunt down the ice machine. I'll be back in a flash."

"Okay, babe," he called from the shower.

I grabbed the ice bucket and left the room in search of the ice machine. Meandering down the hall, I inhaled the acrid smell of burnt popcorn. Patrons bustled about their daily lives arriving and leaving their rooms. I spotted the ice machine at the other end of the hall by the vending machines.

As I reflected back on the past month, I felt relieved, finally having the "female" situation behind us. Admittedly, I still cringed at the thought of that painful stabbing, even though it meant we finally had a peace of mind in our relationship. Julian's demeanor changed, too. He was much calmer and at peace. The fact that he'd dated the "Bitches" was soon forgotten.

I placed the bucket on the tray of the machine and pressed the button that immediately started dispensing the ice. A few of them scattered to the floor. When I bent over to retrieve the escaping frozen chunks, I heard voices—one familiar voice, in particular. I glanced up in the direction of the sound and three doors down from my position a man had his arm wrapped affectionately around a stunning, golden blond-haired woman. They were headed for the stairs. She looked vaguely familiar, but I couldn't place where I'd seen her. She appeared much younger than him. From where did I know her?

They were whispering softly, "They did a beautiful job, didn't they?"

"Yes, I'm so proud of..." Then the conversation trailed off as they moved further and further away from me. My heart lurched into my throat. I quickly covered my mouth, to thwart the possibility of any more sound leaking out. It wasn't the fact that I couldn't be seen here in the hotel by anyone I knew.

It was Logan Cahill, Julian's dad, but the woman he was with was *not* his wife, Nancy.

Chapter Nine

My heart sank. My pulse raced again, but for a different reason now. I couldn't let Logan see me. I quickly squeezed into the space between the candy and ice vending machines, thankful for my slender frame.

Once Mr. Cahill and the "mysterious woman" disappeared down the stairs toward the concierge desk, I made a beeline back to the room, leaving the ice bucket behind. I'd forgotten about my thirst. Wheezing, I flew through the door, met by Julian's rigid body and wrapped him in my arms, never wanting to let go.

He lifted my chin with his fingers. "What's wrong? You're shaking and look like you saw a ghost."

"Hold me, please, Julian."

"Tell me. What happened out there? I'm not going to stop asking until you tell me," he scolded, pulling me tighter into him. Then he hastily released his grip looking down into my troubled and most likely swollen eyes.

Should I tell him the truth? How would this affect the admiration he felt for his dad? I despised Logan at this moment. How could he do this to his family? I couldn't get my head around the blatant disregard he had for his wife, Nancy, with a much younger woman. It was appalling.

Placing his hands on both sides of my face and raising it to meet his worried eyes, Julian sounded more insistent. "Amber, you're trembling. I'm not going to ask again, what the hell just happened out there? You're scaring me."

I had to say something. I wanted to change the subject, but nothing came to mind.

"I—I saw your dad," I quietly stuttered.

With a blank stare, he muttered, "Oh?"

Julian wasn't obtuse. No doubt he comprehended the motive behind his dad's late-night presence in a hotel. After all, we were here for the same reason.

When various emotions crossed his face, he hesitated and closed his eyes. When he re-opened them, there was a pained look. "Was he with someone?"

"This is none of my business, Julian." I grimaced, choosing to avoid any further discussion. "Can we go, please?" I couldn't bear the thought of him learning about his father's infidelity.

"I suppose," he snarled and mumbled something under his breath, but I couldn't make it out. His head dropped.

Our conversation was over, but watching the wounded look on his face, I knew he understood about his dad.

"Let's go," he said brusquely, as he gathered his jacket from the bed and headed for the door.

Our perfect evening…spoiled by the disgraceful actions of his father. Now I understood why he didn't attend the competition tonight. He was out cheating on his wife.

Only a few hours before, we were on top of the world. Right when things were beginning to look promising, an emptiness filled my heart. What would be the effect on Julian? He was so close with his dad, more so than with his stepmom. Now he had no one. Could he overcome this? Would *our* relationship suffer? I dismissed that thought immediately from my head.

As we headed home moments later, my eyes swelled with unshed tears. I tasted the bitterness. A teenage boy needed his father like a superhero needed his little buddy.

We rode home in silence, Julian quietly brooding, I suspect about his dad. Thinking I ought to make some kind of conversation, I decided against it and kept quiet. Instead, I rested my hand on his thigh.

Without taking his eyes off the road, a burdened expression filled his face. What was he thinking? The late night darkness subdued the unpleasant scenarios passing through my head.

"You okay?" I spoke tentatively, deciding to say something after all. The absence of conversation was killing me.

A long silence followed. "I will be," he said eventually and looked lost in thought.

Oh. What did that mean?

Arriving home, he pulled into one of the bays of his garage alongside his dad's car. "Oh look, Daddy's home." He scowled, unable to squeeze any more hostility out of those words if he tried.

Along the worn path, he took me home, completely disregarding the heart on the maple tree.

"Stop," I said, sternly. No way was I going to let him get away with that. I didn't care how hurt he felt.

"What?" he snapped at me.

"The heart, Julian. You didn't touch the heart. Remember? No excuses." I brought his words back to him. "You can't forget to touch the heart each time you pass by."

Reluctantly, he pulled his hand from his pocket, reached up and brushed the tips of his fingers across the heart. "Okay, happy? Let's go," he said, unable to keep the disdain from his voice.

"I suppose," I snarled and kissed the heart. I said a silent prayer in my head and let Julian walk me the rest of the way home. He gave me a quick kiss, said goodnight, and left.

He worried me, but I stayed quiet. Anything I said would be pointless. I had an overwhelming urge to hold him, but instead, I let him walk away. I could tell he wanted to be alone. He needed time to absorb and process this latest unfortunate incident. Oh, my heart tightened for him.

A CRISP AND CHILLY SATURDAY morning came and went without any word from Julian. Against my better judgment, I decided to visit him. I snatched my sweater from the closet and made my way to his house, touching the heart on the maple tree along the path.

His face looked odd when he greeted me at the door. "C'mon in, babe." His voice sounded different, incredulous.

With caution, I walked in and followed him to the living room. "What's going on?"

"Nothing," he said unconvincingly. "Oh yeah, want to see my new tattoo?" His voice dripped with sarcasm.

Julian removed his black T-shirt in record time and turned to reveal a red heart tattoo marring his back left shoulder blade. The letters of my name were written across it in dark yellow ink.

"It's just like your birthmark."

"And in the same spot as my birthmark."

"Yup, I did that intentionally." He plopped down on the sofa and raked his hands through his hair. With a guarded move, I sat down next to him. Something was amiss. I sensed it. He was brooding, and I suspected it was because of his dad.

I draped my arm over his shoulder, careful not to brush against the new tattoo. "Thank you, Julian." I smiled at his thoughtful gesture, but at the same time shook my head at his decision to do this to his body. He'd obviously done this out of spite. How broken he must have felt inside.

"Did you do that this morning?"

"Yup, do you like it?"

"I love it, very sweet, but you do know it's permanent, right?"

"Yup, I surely do." He sneered.

"Does this have anything to do with your dad?"

"Yup, it surely does." He said in a derisive tone. He leaned back and folded his arms behind his head, looking damned proud of himself.

"Is your dad going to be angry you did this?"

"Yup, he surely will and do you know what else, Amber?"

I was afraid to ask but did anyway. "What?" I cringed.

"I don't fucking care what my dad thinks," he snarled.

His impulsiveness was freaking me out. He was not handling this situation very well, at all.

"You're acting strange. What's going on?"

"Nothing." He dismissed me, crossing one leg over the other, resting his ankle on the knee.

"Don't give me that crap, Julian. Your attitude is scaring me. Stop with the *'yups'* and *'surelys'* please." I growled back at him. "I can see that you're hurting, but making rash decisions is not the way to handle this."

"Amber, don't fucking try to tell me how I should act or what I should say when you have no fucking idea what I'm going through!" he shouted. "Is your dad out fucking around with some tramp?" He leaned forward and buried his head in his hands.

"Don't swear at me. This isn't my fault!" I stood and screamed right back at him. "I'm not even sure I know who you are right now with this idiotic attitude. When you sort out your shit, then I'll be happy to have a rational conversation with you. Until then, I'm leaving! Goodbye!"

When Julian made no attempt to stop me, I turned and stormed out of his house. How could he be so cold and callous to *me* for cripes sake?

Along the path, I hesitated at the maple tree. Feeling a rage inside me, I wanted to walk by but remembered making Julian touch it for me the night before. My anger intensified as my body shook. I grudgingly reached up and slapped my palm across it and ran home.

In a huff, I slammed the door after walking inside my house. About to head up the stairs to my bedroom, my mom's voice halted me in my tracks.

"What's the matter, sweetheart?" I looked up and met her worried glance, as she sat on the sofa reading the newspaper.

I broke down into huge sobs. "Julian and I had a huge fight, and I think we might've broken up."

She tapped her hand on the cushion next to her. "Come over here and tell me what happened."

I shuffled over and curled up next to her. I proceeded to tell my side of the story without giving too much away. I couldn't tell my mom we were in a hotel. "Julian is angry over something his dad did and to spite him, he went out and got a tattoo. I told him making rash decisions was not the way to go about it. Sometimes he's as stubborn as a mule. He cursed at me, so I left. That's the gist of it."

"You did the right thing. Give him time to cool off, and he'll realize the error of his ways, honey." She paused. "Let me tell you the story of the time your dad and I had a whopper of a fight."

Oh boy, another story from my mommy. I rested my head on her lap as she folded the newspaper and started in.

"Back in college, we'd been invited to a friend's off-campus party one night and drove my car. There was enough alcohol going around to inebriate an entire army. Well, your father ended up drinking himself into a stupor...real stinking drunk. He had my car keys in his pocket and refused to give them to me when it came time to leave and insisted he drive back to our dorm. I made a feeble attempt to wrestle them from his grip but failed miserably."

She stopped, turned to face me, and tucked one leg under the other. She caressed the hair back from my face and continued. "He jumped into the driver's seat and started the engine. I screamed and threatened him to no avail. Against my better judgment, I climbed into the passenger side. A bad idea, I realized later. I mean, if we'd crashed, two lives would've been lost. He started out on the highway reaching speeds of nearly one hundred miles per hour. I was shaken to my core, screaming to slow down. I told him we were over for good and never wanted to see him again. He laughed a drunken laugh. I thanked the good Lord we made it back to our dorm safely but not before grabbing my keys from the ignition and storming away from him." She stopped. Her blank stare told me she was reliving the ordeal all over again.

I patted her hand, startling her.

She cleared her throat and continued. "Two days went by before he re-appeared at the door of my dorm room. He held a dozen red roses and a box of chocolates in his hand when I opened the door. He apologized until I agreed to take him back. He never attempted anything like that ever again. I found out later that his brother—your uncle Billy—had been diagnosed with cancer the night before the incident. Your dad was going through a rough time with that. I forgave him, and the rest, of course, is history. That's the condensed version." She smiled. "If Julian's anything like your dad, then he needs time to cool off."

"Wow, that's so uncharacteristic of Dad." I sat up and looked at her. "I guess I'll give Julian some time."

"I think that's a great idea, honey."

"Thanks for another great story, Mommy. You always have a knack for making me feel better."

SUNDAY MORNING OVERCAST SKIES turned everything dreary, bringing massive rain. I laid on my bed with one leg crossed over the other staring out the window. Black clouds smeared the heavens, matching my mood. I hadn't heard from Julian since our fight the day before. My heart ached for him. Did I overstep my bounds? Maybe he was right. What *did* I know? He needed someone to understand him right now, not berate him.

Surely he was suffering. His stepmom was never a part of his life, his dad betrayed him, and now I walked out on him. He must be feeling shattered. I needed to know he was all right. Against my mom's advice, I decided to call him. He picked up on the second ring.

"Hi," I whispered.

"Hey."

I let out the breath I'd been holding, relieved that he'd calmed down.

"Um, I'm so sorry about what I said to you yesterday. You were right. What do I know?" I cleared my throat and picked at a stain on my jeans.

"I'm the one who should be apologizing to you, Amber. I said some pretty hurtful stuff. I was a total prick. I didn't think I'd ever hear from you again. I'm so sorry."

I started making circles around the stain with my finger. "Zero chance of that. You'll never get rid of me."

"Glad to hear that, but you do know what you're getting yourself into, right?"

"Ha, ha, you betcha. How are you doing?"

"As good as can be expected."

"Hey, do you want to come over?" I asked.

"No, I don't think I'm in the right frame of mind for visiting. Nothing against you, I just need some more time alone."

"I understand completely. I'm so sorry your heart is breaking.

Have you seen your dad yet?"

"Hell no. I'm avoiding him at all costs," he said bluntly, his voice filled with rancor.

Oh. I could tell he had a lot more healing to go through.

"He may wonder why you're avoiding him. I'm always here if you need me."

"Thank you." He paused. "Hey, I'll see you tomorrow morning. You're riding to school with me, right?"

"Yup, surely am," I said in my most sarcastic voice.

"Very funny, babe."

We hung up.

ANOTHER MONDAY MORNING arrived without any more hoops to jump through. I'd dressed in blue jeans, a light yellow sweater, and my Reeboks, ready to face whatever the world threw at me today. Julian was as sexy as ever in his tight jeans, blue T-shirt, and leather jacket. I just about expired when I laid eyes on him this morning. Had I ever seen him in jeans? I didn't think so. And I know I'd never seen him in that jet-black bomber jacket. I sighed loudly. He shook his head and rolled those dazzling blue eyes at me.

I didn't know what went on in the Cahill house over the last twenty-four hours, but now Julian was acting distant. I knew Mr. Cahill was home, too.

I remembered Robin's words to me; back when I first met Julian...*Why is it that great-looking guys come with so much fucking baggage?* How true those words were right now.

As we stepped through the doors of the school, the public address system buzzed with the news of Julian's and my win at the competition the Friday before. The emphatic sounds of whistling and clapping filled the air as we strolled down the hall to our homeroom. His somber mood improved immediately. Although, it was abundantly clear no one knew the pain that burdened him at this moment. Our secret would stay with us.

Moments later, the bell rang, and we parted ways. I headed to my chemistry class while Julian went in the opposite direction to history.

Walking down the hallway, I heard the distant voice of my best friend.

"Amber." Shelby hurriedly caught up to me.

"Yeah, what's up?"

"Hey, Brad and I are going to have an overnighter at his house next weekend, and we wanted to invite you and Julian. We'd love it if you could come. One other couple, Nate and Darby are coming, too."

Shelby always understood my issues. I cherished her as a true, honest friend, as well as one that I desperately needed in those early days. Maybe I should fill her in on our latest dilemma. Would she be able to help? I opened my mouth to speak but hastily closed it again. I wanted to tell my best friend, but couldn't betray Julian's trust in me.

"What's the matter, Amber?"

"Nothing. Let me talk to Julian, but this sounds perfect."

She tipped her head to the side and narrowed her eyebrows at me. "Okay, let us know."

"I will." I turned and walked away. I knew I'd say something I'd regret later if I stood there a moment longer.

Come hell or high water; this was what Julian needed to take his mind off the troubles with his dad. A night away from home...with me. Now I needed to convince my parents to let me go.

OVER THE NEXT WEEK, the situation with Julian's dad hadn't improved much at all. Mr. Cahill was questioning Julian's rebellious and disobedient behavior of late. He'd shrug his shoulders and remain silent, taking no steps forward. As a matter of fact, I'd guess Julian actually took several steps backward. Unless he confronted his dad, I didn't see the situation improving, either. What's more, I always felt uncomfortable being in the middle of their brouhaha. But, this evening I was going to do my homework at Julian's house. I tried but was unsuccessful in my attempt to sway him to come to mine.

I rang the bell.

"Hi, babe," I said when Julian opened the door.

"Hey." He took my hand and pulled me into the house. With gentleness, he bent down and kissed me on the lips.

"How's it going?" I asked tentatively.

He frowned.

Oh?

We meandered to the kitchen where Nancy was finishing up the dishes.

She looked up at me. "Hello, Amber," she said in her brusque tone—a tone I'd become all too familiar with since I'd known her...Well, at least she used my name.

"Hi, Mrs. Cahill. How are you?"

"Busy," she said while placing a plate into the dishwasher.

"Nancy, we'll be in the den doing our homework," Julian informed her.

Julian took my hand, and together we headed into the study and closed the door. Before sitting down, Julian swept me into his arms and planted a wet kiss on my lips. He took my breath away. I giggled as we sat down on the loveseat and plunged into our homework.

I lifted my history textbook from my backpack. "By the way, how did you do on your report card?" I asked him. "I got four A's and an A+."

He sighed. "You did better than me."

Before I could ask him his grades, there was a commotion at the door. Logan barged into the room holding a piece of paper in his hand. I couldn't make out what it was.

"Hello, Amber," he said cordially.

"Hi, Mr. Cahill. How are you?"

He glanced toward Julian, narrowed his brows, and then turned back to me. "I've had better days," he said.

Crap. Here we go again. Why did I agree to come over here? I glanced at Julian's scowl.

"What do you want, Dad? I assume you're here for a reason."

"You're right. I am," he said, then looked to me. "Amber, would you please excuse us and give me a moment with my son?"

"Um...sure," I stuttered, my heart pounding in my ears.

With a stiff posture, rigid muscles, and corded neck, Logan turned to Julian. "Come with me, please, Julian."

Julian grumbled and followed his dad out of the room. He closed the door behind him.

I felt a tightness in my chest. What was going on now?

I tried, but couldn't make out any of the muffled conversation on the other side of the door, so I opened a textbook and started in on my work.

Seconds later the discussion grew louder. I lifted my head and glanced at the door.

"What's this?" Julian's dad sounded mad.

"What's it look like, Dad?" Good lord, now Julian's antagonizing him.

"Should I ground you for one more week?" Logan shouted. "With grades like this, you'll never get into medical school."

Grounded? So that's why he wouldn't come to my house. It occurred to me that Logan was holding Julian's report card in his hand. Julian never told me what his grades were.

Seconds later the door flew open and in walked Julian. His shoulders slumped forward. He looked dejected.

"I'm sorry, babe. You're going to have to leave. I'll see you in the morning. Okay?" He didn't even look up at me.

"Sure," I said in a flat, monotone voice. It was the only word I could think to say. Without a second thought, I scooped my books into my bag, gave Julian a chaste kiss on the cheek and left. Along the path, I stopped at the maple tree and placed my hand on the heart. I prayed things would get better with Julian and his dad.

THE WEEK DRAGGED BY SLOWLY, but tonight was the sleepover party at Brad's and not a moment too soon. Julian was free to come and go as he pleased. I hoped for the Wyss home to be a welcome distraction from the hell Julian felt within the walls of his own house.

I met Julian at his house after convincing my parents to let me spend an overnight at Brad's. They seemed to relax when I mentioned Brad's parents would be there supervising us.

I never knew what I was going to walk in on at the Cahill's, but on this particular evening, his dad wasn't home. I breathed a sigh of relief.

"Ready to go?" I asked.

"Yup, let's go, babe." He sounded happy; no doubt relieved the grounding was over.

He never divulged the reason behind the heated argument with his dad from the week before, and I didn't ask. An explanation had to come from him when he was ready.

Brad lived in Castle Rock, south of Castle Pines along I-25. He and Shelby had dated since their sophomore year. They became an awesome couple for Julian and me to hang out with. Brad was, to many girls, a heartthrob himself. Not the caliber of Julian, but a hot-looking guy nonetheless. With short black hair, serious blue eyes, and a six-foot frame, he was the complete package.

Fifteen minutes later, with our overnight backpacks in tow, we were greeted at the door by Brad's mother, a short, slender woman with shoulder-length, spiky red hair.

"Welcome Julian, come in." Looking at me, she extended her hand. "And you must be Amber. Welcome, dear. You both sounded wonderful at the talent competition a couple of weeks ago. Congratulations on the win."

I nodded and thanked her with a firm handshake. "Your home is beautiful, Mrs. Wyss. Thank you for inviting us."

"My pleasure, Amber. We always love when Brad's friends visit us."

"Hey, Mrs. Wyss, great to see you again." Julian gave her a brief hug.

She smiled, turned, and made her way to the kitchen.

Julian and I found our friends in the family room. I wasn't sure where Brad got his height from because his mom couldn't have been five feet tall if that.

A loud crackle and pop from a log burning in the fireplace against the far wall made me jump. One of the embers escaped and landed on the carpeting beside the stone hearth. Brad jumped up from the sofa and stamped it out with the toe of his sneaker and spotted us.

"Hey, you guys. Glad you could make it," he said.

"Wouldn't miss this for the world, Brad," I said.

I looked around at the vastness of the room. There were three different seating areas around a square coffee table. Shelby sat on the overstuffed sofa just vacated by Brad, while Nate and Darby sat arm-in-arm on the adjoining love seat. Julian and I plopped down in the large, overstuffed, pale brown chair between the two with me sitting on his lap.

Mrs. Wyss supplied us with pizza, cheese and crackers and an assortment of snacks and drinks. We ate, talked, and laughed a lot. It made me happy to see Julian enjoying himself. On occasion, Mr. Wyss made unsolicited appearances in the room, as if to make sure we were behaving ourselves.

"Very discreet, Dad!" Brad yelled out.

He was cool, though, joining in our conversation, laughing and joking with us.

For hours, we chatted about sports, school, hiking, and everything else under the sun, having a fabulous time. While Shelby and I "tried" to gossip about our boyfriends, we couldn't help but overhear the guys voicing their grievances over matters they wished girls knew. One by one, they all went through their own lists.

"If you wear a push-up bra and a low-cut blouse, you lose the right to complain about having your cleavage stared at," Brad smirked.

Julian chimed in next, "If it itches, it will be scratched."

We were rowdy and loud, laughing hysterically. I'd even heard Mr. and Mrs. Wyss chuckle from the kitchen.

Our fun evening moved along quickly. Glancing at the clock, I noticed it was two in the morning, and we all decided on sleep. Mr. and Mrs. Wyss had gone to bed hours before and didn't seem to object to us sleeping together in the family room. Of course, they didn't have much say in it at this point.

"Behave yourselves." Mr. Wyss looked daggers at us before trudging up the stairs to bed.

"We will," we all said in unison, knowing full well that wouldn't be the case.

Julian and I managed to snuggle up together on an air mattress while Brad and Shelby slept on the sofa. Nate and Darby brought a sleeping bag and found a spot in front of the fireplace. The television hummed in the background with enough volume to guarantee that Julian and I wouldn't be heard with our veiled intimacy.

With lightning speed, we climbed under the blankets, removed our clothes, and swaddled our naked bodies together.

Julian whispered in my ear, "Thank you for a great evening, babe. Want to have sex?"

At first, my initial reaction was: *Are you kidding?* But after glancing across the room, I noticed Nate and Darby going at it like feral animals while Brad and Shelby were pleasuring each other in an indiscreet way. The blankets covered our exposed nakedness. Who was going to see us and, better yet, who would care?

"Seriously? In the same room as the others?" I admonished.

"Well, if you haven't noticed, they're all pre-occupied at the moment," he spoke under his breath.

"What the hell, okay. By the way, how's the tattoo feeling? Completely healed?"

"Yeah, all is good." His smile dropped.

Crap, I reminded him of a painful topic. I had to learn to keep my mouth shut. I cringed at the thought of his dad ever seeing that tattoo on his back. The fact that he got it out of spite was a situation only capable of ending in disaster.

I cocooned my body around him, and we made sweet, passionate love for what felt like hours, trying to be as judicious as humanly possible. He'd become so great at sex; it was a monumental effort to restrain my screams.

"Hmm, love you, Julian."

"Love you, too, Amber. I can't believe I get to cuddle with you all night. I don't ever want the night to end."

"Neither do I."

With my back to his front, we fell into a deep, blissful sleep as the TV fell silent and clicked off by itself.

I WOKE BEFORE JULIAN, giving me an opportunity to stare at him. Sprawled on his back, right arm above the head, his muscular abs and private area were swathed in blankets. His lips parted slightly, breathing softly. I propped myself up on my side, resting my head in the palm of my hand and gawked at him. He was so sexy and beautiful.

What did I do to deserve this boyfriend?

"Hey," I said as he opened his eyes. "You caught me staring at you."

"As long as it's your beautiful eyes doing the staring, I'll live with it."

"You'd better."

Moving at the speed of lightning, he pushed me to my back, laid his hard-as-steel body on top of me, and pulled the blankets over our heads. "It was most excellent spending a night with you, Amber. If we were alone, I'd hump your brains out right now," he whispered in my ear. The others were still sleeping while Mr. and Mrs. Wyss were moving about in the kitchen.

"Jeez, so romantic, Julian." I punched him in the shoulder. "Bring it on," I teased quietly.

PACKING OUR BELONGINGS and showing our gratitude to Mr. and Mrs. Wyss, we bid our friends a goodbye. Julian and I headed home in the early afternoon after a relaxing morning of idle chit chat. We had a phenomenal time.

Driving home, I decided to tackle a delicate subject. "Are you going to talk to your dad?"

"Why are you bringing that up, Amber?"

Crap. Another faux pas with my damn mouth, but I wanted to know how much longer Julian was going to evade his dad's constant interrogation. It had gone on long enough. "Are you going to spend the rest of your life shutting your dad out? Maybe you should hear what he has to say."

He whipped his head around to me. "What could he possibly have to say that I give a shit about? I still fucking detest him."

So this was how it would be. Pushing the issue with him was certainly ineffective. Anyhow, I didn't want to ruin the wonderful weekend we had, so I sat in silence for the rest of the ride home. It appeared that we'd reached an impasse.

Arriving home minutes later, he asked, "It looks like my parents aren't home. Want to come over?"

Anger forgotten.

"Sure, I'll need to let my parents know that I'm home first and then I'll be right over."

I decided on a quick shower to rid myself of the last twenty-four hours of partying. Going through the motions of washing my hair and the rest of my body, I decided to give him time. He wouldn't listen to my suggestions and, honestly, I was getting tired of his defiant attitude whenever I broached the subject of his dad. He'd talk when he was ready.

Dressed in my dark blue jeans and simple white T-shirt, I made my way over to his house. As he opened the door, I sighed. How he could make sweatpants and a T-shirt look sexy was beyond explanation. When he mentioned that he'd also taken a shower, we laughed.

Julian raised an eyebrow and winked. "Hey, want to fuck my brains out?"

I grinned. "Well, when you put it that way, how could I say no?" He needed me; I was his solace, his comfort. I'd do anything for him.

Taking me by the hand, he dragged me into his family room and spun me around, pressing our bodies together.

I squealed. "What is it about family rooms now?"

He looked down into my eyes. "I'm not sure, but I thought for a change of pace, we could do it here."

We removed each other's clothing and found our way to the Persian area rug in the center of the room. Julian spread a blanket on the floor and in short seconds started invading my mouth. With subtle, seductive kisses, I pounced on his lips with an equal amount of passion back.

Oh, this felt right. I closed my eyes, trying to take in the moment. We'd come so far and experienced so much together. My feelings went deep for him.

He lowered me to the floor and curled the blanket around us. He positioned himself at my opening and with gentleness, eased himself inside me with a low groan.

"God, I can't get enough of you, Amber. What are you doing to me?"

"The same thing you're doing to me, Julian. We're in love."

He smiled and found a steady pace moving in and out with a slow, consistent rhythm.

My heart pounded, losing myself in Julian's passionate ambush of my nipples until they hardened under his assault. I ran my fingers through his hair and pulled him down to my lips. I was thrusting my tongue in his mouth.

Through harsh breathing, he started ramming into me with vigor. He groaned.

"I'm so close, Julian." I started shaking.

Suddenly he stopped and heaved, "Shit!"

"What was that?" I asked.

"Fuck, my parents are home!" He swiftly pulled out of me and started shrieking commands.

"What should I do?" I felt terrified as a tiny giggle escaped from my lips. I was entirely in the buff, and Julian's parents had just stepped from the garage, into the kitchen, only feet between us. This was my worst nightmare.

"Shit, Amber, hide. In the closet, over there." He pointed to a door on the other side of the room.

Grabbing my scattered clothing sprinkled about the floor, I hurriedly scampered across the room to the coat closet. It was a tight squeeze, but I managed to, in record time, dress myself. Pants…check. Bra…check. Shirt…check. With my heart pounding through my chest, I saw Julian drag his pants on and tidy up the area. In my haste to hide quickly, I'd accidentally left the door ajar, allowing me a decent view of the room.

As Julian tried to tug his shirt over his head, I heard the infuriated voice of his father. He'd just appeared in the room, stopped with a jerk and stared at Julian.

"What the hell is that on your back, Julian?"

Oh God, Logan saw the tattoo. Okay, this was my new worst nightmare unraveling.

"A tattoo, *Dad*," he ridiculed in a condescending tone, yanking the shirt down to cover his gorgeous midsection. He moved across the room from his dad.

"Don't take that tone with me, Julian. Where the hell did you get that?"

Logan Cahill was not to be mocked. He looked completely and utterly livid.

As if the situation couldn't get any worse, Nancy stepped into the room from the kitchen. My legs went weak and started shaking while my breathing intensified.

"What's the problem in here?" she asked.

Logan shifted his angry eyes to her. "He's got a goddamn tattoo. That's the problem, Nanc." I saw her flinch.

Logan turned his heated stare back to Julian. "How the hell did you get that? You need parental consent."

Julian ignored him and gave Nancy a don't-you-dare-say-anything glare.

What? Had she given him consent? This was worse than I thought. Why would she do that?

"I don't know what your problem has been lately, but it'd better stop, or else."

"Or else what, Dad?" he said with a crusty tone.

Both of them continued to stand on opposite sides of the room glowering at each other.

"Or else you won't be allowed to leave this house for a month. Don't test me."

I couldn't believe Julian continued to antagonize him. This issue with his dad was deeper than I thought.

"It's that girl," Mrs. Cahill interrupted. "She's a bad influence on him."

I wanted to cry. I couldn't believe what I was hearing. I thought she liked me. Well, the feeling was mutual. Right now I despised the woman.

"Don't you dare talk about Amber like that, Nancy!" There was rancor in Julian's voice. "She has nothing to do with the reason I got this tattoo. In fact, she wasn't all that thrilled with it either in the beginning," he said, rocking back and forth in place.

Mr. Cahill continued, "Then why, Julian? We discussed this and my answer was a flat out no, and you went behind my back and did it anyway."

"Oh yeah, well, Dad, you're a fine one to talk about doing things behind someone's back," Julian hissed.

Mr. Cahill rolled his fingers into a fist at his side, his rage intensifying. "What the hell is that supposed to mean?"

Julian paced across the room, and stood behind the sofa, putting the couch between them as if finding a safer distance from his dad. Contemplating his next words, he shot an evil eye in his father's direction. "Okay, Dad, who is she?" He scowled at him.

I put my forearm in my mouth to stifle my gasp. Oh, this was it. He was finally confronting his dad—in front of Nancy no less…and me. I couldn't believe I was witnessing this. I didn't want to be here. This was none of my business. *Crap!*

Logan stopped abruptly, stepped back, and exhaled. His eyes narrowed as his shoulders sagged. "What the hell are you talking about?" His voice sounded threatening and harsh.

"Don't act like you don't know, Dad."

There was a long silence. Logan dropped his head. His look was one of torment and deception.

"Who the fuck is she, Dad?" Julian hissed at him, placing his outspread hands on the rear of the sofa in a commanding stance, now dictating the direction of the face-off. A spreading tension filled the room.

"What is Julian talking about, Logan?" Nancy glared at him, shocked. "Are you…" she trailed off, eyes heated. Then a sudden realization filled her face. "No. You haven't been seeing…"

"Tell your *wife*, Dad!" Julian interrupted, emphasizing "wife." "Tell her, tell her, go ahead, tell h—"

Interrupting Julian before he could get another word out, Logan balled his hands into fists and yelled, "She's your mother, Goddammit!"

Chapter Ten

Holy hell. His mother? I gulped, hoping nobody heard me. My mind drifted back to the hotel. That was why she looked so familiar to me. Julian was the gorgeous spit-image of his mom. As a matter of fact, I would even go so far as to say she was stunning.

Now more questions surfaced. Why had Julian been told she died? Why was Logan with her? Why did Logan marry Nancy? What did Nancy know? I scanned the room, looking from Julian to Logan to Nancy. Disbelief to embarrassment to hostility covered the faces of the three of them.

Julian missed an entire lifetime with his biological mother. Was that his mom's choice? I scowled at the thought. No, I refused to believe she'd knowingly reject him. After all, what kind of parent did that?

A bitter stare crossed Julian's face. "What? You fucking told me she died. Why would you do that to me?"

Logan narrowed his brows at Julian. "It was to protect her. It had to be this way, and stop with the foul language. It's disrespectful."

Julian's eyes burned into his dad with anger. "I'm pissed, Dad. You've lied to me my entire life." He crossed his arms over his chest, deliberately ignoring Logan's demand to clean up his language. "Why the fuck did she need protection? Huh, Dad?"

I recalled my conversation with Julian about his mom when we first started dating. What if he'd been more persistent in questioning his dad back then? Would Logan have been more forthcoming and given him some honest answers?

Logan's stance stiffened, exchanging heated gazes with Julian. "When you decide to cool down, I'll explain the whole story to you, but not until…"

"You want me to calm down? Put yourself in my shoes, Dad!" he shouted and turned toward the closet just in time to catch a quick glimpse of my bulging eyes.

Nancy interrupted with a high-pitched screech, "Don't, Logan. Stop now. Not another word, I mean it!"

I couldn't help but cringe at the family secrets unraveling before me. At the moment, I felt thankful for my unrestricted view of the room, but also relieved to be shrouded in darkness.

"It's out in the open now, Nancy," Logan said, glowering at her with contempt.

"I mean it Logan, don't!" she screamed, thrusting her boney finger into his chest.

Logan jerked away.

"Trust me; you don't want to do this," she hissed at him. When he narrowed his eyes at her, she blurted out, "Fine. It was me who gave him consent."

Holy crap! Nancy gave Julian consent to get a tattoo…behind Logan's back? Why? I suspect Julian must have asked her.

"You what!" he bellowed at her. "Goddammit!"

"What's going on here? I deserve to know why you told me my mom died sixteen years ago when, in fact, she hadn't. Somebody better start talking…now!" Julian moved in front of Nancy, punching his fist into the sofa.

"I said no!" Nancy yelled.

"I said yes." Julian turned and regarded her with a vile glare.

Logan moved between the two of them, breaking up the impending stand-off, then turned and glared at Nancy. "I've had enough of your control of my life. Julian has a right to know, and nothing you say or do will stop me, especially after your latest confession."

Double crap! Nancy never seemed to be someone you dared to double-cross, but now I was really captivated. What was her motivation in all this? And what kind of dysfunctional vortex had I entered into here? My family never had fights like this.

Nancy flashed her beady eyes at him. "You'll be sorry, Logan."

Logan fixed her with a lethal stare. "Don't you dare threaten me—it's over."

"It'll never be over!" She glared at him with a don't-cross-me look and stormed out of the room. I was not sure from where, but I heard the sound of a slamming door.

Oh my God. What kind of marriage did the Cahill's have? Obviously one based on deceit and deception. My curiosity piqued to new heights, but I was getting restless standing in the closet. On top of this, my bladder was summoning me. Julian remembered that I was here, right?

Julian raised his voice again. "I've been in the dark for my entire life, Dad. What the hell is going on in this godforsaken house? I want the truth."

"Okay, Julian." Logan moved around, sat on the sofa and tapped the cushion beside him. "Sit, please." Julian shuffled over and sat on the adjacent loveseat. I suspect he was trying to keep his distance and allow me a view of the anguish on his face.

Logan leaned forward and shook his head, hesitating, as if trying to find the words. "Your mother was sixteen years old when I got her pregnant. I was twenty-four, and…"

"It's called statutory rape, Dad," Julian interrupted.

Logan let out a deep breath. "Yes, I'm well aware of what it is."

"It wasn't to protect her, Dad; it was to protect you," Julian criticized him as if trying to pick a fight.

Whoa! I remember thinking she looked younger than him. She was eight years younger.

"Stop with the attitude. This is hard enough without dealing with your smart mouth. Do you want to hear what I have to say or not?"

Julian clenched his teeth. "Go on."

Logan stood and started pacing the area and sat beside Julian on the loveseat. Julian flinched.

"Lisa is from a wealthy, prominent family."

"Her name is Lisa?" Julian asked, his face full of wonder. He looked as if he'd found a lost treasure. He had…his mother.

"Yes, Lisa Hayward." Logan dropped his head in shame. "Christ, we loved each other then and still do today."

"Hayward? My middle name." His eyes glowed with sweet recognition, shifting inconspicuously in my direction.

It warmed my heart when he acknowledged my presence. Suffice it to say, I remained still in the dark confines of the coat closet, even though my legs were cramping up.

"Yes, son." Logan took Julian's hand. "Hayward." His eyes filled with emotion.

I remembered Julian mentioning his middle name being Hayward. I figured it had to be a family name, never imagining his moms.

Releasing Julian's hand, Logan continued. "Thankfully, Lisa was able to cover up the pregnancy for nearly eight months. Once her parents found out, they threatened to disown her unless she agreed to give the baby up for adoption. They continued to probe her into revealing my identity. She was heartbroken and refused, knowing the outcome would, most likely, lead to my jail time. The thought of you being raised by another family was out of the question. I made the decision to raise you myself until she was a legal consenting adult. Then we would marry and be a family together. I was already making a decent living on my own."

Julian let out an impatient huff. "So, why didn't that happen?"

"Hear me out. I haven't finished."

"So, are her parents... my grandparents... still alive?"

"Yes, son, although they never knew I was dating your mom back then and still don't know it was me who raised you. They assumed an anonymous family adopted you. You see, they don't know my identity as your father. Lisa has told me about them and shown me photographs, but I've never met them."

"Yes, I guess that would be the case." Julian frowned. "But why tell me she died? I don't understand."

"I was forced to say that."

"Wait, why?" Julian looked as though he was mulling something over in his head. "Where does Nancy fit into all this?"

As Julian said the words, Nancy burst into the room, temper flaring and demand Logan end the discussion. Where was she?

"No!" Logan bellowed.

With heavy feet, she inched across the room and removed the ornate, blue vase from the mantel. She lifted it over her head, and threatened to heave it across the floor.

"Put the goddamn vase down, Nancy. You know what that means to me."

"Then stop talking now!"

With terror in his eyes, Logan rose from the sofa and hurtled himself toward Nancy, begging her to hand him the vase.

"You don't believe me, do you, Logan?" She sneered.

Out of my field of vision, I heard the crash of, what I assume was a priceless vase hitting the floor, shattering into pieces.

In quick seconds, Mr. Cahill hovered over Nancy, pointing at the door. "Get out! Get out of my goddamn house! Now! Everything is out in the open, and I don't care who knows. No more goddamn blackmail."

Blackmail?

"This isn't over, Logan." She grabbed her purse, headed to the kitchen, and slammed the door. Seconds later, I heard a car drive away.

"Blackmail? What is going on here, Dad?" Julian asked, eying the broken vase.

I'd walked into the house of hell. I thought this was something you only saw in the movies.

Making his way back to the sofa, Logan sat and stared in dismay at the broken vase strewn about the floor.

"Lisa was scheduled to deliver you at Denver Medical Center. Following the birth, her parents instructed the baby be put up for adoption. Since Lisa refused to divulge my identity to them, I had to be careful about my involvement."

Logan got down on his knees and started fishing through the broken pottery, examining each piece before placing them in a pile.

"I knew Nancy through my older sister, Jenny. She delivered your cousin Becky and came highly recommended as a respected doctor. I suggested Lisa use Nancy as her OBGYN. She did and immediately liked her, hoping to make the whole process easier. I trusted Nancy when I filled her in on our dilemma. She was glad to help and willing to fill those shoes. I made it known that Lisa's parents must never find out after I arranged to take you home." He ran a hand through his hair. "I didn't realize how unstable she really was."

Julian watched his dad, mesmerized, taking in every word.

Pain and anguish crossed Logan's face, as he examined a piece of the vase. "Lisa's parents signed the adoption papers after you were born, relinquishing any involvement with you. Once blood tests proved me to be your father, I received parental custody. After completing the necessary paperwork, I took you home. Lisa visited frequently when you were a newborn. We planned to marry in the future. Everything was perfect—so I thought." Logan hesitated and let out a deep breath. "That's when my world fell apart, and Nancy blackmailed me."

Julian's eyes widened in complete shock. "What'd she do?"

Logan shifted on the floor to face Julian, wrapping his arms around his knees. "When you were a month old, she approached me out of the blue and threatened to tell the Haywards about me." He grimaced, shaking his head. "She demanded I marry her and prohibit Lisa from having contact with you. Once you were old enough to understand and start asking questions, I was to tell you your mother died. It was the only way Nancy felt assured you'd never search for her, finding out the truth. Lisa was completely devastated at the thought of never being able to see you again."

Whoa! Everything was starting to make sense. It reminded of my conversation with Julian when I asked him if he knew her name. *My dad told me he'd tell me one day, but it was too soon.* This was why it was too early. Logan was waiting until Julian turned eighteen. Nancy threatened Logan to keep quiet. She was as much of a psychopath as the two bitches who stabbed me. At least my misery was short-lived. He'd suffered with her for years.

"And you did this?"

"I had no choice, Julian. I would have walked across burning coals to protect you. If I'd gone to jail, you would have ended up in child protective services, or worse yet; Nancy would have taken legal guardianship of you. The thought of her raising you made me sick. So, I married her. She'd threaten me whenever she could, and did it frequently. I couldn't take any chances of Lisa coming in contact with you." He stopped and stared at the pictures of Julian hanging on the wall. "Christ, Nancy wouldn't even let me show you a photograph of your own mom."

I remembered Julian telling me he'd never seen pictures of her. So, that's why. I suspect Nancy's motive behind it was to keep Julian from identifying Lisa in public. Wow, Nancy had her bases covered. *Bitch!*

"You are my life, my world, my everything, Julian. You are my child."

Logan adored Julian with all his heart. The thought he'd spent the last sixteen years of his life living in holy hell to protect him was true testament of his love.

Julian lowered his head in shame and ran his fingers through his hair. "I'm sorry about my behavior lately, Dad. I had no idea what you'd been going through all these years. I thought you were out cheating on Nancy." He shuffled his position on the sofa. "But why did you continue lying after Lisa was of consenting age? That's what I don't understand."

"I didn't plan to, but Nancy threatened me with lies of abuse and adultery if I told you the truth. She's a sick woman in need of help. Hell, she would have gone so far as to injuring herself to prove her point. My goddamn hands were tied, and I wasn't going to take any chances with your life. At least not until you were a legal adult. Then I was prepared to blow the lid off this charade of a marriage."

"She's in need of a psychiatric ward, Dad. So, what happens now? I won't lose you, will I?" Julian spoke through an emotion-filled voice.

"No. I won't let that happen," Logan said, but I don't think he felt the conviction of his words.

They both stood and hugged. Tears streamed down both their faces. Julian had his dad back. I swallowed past the knot in my throat. What a day.

"When did you start seeing Mom again?"

Julian smiled when he said *mom*. What an uplifting moment for him.

Logan smirked. "I never stopped. I couldn't. I loved Lisa with all my heart and still do. I couldn't imagine my life without her. Nancy never knew I continued to see her either, until now. I had to be extremely judicious about our secret affair. Nancy kept a close eye on your whereabouts, but I was able to be more vigilant with my own." Logan bent down and continued to gather the remaining pieces of the broken vase. "She's my sanity."

"Let me clean it up, Dad."

"Thanks, son." Logan moved to the sofa. He turned to Julian and grinned. "I've kept Lisa up to date on your accomplishments. I've shown her pictures of you, so she's seen you grow up into a wonderful young man, albeit, from a distance. It's been tough on her." Logan paused briefly then his eyes went wide. "Unbelievable, Julian, I've kept this secret from Nancy for sixteen years, and it's you who sees me. I don't know if I should feel condemned or thankful."

"I'll go for the latter, but it wasn't me who saw you, Dad."

Logan stuttered, looking puzzled. "Then…uh, how did you know?"

"It was Amber—she saw you."

I cringed. How was I ever going to face Logan again? Then again, if I hadn't seen him that night, none of these revelations would have been uncovered. I believed in the greater good.

Logan's mouth twisted in anguish. "Oh, so she told you?"

"Yes, but she didn't want to. I demanded it out of her."

"Where was this?"

"I'd rather not say, Dad."

Thank you, Julian, for not giving away our hotel rendezvous to your dad. I sighed. I could only imagine the aftermath of divulging that tiny piece of information. After all, Julian just fixed the relationship with his father; I couldn't bear to witness one more confrontation today.

"Are you okay?"

"Yes. Thank you for being my dad and raising me." Julian scooped up the remaining pieces of the broken vase and placed them in a pile on the coffee table.

He smiled at Julian. "You know, your mom and I were at your talent competition."

Julian stiffened and abruptly lifted his head.

"She beamed with pride at your performance. You get your voice from her. She's a beautiful singer as well. By the way, congratulations on your win. Your mother sobbed with joy. She wanted very badly to give you a hug following your performance."

"Really? You both were there?" Julian's mouth fell open. "That means a lot to me, Dad. When can I meet her?"

I should've known his dad would never have missed the talent show. I thought back to the hotel. I was at the ice machine and overheard Logan and Lisa's conversation. Yes, they were talking about us.

"You will soon, but let me settle things with Nancy first. Okay, son?"

"I hate Nancy. It was because of her that I never knew my mom. She kept me away from her. I'll never forgive her for that."

"I don't know how things would have ended up if she'd never entered the picture, Julian. Lisa was under tight rein with her folks."

"Where is she now?" Julian wrapped the broken glass in a newspaper. He stood and walked to the sofa again. He grinned at me before sitting.

"I'll tell you in due time, not now."

"No more secrets, Dad." They sat, shoulder to shoulder—two handsome men—staring at one another.

"Okay, son."

Julian grinned. "No wonder you looked terrified when I asked to see her grave a couple of years ago."

"Yes, I wasn't sure how I was going to tiptoe around that one, but you were easy to appease."

Julian gave him a sideways smile. "More like gullible, wouldn't you say?"

"No. You've been the best son a father could ask for."

Julian eyed the broken glass wrapped in the newspaper. "Where did this vase come from?"

"Your mom made it for me," Logan said, his voice catching in his throat.

"Fucking bitch," I heard Julian say under his breath, no doubt referring to Nancy.

Closing in on dusk, a disturbance at the front door only meant one thing…my rescue from the closet would be delayed. I swiped at the darkness around me and touched what felt like the vacuum. I gingerly sat down. My legs were sore, and I had to pee pretty bad now. Oh, this felt better.

Logan made his way to the front door, and I heard the exchange of some confusing dialogue.

"Are you Logan Cahill?"

"Yes." Logan sounded polite.

"I'm Carl, Lisa Hayward's father."

Whoa, can this get any more bizarre? They walked into the living room together. Carl looked to be a much older gentleman, possibly in his sixties. He was tall, handsome, and stocky with salt and pepper-colored hair. But, it was not him I noticed first—directly to his left was Nancy. *Are you kidding me? She knew Julian's grandfather?* Nancy must have driven to the Hayward house. What an evil bitch.

"Listen, I'm here to see my grandson."

Mr. Cahill let out a deep breath. I squinted, trying to size up the situation but couldn't see the looks on their faces. "Of course. Have a seat, please, Carl."

"There he is. That's Lisa's child." Nancy stormed into the room pointing at Julian. He'd just finished cleaning the pieces of the broken vase off the floor. She looked pissed as if she expected a riot to break out, but it didn't happen. Karma, I thought.

"My dad told you to leave, so get out!" Julian stood from the floor and shouted at her.

"Don't you take that tone with me, boy."

"Enough. Both of you." Logan stepped between them.

Julian eyed her with contempt and then turned his attention to the strange man.

Carl strolled over, as a smile swept across his face and offered his hand. "How wonderful to meet you. I'm your Grandpa Hayward."

With complete grace, Julian took his outstretched hand and the men greeted each other. "Great to meet you, too, sir."

"Heavens, boy, call me Gramps, please."

Julian's smile stretched a mile wide. Nancy, however, had a look of pure hatred. The whole incident backfired in her face. I wasn't someone who took pleasure in people's comeuppance, but I firmly believed she got what was coming to her.

"Excuse me a moment, Carl." Logan took Nancy by the arm and dragged her outside. I couldn't hear the conversation between them, but Logan re-entered the house alone. Was she gone forever? Somehow, I doubted it.

With his arm, Julian gestured for Carl to sit.

"Thank you, Julian. I'd be happy to." They both sat on the sofa. Logan followed and sat on the cream-colored wingback chair. "I'd love to hear all about you, son, but first I've got to get something off my chest."

"Before you begin, would you like something to drink?" Logan asked.

"No thank you, Logan. I won't take up much of your time. I just want to say my peace, and I'll be on my way." He turned to face Julian. "Sixteen years ago, I regretted shutting my daughter's child out of her life, but I want to change that today," Carl said. "My relationship with my daughter was never the same after we insisted she give her child up for adoption. But here you are, sitting before me, a handsome young man. You look like your mother, Julian. I'm pleased that your father made the decision to raise you. Because of that decision, you will now be a part of my life. I hope we can get to know each other. One lesson I've learned in all this is that family is everything."

"I'd like that, Mr...., uh, Grandpa." Julian's eyes widened.

Carl turned to Logan. "If I'd known you were the father all those years ago, I may have reacted differently. That's all in the past. I can see that you've done a great job raising Julian, and wish nothing but good fortune for the both of you. Your wife filled me in on what transpired here this evening, putting her spin on it. Look, I may be an old geezer, but all my faculties are still sharp, and I recognize when I'm being hoodwinked." He tapped a finger on his head. "I put two and two together and knew I needed to come and see for myself. That's why I'm here."

After Logan spent the next fifteen minutes of the evening explaining the condensed version of the story, Carl stood to leave. "I'll be seeing you again, Julian."

"You bet." Julian gave his Grandfather a proper hug and the house was quiet once again.

Logan retired to his bedroom upstairs while Julian made his way to the closet. He tore open the door and tugged me into his arms.

"I have to pee," I laughed.

He helped me exit the house out the rear sliding-glass door. We threaded our fingers and walked along the path to my home, stopping in front of the maple tree. Together we touched the heart.

He placed his hands on each side of my face and gave me a chaste kiss. "I'm so sorry you had to endure all that, Amber. I didn't realize you'd be in the closet for such a long time."

I think I might've been standing stock still in the darkness of the coat closet for over an hour but didn't mind, considering the outcome. Julian's mom was alive, all was okay with his dad, and he'd soon have a new set of grandparents doting over him. That about summed it up.

I was struck, though, by how fucked up the Cahill family really was. Nancy and Logan's marriage was a deceptive shambles, and Julian found himself trapped in the middle. It's a wonder he turned out as normal as he was.

And then it dawned on me when I thought of how our relationship started—his fear of committing to one girl. He never had a decent role model in that house when it came to relationships. I hoped for a complete mending of his broken years.

I clasped my hands around his head, pulled him down to my mouth, and kissed him tenderly on his lips. "It's alright. I'm so happy for you. She's your mom, Julian. And I've got to pee."

He laughed and punched his fist into the air. "Yes!"

He grabbed me, pressing his body against mine and hugged me as if his life depended on it. His mouth covered mine as he kissed me passionately, our tongues stroking each others. Julian buried his head in the crook of my neck while we rocked back and forth for long minutes. There were no words spoken. He pulled away, looked down into my face, and ran the pad of his thumb across my lower lip.

"I love you so much, Julian."

"Love you, too, Amber," he said, turning and leaving me at my front door.

Feeling scattered, I made my way inside my house wondering what more could happen to me? Life in Castle Pines, Colorado was certainly not dull.

I headed directly to the bathroom.

Chapter Eleven

A fresh blanket of newly fallen snow covered the ground on this joyful, Christmas morning. The snow glistened in the bright sun off the top branches of the maple tree. Gazing out the window of my bedroom, I watched it melt and fall to the ground.

I'd showered and dressed, then downed a couple of aspirin to keep my nagging headache at bay.

My mom and Robin looked up when I appeared in the kitchen for breakfast. They were seated at the island devouring my dad's famous waffles, while he poured the raw batter onto the waffle iron.

"Merry Christmas everybody," I announced.

"Merry Christmas to you, pumpkin. Would you like a waffle?" my dad asked.

"Absolutely, Daddy."

One holiday tradition in the Scott house was the consumption of waffles on Christmas morning prepared by my dad.

"Coming right up," he said, dropping one onto my plate.

Robin swallowed her last bite, dropping the fork on her plate. "Let's get to the gifts," she said. "Hurry up and finish eating, Amber."

"Jeez. I'm eating as fast as I can." I giggled, just as excited as her.

A MUSICAL INTERLUDE rang faintly in my ears when I pressed the Cahill's doorbell. After spending most of the holiday with my family, I headed to Julian's for dinner and the exchanging of gifts. I didn't have to search far to find the perfect gift for him, but had to enlist the help of Mr. Cahill. He was most helpful and thought my idea was great. The anticipation I felt deep in my belly at watching Julian's face when he opened his gift left me beyond excited.

I hadn't seen much of him since the "closet caper" as it became known. That was one of the most uncomfortable moments of my life.

My mouth dropped open when Julian opened the door. I scanned his body from head to toe. Fitted in a pair of black dress slacks, coal button-down dress shirt, and a tie that matched the color of his blue eyes, he looked eatable. I fanned my face, nearly melting right there on the spot.

"You look good." My heart skipped a beat. "Merry Christmas." I scooted over to him and planted a kiss on his soft lips.

"Hey." He placed his hands on each side of my face, kissing me back. "What's this in your hand?"

"My gift to you."

"Oh?" His eyes lit up. "You look beautiful."

"Thanks."

I'd settled on a long sleeve, red wrap dress coupled with my black ballet flats. In my ears, I wore the sparkling diamond teardrop earrings just gifted to me by my parents.

"Love your dress." He bent down and whispered in my ear, "I'd love to take it off you, too." His motive was clear, and I felt instantly aroused.

I playfully punched him. It was so nice to see him in a good mood after a stressful fall semester. It had been a month since Julian found out his mom was alive, although he hadn't met her. There were no immediate plans for that, either. At least not until Nancy was out of the picture. Logan served her divorce papers, but she continued to make his life miserable. He wanted to settle his legal affairs with her before bringing Lisa into the picture. But that didn't stop Julian's harassment about meeting her.

Standing at the edge of the living room, I felt the onslaught of hugs and kisses from Julian's grandparents, cousins, aunts and uncles. I felt like a puppy in a new home, being passed around and squeezed by everyone. I loved his family. They were such a loud, fun-loving group of people and all seemed to like me, too.

As the newest grandparents, Carl and Helen Hayward lent Julian an ear, listening to him ramble on and on, describing every second of his existence. They certainly didn't mind.

Unlike Carl, Helen was a short, slender woman in her late sixties with a pixie white-blond haircut. She shared those same striking blue eyes with Julian and his mom. An eye color so rare, it was almost haunting.

Julian's other grandparents, Grant and Cora Cahill, shared a comicality that kept us all in stitches, bantering back and forth between them. They were a hoot. I could see where Julian got his sense of humor.

Grandpa Cahill wrapped his arms around my shoulders and squeezed me into him. I let out a soft groan, though loud enough to hear.

"Heavens, Grant, don't smother the poor, sweet girl," Cora muttered.

"It's okay. I don't mind." I exhaled quietly when his arms released me. "Merry Christmas, Grandpa Cahill."

"Same to you, Amber. Julian has told us all about you."

I blushed hoping whatever he told them was PG rated.

The outpouring of love I felt from Julian's relatives made me long for my own extended family. Since moving to Colorado, I hadn't seen my aunts and uncles, cousins, or grandparents. I had a much smaller family than Julian's, on top of the fact that they all lived on the east coast. My mom and dad both had one brother. All in all, I had two cousins between my parents. I sighed, wondering when I would see them again.

Following the group down the hall, I stepped into the family room, instantly greeted by Logan's hug.

"Merry Christmas, Mr. Cahill."

"And a merry one it will be." He nodded, no doubt confirming he remembered my secret surprise.

I placed Julian's gift under the beautifully decorated, fourteen-foot Christmas tree. It stood in the far corner of the room next to the stone fireplace. A theme of gold and silver ornaments surrounded the all-white lights of the tree. Logan and Julian spent the past week decorating the house to the nines. A warm iridescent glow filled the room along with the sounds of Christmas music playing on the radio. Very Christmassy. And Julian looked happy. An "on-top-of-the-world" kind of happy.

Logan took Grandpa Hayward aside and began discussing something quietly. I couldn't make out the conversation, so I ignored them and angled my eyes toward the lavish tree.

I squealed when Julian came up from behind, grabbed me around the waist, and swung me in circles. "Do you like the tree?" His boundless energy exhausted me. I couldn't keep up with him, thinking I really must start working out.

"I love it. You did this with your Dad?" A small, disbelieving giggle erupted from me as I shook my head. It astounded me that a couple of men could decorate a tree this beautifully.

"Nah, my dad did the tree. I helped with the other stuff."

"Well, the house looks beautiful."

"Thanks, babe."

Peeking into the kitchen, Helen and Cora were busily preparing the meal. Cherry-glazed pork tenderloin, mashed potatoes, roasted asparagus, rolls with orange butter, and a cream cheese-coconut-pecan pound cake with brown sugar, praline glaze awaited our hungry bellies.

"It smells awesome in here. My stomach is rumbling. Can I help out anywhere?"

"Thank you, Amber, honey, but we've got it covered. Please go visit with Julian," Cora muttered.

As I strolled into the dining room, I glanced at the table decorated with a dark crimson tablecloth accented with gold embossed napkins. Mr. Cahill's finest china surrounded a lovely centerpiece of red berries, pine cones, and three pine scented candles.

THIRTEEN PEOPLE ENCOMPASSED the large table as we sat down for dinner, Julian sitting to my right.

Logan stood and raised his wine glass. "To second chances and new beginnings." He caught Carl's eye and quickly glanced at the clock.

We all raised our glasses in unison, nodding to Logan, and took a sip of the champagne.

To the sound of knives and forks clanging against plates, we dove into the most scrumptious meal I'd ever tasted. The low rumble of cheerful voices surrounded me, feeling as if no one could be happier than me at this moment.

Julian clutched my knee under the table circling his thumb along my inner thigh, driving me crazy.

The dinner conversation ebbed and flowed with a handful of different topics. Julian's grandparents asked about my family and what it was like living in New York. The men talked sports and the upcoming Super Bowl. I received a few scowls from around the table when I told them I was rooting for New England. I laughed. I noticed Logan and Carl speaking softly. I couldn't make out what they were saying but thought I heard Lisa's name. Logan peeked at the clock again. Something was up.

"What do you say we move this to the family room," Logan said. "We have a lot of gifts to get through."

We all rose from the table and found seats around the beautiful Christmas tree. I inhaled the fresh pine scent wafting through the room as I bit into my sugar cookie. Julian tapped on his lap for me to sit. I did. The area glowed with the glimmer of the early evening sun filtering through the windows, along with the twinkle of the tree lights.

One by one, the gifts were opened, wrapping paper flying everywhere. I was giddy with delight at the thought of Julian's reaction to my gift.

Julian shifted me off his lap and rose to retrieve a gift from under the tree. "I'm going next," he said. He moved to his dad and handed the large present to him. "Merry Christmas, Dad." He stood aside, watching, as Logan made short work of the paper to reveal a large box. As he opened it and shifted some tissue paper aside, a rush of air left his lungs.

"Julian, oh my God, how—when ..." he stuttered, unable to find the words to show his gratitude.

Logan reached into the box and pulled out the sentimental vase Nancy had broke the night of the confession. Julian had glued it back together perfectly. No wonder I hadn't seen him in the last few weeks.

It must have been painstakingly tedious fitting all those pieces back together. I was speechless.

Somehow, I was able to lift my gaping jaw with the palm of my hand. After all, I'd seen the sheer number of broken pieces that littered the floor that night.

Mr. Cahill turned and pulled Julian into a tight hug. They rocked back and forth for what seemed like several minutes.

"Thank you, son," Logan said with emotion filled eyes. "Did you do this?"

"Yes, Dad, I remember you telling me what this vase meant to you."

What a perfect gift. When Logan relayed the vase story, mouths dropped on the faces of nearly everyone in the room.

When we all recovered our composure, I said, "My turn." I hopped up off the sofa and grabbed my gift to Julian from under the tree. I flashed a quick, knowing glance at Mr. Cahill, and his answering grin made me smile.

After Julian had returned to the sofa, I handed the gift to him. I knelt on the floor beside him. He fixed his eyes on the wrapping paper. I'd created my own decorative paper of little red Camaros, hearts, and gold stars.

"Love it, Amber."

I smiled. "Thank you. I designed it myself."

Trying to avoid tearing the handmade paper, he slowly removed it to reveal a small flat box. Removing the cover and tossing the tissue paper aside, he stared long and hard at the gift.

"What? Is this …"

"It's a picture of your mom and you, Julian, when you were a baby," I interrupted him.

With Mr. Cahill's help, we were able to find a photograph of Lisa holding Julian when he was one month old. I placed the old picture in a frame I decorated with hearts around the edges. It was the first time he'd ever seen a picture of his mother. I also asked Logan to continue to keep Julian from seeing any pictures of her until after Christmas. It wasn't an easy accomplishment. I knew Julian had been very persistent in his desire to see some. He told me how amazed he was that his dad didn't have any photos of her. It was so hard to maintain the secret, but after watching the look on his face, it was all worth it.

"Amber, how did you get this picture?"

"I got it from your dad," I said, grinning at Logan.

"So you *do* have pictures of her, Dad?"

"Of course, son, I'll show them to you now. I was sworn to secrecy by your girlfriend."

Logan walked around and looked over our shoulders at the photo in the frame. "It looks perfect in this frame." His eyes shined. You could tell there was true love between them.

After giving me a sardonic grin, Julian turned to his dad. "I knew you had to have pictures of her." His eyes then landed back on me.

I shrugged.

After staring at the photo several minutes, he yanked me up into his lap and planted a wet kiss on my lips. There were cheers and applause from around the room. I nearly died of embarrassment.

Only two presents remained under the tree. Julian stood, retrieved one, and handed it to me while I resumed my seat on his lap. I slid my finger under the fold of the paper to reveal a small box. I felt the weight of everyone's eyes glued to me.

From the kitchen, the phone rang. Logan stood and disappeared to answer it. I couldn't hear the conversation, but when he returned, his grin stretched across his face, and he nodded at Carl.

My feminine intuition told me those two were up to something. Julian was too preoccupied watching me open his gift to notice.

I removed the small cover to reveal a delicate, gold chain looped through two diamond-studded hearts. Removing it from the box, I also noticed a gold bracelet with two hearts coiled together in one long string.

"Do you know what the hearts represent, babe?"

"I'm assuming the two hearts that grace our backsides."

"Yup. Your birthmark and my tattoo." His smile touched me deeply.

"Thank you, Julian. I love them. They're beautiful."

Julian placed the necklace around my neck and fussed with the clasp until he was able to fasten it together. I lifted the hearts to my lips and kissed them. He then attached the bracelet to my wrist. I shook my hand, appreciating the sweet, jingling sounds made by the jewelry. It was perfect. I turned and kissed him.

Logan edged around the sofa and picked up the final present from under the tree and handed it to Julian.

"What's this, Dad?"

"Just open it, Julian."

With deft fingers, Julian pulled the wrapping paper away from the small flat box. He removed the cover to reveal some folded Christmas-red tissue paper. I watched as he pushed the paper aside and found a handwritten note. Ever so vigilantly, he lifted the piece of stationery from the box and read it aloud...

"Dear Julian,

Sixteen years ago, I gave birth to the most beautiful baby boy in the world. I held you in my arms, kissed you with my lips, and touched you with my hands. Most of all, I loved you with all my heart and soul, unconditionally. Then, without warning, you were taken away from me. I couldn't hold you. I couldn't kiss you, and I couldn't touch you anymore, but I never, ever stopped loving you.

Now here you are, a handsome young man, all grown up and beautiful, inside and out. Oh, how I've missed you.

Since that dreadful day, I have longed to hold you again and touch you again, and now I get my chance. Julian, please turn around.

Merry Christmas!

I love you,
Mom"

Julian raised his head, and, with a confused look, glimpsed in the direction of his dad.

"Well, turn around, Julian." Logan smiled, gesturing with a twirling finger.

My eyes followed Julian's as he stood and swiveled around. Standing there in all her beauty was his mom. Unbeknownst to us, Lisa

Hayward had tiptoed into the room while Julian was reading her letter. Without a peep from anyone, she stood quietly, behind the sofa where we sat.

I knew it! I knew Logan and Carl were up to something.

I spun back around at the gaping faces in the room. As the sounds of "I'll be home for Christmas" played on the radio, I thought of how apropos that song really was. Lisa was home for Christmas with Julian and Logan. Another perfect gift.

With tears streaming down her face, she cried, "Julian, come give your mom a proper, overdue hug."

In a fraction of a second, Julian darted around the sofa into her arms, practically knocking her over as they embraced. They held each other tight, as though no one else existed within the room, never wanting to let go. Claps and cheers erupted throughout the room. Julian finally had his mother. An uncontrollable sob left his lips. Lisa had her face buried against his shoulder, crying softly. What a sight to behold as tears flowed down my cheeks. I scanned the room until my eyes landed on Logan. A myriad of emotions flitted across his face, melting my heart.

"Mom, Mom, Mom," Julian repeated over and over. "I can't believe you're here."

"From now on, I promise I'll always be here for you, Julian."

"This is the best Christmas present ever!" Julian choked the words out, unable to contain his sniffling. "Thank you, thank you, and thank you."

"Yes, it is," she said. "The best one I've ever received."

Classy, elegant beauty radiated off Lisa when I looked at her. Julian looked exactly like his mom. That was why she looked familiar to me in the hotel. She shared his stunning blue eyes and blond hair. They were unmistakably mother and son. She wore a red V-neck, sheath dress that hugged her tall, svelte figure, though, not quite the height of Julian. Accented with glimmering jewelry, she exuded pure grace.

Standing and moving to Julian and his mom, I extended my hand to her. Lisa reluctantly released Julian and pulled me into a warm embrace.

"Hello, Amber, it's a pleasure to meet you, too. I've heard so much about you. I know how happy you make Julian. Thank you for that." She patted her hand up and down my back.

Lisa was a breath of fresh air. A sharp contrast from the cold, calculating person Nancy was. My mind drifted back to the hotel debacle and how angry I felt toward Mr. Cahill that night. What a difference that reckless moment made, now that we all knew the truth. I couldn't be happier with the way things turned out. Though, I'd have given anything if Julian could've avoided those few weeks of hell he went through, loathing his dad.

I hugged Lisa back. "Same to you."

WE ENTERED THE STARK, cold, Cahill cabin on New Year's Eve. Julian took me to his family's camp on Shadow Mountain Lake to ring in the New Year. I wondered how many times Lisa and Logan had driven here for the same secretive privacy. I dismissed the thought.

The bitter cold filled my lungs as we entered through the door. My body shivered uncontrollably—even through my many layers—until Julian ignited a log in the fireplace. Meanwhile, he rubbed my shoulders to my fingertips before warmth spread to my extremities. We laughed about our situation. "Sorry, babe, there's no furnace, so we'll use the heat from the fireplace and our own bodies. Okay?"

The meaning behind those words was implicit. The instant arousal I felt at the thought of snuggling up next to Julian's bare body made me warm and tingly.

After gathering a comforter off his bed, we nuzzled together on the floor in front of the fire. From under the blanket, we removed our clothes and pressed our naked bodies together. As the burning wood hissed and crackled, we spent the whole evening making love to each other. At the stroke of midnight, we kissed long and hard, like it was the last time we'd ever do this.

It was a perfect New Year's Eve, my best ever. My love for Julian went beyond anything I could describe. This gorgeous, sexy guy was mine...forever.

"I love you, Amber."

"Love you too, Julian. So tell me...how's life with your mom?"

"She's the most perfect mom in the world. Now I know what it feels like to be a complete family…like yours." He rolled over and gave me a chaste kiss on the lips. "I love her so much, babe."

Julian went on and on about all the conversations they'd had in the last week. They were getting to know each other. It was a delight to see and hear. He looked so happy.

Logan and Lisa brought out all the photo albums, and Julian spent hours proudly showing them to me. Instead of feeling a sense of dread at the thought of losing him, our relationship was better than ever.

I rolled to my side, facing him and rested my head on the palm of my hand. "So…what are your dreams for the future?"

He curled his body into the fetal position, facing me and looped his legs around mine. "You really want to know?"

"Of course," I said, making circles in his chest hair with my free hand.

"I'm going to marry you first."

My hand stopped, and my eyes popped out of my face. *He wanted to marry me?* "And…second?" I sputtered.

"Then I'd like to become a doctor, an MD."

"A doctor of what?"

"I'm intrigued by the brain, so probably something to do with neurology. How about you?"

"Um, I'll just be happy being married to you, loving you…," I paused and then continued, "to the stars and back," I finally said and grinned at him. "I'm not really sure what I'd like to do." I couldn't envision my future beyond tonight.

"Love that. I'll love you to the stars and back, too."

The holiday season of 1998 would go down as one of the most memorable I'd ever had in my life. I'd never been happier. I knew Julian felt the same way. He was getting a second chance at life with his mom.

Chapter Twelve

1999. The much anticipated New Year was here and the promise of new adventures for Julian and me.

As I made my way down the hall to my locker, I felt a tap on my shoulder. It was the first day of classes after Christmas break. Trying to get back into the mindset of school and upcoming mid-term exams were stressful, to say the least.

I turned to see Shelby. "Did you hear the news, Amber?" she asked.

"I don't know. What news are you talking about?"

"Mitzi Carlisle," she went on.

I admitted I was curious, but at the same time, didn't care. Why should I give a damn about the evil girl and her bitch friend Bianca?

"What about her?" I asked with an emotional void in my voice. We moved along toward my locker.

"She committed suicide."

I stopped short. "What?" My heart lurched into my mouth. "When?"

"They found her on New Year's Eve. She hung herself."

"Oh my God. How?" I started shaking. "I thought she was locked up in the detention center."

"I heard she was released on bail and home for the holidays. She did it at home." Shelby wrapped her arm around my shoulders, eyeing me with concern. "Are you okay, Amber? You're white as a ghost."

Mitzi's twisted mental state was more disturbed than I'd originally thought. I felt lucky to be alive. I thought back to some of our conversations…or should I say…verbal lynchings. Was there any sign then that would indicate she was suicidal? *He belongs to all of us.* My whole body shook at her words. Was this my fault? If I hadn't come along, would she still be alive? Would she have a chance with Julian? He almost had sex with her, but didn't because we started dating. No, I refused to take the blame for this.

"I'm fine. Thanks for telling me, Shelb."

"Okay, see you later." She disappeared down the hall to her next class.

I opened the door to my locker. I stared blankly at the contents of locker 315. The unwelcome vision of the last time I saw Mitzi loomed heavily around me. She was right here, pummeling her foot into my ribs. I shuddered, grabbed my textbook and scrambled off to study hall.

To take your own life was a desperate, selfish act. There was nothing more final than death. The heartache her family must have been experiencing, filled me with so much pain and sorrow.

As cruel as she acted toward me, my heart broke for her family. After Bianca's arrest, her family moved out of the area, but I hadn't heard much from Mitzi's. I needed to find Julian. He needed to know about Mitzi. I scurried down the hallway and found him walking to his locker.

"What's wrong, babe," he asked, reaching up and tucking a stray hair behind my ear.

Out of breath, I grabbed his arm. "Julian, Mitzi committed suicide."

"Really?" he said with a condescending tone.

"Yes. I'd like to pay my respects to her family."

His eyes widened. "Are you serious?" He stretched out the last word for emphasis.

"Yes. It's the least I can do."

He grasped my shoulders and spun me around to face him square on. "Amber, are you insane? She tried to kill you."

"I know, but I need to do this."

He closed his eyes and shook his head.

Now we had another hoop to jump through—the suicide news of

Mitzi. I wasn't sure how much more we could endure. Just when things were settling into a nice rhythm, another struggle came our way.

"THAT'S HER FAMILY'S HOUSE, Julian," I spoke loudly making Julian jump as we turned down Mitzi's street. We made the fifteen-minute drive to the Carlisle home in Castle Rock.

Against my better judgment and Julian's warning, I needed to share my heartfelt sympathies with her family. He refused, but I managed to convince him to go with me.

Pulling into the driveway of the house, Julian looked uneasy. "Are you sure you want to do this, Amber?"

"Yes."

"You're a better person than I could ever think of being. After the way they treated you, you still care." His admiring look took me by surprise. "That's one of the things I love about you."

The low growl of a huge German Shepard startled us as we made our way up the sidewalk to the Carlisle house. Julian tugged me to his side after ringing the doorbell. The house—no more than an unkempt shack with muddy hand-prints covering the door—looked like it hadn't seen a coat of paint in its entire sorry life.

A heavy-set woman with jet-black, mussed hair opened the door. "Can I help you?" She looked ragged and untidy.

"Hi, Mrs. Carlisle, I'm Amber, and this is Julian. We were classmates of Mitzi's and wanted to express our—"

"Get the fuck off of my property, you bitch!" Her fierce rampage drove me back against Julian. She turned her beady eyes toward him, drew in a deep smoldering breath and continued, "You too, you disgusting piece of garbage. It's because of you two that Mitzi took her life," she spat at us.

My scalp prickled. I froze, shocked to my core.

"Let's go, Amber…Now." Julian pulled me tighter against him.

Sadness filled my eyes as tears streamed down my face. "We—we wanted to say we're sorry for your loss," I stuttered through my sobbing.

"Your sympathy means nothing to us. Nothing!" she screamed.

"Now get out of here before I call the cops!" She slammed the door in our faces.

Julian clutched my hand and pulled me to the car. I couldn't believe she blamed me for her daughter's suicide. What the hell did I do except defend myself against her wrath? My stomach roiled.

"C'mon, let's get the hell out of here. That whole family is fucked up. Don't let her get to you." Julian opened the passenger door and ushered me in.

"Well, it does, Julian. I can't pretend it doesn't bother me. I should've listened to you. Dammit."

We left without a backward glance, driving home in silence, never mentioning her again. We never attended the funeral. In all likelihood, we would have been thrown out of there, too.

IT WAS THE FIRST WEEK OF FEBRUARY or better known as "midterm week" when I headed out of my English class to find Julian. I had another excruciating headache and wanted to go home and lay down.

In the last two weeks, the pressure of studying for my tests had caused a few migraines.

"How was your exam?" Julian eyed me with a discerning gaze, coming toward me down the hall.

Clutching my head, I said, "Fairly easy, but I've got another headache. Could you take me home?"

"You do look run down. It's your third bad headache since exams started, Amber."

I winced in pain. "I'm sure it's the stress of the exams."

"We need to get away and have a relaxing day together. How about I take you hiking this weekend?"

"Sounds fun, but right now I'm tired and need to lie down. Please take me home."

"Okay."

I made a quick stop at my locker and grabbed my science textbook for my test the next day. Before heading out, Julian returned one of his borrowed history books to the library.

"Ready?" he said.

"I've got everything. Let's go."

I pushed open the front entrance doors of the school and made my way down the three steps leading to the bus zone. Before I could catch myself, my left leg numbed, tripping over my own two feet. I ended up doing a face plant on the pavement. My book bag flew out of my hands and tumbled across the blacktop.

In seconds, Julian was by my side. "Christ, Amber, are you alright?"

"I tripped. Crap, my nose is bleeding."

Taking a handkerchief out of his pocket, he wiped my nose with a sweet gentleness.

"What did you trip on?"

"I don't know. I just went down. My left leg felt like it was asleep," I said. "It's sore, but the feeling is back now."

Minutes later, Julian dropped me off at my house. I told him I wanted to be alone. "I'm going to lie down, okay? I'll see you later."

Begrudgingly, he went home.

DARKNESS SURROUNDED ME when I woke in my bed, and I still had head pain. Cripes, what was wrong with me? Why couldn't I shake this monstrous headache? I shuffled my way to the medicine cabinet, swallowed down a couple of painkillers, and went downstairs.

"There she is. We didn't want to wake you, honey. Would you like me to warm you something for supper?" Mom looked at me, concern etched in her face.

"Sure, Mom. I can't seem to get rid of this horrible headache. I just took some pain meds."

"Give them time to work."

"Okay."

She warmed me some beef stew in the microwave. I staggered over to the bar stool and sat down at the island.

"Are you okay, sweetheart? You look sick. How did you get that bruise on your nose?" She placed the warm stew in front of me.

"I fell at school. I feel awful, Mom."

It only took one bite of the stew before I had to hop up and run to the bathroom, depositing every bit into the toilet. Mom followed closely behind.

"You feel warm, Amber." Hunched over behind me, she draped a cold washcloth on my neck. "Seems you have a touch of the stomach flu. Let's get you to bed."

"Thank you, Mommy." We made our way to my bedroom, and she lay down with me, caressing my head until I fell asleep.

THE FOLLOWING MORNING, I looked as though I'd been hit by a Mack truck with swollen eyes and a bruised nose from my fall the day before.

"Honey, you shouldn't be going to school today." Mom placed the back of her hand on my forehead. "You still feel warm."

"Yeah, you look like hell," Robin added.

"I have another exam that I can't miss. I'll tough it out."

Julian looked at me oddly when he rang the doorbell. "You look tired. I called your house last night, and your mom said you were asleep and not feeling well."

"Well, at least you're on board with everyone else." I must have looked like shit. "I got sick last night and still have a massive headache."

"I'm worried about you." His concern was sweet. "If you're up to it, I'll take you hiking tomorrow to Bighorn Mountain. It's a perfect time of year to hike there, and I know about a great trail I think you'll be able to handle. The fresh air will clear your head. It's a short drive outside Denver."

"Sounds like what I need." I tried to smile, but couldn't and rubbed my temples instead.

"Great, let's get our last exam over with and get you back home to rest."

I FELT PUNCH-DRUNK with delight thinking about my hike in the mountains with Julian today. I slept well, and for the time being, I even felt better, though the throb in my head continued intermittently.

I didn't want to ruin the plans Julian had for us, so I decided to grin and bear it. I took a couple of painkillers and hoped for the best. Maybe fresh air was what I needed.

"Hi, Mrs. Scott, I'm here to pick up Amber." My mom met Julian at the door.

Looking over her shoulder, I squealed, "Hey, great-looking."

His eyes widened. "You look better."

"I feel a little better, too."

Motioning with her arm, my mom waved him in. "Lyle and I had the pleasure of meeting your mom last week. What a darling person she is. You must be thrilled."

"Thank you, Mrs. Scott. I am. You never know when life is going to throw you a curve ball."

"Isn't that the truth," she said.

Making her way down the stairs, Robin moseyed over to us standing in the foyer. "Hey, what's up?" She gave Julian a fist-bump.

"Not much, Robin. How 'bout you?"

"Well, I'm waiting to hear if I got accepted at the University of Colorado, my first choice college."

Julian's eyes lit up. "That's where I want to go, too. I'd like to go into some form of neurology. Possibly become a neurosurgeon. What are you majoring in?"

"Wow, cool. Right now, I'm thinking about majoring in biology, maybe research in genetics. That area has always fascinated me." From the entry table, Robin snagged a pamphlet and handed it to him. "This is some information about the biology program."

Julian studied it for a moment and handed it back to her. "Awesome. I'm sure you'll get in. They have a great science program."

"I hope so. Where are you two going?" she asked.

"I'm taking Amber hiking to Bighorn Mountain. It's about an hour's drive northwest of here. Would you like to tag along?"

"It does sound tempting and might relieve the pressure of school exams. Do you mind, Amber?" She turned to me with her "pretty-please" face.

I wrapped my arms around Julian's waist. "Of course not, sis. I'd love to spend the afternoon with my two favorite people."

"Alrighty then. Let me grab a few things, and I'll be right with you." She disappeared upstairs and reappeared a few minutes later with a camera strapped around her neck. She'd changed into sweat pants, a hoodie, and pair of sneakers.

Spending any amount of time with Robin before she headed off to college would always be on my priority list. I'd miss her so much when the time came.

Mom smiled. "Okay, please drive carefully, Julian. Will I see you three for supper?"

"Yes, Mom," Robin and I said in unison as we headed out the door giggling.

I clambered into the front seat of Julian's Camaro while he held his door open for Robin to climb in the back. Moments later we were headed northwest toward Denver. The sun provided perfect warmth for a day of hiking. Julian switched the radio on and the sounds of the "Macarena song" came on.

Robin shook her head in disapproval from the back seat. "Ugh, turn the station. I can't stand that song anymore."

Julian switched the radio off, turned to me and asked very sweetly how I was feeling.

"Good," I lied. My head still hurt. I didn't want to wallow in my self-pity, so I changed the subject. "Are you ever going to wipe that happy smile off your face you've been sporting for the last month?"

"I can't help it," he said grinning like the Cheshire Cat from "Alice in Wonderland." Though, his look told me there was something more he wasn't telling me.

"What?" I playfully mocked.

Looking damned pleased with himself, he said, "Nancy is finally out of our lives. My dad got her to agree to a divorce this morning. I think it's costing him dearly, but he seems satisfied. My mom will be living with us permanently." He looked at me as if trying to gauge my reaction.

I bounced up and down in the seat, clapping my hands. "That's great! I'm so happy for you."

"Yeah, that's super, Julian," Robin said.

Julian's respect for his mom went beyond any kind of

unconditional love. It was more of a profound bond and deep connection between them.

BIGHORN MOUNTAIN STOOD TALL in the distance from the beginning of the trailhead. Through the heavily forested slope, I could almost see the summit. We wouldn't be hiking that far. Julian was only going to an open field to view the sheep. The sheer enormity of the snow-capped mountains took my breath away. The picturesque landscape was spectacular.

Julian parked the car along the side of the road. Gazing ahead at the trail, I noticed we'd be bushwhacking our way through tall weeds.

We retrieved our hiking gear from the trunk and started up the dirt path on foot, Julian in the lead. He looked every bit the hiker with his multi-pocketed hiking pants. Each compartment held a map, compass, and binoculars. He wore a long sleeve shirt under a windbreaker, a hat, some gloves, and hiking boots. Strapped to his back was all the necessary hiking gear along with water bottles and energy food. He thought of everything. I smiled. What would I do without him?

Robin and I rolled our eyes as we followed him up the trail. We were strutting-our-stuff in sweat pants, sweatshirts, winter coats, and sneakers. We stood out like a couple of mismatched hiking wannabe's, looking like we'd never hiked a day in our sorry lives.

"I've hiked this trail on a few different occasions and each time I've seen a herd of Bighorn sheep. They're indigenous to this area...hence the name *Bighorn Mountain*." Julian grinned, easing comfortably into the role of tour guide.

Robin and I laughed at him.

"Are you two having a good laugh at my expense?"

"No way, Julian. We wouldn't do that." With a swipe of our hands in the air, Robin and I high-fived.

Julian clued us in about the trail's increased difficulty as we climbed higher. He wasn't kidding. The flat, cleared dirt path at the trail's beginning had now transformed into a steep, rock-laden hike over boulders and tree roots. At times we held on to tree limbs scaling the cliff. I was beginning to wish I had hiking boots.

With Julian in the lead, followed by Robin, then me, we made our way across a narrow, jagged ledge. The path—no more than ten feet wide—dropped off into a deep ravine on each side. Ahead, we entered a vast, open meadow and spotted nine Bighorn Sheep grazing in the tall prickly-stemmed grass. They stood about fifty feet ahead of us spanning the entire open pasture. It was an awe-inspiring sight.

"See, there they are. Cool, isn't it?" Julian looked at me with fascination.

"Yes, very cool," Robin said. "I'm so glad I came here with you two. It's just what I needed."

My head began to feel better. Maybe it was the altitude. "I agree. I'm enjoying it, too."

While Robin and I rested in the open field, taking in the magnificent scenery ahead of us, Julian pulled three water bottles and chocolate energy bars from his backpack and handed them to us. He retrieved a map of the trail from the outer pocket of his pants as one of the sheep turned his gaze toward us. I froze.

"Sometimes you can approach them," Julian said.

"I'm not sure I'd feel comfortable doing that," Robin said, moving slowly toward Julian and me. She looked terrified, but turned and took a bunch of pictures.

I quenched my thirst with a generous sip of water. "I'm with you, Robin. I'll admire them from afar...thank you," I said, tucking myself under Julian's arm. He grinned.

"Look at the baby sheep over there. They're so furry and cute." Robin cooed.

"I love how the horns twist around their ears." I pointed at one standing to my right, "Look at the horns on that one. They wrap around the ears and meet under the chin, in the shape of a heart." I glanced up at Julian. He smiled at me.

"Always a heart reference, babe. Your birthmark and my tattoo."

"Yep. Forever." I tilted my head at him. His breath hitched.

"According to my map, we've hiked about a mile. We should probably head back." Julian released me and tucked the map back into his pocket.

Not looking forward to the hike over the rocks on the way back, I said, "I'm kind of tired anyway. Okay with me." I yawned.

"Thanks for bringing me along guys." Robin finished her energy bar and shoved the empty wrapper in her pocket.

"Anytime, Robin." Julian beamed.

"Before we go, would you take a picture of Amber and me with my camera, Julian?"

"Sure, love to."

With the Rocky Mountains in the background, Robin and I stood arm-in-arm while Julian snapped a photo of us.

"I want a copy of that, too, Robin," I said.

As we turned to head back, my head began to pound again. Damn. Deep in the recesses of my brain, I knew something was wrong.

Julian made easy work of the boulders, side-stepping where needed while I followed directly behind him, trying to navigate the tree roots and rocks with my sore feet and throbbing head. I wasn't sure how much further I could go before needing a break. Instead, I willed myself to forge ahead.

Moments later, as we reached the narrow rock ledge, the wretched pain intensified in my head and my vision blurred. Then without warning, my eyesight completely vanished.

"Julian, stop! I can't see! I can't see!" I screamed.

"Amber!"

Abruptly my left leg went completely numb. I stumbled, fell, and began tumbling down the sharp slope of the rocks.

I heard Robin scream, "Oh my God, Julian, she's heading for the cliff!"

Not only could I not stop but was picking up speed, feeling myself topple over and over.

"Amber!" Julian shrieked.

I plummeted down the rocks screaming, "Help me, help me!" I couldn't see. Everything was black. I didn't know where I was and couldn't stop tumbling. I felt a sudden jolt of pain as my arm slammed hard against a rock. My head and back both hurt. A terrified feeling swept through me. I knew, at this moment I was going to die.

No, please, God. I beg you, not like this, I prayed.

I wasn't sure what happened next but felt a hand grab my left arm at the wrist making me stop with a quick jerk. I was dangling in mid-air. My feet flailed about, trying to latch on to any solid ground beneath them, but nothing was there. My head felt a sudden dizziness.

"Amber," Julian grunted.

"I can't see! Help me!" I screamed.

"I've got you, and I'm not going to let you fall, Amber. Robin, see if you can grab hold of her other hand or a piece of her clothing." Rough edges of panic pricked Julian's voice, fighting for air.

"Amber, what's wrong?" Robin sounded hysterical, terrified.

"Help me, help me! I don't know, Robin."

"Amber, can you grab Robin's hand?"

"I can't see anything, Julian."

"Just raise your right hand and reach out."

Panicked, I grabbed at the air but felt nothing.

"Reach toward my voice, Amber!" Robin shouted. I lifted my hand and thrashed about, trying to grab onto anything.

"Over here."

"Be careful, Robin. We don't need you going over the ledge, too." Julian warned, panting heavily.

"I love you, Julian. I love you too, Robin. Tell Mom and Dad I love them, too," I cried, resigning myself to my fate.

"We all love you too, Amber." Robin started bawling. "Stop talking like that. Nothing is going to happen to you. Julian and I are going to save you. Just snag my hand. Please, Amber."

I made one last attempt to grasp onto Robin when I felt the warmth of her hand in mine. *Oh, thank God.*

"Okay, help me lift her." I could hear Julian out of breath, groaning.

"I'm trying," Robin grunted.

Little by little I felt myself inch upward until I felt the firm, steady ground beneath me again. I was safe, resting on my back.

"Thank you, thank you, thank you, guys, but I still can't see. I'm scared." A sickening doom filled me. What was wrong with me? I cradled my hands around my scalp. "My head hurts."

"I'm scared too, Amber." Robin whimpered.

"I don't feel very good."

"Amber ... Amber ... Amber," Julian's voice sounded distant and hollow.

"I'm really sleepy." I could barely hear my slurred voice.

"Amber!"

The ethereal voices were slowly fading away.

"Robin, we've got to get her out of here and to the hospital now!"

"I know Julian. What should we do?" she cried.

"Can you carry my backpack?"

"Of course, give it to me."

I felt myself move upward into Julian's arms. He was moving fast. Silence.

Chapter Thirteen

I opened my eyes. My head ached, but I'd regained my sight. I was in the hospital. I'd been here before, after the stabbing incident at school. There was a sign on the wall in bright red letters that read: Emergency. I saw white…everywhere—blankets, walls, and curtains— except for the darkness outside my window. How long had I been asleep?

My mom sat on my bed, caressing my head. "Amber, honey, how are you feeling?" she asked.

"I hurt everywhere, Mom." I lifted my head and looked down and examined my arms resting on top of the blankets. Bruises, scrapes, and bandages covered them. I burst into tears. "What's wrong with me, Mom? I'm scared."

"Shh, pumpkin." My dad pushed up from the chair next me. He looked weary, repeatedly rubbing his forehead.

"Hi, Daddy." I sobbed.

"Hey. We were worried about you. You've been asleep for a few hours."

"How did I get here?"

My mom leaned over and kissed my forehead. "Julian and Robin brought you. You're in Denver Medical Center."

"Where are they now?" I sniffed.

"They're in the waiting room," she said. "They filled us in on what happened."

I noticed an IV in my arm and wires and patches attached to my head. My head ached. I willed for my headaches to stop.

"Why did this happen to me, Mom?" I began shaking uncontrollably. "Please make the pain stop."

"Try to relax, honey," she said as her chin trembled. Her eyes were puffy. I could tell she'd been crying.

My dad squeezed my leg with his hand. "The doctor wants to do an MRI of your brain. Are you up for that, pumpkin?"

"What's an MRI?"

"It's a way of taking pictures inside your brain."

"I'm scared, Daddy. Will it hurt?"

"No, it doesn't hurt, and we won't leave you. You're in good hands."

"Okay, then." I let out a shaky breath. "Can I see Julian and Robin first?"

Before I got the words out of my mouth, I caught both of them in my periphery vision. They strolled into the room and circled my bed. Julian's face filled with anguish.

"Hey, Amber," Julian spoke softly in my ear as he bent over and kissed me on the cheek.

"Hi."

"How are you feeling?"

"Awful, scared and sore." I brushed my fingers against the bandage on my arm and winced.

Julian closed his eyes and shook his head.

"What happened? The last thing I remember was you two saving me."

Robin grabbed my hand. I flinched when a stinging pain shot through my arm. "You terrified us. After Julian saved you from the cliff, you had a seizure. Your whole body convulsed, but Julian cradled your head to keep you from hurting yourself. He saved your life."

Julian grimaced. "You helped too, Robin. I couldn't have done it without you there. Thank God you went hiking with us; otherwise, I couldn't have saved her alone."

I glanced up at Julian's face. The skin bunched around his eyes and his jaw quivered subtly. He looked tired. Very tired.

"Thank you," I said, choking back tears.

"I'm glad I was there, too," Robin said. "But you saved Amber from going over the cliff. You saved her life!" Pinning her wide eyes at Mom and Dad, she continued, "He grabbed her arm just before she went over the cliff. It was the most amazing and incredibly brave thing I've ever seen in my life. It was like he was superhuman, almost God-like." Robin rounded the bed to Julian and wrapped him in her arms, not letting go. "Thank you so much."

"Thank you, Julian." Mom's voice cracked with emotion as she glanced at him.

Robin clutched her sweater tight against her. "He sprinted down the mountain with her in his arms, put her in the car and drove here."

Barely able to lift my arm, I grasped Julian's hand and gave it a gentle squeeze. "The doctor wants to do an MRI of my brain."

"Magnetic resonance imaging," he smiled. It was nice to see him finally smile. "It's a scan of the head that uses magnets and radio waves to create images of your brain."

"How did you know that?"

"All the medical journals I read. I want to be a Neurosurgeon some day, Amber."

"And you will, Julian, I know it." I wished he could fix whatever anomaly was happening inside my head right now.

I heard a soft knock on the door. A doctor dressed in green scrubs approached my bed. "Hi, Amber, I'm Dr. Trevor Korrick. How are you feeling?"

Dr. Korrick had bushy gray eyebrows, light stubble on his face and a pleasant husky voice. Right away, I liked him.

"Not very good, Dr. Korrick. I want my headaches to stop."

"The transport team will be here shortly to take you for an MRI. Are you ready?"

"Yes."

Moments later, two patient transporters wheeled a gurney into the room. They eased my broken body onto the stretcher, explaining the entire procedure to me and my parents. As they pushed me out the door, I glanced back and saw the pain of four long faces.

"Don't worry. I'll be right back, guys," I reassured them.

A tear tumbled down my mom's face. "We'll be right here waiting, honey." Her voice sounded soft and weak.

MONDAY MORNING came with a thin coating of snow covering the ground. I'd spent the last twenty-four hours watching TV, eating, sleeping, and waiting for the results of my MRI. I tried to process everything that was happening to me all at once. I couldn't believe another wrench had been thrown into the mix.

During my overnight hospital stay, I experienced another seizure—a grand-mal scale. I'd been prescribed medication to control them. Once again, my mom took a leave from work to stay with me, as she did during the stabbing incident. My dad took the day off as well.

Lying on the sofa in the living room, I couldn't quell my wavering thoughts. My nerves prickled tenfold waiting for a call from Dr. Korrick's office. I'd be lying if I said I wasn't scared to death. Luckily, I suffered no broken bones from my tumble down the mountain but received fourteen stitches to close the deep gash on my arm.

Moments later the phone rang. I quivered in pain shifting my body to sit up. My heart started pounding. Was it the results of my MRI? I closed my eyes and mumbled a silent prayer to myself, *Please let me be okay, please let me be okay.* I repeated over and over.

Looking back on my life since moving to Colorado, I felt like I'd been on a carnival ride with no end in sight. What more could happen to me?

"I'll get it!" Mom yelled from the kitchen.

I couldn't make out her part of the conversation, so my attention resumed with the movie on TV. She exited the kitchen to the garage, while I listened to the closing musical credits to *Toy Story.*

"Amber, honey." My mom and dad strolled into the room from the kitchen. My mom sat on the sofa next to me, caressing my cheek.

"What is it?"

"Dr. Korrick's office has made an appointment for all of us to come in for a consultation."

"Why, what's wrong, Mom? Does he have the results of the MRI?" I began shaking again, and the ache in my head returned.

"Yes, the MRI shows a large mass in the right front hemisphere of your brain and they want to do a biopsy to determine what it is."

My breath left me in a rush. "No!" I wailed. "Am I going to die?" I started to hyperventilate.

Wrapping her arms around me tightly, she said, "Calm down, honey. Bend over at the waist and take slow, steady breaths."

I pulled my legs up against my chest and wrapped my arms around them and rocked myself back and forth. All I thought about was the fact that I had a mass on my brain. I was numb to the pain in the rest of my broken body.

No. No. No. I can't die. I'm too young.

"Dr. Korrick needs to find out what kind of mass it is," my dad said as he settled on the couch to the left of me and draped his arm around my shoulders. "He'd like us to come down to his office this morning. Are you up for that?"

"I'm scared, Daddy. Will it hurt?"

"I don't think so, pumpkin."

AFTER TWO WEEKS OF BITING MY NAILS down to the cuticle and wearing a circular pattern in the carpet of my bedroom, I tried to remain upbeat, but my hopes were dashed when the biopsy results confirmed the worst. A glioblastoma, multiforme, grade IV tumor was growing on my brain. In other words, I had brain Cancer. The big "C."

"Oh my God, no!" I cried, squeezing my mom's hand. A legitimate, honest-to-goodness panic rose in my chest. Up to this point, I'd survived moving across country, harassment at school, a stabbing, and falling down a cliff, but this was different. This was cancer…stage four! I screamed in my head.

I'd sobbed nonstop trying to absorb the terrifying news but decided to do whatever it took to survive. I knew it was bad when I'd heard my mom and dad crying secretively in their bedroom. Grade IV was the worst kind of tumor. As horrible as it was for my parents, Robin took the news the worst. She was inconsolable.

"No. No. It can't be true," she screamed, pounding her fists into her thighs. I worried about my big sister. While I was home sick, she'd been so attentive to me. We sat and talked while I lay in my bed. She brought me things to read and even gave me a pedicure. I told her I would fight hard to beat this.

Now I found myself sitting on the sofa waiting for Julian's visit. For the last two weeks he'd stopped in every day after school and spent the whole afternoon and evening with me. Either he played his guitar and sang, read to me, did his homework, or just sat quietly. I couldn't imagine what I'd do without him. He was my solace. My balm. My cure. But, he needed to hear the results, and I needed to be the one to tell him. My chemotherapy was scheduled to start soon, so I needed to impart the full scope of my brain tumor on him before then.

My head still donned the bandage from where Dr. Korrick opened my skull to do the invasive biopsy. Because of the tumor's location, it was inoperable. The only other options were radiation and chemotherapy. We opted for those. I admitted, I was frozen with fear but decided to be strong and brave for everyone. I could fight this. Couldn't I? How did I do that when faced with an uncertain future? My prognosis was not good, but I believed in miracles. Would I beat this or would it beat me?

I'd showered and dressed in comfortable sweats when the doorbell rang. It was the first time I'd worn something other than my pajamas in more than a week.

"Hi, babe," Julian said as he lowered his head to kiss me. I'd never grow weary of his tender lips on mine or the intoxicating scent of him.

"C'mon in." I took his hand and dragged him to the sofa. I sat on his lap. He snaked his arms around me, holding me tight against his chest. I turned to face him and took a deep, shaky breath. "The biopsy results came back."

His expression turned somber. "By the look on your face, I can tell it's not good, Amber."

"You know me so well...too well." I felt a deep sorrow for what I was about to tell him, gnawing at me to my soul.

"Well, what is it?" he asked with quivering lips.

"It's a grade four tumor, Julian." My throat tightened trying to push the words from my mouth.

He looked heartbroken. "What type of tumor?"

When I filled him in on the extent of my cancer and diagnosis, his eyes glossed over as tears threatened to fall.

"I'll be okay—really. I'll be strong for you. I'm going to fight this with every fiber of my being. Please don't cry."

I leaned my head against his shoulder and cuddled into him as he held me tight. We cried for a long time, never letting go of each other. I closed my eyes as he kissed my neck with soft sensual kisses, making me feel as though this was all a sick dream.

"You are the bravest person I know, Amber. I can't imagine my life without you in it," he whispered.

"You're making me weep."

He tucked a stray hair behind my ear. "I'll be there for you every day, anytime, anywhere you need me."

"I'd love that, thank you. Love you so much."

"Love you, too."

JULIAN TAGGED ALONG with my mom for my first chemotherapy treatment. With hands knotted together, we toddled along the lengthy corridor of the Denver Medical Center and entered the elevator. My hand trembled when I pushed the button for the ninth floor—the neurology floor. Julian was uncharacteristically quiet. What was he thinking? My life as I knew it was about to change. Dr. Korrick informed me the treatments would completely drain my body of all strength and energy. Was I ready for that?

After a routine blood test cleared me for my first treatment, Mom, Julian, and I were escorted to a private room. A calmness encompassed me when my attention shifted to an overstuffed chocolate brown reclining chair. I shuffled onto the soft cushion and made myself comfortable. My mom pulled another chair up alongside me and held my right hand. I think she was more nervous than me. Julian stood on the opposite side, took my other hand and linked our fingers together.

A friendly looking nurse—she appeared to be in her late thirties—with a pageboy style haircut introduced herself, "Hi, honey. I'm Nurse Maribelle Hayes," she said with a southern twang to her voice, making me smile. She placed a pillow on my lap and asked me to position my left arm on it. I did, reluctantly letting go of Julian's hand. He stepped back giving the nurse room to tend to me. She wheeled a machine hanging on an IV pole over to my chair. Next to the machine was a bag with clear liquid in it. She placed a tourniquet above my elbow and tapped the inside bend of my arm.

"Just lookin' for a good vein. First time, darlin'?"

I swallowed hard and nodded to her.

"You'll do just fine, honey."

With my mom and Julian looking on, I squeezed my eyes shut as Nurse Hayes' skilled hands inserted the tip of the needle into my arm. All at once, the medicine was flowing through my body, making me well again. I opened my eyes in time to see the tear-stained cheeks of my mom's face.

"I'll be right back," Nurse Hayes said. She turned and left. Julian resumed his place at my side and clutched his hand with mine again.

"Please, don't cry. I'll beat this, Mommy."

"I'm sorry, honey," she sniffled.

"You are very brave, Amber," Julian murmured. "To the stars and back."

I blew kisses at him as he held my hand, never letting go until the bag was empty. "To the stars and back."

DAY THREE HAD COME AND GONE. The first two after my chemotherapy treatment made me so dreadfully sick I was unable to get out of bed. I cringed at the thought of eight more weeks.

Julian sat quietly with me, caressing my back and muttering sweet memories of ours in my ear. I only heard half of what he was saying, though. I was in and out of sleep but heard him softly weeping on occasion.

I had to fight. I had to fight … for Julian's sake. I repeated those words over and over in my head. I didn't want to leave him. Ever.

ROBIN AND MY MOM accompanied me at my next two chemotherapy treatments. I dreaded this. I'd have four semi-good days before I was back for another treatment. Robin was grossed out by the needle while my mom brushed the back of her fingers along my cheek. Her touch felt comforting. They sat on opposite sides of my comfy brown recliner waiting for the medicine bag to empty when Robin's head darted up, startling me.

"Guess what?" she declared, her voice singsongy.

"What?" My mom and I said in unison.

"I wanted to wait until we got here to put an upbeat tone on this. Ready?"

"Yes. Yes. Yes. What is it?" I implored her.

"Well, my acceptance letter came in the mail today from the University of Colorado," she said, bouncing up and down in her chair like a ping pong ball.

"Congrats, sis. I knew you'd get in."

Mom reached across the chair to her for a hug. "Yes, congratulations, honey. That's excellent news."

Robin looked happy. It made me wonder if I'd ever experience the same joy. I swallowed back tears and smiled.

CANCER WAS MY LIFE NOW—weekly chemotherapy and now the start of radiation treatments—keeping me bedridden with wretched vomiting. When I could muster enough strength to look in the mirror, staring back at me was an unsightly excuse for a sixteen-year-old girl. Why me? My hair had completely fallen out, my face was puffy, and my skin blotchy. The skin on my arms stretched so tight; I swore you could see right through to the bones. This horrible disease was taking its toll on me. I had to continue to fight.

I looked forward to Julian's visits. He always kept me informed, explaining medical terms I didn't understand. His presence meant the world to me.

When he wasn't comforting me, my mom, dad, Robin or Shelby would sit alongside my bed and caress my aching head. Each time Shelby visited she'd bring me a different silk bandana to wear on my hairless head.

"Here's a sunshine yellow one for you, girl," Shelby said, plopping herself down on my bed.

"Thanks, I love it. Could you help me put it on?"

"Sure, love to."

It took her all of thirty seconds to wrap the silk bandana around my head and knot it.

"Oh Amber, you look so beautiful. I miss you so much at school."

"Miss you too. I'll beat this. I promise."

She dropped her head, as if to hide the tears forming in her eyes. She was my best friend. I loved her. I was so grateful to have such loving family and friends surrounding me.

"I gotta get going. I'll see you tomorrow."

"Okay, Shelb. Thanks for coming over."

Being home, lying in bed, I fixated on this dreadful tumor in my head. When did I start feeling symptoms? Could it have been caught earlier? If so, would I have a better outcome?

Then I thought back to the school stabbing. I remember the pain in my head after being shoved against the lockers with such force. I had headaches for weeks following that incident. The doctor diagnosed it as a mild concussion, prescribing pain medicine, and essentially sent me on my way, never taking an x-ray. Was this atrocity in my head then? Maybe I wouldn't be in this predicament if they'd just taken a damned x-ray. I frowned.

APRIL BROUGHT WARMER WEATHER. Six weeks into my chemo treatments and a scheduled CT-scan confirmed no change with the tumor. Plus, the ongoing seizures started causing problems with my cognitive thinking. My speech became slurred and sometimes unintelligible. Hope was fading for me. I couldn't bear to see that pain cross Julian's face again. It was bad enough enduring the tears of my family.

I never went back to school. The weakness in my right side and the non-stop seizures—that continued to plague the doctors—kept me homebound. Julian filled me in on what I'd been missing in school, but I was too sick to care.

Today was a pretty good day though, as my mom laid in bed with me. I didn't remember much about my seizures, but she expressed her concern that I should be admitted to the hospital.

"Please let me stay home, Mommy. Please." The thought of dying in the hospital gripped me with fear.

"This is a decision Dr. Korrick should make, honey."

Sobbing uncontrollably, I pleaded, "I don't want to go to the hospital."

"Stay calm, sweetheart, okay?"

"Don't leave me alone, please."

I heard my mom silently crying. "We won't, we won't," she repeated until I fell asleep.

THE MAPLE TREE LEAVES started budding. I knew it was late April, as temperatures climbed into the seventies. Plus, it was the end of my chemotherapy treatments. I longed to be outside and enjoy the warmer weather. It was four days after my final treatment. I'd lost nearly twenty pounds, but my appetite finally returned. I was hungry for the first time in two months.

Julian joined my family for dinner. It was like nothing was amiss. Conversation ebbed and flowed around the table. No one mentioned my cancer as if it didn't exist. I wished that was the case.

"Everyone is asking about you at school," Julian said, placing his hand on my thigh.

Robin peeked up from her bowl of chicken stew. "Yeah, I've had quite a few friends ask how you're doing as well, Amber," she mumbled, looking sad. I worried about her. She was slowly withdrawing from everything and everyone, her peppy spirits taking a nosedive. I knew it was because of my sickness.

"I hope I can go back soon."

"Not until we can get your seizures under control, honey," Mom said.

"What would you like to do for your birthday next week, pumpkin?" Daddy asked.

"I'd like to spend it here with all of you, okay?"

"Sure. Whatever you'd like," Mom said.

I'd never seen so many somber faces in my life when muttering those words. The reality of the matter was the fact that this might be my last birthday and I wanted to spend it with my family.

A WEEK LATER, my second scheduled CT-scan confirmed the tumor was still growing rather than shrinking. The light at the end of my tunnel was vanishing. Dr. Korrick decided to change my course of treatment when my body recovered enough to handle another round of chemotherapy. For now, I felt pretty good, but unsettled and frightened at the thought of going through more treatments. I must not give up. I needed to remain resilient. My mantra never ended, but that never stopped me from crying…all the time.

I WOKE ON MY BIRTHDAY with a headache. I had them all the time now with some days worse than others. Julian perched himself on my bed, soothing my forehead with his gentle touch.

"Hey, it's the fifth of May. Happy Birthday, Amber. I have a gift for you." His breath grazed my ear.

I opened my eyes. "Really, what is it?"

"Do you feel strong enough to sit up?"

"Sure, can you help me?"

Wrapping his arms around me, he helped me into a sitting position, then handed me a small box. "Here, happy seventeenth birthday."

I struggled to unwrap the beautiful, birthday paper with my weak fingers to reveal a small ring-sized box.

He smiled. "Open it."

Puzzled, I slowly raised the lid, revealing a beautiful heart-shaped diamond ring. "What's this?" I sniffled.

"I want to commit my love to you, Amber—a secret promise between you and me. It will only mean something to us."

I stared at the gift, then back to his face. "Look at me. I'm a complete mess."

"You're beautiful to me, Amber. You're the most beautiful girl in the entire world, and I want us to be together, forever. We'll make it official when we're older."

I launched myself at him, wrapping my weak arms around his neck. "I love you. Thank you for the best birthday gift ever. To the stars and back. Forever and ever," I cried. The thought of spending the rest of my life with him made me the happiest girl in the world.

"I love you, too." He took the ring from the box and slipped it onto the ring finger of my left hand. It fit loosely, so he moved it to my middle finger. "To us, forever."

"Back atcha." I smiled.

"I have another surprise for you. Are you up for it?"

"Nothing could possibly top this one, but I'll need help getting up."

At my request, Julian carefully slipped one of the silk bandanas gifted to me by Shelby over my head—a lovely blue one mixed with shades of turquoise. He cradled me in his arms. I wrapped mine around his neck and sank my head into the curve of his shoulders, breathing him in. I'd never forget his heady scent.

He carried me down the stairs to a roomful of my extended family. Wide-eyed, I saw my aunts and uncles, cousins, and both sets of grandparents. They all flew here from New York to celebrate my seventeenth birthday with me.

"Surprise!" The room went from pin-drop silent to an outcry of voices as Julian set me down on the sofa.

I was speechless when my eyes locked onto my mom across the room. Both hands were clutching her heart. "Thank you," I mouthed the words to her.

Standing to my left were Lisa and Logan, smiling affectionately at me. Standing arm in arm, it was nice seeing them both happy. After the sixteen years of the hell Nancy put them through, they both deserved to be together, raising their son. And he was going to need them more than ever if, God forbid, I died.

In short seconds, my parents folded me in their arms. "This is the best surprise birthday present ever, Mom and Dad. Thank you."

"We thought it was time for all your relatives to pay us a visit," my mom said.

I knew deep in my heart this would be the last time I'd see any of them. A lump formed in my throat at the thought.

I glanced up, and standing before me were my mom's parents. "Grandma and Grandpa Cashmen, thank you for coming to celebrate my birthday with me. I appreciate it more than you know."

"Goodness, sweetheart," Grandma choked back her words, "of course we wouldn't miss your birthday."

"Everyone wanted to see you, Amber. You're a special girl who's been dealt an unfortunate hand in life." Grandpa Cashmen approached and gave me a tight hug.

"I'm so glad you're all here. Thank you for coming."

Robin padded across the room and sat down on the sofa next to me, draping her arm over my shoulder. She looked happier than she'd been in recent weeks. "I have something for you, sis." She smiled and handed me a small flat box. "You said you wanted a copy, so here you are."

I scrunched my face at her. To what was she referring? After removing the elegant paper, I tugged open the cover, shuffled the tissue paper aside, and my eyes darted to hers. Inside was a framed photo of her and me standing in the meadow of Bighorn Mountain. Our arms drooped loosely over our shoulders with beaming smiles on our faces. My head dropped.

"What's wrong?" she asked noticing the sadness in my expression.

"This was just before I fell and Julian saved me."

She tugged me into her arms. "Don't think about that."

"Thank you," I said, embracing the photo close to my heart then handed it to Julian. "Look, you took a great picture of us."

He stared at it for a long time. "It's a great one of you two." Handing it back to me, he asked if I wanted anything to eat. I shook my head. My appetite had vanished once again.

Julian stood and disappeared across the room toward the spread of food on the table. In the meantime, each of my relatives took turns tugging me into their arms, softly expressing their get well wishes to me.

Lisa took the seat beside me. "Julian has been inconsolable lately, Amber," she said. "He's having a hard time with all of this. I just thought you should know. We're all praying for you every day and night that you can beat this awful disease."

"Thank you for telling me. I'll do my best to make him understand everything will be all right."

"You are such a strong, courageous girl, sweetheart," Lisa said as she took my hand with both of hers and pulled it to her heart. "I can't begin to tell you how much you mean to our family. It breaks my heart to see you going through this. It just isn't fair." Her lips quivered as she stood and resumed her place next to Logan.

I nodded. I didn't know what else to say to her without completely losing it. Julian re-entered the room and quickly reclaimed the seat to my right, vacated by his mom. She winked at me.

"What did you just tell her, Mom?" I suspect he noticed her wink.

"I just told her how much we were praying for her to get well soon."

Julian's somber face turned to me. "I pray for that more than anyone."

As the party died down, my body felt tired from exhaustion. I wished everyone a goodbye as they all headed out to their hotels. After the last of my relatives had left, Julian carried me back upstairs to my bedroom and laid me gently on my bed.

Kissing my lips, he said, "I'll see you tomorrow, bright and early, okay?"

"Okay."

Before he could get out the door of my bedroom, I called him back. He turned and made his way back to my bed.

"I'll be all right," I said. With a knot in my throat, my lips trembled in an attempt to reassure him. "You must know that I will always be with you."

Okay was the only word he muttered.

We each kissed my ring. "To us, forever," I cried.

I lay on my side, curled up with my pillow and sobbed as he shuffled out the door of my room. My heart clenched watching him bury his face in his hands, no doubt unable to hold back his tears. I wiped my nose with the back of my hand, kissed my ring, and closed my eyes.

Chapter Fourteen

The maple tree leaves fluttered in the breeze, growing toward their summer ripeness. May was in full swing, but not with any good news in regards to my cancer. I grew weaker every day, spending most of my days in bed, unable to withstand another round of chemotherapy.

I hadn't gone back to school and didn't see myself ever returning. I tried to remain optimistic when others were around, but spent my alone time thinking about what my future held. I didn't need to possess a medical degree to know I wasn't going to beat this. I should be angry, but I knew better than to spend my remaining days in this life miserable. I was already going to be sick; I sure as hell wasn't going to be bitter as well. Making the most of each day I had left was of utmost importance.

I loved when the weekends came. They were times I knew I would see Julian for most of the day. However, while lying in bed, my hopes were dashed this Saturday morning when the phone rang.

I delicately pushed myself up to see Julian's name on the caller ID. I dragged my legs over the side of the bed and picked up the handset. "Hey, sexy," I slurred.

"Hey, beautiful. How are you feeling today?"

"Same as yesterday, not much better. Can't wait to see you."

"I can't come over until later. Will that be okay?"

I tried unsuccessfully to hide my disappointment at the thought of not seeing him. Julian kept me fighting. If I didn't have that, then I would lose the will to go on. I'm sure he picked up on it, too. "Yes, that's okay."

"You don't sound convincing, Amber."

"Yes, Julian, I'll be fine." I snapped at him.

Silence filled the air on the other end of the phone. I sensed his anguish. "I'm sorry, but I've got something special planned for you, so can you hold tight until then?"

Something special? Now guilt invaded me for my stinging tone. "Yes, I can wait, but what are you planning?"

"You'll see. I'll be over later."

After we hung up, the letdown I felt suddenly lifted.

I was tired, no longer able to resist the struggle with my droopy eyelids, and once again fell into a deep sleep, dreaming of surprises. In fact, I'd slept most of the morning and afternoon away until I felt warm hands nudging me.

"Hey, sis, are you awake?" I felt the bed shift as Robin whispered in my ear.

"Yeah, I'm awake. What's up?" I said groggily.

"Julian sent me to get you up and dressed."

"What? What are you talking about?"

"C'mon, we need to find you something beautiful to wear." She stood and moved to my closet, returning moments later with one of my favorite dresses. "Here, put this on."

I eyed her with a mock stare. Beautiful was not on the agenda for me. "What's going on?"

"Just get up, Amber. Do you need help?"

"Yes, but tell me why."

"You'll see. It's a surprise."

The sparkle in her eyes told me something was up. A thousand scenarios passed through my head as Robin pulled my hands and helped me stand. I leaned on her for support.

She wrapped her arm around my waist. "Do you remember our conversations about Julian when you started dating him?"

"Of course, how could I forget your ridiculous assumption that he was going to break my heart?"

"Well, I was wrong...very wrong. He's been such an awesome, great guy and he loves you so much."

"Tell me something I don't know, sis. I'm afraid he's going to miss me too much when I—"

"Don't say it, Amber," Robin interrupted me. "I can't bear to think of you not being here. You're going to get better. You have to. I love you so much." She walked me to the bathroom and eased me down on the shower stool. "Bath or shower?"

"Bath, please." I didn't have the strength to stand for a shower. "I'm not going to beat this disease. You need to realize that."

I raised the dead weight of my arms in the air, and she dragged my nightshirt over my head. "How do you know? Miracles do happen."

I leaned on her and stood while she tugged my sweatpants down my spindly legs. "I don't want you to die. You can't die," she choked on her words.

"I don't want to die either, but I'll be okay, and so will you." I resigned myself to the inevitable thought that I wasn't going to live a long life. God had other plans for me, and I had to accept that.

In short minutes, Robin helped me bathe then towel off. Over my head, she slipped the amber-colored dress I wore to the talent competition back in October. It hung loosely off my thin frame now. She applied makeup to my face and wrapped my head in one of my yellow silk bandanas while I sat on the stool of my vanity. I glanced in the mirror and felt beautiful for the first time in a long while when the doorbell rang, making me jump.

"That's probably Julian," she said, standing back to appraise me. "You look beautifully dainty, Ambie. Let me help you." Robin tucked her arm around my waist and boosted me to my feet. On wobbly legs, we shuffled down the hall to the stairs. At the bottom stood my parents, along with Logan and Lisa, all looking up with adoring faces. Robin helped me down, one step at a time.

As I reached the lowest step, from around the corner, Julian appeared, dressed in a black tuxedo with a soft yellow shirt and cummerbund. He looked very handsome.

In his hand, he held a beautiful corsage with three scarlet roses and slipped it onto the wrist of my left arm.

A smile swept across his beautiful face. "You look stunning, Amber. Ready to go?"

"You look like your normal sexy self, Julian Cahill. Hey, where are you taking me?" I slurred.

"You'll see. Come, I'll help you."

Before we headed out the door, the parents prompted us for posed pictures. Julian held me close to his side followed by photo after photo in front of the fireplace. I hadn't smiled that much in a long time. Leaning against him, I breathed in his musky scent. Oh, he smelled good. Could you bottle that for me in heaven?

My eyes went wide when he opened the door and waiting in the driveway was a jet-black limousine. Were we going to a fancy restaurant for dinner? "Oh my God, Julian, I've never been in a limousine before." The smile he wore earlier never left his lips.

He opened the door to the limo and helped me shuffle across the seat. There was enough bench-seating inside to seat six people, but we had the whole car to ourselves. I was giddy with delight at the prospect of what lay ahead for our evening. I had no idea what he'd planned, and frankly didn't care, but whatever it was, had me feeling better than I had in weeks.

He pressed his body against mine, snaking his arms around my waist. His nose brushed against my neck, breathing me in as the car pulled away from my house, moving along Aspen Court.

"Where are we going?"

"It's a surprise. You'll have to wait." He hesitated, staring into my eyes. "If at any point during the evening you want to go home, then promise you'll tell me and we'll leave, okay?"

"I promise," I lied. Julian had gone all out to make sure this evening was perfect for me; the thought of wanting to go home was not a possibility, no matter how I felt.

Ten minutes later, the limo pulled up outside the front entrance of the high school. *What?* The parking lot was full with nary a space available.

"We're here. Let me help you." Julian's smile turned to something unreadable. He looked nervous. What did he have up his sleeve?

In short seconds, Mr. Limo Driver opened our door and Julian wiggled his way out. He turned and looped his arm around my waist, easing me out of the car. I snuggled against him for some much-needed support for my broken body and together we limped to the front doors of the school.

"It's a good thing you work out. Bet you didn't think you'd have to carry me all around."

"I'd carry you across the world if it guaranteed you'd get better."

And in that moment, I knew I'd let him.

My excitement was palpable. It had been close to three months since I'd stepped foot in Castle Rock High School. I missed my friends, but was not well enough to attend.

We walked up the three steps into the school, where the halls were quiet, ill-lighted, and empty. *How odd*, I thought. The parking lot was full; however, not a soul was around.

At a slow pace, Julian escorted me down the hall toward the closed doors of the auditorium. Maybe we were going to a show of some sort. I tried unsuccessfully to interpret the look on his face. Was he expecting something?

At once, the doors opened wide, and as we stepped through, I nearly fell backward when the large group yelled, "Surprise, Amber!" I was thankful Julian was holding me up because I'd have collapsed from the booming vibration coming at me from all my friends.

"Welcome to your junior prom, babe." His lips brushed against my ear.

Tears filled my eyes when I looked around. Hanging on the wall straight ahead was a banner that read: *Welcome back, Amber* and overhead written in twinkling lights were the words: "*Nights in White Satin.*" It was like all the stars aligned together in an endless, inky black sky. My head swung around to Julian. "Thank you. I love you so much." Emotion took over my body. I was a complete wreck.

"You couldn't miss your prom, babe."

"You did all this for me?" My voice sounded incredulous.

"I had help from all these friends." He gestured with a swing of his arm around the room. Everyone gazed at me, genuine love in their faces.

"I thought the prom was in June?"

"Not this year. We moved it up, so you could be here."

I had the best boyfriend in the world. I loved him more than I could ever express in words.

I glanced around the room. Panels of white satin cloths draped from the walls to the center of the ceiling where a shiny mirrored disco ball spun above us. It was beautifully breathtaking.

Tables covered in sable black linens were set with white plates edged in gold.

Hundreds of translucent, helium balloons with trailing iridescent, gold ribbons, were attached to a weighted centerpiece on each table.

A DJ, stationed in the far corner of the room, played soft music while a photographer stood against the adjacent wall, capturing lifetime memories.

Shelby made her way to me first. "Hey girl, how are you? Love the bandana. It goes great with your dress."

"I love all of them. I had a hard time trying to decide which one to wear. Robin chose this one." I gave her a quick hug. "Thank you for being my best friend through all of this." My lip trembled as I released her and resumed my place at Julian's side.

She grabbed my hand and opened her mouth to speak. At a loss for words, she closed her eyes and shook her head. Abruptly, she turned, covered her face and walked away sobbing. My heart broke for her. *Damn this disease!*

I wiped a stray tear from my cheek with the back of my hand, as my classmates inundated me with hugs.

"If all of you wouldn't mind, I'd like to dance with my beautiful girl." Julian scooped me up into his arms and took me to the dance floor. The music stopped and Julian set me down gently.

"Crap, Julian, I guess we'll have to wait until the next set."

He pulled me into him, my front to his, and glanced down into my eyes as a stray tear fell down his beautiful face. "This next song is for you."

What?

Bathed in the glow of a single spotlight attached to the ceiling, we stood alone on the shiny hardwood floor.

I heard a familiar tune. The soft strains of "Nights in White Satin" filled the room, except it wasn't the music of The Moody Blues. It was Julian and me singing from the night of the talent competition. Our performance was being played back through the PA system of the auditorium. Julian tugged me close to him, holding my weak and wobbly body against his. He started dancing slowly, making me mirror his movements. Alone in our own world, we swayed back and forth to our rendition of the song, the music of our guitars and soft harmony of our voices.

I shoved my lips against his ear. "We sounded really good, didn't we?"

"Yes, we did, babe."

"Thank you for this beautiful evening, Julian."

"I couldn't let you miss your prom."

I cried thinking about how much I loved him, praying he'd be okay without me. I snaked my arms around his waist and squeezed him tighter against me as the final notes emerged from our guitars. He placed his hands on each side of my face, lifted my chin and gave me the sweetest of kisses. My body must have looked like a rag doll after leaving the dance floor.

After that emotional outburst, we headed to the head table, cheers and applause following us. This boyfriend of mine loved me. It was daunting to think of all he did to make sure this evening was perfect for me.

I ended up picking at my food. I wasn't hungry, but Julian ate enough for the both of us. "Were you starving?" I giggled at him.

"Yep," he said glancing at my plate. "Is that all you're going to eat. You need food to keep your strength up."

I frowned. I wished that was true.

"I'm sorry, babe. I was just teasing you."

"It's okay," I said, because it was.

Moments later, we posed for our picture against the backdrop of a moonlit ebony sky filled with flickering stars.

I didn't have the heart to tell Julian I was exhausted from all the activity. Thank goodness, he picked up on it and suggested we say our goodbyes.

I hugged my friends and shed more tears before exiting the school for the last time. A gut-wrenching sadness swept through me to my core. I felt like my life had just begun here.

We left the halls of Castle Rock High and climbed into the waiting limousine parked in front of the school. I retook one last glance back at the place I'd spent such a short amount of time but had tremendous memories.

I rested my weary head on Julian's shoulder and closed my eyes until the limousine pulled away from the curb.

"Thank you, Julian. This was the most romantic and best night of my life."

"You're very welcome. I love you so much, Amber, it hurts."

"I know. I love you, too. To the stars and back."

"Yes, to the stars and back."

Chapter Fifteen

Two Months Later — July 1999

Julian

My bedroom was a place where I could escape the reality of the outside world. On this particular morning, I laid on my bed sobbing, unable to stop thinking about Amber as if it were the end of the world. For all intents and purposes, it was for me. Fuck this goddamn disease ravaging her body. I couldn't believe the love of my life was suffering like this and there was nothing I could do to stop the pain.

Amber was bedridden and slept most of her days now, even missing Robin's high school graduation. It upset her deeply, but she knew she couldn't sit for extended periods of time.

She had trouble swallowing and only ate small amounts. Her health declined rapidly while her tumor continued to grow. It was clear the end was imminent.

Her lethargy made her confused, sometimes unable to recognize me or that I'd even visited. That hurt the most, but I continued my daily visits. Most of the time, she perked up when I was near and responded with a smile when I sang to her. I brought her a teddy bear, which she loved and cuddled with all the time. So, in some way, I knew she remembered me.

I preyed on her good days, one of them having been two weeks before, deciding to surprise her with a visit to our favorite place. It was a beautiful, warm sunny day, perfect for what I had in mind...

"Are you up for a ride in the Camaro?"

"Yes, it'll feel good to get out. Where are you taking me?"

"It's a surprise, but you must promise to tell me if you want to go home, okay?"

"Spending time with you is all I want to do, Julian."

She'd read my mind.

I pulled into the parking lot of Windsong Lake and found a space with a short walk to our favorite spot.

"I know where we are. It's our favorite spot. We've been here many times." Her voice sounded hoarse and weak, but her eyes shined bright with excitement. With her failing memory, I was thrilled she was able to recall our many visits.

After I had grabbed a blanket and food from the trunk, I opened her door and lifted her from the front seat of the car. She wrapped her arm around my shoulder so close I could breathe in her intoxicating scent. She was thin with barely any meat on her bones. Very slowly I helped her walk through the gate, to our spot along the rock laden shore. Then she kissed me, her sweet lips on mine. She smelled heavenly. I knew until I took my final breath, I'd never forget that scent.

She was too weak to hold herself up alone, so I sat her down on the warm sand while I spread the blanket. She managed to crawl onto it. I sat down beside her and wrapped her in my arms. We remained like that for several minutes. I snuggled into her and kissed her soft lips. She welcomed my tongue and thrust hers in deeper.

She pushed herself back, panting. "Julian, this is perfect."

"There's something I'd like to do. I hope you're up for it."

"What do you have planned now?"

From the pocket of my shorts, I produced two rings engraved with our names on the inside. The exterior of both wrapped with rings of color—symbolic of the candy she gave to me on our first date—interspersed with red hearts.

I gave one of them to her. "This ring means we are connected in our hearts forever. Just like the heart on the maple tree."

Her bright blue eyes lit up. She stared long and hard at it. "I love it. It reminds me of Life Savers and hearts." She read my thoughts, beaming with her beautiful smile. "But you already gave me a diamond ring for my birthday."

"That was more of a promise ring. This one connects our hearts forever."

"Like after I die?" she said, choking on her words.

Once again, she read my mind. "Yes," I whispered to her.

"Okay. We will be connected in our hearts forever and ever."

"I will wear this forever, Amber. Never take it off."

Her lips started quivering. "I don't want to die, Julian. I'm trying to be strong for everyone, but I'm scared."

"I'm right here for you, and I won't ever leave your side, okay?"

"You do realize I'm not going to beat this disease, don't you?"

Hesitating, I lowered my head. I knew the diagnosis was not good but didn't want to convey that to her. I didn't want to face the truth, either. "Stop talking like that, Amber. You need to be strong and stay positive."

We both began weeping soft steady streams of tears.

"How much do you know?" she asked, knowing full well that my interests laid in neurology.

"I've been trying to read everything I can about your type of tumor."

"Well, what have you learned?"

"Not much," I lied.

She eyed me skeptically. "Julian, you must promise me you will realize your dream of becoming the doctor you've always envisioned. You'll be the best. I know it."

I chuckled. "Well, I'm not so sure I'll be the best, but I'll try, just for you."

"Thank you. And you *will* be the best. I know you will. You also have to promise me that you'll be happy, too."

"I promise, Amber." Although without her, this was a promise I wasn't sure I could keep. A lump formed in my throat. I didn't want to break down in front of her. God knows I'd done it enough in my alone time.

"I will always love you, Julian. My life may be cut short, but you've made this past year the best of my life."

"I'll always love you, too, Amber…always." Pain shot through me to my core. *Hold it together, Cahill.*

We slipped the rings on each other's right hand, ring finger and kissed long and hard.

"There is one more thing you could do for me." She smiled her beautiful smile…the one I'd never forget.

"Anything, what would you like?"

"I'd like you to make love to me…here. Right now, please."

"Oh, Amber, I'd love nothing more than to do that with you, but are you strong enough? I don't want to hurt you."

"If my body couldn't withstand it, at least I'd die with a smile on my face." She smirked.

She could still be funny in light of her illness.

"What the hell, let's do it."

It was absurd how much I loved her. And I was sure this would be our last hurrah. Our end piece. Our parting song. Our farewell performance. The culmination of our entire relationship would end as it began…Loving her.

I glanced at my surroundings, and except for a couple in the distance at the far end of the lake, we were all alone.

"Are you sure, babe?"

"Yes, I've never been surer of anything in my life."

"Okay." I lowered her to her back, bent over and kissed her. She kissed me back. Her lips felt soft. As always, I was instantly aroused. She always made me ready for sex, but this time we would make slow, passionate love to each other.

"Please, Julian, make love to me now."

Wordlessly, she sat up and lifted her arms while I grasped the hem of her shirt and raised it over her head, grazing my fingertips up her thin torso. She shivered. I wasn't sure if she was cold or aroused.

"You okay?" I asked.

"Yes. Totally okay." Her breath hitched.

Her body was a mere shell of what it used to be. But I knew beneath that sick exterior was my beautiful Amber.

She looked me in the eyes. I read her thoughts to undress me and nodded. She hooked her hands at the bottom of my shirt and tugged it over my head. She popped the button of my shorts and lowered the zipper, intentionally skirting her fingers over my erection. I groaned. Christ, she knew how to turn me on.

I laid on my back, lifted my torso and she removed my shorts and boxers in succession, tossing them aside.

Lying on her back, I shifted between her legs and eased myself into her. She groaned. This felt heavenly. I knew I didn't have long before she'd weaken, so I started moving slowly, not stopping until we both reached our climaxes together.

I collapsed onto the ground beside her, trying to catch my breath. "Feels like I have sand in my butt crack." I grimaced.

She laughed the sweetest sound I'd ever heard. I'd never forget that sound.

"Thank you, Julian. I love you to the stars and back."

I tapped on her nose. "To the stars and back, babe."

"Every time you look to the heavens and see a million stars, I want you to think of me."

"I'll be thinking of you a lot more than that, Amber. But, I promise, whenever I gaze at the stars, you'll be in my heart. I'll never forget you." In a roundabout way, I knew we were saying our goodbyes to each other.

"Back atcha, Julian. I'll never forget you, either."

We cried long and hard, a cleansing, purifying cry until all that was left were dry heaves.

JULY MOVED INTO AUGUST. The Scotts arranged round-the-clock hospice care for Amber in their home to keep her comfortable. The extra help enabled the family to spend more quality time with her.

I was reading an article in one of my medical magazines when Mr. Scott called my house to inform me that Amber was nearing the end of her struggle.

"She's asking for you, Julian. Come over as soon as possible," he said through a hoarse voice.

"Of course, I'll be right there."

A soft breeze carried the musky scent of pine in the air as I hurriedly made my way to the Scott home on this sunny Saturday morning. My parents followed close behind. The deep blue sky overhead cast a peaceful shadow below. It may have been warm outside, but a stinging chill swept through my body. A lump developed in my throat when I passed by the maple tree and touched the heart. The increased pulse of my heart through my chest kept me on edge. I knew this day would come, but wasn't prepared for the unwelcome pain and agony of the inevitable. I couldn't bear to say goodbye to her. I wanted someone to pinch me and tell me this was all a horrible nightmare.

With shaky legs, I made it through the door and up the stairs to her bedroom where she laid still, wrapped like a cocoon in her quilt. Was I too late?

Through half-opened eyes, Amber opened her mouth to speak. A raspy, gurgling sound came out. "Julian, where are you?"

"I'm here, Amber." I laid my head down on the bed beside her and cuddled her tight to me while caressing her face with my fingers. My throat tightened, again. I couldn't hold back the tears flowing down my face. My parents tugged Lyle, Elizabeth, and Robin into their arms, comforting them with hugs.

"Maple tree," Amber slurred, barely able to speak, but I knew what she meant. "Take...me...to...tree, Julian."

"What is she saying?" her mom asked through glassy eyes.

I let out an uncharacteristically loud sob. "She wants me to take her to our tree. Would that be okay?"

"Yes. Yes. Do what she wants." Lyle sniffed and cleared his throat.

"Okay, Amber," I said and maneuvered my trembling arms under her. I lifted her crippled, lifeless body and cradled her in my arms, holding her close to me. She was light as a feather. Her arms drooped across her body while her head lolled against my chest. I buried my nose in whatever hair she had left and inhaled deeply committing her scent to memory. I'd never forget her.

With everyone following, I carried her down the stairs and out the front door.

"Where are you taking her?" my mom asked.

"You'll see," I said, sobs threatening, again. I looked deeply into her hollow eyes as I carried her down the path and stopped at the maple tree. "We're here, Amber," I whispered softly in her ear.

Everyone circled the tree as she opened her heavy-lidded eyes and with every ounce of energy she had, raised her hand and touched the heart. Then her arm weakened and tumbled to her side. "I'll see you again," she slurred, her voice hoarse. "I...love...you. Yu ... ave...destin-y...eightee...year," were the last words she spoke to me...each a struggle to push from her lips.

"I love you so much it hurts," I cried.

"We all love you, Amber." Robin, her mom, and dad cradled her head and stroked her arms.

As I hugged her close to my chest, her breathing labored, growing more and more shallow, until no more breaths came.

My sweet Amber died on the second day of August, in my arms, at the age of seventeen. I stood there, stunned, and caressed her beautiful face, willing her to come back to me. I felt numb. Life would never be the same again. Her mom, dad, Robin, and my parents surrounded her. We all cried heaping tears of sorrow.

I carried Amber back to the house, up the stairs and laid her down on her bed. She was gone. *Forever.*

"I can't believe my sister is gone." Robin sniffled and cried as she collapsed to the floor. "She was my best friend. No! She can't be gone! Dammit, she can't be gone!"

I gave her one last kiss and struggled to push my listless body up off the bed. I dragged my legs around to Robin and helped Amber's dad lift her into his arms. Seconds later, Mrs. Scott joined us. No one said a word as we all rocked back and forth, trying unsuccessfully to comfort each other.

"Thank you, Julian, for being here for her all the way to the end. I know how much it meant to her." Mrs. Scott sniffed through her anguish. "Would you say something at her funeral?"

"There is no other place I'd rather be, except here for Amber. Of course, I'd be honored," I hiccupped, unable to push down the lump in the back of my throat. I felt the arms of my parents wrap around me moments before I crumpled to the floor.

AUGUST 6, 1999 was a day like no other. With hundreds in attendance for Amber's funeral, I couldn't believe four days had gone by already. Four long days without her, the love of my life—it felt like an eternity. Numb was the only word to describe my feelings.

The sun shone brightly in the aquamarine blue sky—one of her favorite colors. Her entire family, along with a huge crowd of classmates, filled the surrounding site of her grave. The outpouring of love and adoration was overwhelming.

Settled on a chair alongside the grave, I looked up and caught Robin stumble her way over to me. She plopped down on the empty seat beside me.

"I can't go on without her, Julian. The pain is too much," she cried loudly.

"I know. I know," I said. "I'm feeling it, too." I reached over and wrapped my arm around her, pulling her to my side. I leaned my head against hers, feeling the melancholy in her tears. "We will always cherish the memories of her."

"Before you came to the house on the day she died, my mom, dad and I sat on her bed and talked with her. She told us how much she loved us, but it was time for her to go. She knew, Julian. She fucking knew it was her time," she cried, anger emanating from her body. "Then she asked to see you."

"Shh. I know. The pain is insufferable."

"I want her back, so bad." She buried her head in my neck and cried. "I can't handle the pain."

"If you ever need a shoulder to cry on, please don't hesitate to come over to my house. Okay?"

"Thanks, Julian. I will." She raised her head and met my eyes. "I will never forget how happy you made her. She loved you so much."

"She made me happier. I loved her, too. More than you could know."

We sat and held each other until the service began.

A few classmates expressed their deepest sympathies with some endearing words.

Amber's best friend, Shelby, approached the microphone, choked with tears. "Amber was my best friend," she cried. "I remember the day we met—she was so concerned about how she was being treated by others. Little did she know, she was the envy of every girl in the school." Shelby looked at me and smiled. "I will miss her bubbly personality, her wit, and her thoughtfulness, but most of all, I will miss her." She looked to the heavens. "I love you, girl."

She buried her face in her hands, turned and sat amongst the crowd.

After Amber's grandpa Scott read the eulogy, it was my turn to approach the microphone, but instead, I retrieved my guitar from its case, grabbed a stool, and pulled the mic stand to my mouth. I sat down and cleared the knot in my throat.

"I wrote this song for Amber while she lay sick in her bed. She always smiled when I sang it to her. It's called "Memories in Your Mind." I hope you like it as much as she did."

I took a deep breath, closed my eyes, and started to sing.

Don't forget the summer days,
The sunny warmth, the golden haze.
Sunlight shining through the trees,
The soft wind rustling through the leaves.

Don't forget the starry nights,
The endless sky with endless lights.
Sparkling in an eternal sea,
For lovers like you and me.

Precious memories in your mind,
Like aging roses fade with time.
No matter what you say or do,
I won't forget about those of you.

Don't forget our favorite song,
It seemed they played it all day long.
And just for us the notes did rise,
Gazing in each other's eyes.

Remember how much we cared,
Happy at the same time scared.
All summer days turn to fall,
And nothing then is left at all.

Precious memories in your mind,
Like aging roses fade with time.
No matter what you say or do,
I won't forget about those of you.
Amber, baby, I'll always love you.

When I strummed the last note, I slowly opened my eyes and spoke my next words into the microphone, "Angel now, to the stars and back, I'll never forget you."

Tears flowed down the faces of nearly everyone in attendance. Shaking uncontrollably, I got up from the stool and saw Lyle, Elizabeth, and my parents approach me from the left.

"Julian, that was so beautiful," Mrs. Scott said through misty eyes. We hugged for a long time.

"Thank you. I wrote it just for her. God, how I miss her." I whimpered as Elizabeth stroked my arm with a soothing touch.

I broke at that moment. My mom and dad caught me before my legs collapsed to the ground. I hurt so badly.

"Julian, we all feel your pain, honey," my mom said, holding me up by my elbow.

"I don't know how to handle the ache I'm feeling right now." I bawled.

ALONE IN MY BEDROOM, I spotted a photograph I took of Amber only a few months before. She was alive, happy and full of life. How would I go on without her?

I sank to the floor, pounding my fists into the carpet. "Why, God, why?" I screamed. My tears manifested themselves into torrents of rage. I rocked back and forth on my knees, rifling my fingers through my hair.

"Shh, Julian, I understand honey. The pain is unbearable," my mom's soft words washed over me. She tugged me into her arms and pulled my head to rest on her shoulder.

"Why, Mom? Why Amber?" I was a blubbering mess, my body convulsing.

"I don't know, Julian. God works in mysterious ways. I guess this was the plan he had for her. Always remember, your soul shines the brightest in its darkest hour."

"It's not fair!"

"I know. Sometimes life isn't that fair." She paused. "I missed sixteen years of your life. Look, if there is anything your father or I can do, we're here for you."

Yes, if anyone could understand how life can deal you a shitty hand, it was my mom.

I couldn't control my raw emotions as we rocked in each other's arms for several hours. At least it felt like that.

"I love you, Mom. Thank you for being here for me. I can't imagine how much harder this would have been without you."

"It will take time, but you will recover, darling. God never gives us more than we can handle. And who knows, maybe you'll find another special girl out there. Someone just as sweet, kind, and extraordinary as

Amber was."

"I hope so, but I can't believe there could possibly be anyone as perfect as she was."

THE ONLY HIGHLIGHT of that summer was my parents' wedding. They contemplated postponing it until the spring, because of Amber's death, but felt it may help ease my pain. Though it was only a temporary reprieve as the ache I felt returned shortly thereafter.

My dad chose me as his best man, and except for the Scotts, it was a small affair with immediate family in attendance. Lyle, Elizabeth, and Robin—all heart-warming smiles—looked on as my parents united together in marriage. From time to time, the pain showed in their faces. How brave for them to be here.

Mom and Dad had the life they'd always dreamed of...for sixteen years. They looked happy. It was bittersweet for me, though. A life I desperately wanted someday but would never have with the girl I loved. She was gone. I'd never see her again. The thought made me curl up in myself because Amber should be here. After all, it was because of her that my parents found their way back to each other. I was sure she was here in spirit looking down on all of us, though.

I smiled for the best parents in the world regardless of my agony.

In the course of time, the only moments I felt any comfort were the nights when I'd sit outside, gazing at the stars, thinking of my girl. I'd feel a shiver and knew it was her smiling down on me. I smiled back.

THE FIRST DAY of my high school senior year came too soon. My classmates greeted me with warm embraces. Unfortunately, I wasn't as kind in return. I was still angry; an ugly, nasty anger.

"Leave me alone! No, I don't want to go out on a date or want your fucking comfort." I was a total prick, my emotions still pretty raw. Thankfully, they all understood and allowed me space and time to finish my grieving. But, do you ever finish grieving? Would there be a day when I could smile and laugh again? It didn't exist in my mind.

I couldn't focus for the first month, and my grades suffered because of it. That's when Amber's words came back to me... *Julian, you must promise me you will realize your dream of becoming the doctor you've always envisioned.* I knew what I needed to do and that involved getting my act together, buckling down, and start working toward that goal. I did and never looked back. I couldn't fathom ever dating again, and instead, put every bit of myself into my education.

The following January, my acceptance letter arrived from the University of Colorado...my first choice college. Along with a plethora of scholarships, I received the first annual Castle Rock Heroism Award for my immediate medical aid during Amber's school stabbing incident. In reality, I would have walked across burning coals to save her that day.

Later that spring, the release of the class rank list revealed me Castle Rock's valedictorian. Amber would have been the salutatorian. We often teased each other as to who would hold the number one spot. I would give anything for it to be her reading the valedictory speech at our graduation. Instead, there would be an "empty chair" memorial representing her.

"We're so proud of you, Julian," Mom said when I told her of my class honor. "I know how difficult it was for you this past year, but you persevered." She went on, "I can't imagine how different it would be if I weren't a part of your life right now, sharing this incredible accolade with you in person, instead of from afar."

"Thank you, Mom. I can't comprehend that thought, either." I smiled and thanked God every day that Amber spotted my parents in the hotel that night. Our secret rendezvous could have unraveled but instead was trumped by the fact that my parents were sharing the same tryst.

OUTSIDE THE WINDOW, thick clouds shuttled across the sky when I took my place on the stage seated to the left of the podium. I watched the processional of all five hundred sixty-two classmates—a widespread mass of maroon graduation gowns—enter the Castle Rock High School auditorium for graduation 2000. The sound of the school band playing "Pomp and Circumstance" pounded in my head. Tears sprang to my eyes as I glanced down at Amber's graduation gown draped over her empty chair. I'd placed a yellow rose on top of it earlier.

I forced myself through the usual motions of the ceremony—clapping where necessary, smiling when appropriate, and shaking hands with classmates after receiving their awards.

The ceremony droned along slowly when Principal Dodds approached the podium and spoke into the microphone. "This year's valedictorian of Castle Rock High School is attending the University of Colorado in the fall with future plans of medical school and becoming a doctor of neurosurgery." He went on as the crowd gasped, "He had a difficult junior year caring for his dying friend all along with maintaining a 96.4 average. He's the true embodiment of what a hard-working student can attain."

Dodds started reading the long list of my achievements and scholarships, and all I could focus on was the fact that Amber wasn't here. She should've been seated right next to me on this stage. Almost a year had gone by since her death, and yet I still found every day a struggle. I promised her I'd be happy, but it was a fight just to smile. She was probably scolding me from heaven right now. I knew life would get better, but when?

"Please put your hands together and welcome Julian Cahill," Dodds commanded, shaking me out of my wandering thoughts.

I remembered making my way to the podium amidst the deafening applause but not much of anything else. I did notice my parents sitting in the front row to my right. Amazingly, Amber's parents and Robin sat to their left. How brave of them to be here. It was then that I knew what I had to do.

I waited for the clapping to die down before I began. I hadn't prepared a written speech, making the whole experience a monumental effort until my thoughts turned to Amber and I instantly calmed.

I started by welcoming the usual surfeit of people—principal, student body, parents—then proceeded into my parting words...my goodbye, the final farewell. I touched on different key points from my thirteen years at Castle Rock, trying to maintain my composure.

Midway into my prose, my words drifted to Amber. "This should have been Amber's speech, not mine," I said. "She was the strongest person I'd ever known. It would be remiss of me to ignore how brave and courageous she was through her cancer. I am bound and determined that she never be forgotten." I gestured to the *"empty chair,"* then looked to the heavens. "Congratulations, sweet girl, we all miss you."

I finished my ten-minute speech by explaining how I made her a promise that I intended to keep. "So, look me up in about fifteen years if you ever have a neurological disorder." I finished with a humorous flourish and grinned. It felt good to smile. I'm sure she had everything to do with that, too.

I received a standing ovation. Fresh tears streamed down my mom's cheeks as she stood, joined by my dad, Lyle, Elizabeth, and Robin, slapping their hands together.

Moments later, Principal Dodds announced the presentation of the diplomas.

"Julian Hayward Cahill," announced Dodds. I approached him with my hand extended as he awarded me my diploma. "Congratulations, Julian, best of luck to you in your future endeavors."

"Thank you, sir."

For the rest of the graduation, I stood, stoic, only slightly interested in the presentation taking place in front of me, going through the motions of shaking hands with the rest of the student body as they shifted from right to left across the stage.

The moment to award Amber's diploma to her parents finally arrived. Breaking protocol, I approached the microphone and swallowed to push down the lump in my throat. "It's my honor to present Mr. and Mrs. Lyle Scott with the most distinctive diploma of all." I hesitated, choking back tears. "Amber Lynn Scott." I enunciated each syllable of her name. To roaring applause, and a flash of lightning across the sky, (I grinned. Amber was here,) Elizabeth and Lyle stood and approached the stage from the right, slowly making their way across the floor to me. Robin stayed seated. She looked as though she'd lost a lot of weight. I watched her head drop into her hands and start bawling uncontrollably. I could tell she didn't have the strength to come up on stage. My heart broke for her.

Through tears and soft crying, I saw Elizabeth press her hand against her chest. When she removed it, I noticed the heart necklace I'd given to Amber for Christmas, draped beautifully around her neck.

When she reached me, I graciously handed Amber's diploma to her. I didn't have the strength to say anything else.

"Thank you, Julian—she would have been so proud."

"It's my pleasure." The strangled sob of my voice echoed throughout the auditorium.

My eyes met my mom's. From where I stood on the stage, I saw her mouth the words, "I love you."

PART 2

Chapter Sixteen

Seventeen Years Later - 2017

Julian

Destiny? At the conclusion of the tour with the incoming medical students, I dashed back to my office to gather my car keys and head for my parents in Castle Pines. Christ, I couldn't stop thinking about the young blond girl. Who was she and why couldn't I get her out of my head? She was stunning. Those eyes, those goddamn eyes, were beautiful. She was tall, slender, and had a quiet beauty about her—like someone else who would always have a place in my heart. I shook my head, trying unsuccessfully to forget her. So many years had passed since my sweet Amber died.

I shrugged off my white coat and hung it on the rack behind the door of my office. I crossed the room and grabbed my keys from the top drawer of the mahogany desk Mom and Dad had gifted to me after receiving my doctorate. It was a day I'd never forget as they looked on with pride…

"Dr. Julian Cahill, Neurosurgery." I stumbled in my attempt to cross the stage to be hooded. The audience echoed a collective sigh of relief when I regained my balance. I'd finally graduated. I was now an MD, the end result of the most difficult thing I'd ever done in my life. Eight long years of college and medical school and I still had to complete my residency requirements. I admit, there were times I wanted to call it quits but forced my thoughts to Amber and found a renewed strength to finish. You could say fight or flight per se. And fight, I did.

I SHOOK MY HEAD thinking about the thirty-minute drive to Castle Pines at the same time a knock on the door startled me. With keys in hand, I straightened myself and headed to the door.

"Damn, I've got to get down to my parents' house," I snarled to myself. The tour took longer than anticipated. My parents were expecting me within the next fifteen minutes. That wasn't going to happen, and now I had another delay.

I pulled my phone from my shirt pocket and dialed my mom.

She answered on the first ring. "Hi, Julian."

"Mom?"

"Yes."

Opening the door, I jerked backward at the intense, arctic blue eyes staring back at me. Stunned silent, I thought I'd opened the door to some kind of time warp of my past. It was her—the girl from the tour. The girl who could have been Amber's look-alike—Destiny.

"Julian? Are you there?" My mom's voice filled the void inside my head.

"Uh...hold on, Mom." I lowered the phone, covered the talk piece with my hand and greeted the young girl. "Come in. Please, take a seat. I'll be with you in a moment," I told her and resumed the conversation with my mom. "Hey, wanted to let you know I'm going to be a little late," I said, watching the young lady stride across my office and sit on the brown, suede couch. She crossed her legs and rested her hands in her lap. She took a quick glance at me before her eyes dropped to her hands, looking anxious.

"Okay, Julian. How late do you think you'll be?"

"Uh...probably won't be leaving here for another half hour."

Examining the stunning young woman seated on my couch, she began tapping the tips of her fingers together.

"Okay, we'll hold the celebration until then."

"Thanks. See you soon."

I hung up. The attractive, blond girl raised her head and roamed my body from toe to head. Over the years, I'd come to recognize that—all too familiar—gaze. She was sizing me up.

She stood and approached me with an outstretched hand, exhaling quietly, "Excuse me, Dr. Cahill, I don't know if you remember me, but I'm—"

"Destiny. Right?" I broke her off and took her hand. Of course, I remembered her. I hadn't been able to get her out of my head since seeing her only moments ago in the hallway. If possible, she was even more beautiful up close.

"Yes, that's right," she said with a bewildered stare.

I released her hand abruptly when the hair stood up on the back of my neck. "Can I help you with something?" I asked, sidestepping her and settling myself on the corner of my desk. I sensed her eyes following me.

I roamed her body as she stood there staring at me. She had gentle curves, full lips, and gorgeous long blond hair that fell across her breasts. But those hauntingly beautiful blue eyes—the same eyes that completed Amber's face—were stunning. Except, she wasn't Amber. Who was she and why was she here? A haunting tremor stirred in my soul.

She tucked a loose strand of hair behind her ear and cleared her throat. "I'm sorry to bother you. I can see you're quite busy, so I'll come back another time."

As she turned to exit my office, I stood and grabbed her by the arm, unable to let her go. "You came all this way, and now you want to leave?" I snapped. *My time is valuable,* I screamed at her in my head. *Quit being a prick, Cahill.*

Her mouth turned downward. She'd seen right through me.

"Please, stay." I sounded more cordial and motioned for her to sit back down. "I'm done for the day and was just heading to my parents' house—"

"In Castle Pines?" she interrupted me and inhaled sharply as though trying to catch her breath. She narrowed her eyes and shook her head, confused like she didn't know who spoke her own words.

After recognizing the fact that we continued to finish each other's sentences, I asked, "Yes, how did you know?" *Stalker.*

"I'm not sure, but feel like I know you," she said. "Something kept telling me to come here. I asked the nurse where your office was, so here I am."

She had a sweet melodic tone to her voice. I couldn't get over the fact that she was a carbon copy of Amber.

Hesitantly, she made her way back across the room to the leather sofa and immediately sat down.

That was when I caught a hint of her intoxicating scent. Christ, who was she? She moved with a cute swagger. I shook my head again, questioning the motives behind her sudden appearance here.

Following her, I resumed my position on the corner of my desk, folding my arms and crossing my feet at the ankle…my intimidation pose. "I'm sorry, but I don't know you. You must have me confused with someone else."

Her lip trembled. "Please," she begged. "I feel as though someone sent me here, and I have to find out more."

Why the heck, did she feel the need to talk some more? I didn't know her. End of story. She was just one more female ogling me, wanting more. It had been the same damn story my entire life. Though, I was thankful for my good looks. It was a loving reminder of how much I resembled my mother.

I gave her a glowering look. "Before divulging any information about myself, I want to know about you." Okay, I regretted that I sounded harsher than I intended.

Cringing, she took a deep, shaky breath and started in as if the information she'd divulge to me would solve the mystery. "Well, I'm eighteen years old and have lived in Colorado my entire life." She shrugged her shoulders, as though she didn't know what else to say, but continued, "I live with my parents in Boulder and will be a freshman at the university this fall, but you look familiar to me. As soon as I saw you, I knew I had to figure out why."

Maybe I knew her parents. Over the years I'd rubbed elbows with a number of dignitaries. Maybe her parents were some of them. Her clothes looked expensive. I suspected they had money.

"What are your parent's names?"

She looked puzzled. "Um…Marcus and Cynthia. Why?"

The names didn't ring a bell. "No reason. I thought I might know them."

I didn't have any siblings, so she wasn't mistaking me for a brother. I wanted to tell her to leave. This conversation was going nowhere, and I was late for dinner at my parents. I hadn't seen them for several weeks and was anxious for this meaningless discussion to be over.

And she was young. Very young. How old did she say she was? Eighteen? Christ, she was barely legal. I calculated that she was born in 1999, the year Amber died.

Just for the heck of it, I asked the date of her birthday.

"August sixth," she said nonchalantly.

I gasped inwardly.

"What's wrong, Dr. Cahill?" She undoubtedly noticed my frenzied look.

Christ, she was born on the day of Amber's funeral. "Well, that's a memorable day for me," I said. She didn't need to know anymore. Plus, I was starting to feel uncomfortable and edgy with her.

"I'm sorry. Look, I know you're heading out, so maybe we can talk some other time. Would that be all right?" she asked, looking like a lost kitten.

The silence between us was all too brief when I regained what composure I had left. "I'm not sure that would be a good idea." I stood and headed to the door.

Her pathetic sad face was back. What did she want from me?

"Look, I've got to get moving, so if you have nothing more to say…" I stopped, silently urging her to continue. That sullen look had me quailing.

Her face flushed. She stood and smoothed her hands down the front of her dress. "No. Thank you for your time, Dr. Cahill," she said, sounding as if a sob was trapped in her throat. "I just thought I knew you, but I guess not."

I opened the door and watched her stumble as she crossed the room.

"Is everything all right? Do you need to sit down?"

"I'm okay," she snapped and quickly exited my office, heading directly to the elevators.

The light coming from the window at the end of the hall surrounded her lithe figure like an aura, almost as if she were an apparition. I stared at her as she walked away. In a roundabout way, I didn't want her to leave. But what more was there to say?

She looked back once with a smile on her face that nearly took my breath away as she entered one of the elevators. As the doors closed, one disconcerting thought went through my head… *Why does she have such a striking resemblance to Amber?* I couldn't bear to be reminded of all that shit again.

I DECIDED TO DRIVE the Mercedes Coupe down home to Mom and Dad's. It'd been a while since I'd seen them. Except for my on-and-off relationship with Sarah Andrews, my so-called social life was non-existent. This was always pointed out to me. Today would be no different. I always made excuses, but the truth of the matter was that I worked to numb the sobering thoughts of a lasting relationship. I knew I'd never get married, but didn't have the heart to tell my parents. Lying was my ruse. I couldn't imagine myself with anyone but Amber—even after all these years. It was my life, my decision, and I was okay with that.

Leaving the Denver skyline behind me, I headed south on I-25 to Castle Pines, which would take a little over thirty minutes. The burnt-orange sun peeked over the horizon, reminding me of the multicolored skies along the shores of Windsong Lake.

With the heavy Friday traffic, I had more than enough time to think about how the impending conversation with my parents will unfold. I suspect questions surrounding my social life would pop up.

Thoughts of Destiny surfaced unexpectedly in my head. *Why the hell am I thinking about her?* I shook my head and glanced at the distant mountainside to my right. Would Destiny enjoy hiking? *Get the girl out of your head, Cahill!*

I rubbed the back of my neck. Fuck! Why couldn't I get the image of her out of my brain? Since her earlier appearance in my office, my head had been in a tailspin.

Pulling into my parents' driveway thirty-five minutes later, I glanced at the Scott house. It was the same ritual for me every time I came home. I'd let my car idle while I sat, staring at their home, remembering all the good times.

A distant voice calling my name knocked me away from my wavering thoughts. I turned to my childhood home and caught a glimpse of my mom standing at the front door gesturing to hurry up with a swing of her arm. *I'll have to see the Scotts another time,* I mumbled to myself. After all, I was already over an hour late. I finally silenced the engine and headed for the door.

"Hi Mom, how are you?" I kissed her cheek, gave her a hug, and strolled inside.

As I glanced toward the living room, my mind strayed to the day of Amber's and my sex rendezvous on the Persian rug. My parents walked in the door minutes later, nearly catching us in the act. Amber ended up hiding in the closet for over an hour. I laughed to myself.

"I'm good. We're both good. It's great to see you. What's so funny?" she asked.

"Just remembering the past. You look beautiful as always. Did you change the color of the door? It looks different."

"Thank you." She hugged and kissed me back. "Yes, your father freshened up the red paint. He insisted it was the same color, but I begged to differ. And you confirmed it for me. Happy birthday, honey. Long time, no see."

"Thanks," I said in my most sardonic tone.

"Oh, Julian, when are you going to enjoy a birthday again?"

"I don't know. Maybe I should change the date, huh?"

She ignored my sarcastic comment. "How is everything with you? Still working too hard?"

"Always."

A look of concern crossed her face, the kind of look every child is familiar with. "You're going to burn yourself out."

"Maybe." I ignored her parental glare and changed the subject. "Hey, I was thinking about the Scotts. Do I have time to go say a quick hello?"

Taking me by the arm, she dragged me down the hall. "First, I have something to show you."

Rounding the corner into the dining room, I lurched backward. My ears rang with the sound of cheers.

"Surprise!" they all yelled.

My eyes went wide. My dad, Lyle, and Elizabeth stood when I came into view. Laying a hand over her heart, Elizabeth sighed deeply.

My dad approached me. We patted each other on the back and hugged.

"Happy Birthday, Dr. Cahill," he said.

"Thanks, old man. A bit more white since the last time I saw you," I teased, ruffling his hair.

"Hey, just because there's snow on the roof doesn't mean there's no fire in the furnace. Just ask your mom."

I laughed. "I'll have to remember that one."

I turned my focus to Lyle and Elizabeth, standing with outstretched hands. I made my way across the room and engulfed Elizabeth into my arms.

Hi was the only word I could mutter. A lump swelled in my throat.

"Happy birthday, Julian." Elizabeth's voice cracked with emotion.

I extended my hand to Lyle. He grabbed it and pulled me in for a hug, "It's been way too long since we've seen you, son. You look well."

"I'm sorry I don't get down here that often. I promise to change that," I said. "Shall we all sit?" I motioned for everyone to find a seat around the table.

Elizabeth sat to my right and patted my arm. "We understand

you're busy. Incidentally, we read in the newspaper that you're being honored at the American Medical Association awards banquet. Congratulations, Julian," she exclaimed.

I rested my hand on hers. "Thank you. It will be at the Denver convention center next month," I informed her, always happy to talk about my work. I hoped she and Lyle didn't feel the need to attend. Most likely it would drone on into the late evening. *Hmm, I've got to write my speech for that.*

"You know, she would have been so proud of you."

"I hope so. I did it because of her." I told both of them. There wasn't a single day that went by when I didn't think about Amber.

"We want—" Lyle stammered. "No, *she* would want you to move on with your life."

"I'm okay—really," I said, determined to make them believe me. *Christ, here we go.* Did I look that pathetic? Why was everyone so hell-bent on the trajectory I chose for my life? Evidently, an unmarried, thirty-five-year-old male meant certain doom. I laughed internally. That was far from the truth. *Well, sort of.* My education and work were not conducive to a family life. *Get them off your back with this shit.*

"How's Robin?" I asked, changing the subject. During my senior year of high school, I lost touch with her. I'd never forget how distraught she was on the day of Amber's funeral. I knew she suffered from severe depression soon after. She delayed her college education by a year, but eventually attended the University of Colorado and earned her degree.

"She's well." Elizabeth beamed. "We have our first grandson. He's our pride and joy. Camden will turn one next month. She's having a party for him, and I'm sure she'd love for you to be there."

"Great. I'll have to check my schedule." Unconsciously, I gazed at my watch. It was moving on toward seven.

"She's happy, Julian. She's working as a geneticist at Broomfield Hospital. She loves it." Elizabeth was all smiles in her white blond hair.

I remembered Robin's fascination with the field of biology when she mentioned it to me years ago...on a day I would never forget. Amber nearly fell to her death when the three of us went hiking in the mountains. If Robin wasn't there to help, I wasn't sure I would have been able to save her myself. "I'm happy for her," I said. "What's her husband's name again?" I asked, pushing the pain of that day out of my head.

"Liam Spencer," she said proudly.

"Ah, that's right. And they live in Broomfield?"

"Yes, in a nice neighborhood."

"I'm in Denver, not far from her. I'll have to get back in touch."

"She'd love that, Julian." Elizabeth handed me a card with Robin's cell number on it. I tucked it in my wallet as she reached under the table and fetched a bulky bag.

"Lyle and I have a couple of gifts for you."

"You shouldn't have," I said when she handed them to me. "Two?"

She blushed and started fidgeting with her napkin. "You'll see."

"Your dad and I have a couple for you as well, honey," Mom chimed in.

"Thank you, Mom."

I glanced around the table as eight eyes stared at me making quick work of the wrapping paper of the larger box. I opened it to reveal the trophy Amber and I won at the talent competition all those years ago. I trailed my thumb across the inscription on the plaque. *Castle Rock High School Talent Competition, First Place.* A knot formed in my throat. I remembered how beautifully she sang.

"Thank you," I whispered.

"We thought you deserved to have that."

"I remember that day like it was yesterday." My life changed forever that night, although I couldn't divulge to them the real reason it was so unforgettable. The whole hotel fiasco would go down forever in infamy.

Lifting the second, much smaller box, I shook it, affirming no rattle. After slipping my finger under the tape, the paper fell away easily. Gazing at a small white box meant for trinkets and the sort, I opened it and sucked in a quick breath.

"Wow," I said. Under the spring-loaded lid of the box was the heart-shaped diamond ring I'd given to Amber on her seventeenth birthday. We pledged our love to each other that day.

"You gave her that ring, didn't you?" Elizabeth asked.

"Yes, but I thought it was on her finger when you laid her to rest."

"It was, but we removed it." She grabbed my hand and made eye contact with me. "We thought it was a good time for you to have it back."

I looked around the table at all the heads nodding along when she spoke, as if I couldn't understand the motive behind this gift. My mother was already pressuring me to find someone to settle down with; I didn't need it from anyone else.

Elizabeth placed both of her hands over mine and smiled. "Please give it to someone special in your life."

"I'd already given it to someone special."

"Keep it, Julian. It's yours. Do with it as you please, with our blessing," Lyle added.

I sat, moving my eyes from Elizabeth to the ring and back, awed by how courageous she and Lyle had handled Amber's death. Christ, it had been eighteen years and still felt like it was yesterday for me. I shook my head and scowled at myself. Maybe it *was* time to move on with my life. But…with who?

Elizabeth leaned forward, studying the ring. "It has spent the last eighteen years in her jewelry box. I'd forgotten about it. After your mom called to invite us to your party, I thought this would be a perfect time to part with it."

"Thank you." I bent over and kissed her on the cheek. Apparently, her eyes caught sight of the multicolored ring on my right hand.

"Did you also give her one that looked like that?" She raised my hand and examined it closely.

"Yes," I said automatically.

My mom glanced at me, confused. "I never realized you gave her rings, Julian."

"I gave her the diamond on her seventeenth birthday, the other at a later time."

"How come your father and I never knew this?"

"It's a moot point now, don't you think, Mom?"

She narrowed her eyes at me, got up and disappeared into the kitchen. I shook my head and lifted the ring from the box. I twisted it between my fingers, knowing it touched the finger of the girl I loved. Unconsciously, I lifted it to my nose and inhaled, hoping to draw in a whiff of her scent. At the time I'd given it to her, I remembered quietly praying it would give her a renewed strength to get better. How naïve I was.

"You loved her, didn't you?" Elizabeth asked.

I fidgeted in my chair. Were we treading in a forbidden area? Where was she going with this? Even though eighteen years had passed since Amber's death, my relationship with her would always remain deep in the recesses of my brain—personal and left alone.

"We loved each other," I replied casually.

"Despite the troubles she experienced in the year before her death, she was infinitely happy. And it was because of you, Julian."

I puffed out a breath and told her thank you.

I continued to open gifts from my parents when Mom reemerged in the room with a birthday cake. The glowing flame of the number three and five candles sat on top. The four of them broke into "Happy Birthday."

"Make a wish, Julian," Mom pleaded.

Christ, what was I...twelve? Of course, my only wish couldn't come true—Amber was gone forever.

The fumes of the candle wax filled the room, leaving a trail of smoke when I blew both candles out.

"Thank you, Mom and Dad," I said.

Nervously, I grabbed the salt shaker and started twirling it in circles. Mom stood and plucked the used candles from the cake, depositing them in the kitchen sink. She returned with five plates and forks.

"How was work today?" Dad asked.

"Only one surgery this morning. I guided a tour for the incoming freshmen this afternoon. Speaking of which...," I said, catching the focus of eight eyes around the table. "A young girl, who had an uncanny resemblance to Amber, stopped into my office this afternoon and claimed she knew me," I snorted.

"Wow, amazing." Elizabeth perked up. "You say she looked like Amber?"

"Yep. She could've been her identical twin."

Elizabeth gasped.

Mom's eyes went wide as she cut a slice of the chocolate cake decorated with a surgeon's stethoscope. She placed it on a plate and handed it to Elizabeth. "You're kidding."

"Dead serious."

"She just appeared in your office?" Dad asked.

"As I said, she insisted she knew me. She was one of the female students on the tour I led earlier in the afternoon."

Elizabeth leaned in closer to me, her eyes glued to my every word. "Really! What was her name?"

"Destiny...something. I can't remember her last name. And get this..." I paused, "I asked when her birthday was and to my astonishment, she said August sixth. She was born on the day of Amber's funeral."

"Same year? How coincidental," Mom said, plating another slice of cake and sliding it in front of Lyle. "How did she know you?"

"She had no idea and neither did I. Once I got past the shock of her striking resemblance to Amber, I told her I thought she was mistaking me for someone else."

Elizabeth nibbled on a bite of the chocolate cake and set her fork down. She looked as though she was mulling something over in her head. "Well, I'm intrigued, what else did she say?"

"Not much. That's the point. It was a senseless meeting." I said, and cut myself a slice of cake. I grabbed a fork and dove in. "Mmm, delicious, Mom."

"How odd," Lyle said.

"Exactly. She didn't say much of anything else and left." I shook my head, unable to get her out of my thoughts.

"How's Sarah?" Mom asked, changing the subject. I wasn't sure if it was intentional or not.

"Good. I haven't seen her in a few days. I think we're getting together tomorrow."

"Bring her around. We haven't seen you two together in a few weeks."

And there it was. It didn't matter who I was dating; Mom was always hoping to get us married. I didn't have the heart to tell her it wasn't going to happen, but I admired her tenacity.

"We'll see. I'm busy, Mom." She eyed me skeptically.

Elizabeth peeked up from her forkful of cake. "Yes, Julian, we'd love to meet this Sarah. Your mom has told us all about her."

I glowered at my mom. "It's nothing serious. We've just been out a few times."

Mom raised an eyebrow at me. "For two months, Julian."

I rolled my eyes. "And leave it to you to be counting."

The rest of the evening zoomed by too fast. I resolved to stay in touch with the Scotts from now on and promised to contact Robin when my busy scheduled allowed.

Lyle shook my hand when I stood to leave. "It was wonderful seeing you again, Julian. Don't be such a stranger next time."

"I won't." I thanked both of them and gave everyone a hug goodbye. "Thanks for a great birthday, Mom and Dad."

It was going on nine in the evening when I walked out the door to my car. In the darkness, my eyes caught a glimpse of the moon glistening through the leaves of the maple tree. "What the heck," I told myself. I hadn't checked our initials in quite a few years.

Fishing my phone from my pocket, I pressed the flashlight button and headed straight to the tree. My heart started pounding outside my chest and a sensation of warmth spread throughout my body. I noticed fresh grass had replaced the tattered and worn path between our houses.

Reaching the spot where Amber took her final breath, I stood, facing the tree and glanced at our initials carved into the trunk. They looked weathered but still visible.

Taking a deep, shaky breath, I traced the A and S of Amber's name and did the same with the J and C of mine, feeling an instantaneous weakness in my legs. I then raised my hand and placed it on the heart. The hair on the back of my neck stood up at the same time I felt an electrical current run through me. *What the hell?* I pulled my hand away quickly. Was Amber here watching over me? I grinned, looked briefly to the heavens, and then headed to my car.

When I opened the door, my phone dinged with a text. I glanced down, reading the name on the screen.

Sarah: Sorry to interrupt your evening, but could we get together tomorrow evening?

Me: Possibly. I'm at my parents. Heading home now. Will text when I get there.

Sarah: Okay.

DEEP IN THOUGHT, I arrived at my place in the city forty-five minutes later. I couldn't get my head around the unsettling thoughts of Destiny and why she intrigued me. Her striking resemblance to Amber—that had to be it.

As I punched in the elevator code for my penthouse and headed up to the twenty-seventh floor, apprehension and panic rattled me to my core.

I placed the trophy beside my photo of Amber on my hutch and then hunted down a beer from the fridge. I popped the top and relaxed on the sofa, letting out a deep breath.

"Christ, I can't bear to open old wounds," I muttered as the sound of my voice reverberated in the large living room.

I pulled my phone from my pocket and stared at the text from Sarah. Should I text her back now? It was close to ten.

Me: Home. What time tomorrow? My place okay?

A long silence followed, so I set the phone down and tuned the TV to a repeat episode of *Seinfeld*. She was probably in bed.

I tugged the ring box from my pocket, examining it again as my mind drifted back to the day I gave it to Amber. It was her seventeenth birthday. She lay weak in her bed but so beautifully strong to me. God, how I missed her.

I almost nodded off when my phone chimed with an incoming text. Grabbing it from the coffee table, I swiped it awake and looked at the time on the front...just before midnight.

Sarah: Sorry, I was out and missed your text. Your home sounds perfect. What time would you suggest?

I texted her back suggesting a seven o'clock dinner.

Sarah: Okay, can't wait to see you.

Making decent money now, I could afford a housekeeper to clean my home once a week. I'd employed Carolyn to do some light cooking as well. She prepared lasagna for my weekend meal and an extra week's worth of food I'd find in the freezer. Also, I thanked God she worked for me on Fridays. The place was clean for Sarah's visit the next evening.

Before settling into bed for the night, I paced in front of the floor-to-ceiling windows of my living room thinking about my life. With the exception of my work, I felt my existence had no direction. Maybe I shouldn't have invested so much time and effort into becoming a successful doctor. I loved my work, but where did it get me? An obscenely high paying job with no one to share it with…that was where.

I shook my head and decided to sleep, but that didn't happen as easily as I'd hoped. My thoughts wandered all night to Destiny. *What the hell?* She was interrupting my sleep now.

SATURDAY MORNING CAME WITH A JOLT. I climbed into the shower and let the hot water scald my sleep deprived body.

The weekend was upon me and always a much-needed time to unwind. Work was stressful and the days always long. I always cherished my days off.

I enjoyed my spacious home. I'd looked for a place with a wide-open view of the Rocky Mountains. The distant white peaks reminded me of Amber and our love of hiking. I'd moved in here last December, just before the holidays. The last eight months were spent furnishing the place, to fill the emptiness, both within my living quarters as well as within myself. I would eventually want to purchase a home, but this place suited my needs for now, plus it was close to my job.

I went to the gym in the basement of my building and somehow pulled off my usual workout. Since I'd been a teenager, I never wavered from my desire to keep fit. It was as much a part of my daily routine as breathing was to living. I was borderline obsessed with good health and exercise.

The day flew by remarkably fast. I stopped at the office to take care of a few time-sensitive issues and popped in to check on one of my patients.

It was nearly six before I'd made it back to my place, still needing to heat up the pasta dish. Cooking was not my forte; that's why I enlisted the help of Carolyn. She was an outstanding cook and respected my desire for health conscious choices. I grabbed a couple of plates, some silverware, and napkins, laying them on the kitchen island. I pulled the lasagna from the fridge and placed it in the oven, then headed to the bathroom for a quick shower.

The doorbell rang promptly at seven. Sarah was here. I made my way to the foyer and opened the door. "Hey, how you been? C'mon in."

"Hi," she said softly and stepped through the door.

I bent down and gave her a chaste kiss on the lips. "Hungry?"

"Starving. You eat so late in the evening."

My eyes fixed on the paper bag in her hand as she strode across the living room. She stopped and gazed out the floor-to-ceiling windows.

"What's that in your hand?" I was intrigued.

"A birthday gift," she said, without taking her eyes off the scenic view.

"Well, thank you."

"I can't get enough of this gorgeous view you have of the Rocky Mountains."

"That's why I chose this place." I grinned and joined her at the window, draping my arm over her shoulder. She looked beautifully sexy. I became instantly aroused.

"Let's eat," she said, fixing her blue eyes on me.

"Would you like to eat at the kitchen island or in the living room?"

"Living room, please."

I released her and strode to the kitchen. She followed and sat on a bar stool. I felt her watching me when I opened the fridge and retrieved a bottle of Chardonnay.

I tilted the bottle, showing her the label. "Glass of wine?" I asked. "Sure."

I poured each of us a glass and pulled the lasagna from the oven. Sarah stood from the island and padded across the living room to my hutch. She lifted the photo of Amber and appeared to be studying it.

"Who's this?"

"Her name's Amber." *The only girl I've ever loved.*

"A sister or relative?"

I snorted. "Uh, neither."

She gave me a disapproving look, carrying the framed picture over to the island. "You're being very evasive. Can you expand a bit more on your responses?" She plopped back down on the bar stool and stared at the picture. "She's beautiful."

I sighed. "Yes, she was."

"Was?" Her eyes flicked upward to me. "Julian, what is going on?"

First off, Amber's photo had lived on the shelf of my hutch for as long as I could remember. When I'd changed residences, it moved with me. Of the few women I'd dated over the years, Sarah was the first to mention it.

I ran my hand through my hair. "What would you like to know?"

"Well, if she's not a sister or relative, why do you have a picture of her? She's not a girlfriend unless you're robbing the cradle." She chuckled.

I hadn't discussed Amber with any of the women I'd dated and didn't want to start now. It was too painful for me. I could tell Sarah wasn't going to give up though.

I took a deep breath and exhaled. "She was a girl I dated back in high school," I replied automatically while cutting into the casserole.

She narrowed her eyes at me, looking dumbfounded. "So, why are you still displaying a photograph of her?"

"She passed away shortly after I took that picture."

Sarah gasped, pressing a hand to her mouth. "Oh my God. What happened?"

"She had a brain tumor."

"And you're a neurosurgeon. Coincidence?" she asked, her words barely audible.

"Maybe. She inspired me to become the doctor that I am."

She carried the photo back to the hutch and positioned it in its rightful place, then turned to me and frowned. "You loved her, didn't you? That's why you still have her picture displayed."

Sarah was a breath of fresh air next to the other women I'd dated. She was beautiful, smart, honest, caring and had an uncanny zest for life. I always felt relaxed when she was around. But could I love her the way I loved Amber? That was the million dollar question.

"Yes," I said softly, as she returned to the bar stool and sat down. I looked at her, trying to gauge her expression.

She closed her eyes and subtly shook her head. I wished I knew what she was thinking.

I put my forefinger under her chin and lifted it. "Hey, look at me."

When she opened her eyes, they filled with resolve. She straightened her shoulders and cleared her throat. "What do you say we eat?"

"Good idea."

"WHAT'S THIS?" I asked, opening Sarah's gift. Inside the box was an Olympus camera. I sat there, bewildered. Why was she giving me such an expensive gift?

It was so many years ago, but I still remembered the roll of Lifesavers candy Amber gifted to me on my sixteenth birthday. It was simple, small and...*inexpensive*. Perfect, just like her.

"It's a birthday gift," she said. "I thought you could use it when you were out hiking." She waved her arm toward the window. "You know...take pictures of the mountains."

"It's too much. I can't accept this." Was she trying to buy my love? Maybe that's what she was thinking.

She looked dejected. What was it about that woeful look on a woman's face that made me flinch? First Destiny and now Sarah. She was obviously expecting something I was unable to give her.

"Where do you see our relationship?" I asked her.

She shrugged her shoulders, her face laced with confusion. "I don't know, but a girl can always hope."

Hope for what? Could I see myself going further with her? Of all the women I'd dated since Amber's death, Sarah was the only one I'd dated steadily. *Christ!* I shook my head thinking about my "player" days. Amber cured me of that behavior. Was that where I saw myself headed again? *No!* It was time for me to move forward and stop all this shit. But was Sarah meant to be there with me? Could I fall in love with her?

"Thank you," I said and gave her a kiss.

She wrapped me in her arms and deepened the kiss. "Shall we move this to the bedroom?" she suggested after ambushing me on the sofa. She was all hands and lips, rubbing herself along my erection. God, she was a good lover.

"Absolutely," I panted, trying to regain my equilibrium from the throes of passion. I scooped her up into my arms and carried her to my bedroom. After planting her feet on the floor, I placed my hands on each side of her face, bent down and trailed kisses along her jaw. I released her and unbuttoned her blouse.

"Oh, Julian," she moaned softly.

"Yes." I slipped the blouse off her shoulders, grazing my fingertips down her arms, reminding me of all the times I'd done this with Amber. Her body was perfect.

Abruptly my mind began to wander to the circumstances surrounding Destiny's appearance in my office the day before. Why couldn't I get her out of my head? It was starting to aggravate me. Should I have agreed to get together and talk? All she wanted was to unravel the mystery of where she'd known me from—an innocent conversation.

"Julian?" Sarah startled me out of my thoughts.

"What?" I said, feeling my face flush with embarrassment. For God's sake. Why the hell was I thinking about Destiny at such an inopportune moment?

She released me and pushed herself back. "You've been acting distant all evening. What the hell?" She raised her voice then dropped her head. "Is it her? Amber?"

I stood there gazing down at her. I felt numb, unable to communicate my feelings into words. It wasn't Amber on my mind…it was Destiny—a girl I didn't even know. She was disrupting my life and it was pissing me off. I closed my eyes and shook my head, disconnected and speechless.

"Julian, talk to me. Please."

"Sarah—," I hesitated, rubbing the back of my neck.

"Forget it!" she hissed at me. "Right now I don't feel like competing with your dead girlfriend."

She buttoned her blouse, turned and headed out of my bedroom in a huff. I followed closely behind her, grabbing her arm. She yanked it from my grip.

"Don't. Let me go."

My throat tightened. I knew if I let her walk out the door, it would be the last time I'd see her. This was the defining moment of our relationship.

She stormed across the room toward the door.

"Wait," I said sternly.

She turned and scowled at me. "What?"

I retrieved the camera she'd gifted to me from the sofa, slipped it into the bag and handed it to her. "Here, I can't keep this, but thank you."

Thank you? What a total asshole I was. This beautiful woman was walking out on me and all I could say was *thank you.*

Without a word, she snagged the bag from my hand and left. She was gone and I let her go.

I shuffled to my couch, sank down and plopped my head into my hands, rifling my fingers through my hair. What the fuck have I done? *You prick, Cahill.* I repeatedly beat my fists into the cushions.

"I need a goddamn drink." My voice bounced off the walls of my living room.

I headed to the fridge to hunt down a beer. I popped the top and glanced at the clock: Eight thirty. I pulled my phone from my pocket and dialed Sarah's number. My finger hovered over the green call button.

Chapter Seventeen

Destiny

What a bastard! When the elevator doors closed with a hasty swoosh, my mind went into overdrive. Dr. Cahill wouldn't give me the time of day. And to top it off, he was blatantly rude. *What did you expect, Destiny? You barged into his office and practically demanded answers.* He was a doctor for God sakes. But, where did I know him from? It was driving me crazy. I pounded my fist into the air, determined to uncover this mystery, not even sure why it mattered. Except…it did.

My heart lurched into my throat as the elevator plunged downward, making me feel lighter in an instant. I stared at the numbers above the doors, descending one by one; thinking about my devious behavior after leaving his office. I'd turned and deliberately gave him my all-white-teeth, Destiny Bradshaw, look-of-superiority smile, feeling thoroughly pleased with myself. He gasped. It was my attempt to mask the hurt I felt from his dismissal of me. No way was I going to let him think he had the upper hand. I chuckled arrogantly to myself.

In a huff, I dashed to my car, climbed behind the wheel and coasted out onto the highway. Through the late afternoon traffic, I was home minutes later to my quiet neighborhood on the west side of Boulder, Colorado.

The Taj Mahal had nothing on the sheer size of my parent's house. Comparatively, it was big, but it was also my safe haven. My dad was the president and CEO of his own software company. At times I wondered why we needed something this enormous.

BOXES, SUITCASES, BOOKS, AND CLOTHES littered the floor of my bedroom. I'd be college bound in another two weeks, meaning I had to begin packing.

Folding a pink lacy blouse lying on the floor, my eyes shifted to my laptop. I jammed the blouse into my overloaded suitcase and sat down at the computer. I wiggled the mouse, and the screen sprang to life. After opening Google, I typed *"Dr. Julian Cahill"* into the search box. A myriad of links filled the page about his career along with a few photos of him shaking hands with people I didn't know. I clicked on the top link and started reading: *Neurosurgeon, Dr. Julian Cahill receives top award.*

The article talked about the American Medical Association awards dinner scheduled for sometime next month. Dr. Cahill was being honored for his development of life-altering treatments for brain cancer patients diagnosed as terminal. Blah. Blah. Blah.

No, this had nothing to do with my recognition of him. I clicked the back button and scanned through the rest of the links. Nothing popped out at me. I went back and moved the mouse over some pictures and click on a few of them.

Cripes, he's a gorgeous man! I wondered if he was married. I hadn't noticed a ring on his left hand while sitting in his office. A man that great-looking surely must be dating someone.

Nothing familiar popped out at me, so I shut the computer down.

My stomach started rumbling. It was closing in on suppertime. A hint of basil filled the air as I headed downstairs to the kitchen.

Mom stood at the stove stirring a pot, looking up when I strolled into the room. "Ready for supper, honey?"

"Yes, I'm starving. What smells so good?"

"We're having chicken soup." She carried the pot to the island and set it down on a trivet. "How was the hospital tour?"

"Good, but I don't think I'll go into that field. Too much school."

She scowled her blue eyes at me, tossing her sun-bleached hair over her shoulder. "You don't get anywhere in life without a little bit of hard work."

"I know. I know." I waved my hand, dismissing her. "I'm thinking about astrophysics again," I said, placating her.

My parents were stricter than most, which, at times, posed problems for me. For all intents and purposes, they had a good reason for their over-protectiveness. The death of my older brother from a car accident eight years earlier had completely devastated them. It seemed they didn't stop crying for weeks afterward and in turn, have kept a tight leash on me.

As my only sibling, Timmy was nine years older than me. He spent most of his time with friends, so I only remember bits and pieces about him. He'd recently started college and was home on a break when he took me out for ice cream one evening. Another driver ran a red light and hit us broadside. Timmy was killed instantly. I survived with a deep gash to the right side of my head, above the ear.

Unconsciously, I reached up and felt the scar. Luckily my hair covered it.

The accident was a clouded memory, but I cherished the gentle care received from all the doctors and nurses during my one night in the hospital. It was a comfort to me as well as to my parents.

Nothing got by mom though—or as my dad referred to her as his "beautiful as 'Cyn' " wife (always a play on words with him)—so it was useless to try to hide any detail no matter how insignificant. She needed to know my every move. I loved her, but the rigid restraints she imposed on me were suffocating.

I sat down on the nearest bar stool of the island and started tapping my fingernails on the smooth surface. "By the way, the doctor who guided the tour looked so familiar to me, but I couldn't place him. Do you know a Dr. Julian Cahill?"

She gathered some bowls and silverware from the cupboard and placed them on the island. "No, the name doesn't ring a bell to me. Maybe your dad knows him."

"Know who?" My dad appeared and sat on the bar stool next to me.

"Dr. Julian Cahill," I said, turning to him.

In his free time, Marcus Bradshaw always had a disheveled look about him. My dad wore old, wrinkled T-shirts and god-awful, worn jeans when he wasn't working. He had enough money to buy high-end clothing but always preferred his comfort to style. I loved that about him.

"Nope, the name doesn't sound familiar to me," he said, placing his napkin on his lap. "Why do you ask?"

"No reason. I just thought I knew him. That's all."

"How was the tour today, pumpkin?"

"Not my cup of tea, Daddy. I guess I'll go back to my original interest in astrophysics."

"Okay. Whatever makes you happy." He leaned over and planted a kiss on my cheek.

I STARED BLANKLY at my computer screen, again. Picture upon picture of Dr. Cahill filled the screen. He was quite the handsome man in a "Greek God" sort of way. Why did I have this insatiable need to find out who he was? It drove me insane.

I knew he was from Castle Pines so I typed *"Julian Cahill, Castle Pines, CO"* into the search bar this time. One of the links revealed an address on Aspen Court, and age of thirty-five, but nothing out of the ordinary.

"Thirty five?" I said out loud, my eyes bugging out of my face. No way did he look thirty-five. Twenty-five was stretching it, but certainly not thirty-five.

His profile wasn't coming up on any social media sites either. *Crap!* I'd gotten nowhere. Maybe I didn't know him after all. I wished I could shake this uneasy feeling.

It was moving on toward eleven and my head ached. I closed the lid of my laptop and crossed my bedroom to the window. I stared with wonder out into the darkness of the night. The brilliant light of the full moon cast eerie shadows below against the star-filled sky.

Stargazing was something I'd loved since I was a little girl. When my mom tucked me into bed, I'd always sneak back to the window. After naming as many constellations as possible, I'd slip back under the blankets and dream of flying to the stars. It was most likely the reason for my interest in astrophysics. Something about the stars intrigued me.

I sighed and climbed under the paisley-colored comforter of my bed. Tomorrow would bring a new day of questions into the mystery of Dr. Cahill, but for now, I needed sleep.

> My sister and I are playing dolls on the floor of our living room. Our living room has a dark blue rug and it feels nice on my knees. My doll is wearing a yellow dress along with a yellow bow in her hair. A small neighborhood boy is playing the daddy. I don't know his name, but he plays really nice. My sister takes my doll and I tell her to give it back to me. I go to the kitchen to tell Mommy, but I can't find her. Instead, there is a different Mommy cooking something in our kitchen. She says her name is Lizzy. I go back to my sister and tell her to give me my doll back or I will leave. She tells me not to go. I forgot my sister's name and I feel scared. Really, really scared. Then I remember that I don't have a sister. I try to take a breath, but I can't.

I woke up gasping for air. *What the hell was that about?* The clock said three fifty. I sat up and dangled my legs over the side of the bed, trying to regain my composure. I sucked in a deep breath and exhaled a jagged puff of air. The night light on the wall provided enough light for me to see my way to the bathroom. I popped a couple of painkillers in my mouth and gulped down a refreshing glass of water. Minutes later, I pushed the dream out of the recesses of my brain and went back to bed.

IT'D BEEN TWO WEEKS since the day of the tour with no new answers in regards to my obsession with the mysterious Dr. Cahill. Still intrigued, I found myself lying awake night after night, dwelling on my research. What was I missing?

I wondered if he was feeling the same compulsion. I doubted it. He's the one who asked me to leave his office. That hardly warranted the same crazed madness I'd been going through.

Today, I needed to make a trip to the hospital to collect my immunization records for college. I would be moving into my dorm tomorrow. I couldn't wait.

After breakfast with my parents, I dragged on a T-shirt emblazoned with the University of Colorado across the front—my new home for the next four years—along with a pair of shorts. I put my hair up into a messy bun and applied a little lip gloss. I didn't look my best but convinced myself it would be a quick trip.

Minutes later I was out the door and heading to the hospital. Finding a parking space next to the section reserved for doctors, I pulled in alongside a sporty Mercedes. It was a warm, sunny day, but I felt a slight chill on the back of my neck as I climbed out of my car.

I entered the hospital and headed toward the bank of elevators, pressing the up button. A gnawing sensation in the pit of my stomach kept me on edge. When the doors opened, I scooted inside and pressed the button for the fifth floor. The elevator lurched upward, stopping at my floor. I exited and found my primary physician's office easily. I waited, making small talk with the receptionist while she made a Xerox copy of my records. With the necessary papers in hand, I turned and headed back out.

"Thank you, Dr. Schwebel," I said, waving my hand when he appeared in the waiting room.

"Good luck at school, Destiny," he responded.

"Thanks."

I made my way back down to the first floor and was leaving the elevator when I saw him. I stopped in my tracks, my muscles going rigid. It was Dr. Cahill. I fixed my eyes on his smoking body as he headed toward the revolving exit door. Despite his scruffy appearance, he was still one sumptuous-looking man. I suspected he'd just pulled an all-nighter. Part of me wanted to give him a piece of my mind, while the other wanted to run my hands up his body and squeeze his muscular biceps.

Abruptly, he flinched, whipping his head around toward me. In a flash, I ducked behind the lobby desk, dropping my paperwork, and watched as they seesawed to the floor.

Perhaps this was a bit melodramatic. On the other hand, why didn't I want him to see me?

I scooped up my papers, stood and caught a glimpse of Dr. Cahill scurrying out the exit. Hurriedly, I crossed the lobby and spun through the revolving door in time to see him open the door to his car. I recognized the Mercedes emblem on the front. *Nice car.* I'd parked beside him.

My mouth went dry and my scalp prickled. I took a deep breath in an effort to calm myself. Then, a devious idea entered my head. Once he eased out of his space, I darted to my red BMW, opened the door, climbed in and sped out of my space like a hotrod on a drag strip. Moments later, I found myself following him, staying two cars behind. "What the hell am I doing? What if he sees me?" I muttered out loud. Surely I could be arrested for this. Wasn't stalking a crime? An anxious giggle erupted from my belly.

Dr. Cahill moved east along Sixth Avenue and took a quick left onto Lincoln Street. The car in front of me made a right-hand turn leaving me smack-dab behind Dr. Cahill. I eased off the gas to lengthen the distance between us. Several blocks later, he took a right onto East Seventeenth Avenue. I followed. He drove along for another mile before pulling into the underground garage of a red brick, upscale skyscraper. Wow. The enormity of this building was breathtaking. Mentally assessing the height, there had to be more than twenty-five floors.

I pulled off onto the shoulder and took in the surrounding landscape. Across the street, a beautiful park surrounded a lake. In the distance, the Rocky Mountains stood majestic and proud.

Looking back at the building, above a stained glass window, a sign read: The Zenith, Condominiums in the Park. The entrance showcased a steel door with intricate welded iron patterns weaved throughout it.

I felt like a first class spy, sneaking around, snooping into the mysterious life of Dr. Cahill. The adrenaline rush was exhilarating. My heartbeat hammered in my chest while a knot formed in my belly.

I waited fifteen minutes—giving Dr. Cahill time to reach his home—before exiting my car, crossing the street and entering the lobby. Shiny marble floors and abstract artwork greeted me inside the elegant building. Situated next to a bank of three elevators were two Victorian overstuffed armchairs facing a round, sable black, pedestal table with four clawed feet.

I nervously approached the concierge desk, trying desperately to act nonchalant. Surely the sweat pouring from my upper lip was giving me away. I wiped it away with the back of my hand and cleared my throat.

"Excuse me. Could you tell me where Dr. Julian Cahill lives?" I asked the too-thin woman with hollow, sunken cheeks and pale skin. She looked as if she hadn't eaten in a week.

She arched her thinly plucked brow at me, no doubt scrutinizing my appearance. *Damn. I should've dressed better.* "Dr. Cahill lives in the penthouse on the top floor, but because of restricted access, you must have his permission to visit."

The voice in my head screamed: *PENTHOUSE!* He lived in the *penthouse?*

"Okay, no problem," I said politely, not able to believe the information she'd just, so freely, given out to me. Perhaps her brain was deficient from lack of nourishment. I wasn't planning to visit, but now knew where Dr. Cahill lived.

"Would you like me to give him a call?" she added.

Oh God! No! "Thank you, but I'm in a hurry." I turned and flew out the door before my shaking hands could give me away.

Hopefully undetected, I lurked around toward the rear of the building, immediately noticing the entrance to the underground garage. The gate lifted automatically when I passed by, so I slinked inside. There was nothing unusual about the layout. A bank of three elevators lined the florescent lit wall at the far end of the parking area. The one on the far right said penthouse above the door with a numbered touchpad along the side. The other two were accessible to everyone. This gave me an idea.

"DID YOU GET YOUR IMMUNIZATION records, Destiny?" Mom asked when I walked in the door forty minutes later.

"Yep. Right here." I handed the papers to her standing at the kitchen island putting dishes away.

She briskly scanned them and handed them back. "Are you all

packed?"

"Almost. I'm excited, Mom."

"I hope so," she said, grabbing a few glasses. "Could you put these away up there?" She pointed to the top shelf of the cupboard, squinting at me with a hard smile. "You *are* taller than me."

I grinned and placed the glasses in the cupboard, then headed to my bedroom. My stalking rendezvous would remain a secret from her. She'd probably ground me if she knew what I'd just done.

MY APARTMENT-STYLE college dorm room was white, barren, and depressing—a typical college room. There were two bedrooms separated by a fully-applianced kitchen. Today was move-in day for all first-year students at the university and I was lucky enough to have won a lottery draw over the summer for a single room. I'd be in the suite with two other girls but have my own room.

My mom helped me decorate my room, putting a personal touch on it while my dad broke down empty boxes. Burgundy curtains now hung in the window and a gigantic tapestry was tacked to the empty space above my headboard. My dad nailed a bulletin board to the wall above my desk. Once we placed all my photos on my desk and rolled out an area rug on the floor, we were done. Looking around, the room had a cozy feeling.

After eating lunch at a nearby restaurant, my parents dropped me off at my dorm to say goodbye. Before they left, we hugged and kissed each other as if it'd be the last time we saw each other. A knot formed in my stomach, on the verge of tears.

"Call us on Monday and let us know how your first day went," Mom said, choking back tears.

"I will, Mom. Thanks for all your help today." I gave my dad another tight hug and kiss. "Bye, Daddy."

"We'll miss you, pumpkin." His lips trembled. "Work hard."

"I will. I promise."

I watched as they drove out of the parking lot and disappeared from view. This was the first time I'd ever lived away from home and part of me was scared to death. I took a deep breath, exhaled slowly and marched back inside, spending the rest of the afternoon organizing my knickknacks and thinking about Dr. Cahill.

Interrupting my obsessive thoughts, a flurry of activity outside my room startled me. Investigating the noise, I noticed my suitemates had arrived, and as it turned out, both were from the Colorado Springs area. They graduated from the same high school and knew each other—leaving me at a disadvantage already.

A girl with blond hair, hazel eyes, and pale skin approached me with a warm smile. "Hi, I'm Chloe Whitten," she said, extending her hand.

I took it and introduced myself, "I'm Destiny Bradshaw. It's nice to meet you, Chloe."

I turned to the other girl, whose flawless beauty entranced me. With a dark complexion, big brown eyes, and jet-black, long, wavy hair, she was stunning. I suspected she was into high fashion.

"Hey, I'm Gabrielle Sanchez, Gabby for short." Her voice was low and gravelly.

"Nice to meet you, Gabby. Forgive me for staring, but your hair is gorgeous." I blushed.

"She's a model, Destiny," Chloe blurted out.

"Wow, cool." I raised an eyebrow, my suspicions confirmed.

"Where are you from?" Gabby asked.

"Boulder."

"Oh, cool," she added.

I nodded, then excused myself and wandered back to my bedroom to do more organizing in my closet.

Chloe and Gabby's parents left soon thereafter and the three of us spent the rest of the afternoon chatting and getting to know each other. I instantly loved both of them, deciding it was going to be an exciting year.

College was everything to me. The thought of being unsuccessful was never an option. I'd dreamt of going to college since my freshman year of high school.

I declared my major in astrophysics. My interests laid in the physical nature of the stars. I could receive a bachelor's degree and then decide what to do beyond that.

Along with several scholarships, I'd qualified for advanced placement in my honors physics class. Successfully completing a few AP classes in high school, I was able to transfer eighteen credits, essentially making me a second-semester freshman.

MY ASTRONOMY CLASS met at eight in the morning in the planetarium. My excitement was palpable as I prepared for the first day of classes.

I brushed through the weight of my long, wet hair, applied some makeup then dressed in a pair of white knee-length capris and navy blue camisole. I completed the outfit with my denim jacket and sneakers.

I headed out the door to make the trek across campus. Walking into the round room, I sat along the back row. The seat reclined while the observation of the stars projected on the surface of the dome. It was like sitting outside under the stars on a dark night. I was able to pick out the Milky Way and most of the constellations from the many nights of stargazing I'd done in my younger years. A cool shiver skimmed my back.

Professor Jenkins spent most of the class going over the course syllabus and the grading system he would use throughout the semester.

Later, an exhaustion spread through my body after finishing classes for the day. I had one last stop at the library to buy a calculus book for my upcoming math class, and then I'd head back to the dorm. I walked through the library doors, and my breath hitched at the massive room. Immediately, I noticed a group of computers enclosed within a soundproof glass enclosure to my left. My thoughts drifted again to Dr. Cahill. I'd finished my homework earlier and decided to log on to one of the computers.

In the search bar, I typed: *Julian Cahill, biography*. A series of links popped up on the page—none of which looked promising into unlocking my mystery. Most were about his expertise in neurosurgery.

"Wait," I said a bit too loudly as heads turned toward me. "Sorry." I blushed.

I knew he lived in Castle Pines and based on his age, I calculated that his graduation from high school would have been in 2000. If I could get a hold of his yearbook, maybe that would shine a light on my dilemma. I'd exhausted every other path.

I typed: *high school for Castle Pines, Colorado area.* At the top of the page, a map popped up with a link that read: *Castle Rock High School.* I knew that many libraries carried yearbooks...could this one? I scurried out of the room, my purse banging against the glass door making heads turn again. *Slow down, Destiny.* My heart began pounding once again. My confidence spiked at the thought that I'd finally hit on something.

At the front desk, after asking where the yearbooks were shelved, the librarian directed me to a room upstairs. She told me the only schools included were those of the surrounding areas. I crossed my fingers Castle Rock would be one of them. Taking two steps at a time, I crossed the room to the back wall, noticing all yearbooks were alphabetized. I scanned the row until I hit the C's. Scrolling my finger across the spine of the books, it stopped at Castle Rock High School. *Yes!* I pumped my fist into the air. What were the chances? The first year listed was 1958. I jumped forward forty-two years until my finger hovered over the year of 2000. My hands shook as I pulled the thick book from the shelf.

This could lead to another dead-end, but at the very least, I had to find out if anything jarred my memory.

I headed to an empty table and sat down, brushing my hand across the front. A build-up of static electricity zapped through me. *Ouch!*

I carefully opened the hard covered book and flicked through to the senior picture pages, stopping at the letter 'C.' My finger trembled as I landed on Julian Cahill's picture in the second row, third from the right.

Wow! He must have been one popular son of a bitch. He was positively gorgeous with long blond hair and blue eyes. The hair stood up on the back of my neck as my scalp prickled. He looked familiar, but nothing jumped out at me. I decided to look through the book from the beginning. I flipped through to page one and started in.

There were candid photos on the first three pages and then a table of contents page. I did a quick scan through the titles and turned the page.

My eyes repeatedly blinked as I stared into the face of a girl who looked exactly like me, as if I'd glanced in the mirror. "Oh my God!" I blurted out. All alone, I was sure my outburst fell on deaf ears.

On the top of the page, it said: *In Memory Of.*

I couldn't lift my eyes from hers. She could have been my identical twin—right down to the length of her blond hair, full lips, and bright blue eyes. Me. Me. Me.

Underneath the picture in italics it said: *Amber Scott, May 5, 1982-August 2, 1999.* Wow, she died a few days before I was born. Below her name a few lines from a poem were written.

Precious memories in your mind,
Like aging roses fade with time.
No matter what you say or do,
I won't forget about those of you.

For the third time in as many minutes, I puffed out a deep breath. I recognized those words, but that wasn't what made me gasp. Below the poem was Julian Cahill's name. He'd written that verse. I flipped back to the table of contents. With my forefinger, I scrolled down the list until resting it over *Prom.* Page three-hundred five. Bringing my shaky hand to my forehead, I wiped the sweat away. I turned to the prom page, noticing the theme title immediately: *"Nights in White Satin."* I swallowed hard. There were a number of pictures on the next four pages, but only one stood out. There, standing in a spotlight was Julian Cahill dancing with the shell of a girl. She looked deathly ill. At closer inspection, I noticed it was her. It was Amber.

Fishing a pen and paper from my backpack, I jotted down her name, birth, and death dates. I tugged my phone from my pants pocket, took a snapshot of the page, then placed the yearbook back on the shelf and headed downstairs. I hurriedly purchased my calculus book and jogged back to my dorm. My earlier exhaustion had vanished.

Throwing everything on the floor when I walked through the door, I fired up my computer and typed Amber's name into the search box.

The page filled with her obituary. My heart shattered for this girl who died at such a young age. But obits rarely mention the cause of death. It listed her parents as Lyle and Elizabeth Scott and a sister, Robin. Her funeral took place on August 6, 1999. My goddamned birthday.

"Fuck!"

"What's wrong, Destiny?" Chloe abruptly appeared in my room.

"Sorry. Nothing Chloe."

"You're white as a ghost."

And that was the operative word—ghost.

"I'm fine. Really."

She turned, leaving me alone and headed out to her car as I pressed my hands against my temples and closed my eyes, trying to fit the pieces together. Then it dawned on me. I pulled my knees up to my chest and circled my arms around them. I sat there rocking back and forth, trying to catch my breath. Could it be true?

Throughout my life, I'd felt like I lived another life. "Oh my God! I'm her! I remember!" I squealed out loud. "I was Amber and the gorgeous Dr. Julian Cahill was my boyfriend!"

Chapter Eighteen

Reincarnation. The thought of it had me reeling. I felt ill as I read through a few more articles about Amber on my computer. That's the reason Dr. Cahill looked so familiar to me. From the shocking look on his face when I appeared in his office two weeks before, he looked like he'd seen a ghost. He had. But, why would he just dismiss me?

Get real, Destiny. Not everyone believed in reincarnation. I still had a massive job ahead of me, convincing him of who I was.

I had a plan, and it was time to set it into motion. The clock said five o'clock when I grabbed my backpack, stuffed it with water and a few snacks then asked Gabby if she had a pair of binoculars.

"Yep. I use them for concerts. Why do you need them?" she asked, eyeing me with concern.

"Um..., you'll see."

Moments later, I grabbed my keys and made a straight line toward the door.

"Nothing illegal!" she yelled from the dorm as I jumped in my car.

Ignoring her, I inserted the key in the ignition, fired up the engine and headed down the highway to the Zenith Condominiums.

When the gate rose, I pulled into the underground garage and backed into a parking space giving me a clear view of the elevators and touchpad to Dr. Cahill's penthouse. I breathed a sigh of relief when I didn't see his car. Keeping out of sight, I raised the binoculars to my eyes and focused. I was set.

Placing them on the dashboard of the car, I then flipped the radio on, and the hushed sounds of Taylor Swift rang through my car. Sitting on the front seat, my physics textbook summoned me to study. I eyed it with contempt, but picked it up and started reading.

An hour later a black car pulled into the garage and parked in a spot reserved for management. I watched as a heavy-set woman exited the car and disappeared into an elevator. It wasn't Dr. Cahill, so I resumed my reading, continuing to wait.

My stomach started to rumble. I reached into my backpack and fished out my water, banana, and bag of chips. I scarfed them down as I looked at the time on my phone. Three hours had passed. The sun must have set by now, but I was shrouded in darkness, only lit by the overhead fluorescent lights. Maybe this was a bad idea. No, I refused to give up, scolding myself when the familiar roar of a Mercedes rolled into the garage. It was Dr. Cahill. *Finally.*

I whispered a silent prayer of thanks for the garage's muted light when he pulled into a spot two vehicles away from me.

He exited his car and crossed the garage to his elevator. As he lifted his hand to the touchpad, his head jerked around in my direction, looking spooked. *What was that about?* He'd done the same thing at the hospital.

I crouched down in my seat, peeking through the bottom of the windshield.

He shook his head and turned back around. I raised the binoculars to my eyes. It was like I was standing right next to him. The numbers were huge and crystal clear.

He pressed 2 6 2 3 7 and the door opened with a whoosh. He disappeared inside while I quickly jotted the access code down in my notebook. I was so proud of myself, but also a little shocked at my illicit behavior. What was I thinking? I didn't care because the first part of the plan had come together perfectly.

I SLAPPED THE SNOOZE BUTTON of my alarm clock. Tuesday morning had come with a loud shriek, waking me from an all-too-brief night's sleep. I laid awake for hours during the night thinking about the few memories I'd had of my past life. That must have been what that bizarre dream was all about. How would I convince Dr.

Cahill of my identity? The weekend seemed a more logical time to reveal myself to him. The odds were he'd be home. Plus it gave me a week to do more research.

The clock read seven in the morning as I hauled my body to the shower. Washing my long tresses, a vision of my previous life popped into my head. Closing my eyes, I saw myself in the Rocky Mountains and the dirt path along which I was hiking. Abruptly, the vision faded when my head started to ache.

I switched off the water, dried myself and fetched a couple of aspirin from the medicine cabinet. From my dresser, I dragged on some knee length shorts and a T-shirt and headed out to the kitchen. Gabby was sitting at the table scarfing down a bowl of cereal when I walked in.

"Did you have success with my binoculars?" she asked.

"Yep." I sat down and prepared myself a bowl of Cheerios and glass of orange juice.

"Destiny—" Gabby eyed me suspiciously, her voice laced with disapproval.

"What?" I sighed, rubbing the pain from my temples and trying to evade the direction of her questioning. "Don't worry, Gabby. Nobody got hurt."

"Who got hurt?" Chloe asked, appearing in the room. She placed two slices of bread in the toaster and sat at the table next to me.

"Nobody," I complained, taking my bowl to the sink. *Honestly, lighten up.*

"Well, don't take it out on me." She narrowed her eyes at me.

"Then mind your own business," I snapped, giving both of them the brush off and storming back to my bedroom. I didn't appreciate the confrontation.

"What the hell's up with you?" Chloe yelled.

"I don't need your third degree, okay?" I snatched my backpack from my bed and stormed out, slamming the door behind me.

TUESDAY'S CLASSES went from eight until two thirty, beginning with calculus and ending with physics. Later, I went to the library to study and do homework. I couldn't go back to my dorm. I was still feeling the sting of my roommate's disapproval of me.

Two hours later I pulled my phone from my pocket, swiped it awake, noticing the time...four fifteen. I'd completed my homework and decided to continue my research into the life of Amber Scott.

I sat at a vacant computer and wiggled the mouse. When the screen came to life, I clicked on the Internet icon and typed in her name. Several links popped up with her obituary. I scrolled down the page until I came to an article about a stabbing at Castle Rock High School. I clicked on the link and started reading.

My hand went to my mouth. This poor girl was stabbed in the abdomen by a couple of her classmates over a boy. Was the boy Julian? The article went on to explain how she'd been ambushed in the hall moments before the first-period bell. The teens had been charged with two counts of attempted homicide and remained in custody. It told about authorities not identifying them by name because of their ages.

Holy crap! I was born with a scar on my belly, and none of the doctors had an explanation for it. I lifted the hem of my shirt and studied the two-inch mark. I brushed the tips of my fingers over it, and a vision appeared in my head. I shut my eyes tight and willed my brain to remember the attack. I let out a deep groan when a stinging pain shot through me. My eyes flicked open. I remembered. That was it.

I hit the back button and scanned the page for more articles. Nothing stood out to me. Her obituary mentioned a sister, Robin Scott, so I did a search on her.

The first link cited an address in Broomfield, Colorado, and age of thirty-six. It also mentioned a Liam Spencer. I suspected he was her husband. I typed her name in the box on the social networking site. The search revealed a Robin Spencer at the top of the page. When I clicked on it, my heart skipped a beat. I recognized that beautiful face. A lump formed in my throat. This was my sister. My beautiful sister. I clicked through some of the images, noticing a handsome dark-haired man and adorable baby.

I closed my eyes, forcing my brain to remember anything about her. All that kept appearing in my head was her sadness after my death. I remembered seeing her so vividly at my funeral.

I knew I had to tread carefully with all of this. The first person I had to confront was Dr. Cahill, and then we would take it from there. He'd already sent me away once, would he do it again knowing who I was?

ASTRONOMY WAS MY FAVORITE CLASS, I thought as I reclined my chair and stared at the domed ceiling of the planetarium. Yesterday's headache was replaced by a good night's sleep and the knowledge that I was one day closer to my reincarnation revelation.

As Professor Jenkins started discussing some key points regarding the semester's grading system, the lights dimmed, and my mind began to drift. My eyes landed on the Milky Way, thinking of the billions of stars that made up that cluster of sparkling delight.

"That's it!" I mumbled excitedly. Suddenly it dawned on me why I loved the stars so much. I swallowed hard, forcing down a rolling stomach. "The stars," I whispered to myself.

"What?" A guy sitting next to me asked.

"Sorry, nothing," I replied. I really needed to put a muzzle on my internal thoughts.

BACK AT THE DORM right before lunch, I met Gabby in the kitchen preparing a sandwich. She hadn't spoken to me or made eye contact since our spat the day before.

"I'm sorry for my outburst yesterday."

"If you say so," she said, with a dismissive nod.

"Listen; there is something I'd like to show you. Are you done for the day?"

"Yeah," she scoffed, crossing her arms across her chest. "What?"

"Come with me. Please."

It took all of five minutes to walk from our dorm to the library. I held the door open, and together we walked in and headed up the stairs.

"What is going on, Destiny?" she asked, as the heads of three guys turned to gape at her.

"You won't believe what I'm going to show you."

"You're freaking me out, girl," she said.

"See all these?" I asked her, standing in front of the yearbook section.

With perfect posture, shoulders back and exposed neck, she tapped her foot on the hardwood floor. "Get to it, Destiny."

I pulled the 2000 Castle Rock High School yearbook off the shelf and held the binding toward her. "Do you see the year on this yearbook?"

"Yeah. 2000, so?"

"And we're now in the year 2017, right?"

She looked at me as if I had three heads. "Yeah, what's your point?"

We crossed the room to a nearby table and sat down. My hands shook so bad, I had trouble opening the cover. When I did, I thumbed through to the tribute page and shoved the book in her face.

"Look at that girl." I tapped my finger on the photo of Amber.

She slapped her hand to her mouth and yanked the book closer to herself. "Holy shit. You could be her identical twin!" she exclaimed, studying the picture. She lifted her head and looked at me. "She died?"

"Yes. And her funeral was on the day I was born."

"How do you know that?"

"I did a little research on her." I pulled the book back to me again and flipped through to the prom section. "There. Look at them." I pointed to the picture of Dr. Cahill and Amber dancing.

Gabby eyed me skeptically. "What...how...when?" she stuttered, unable to form a coherent sentence.

I filled Gabby in on the whole ordeal from seeing Dr. Cahill on the tour to the stake-out at his condo. I kept the part about me being the reincarnated Amber to myself. I wanted to be careful who I told.

"You do know what you did was illegal, don't you?"

"Yes. I assure you I'm feeling all kinds of guilt for doing that, but I needed to find out how I knew him."

"Why?"

Why? Because he was the love of my life. I screamed at her in my head. "I'm still looking into that," I lied. I had to get her off my back. At least she was talking to me again. "Let's go."

THE MASTER PLAN to reveal my identity to Dr. Cahill was complete. Today was the day. I'd been a bundle of nerves since I woke this morning. Could I go through with it? There was no time to back out now.

I drove to my parents the night before to spend the weekend with them and met my mom's smiling face at the door. I told her and my dad all about my first week of college, except the part about Dr. Cahill. It was a welcome distraction from Gabby and Chloe.

I needed to get away from all the drama with my roommates. They were talking to me again, but there was an unshakable tension between the three of us.

I'd taken my shower, brushed my teeth and hunted for something in particular to wear. From my dresser, I dragged on a pair of light brown Capris and a cream-colored halter-neck blouse. I made my way to the bathroom and dried my hair then applied some mascara and lip gloss. I fished my cell phone from my pocket and glanced at the photo I'd taken of Amber's picture in the yearbook. Yes. My look matched hers perfectly.

"Where are you headed, honey?" Mom asked when I perched myself on one of the kitchen bar stools.

"Out with a guy I met," I said, looking down at my fingers.

She eyed me suspiciously. "Oh. It didn't take you long to meet someone. What is his name?"

His name? Crap, I hadn't thought about that. I had to make something up quick. Glancing down at my fingers, I said, "Um...everyone calls him JC."

By the skeptical look on her face, I don't think she believed me. I ignored her. I know she wouldn't approve of what I was about to do, but I'd cross that bridge later. For now, I needed to get away from her questioning. I grabbed a banana from the shelf and was out the door.

"Later, Mom."

"Don't be out too late."

"Okay."

THE TRANQUIL SATURDAY MORNING air reminded me of

picnics, lakes, and hiking as I dragged on my sweater and clambered into the driver's seat of my car. My clock said nine fifteen. I clutched my stomach as a wave of nausea hit me. I was shaking all over. *Keep going, Destiny.*

Forty minutes later I pulled into the Zenith's underground garage and noticed Dr. Cahill's car. Yes, he was here. All the pieces of the puzzle were fitting together nicely. I smoothed the front of my outfit when I exited my BMW. *There, I look presentable.*

From my pocket, I retrieved the code to his elevator. I raised my trembling hand and pressed 2 6 2 3 7 on the touchpad. The door opened immediately with a signature whoosh sound. I gingerly stepped inside and turned to push the button for his penthouse, only to see my reflection on a smoke-colored glass wall staring back at me. Where were the buttons? Moments later, the doors closed and the elevator lurched, climbing at warp speed, making my knees buckle momentarily. I reached Dr. Cahill's loft in the sky and quickly shuffled out.

The morning sun from a window in the vestibule cast a shadow at my feet, making them glow, almost like Dorothy's in *The Wizard of Oz.*

I glanced around, noticing Dr. Cahill was the sole occupant of this twenty-seventh floor in the heavens, which explained the elevators direct access to the penthouse.

I approached his door, which screamed extravagance. It was a dark, rich, mahogany wood with intricately carved patterns throughout.

And then it dawned on me…What if he was married and his wife answered the door? Maybe I hadn't thought this through. He wasn't wearing a wedding band on his finger when I visited at his office, but maybe he took it off while he was working. *Crap!*

I raised my quivering hand and knocked.

Eight long seconds later, he opened the door, jerking backward. I opened my mouth to speak but was interrupted by his stinging words.

"How the hell did you get up here?" he snapped.

I wasn't prepared for his hostility. For whatever reason, I thought he'd welcome me with open arms. *What are you thinking, Destiny? Of course, he didn't know who you were.*

"Well? Who let you in?" he barked at me.

"Nobody," I said in a small voice. My lip trembled.

"Why are you here?" His voice softened, but his face looked angry.

"Can I come in and explain?" This wasn't going as planned. *Dammit!*

He closed his eyes and shook his head, holding the door slightly open. "I thought we determined that back in my office."

"But I've discovered how I know you since then." My voice sounded squeaky.

"How? Because I don't know you."

"Yes. You do," I stated firmly, taking a deep breath and releasing it. I replayed this meeting over and over again in my head and never once did it pan out like this.

He sighed and raked his free hand through his hair.

"Please. Can I come in?"

Reluctantly he swung the door open and gestured me in with a swing of his arm.

I stepped through the door and tried to catch my breath. "Wow, your place is enormous. It's beautiful in here." On brave impulse I strode across the living room, instantly making myself comfortable in front of the floor-to-ceiling windows. "You have a gorgeous view of downtown Denver and the distant Rocky Mountains."

"Thank you," he said, without emotion.

I turned and met his narrowed eyes.

Start talking, Destiny. I opened my mouth to speak but closed it.

"Would you like something to drink?" he interrupted, civility taking over and offered me a variety of non-alcoholic options. Damn, he knew I was under the minimum drinking age and didn't look all that pleased about it, either.

"Would you have the ingredients for a cranberry seltzer?" I asked sweetly, knowing full well it was Amber's favorite drink. It was on my first date with him when I ordered that drink and his teasing about it afterward.

He shook his head, doing a double take. "Why *that* particular drink?" he asked.

I eyed him quizzically, playing along. "It's my favorite drink. Why?"

"No reason." He shrugged, fetching a bottle from the fridge.

Surprisingly enough, he did have cranberry juice and seltzer water in the house.

He kept his eyes on me when I sat, facing him, on the over-stuffed, half-moon-shaped sofa, a vintage cream and brown with accent pillows in pastel blues. The surrounding walls were brimming with a white and oatmeal-beige glow, creating a warm, intimate space.

"Thank you," I said when he handed me the ice-cold glass. I took a welcome sip. It was delicious.

He grabbed some bottled water for himself and sat on the other end of the sofa. "I think I've been patient enough, Destiny. Please start explaining yourself."

"Okay," I said, trying to decide where to begin. My skin heated from his fury. I dragged off my sweater and set it on the cushion next to me. "I've discovered something about us...myself."

"Quit stalling and get to the point," he snapped at me.

"Dr. Cahill...Julian—," I paused, using his first name, waiting for his reaction.

His scowl deepened.

Damn! Here goes nothing. "I—I'm Amber."

His eyes darted to me as he leaped up from his seat and stumbled backward. "What fucking game are you trying to play here? Get the hell out of my house!" he yelled.

I flinched at his tone. He frightened me. I set my glass down on top of a coaster on the coffee table. "I can prove it," I pleaded with him. "I'm the reincarnated Amber."

"I don't need this shit. Get out!" His voice reverberated off the walls as the veins in his neck strained against his skin.

I shivered, and my skin crawled as if he'd punched me in the stomach. "I had a sister, Robin."

He stood, crossed his arms and looked at me with a seething stare. "What kind of asshole do you take me for? Those are all details you could've gotten off the fucking Internet." He crossed the room and yanked open his door. "Leave. And don't come back. Understand?"

This was not going as planned. I had to come up with something that was personal between the two of us. I closed my eyes and tried to will something to the forefront of my mind, but nothing came. I stood and shuffled toward the door, and then it struck me.

"The maple tree!" I blurted out. "And the prom!" I exhaled, trying to rapid fire some private moments known only between him and me. "You arranged to move the prom to an earlier date for me."

His face was unreadable. What was he thinking?

"The first time we made love was in your family's camp," I added hastily, overwhelmed with my responsive memory, no doubt solidifying our connection.

His posture suddenly stiffened. Inhaling deeply, he shook his head. "How could you possibly know that stuff?"

"It's because I'm the reincarnated Amber. Think about it, Julian."

"I don't believe in all that reincarnation shit."

This was it. My body went limp as if my arms and legs weren't attached to me. I had nothing else. At that moment I realized how painful my death must have been to him.

Dejected, I snatched my sweater from the sofa and headed for the door, gazing at his bewildered face. "I'm sorry. Thank you for your time, Julian." I dropped my head and walked past him out the door, feeling his raging focus on my back.

"Fuck! Wait." He sounded panicked, sucking in a deep breath.

I turned and stared at him as a tear fell down my cheek.

"What now?" I lashed out, disapproval dripping from my lips.

His eyes bulged while his body shook. "You have the same heart birthmark on your back shoulder blade as her."

Wiping my tears away with the back of my hand, I said, "Yeah. What's your point?"

"Is it really you?"

I stood there, arms hanging limply to my side, looking absolutely defeated. "Yes, Julian. It's really me."

"Are you sure? Because I'm in no mood to be jerked around."

I folded my arms across my chest and puffed out a quick breath. "What could I possibly gain by jerking you around?"

His lips twisted in a lopsided smile. Was he finding this amusing?

"Come here," he said, reaching out for me. "You've got five minutes to convince me. Otherwise…"

Slowly, I shuffled to him. Together, we reentered his home. Julian motioned for me to sit on the sofa while he headed to the kitchen. Opening the fridge, he grabbed two bottled waters for us. After handing one of them to me, he started pacing back and forth.

Feeling parched, I twisted off the cap and took a generous sip. "Thank you," I said, slipping out of my shoes and plopping down on the sofa.

"Time is ticking away, Destiny…Go," he demanded without blinking.

Drat! What should I say? I'd already mentioned everything I could think of before he ousted me from his home only moments ago. My palms began to sweat as my brain cells misaligned.

"Ask me anything you want," I blurted out. *Memory, don't fail me now.*

He started to speak, but huffed out a breath first. I suspected he was trying to think of something capable of tripping me up. "All right. What was Amber's favorite phrase?"

I slammed my eyes shut, trying desperately to remember, but nothing came to mind. "I-I…"

"Just as I thought," Julian butted in, with a scowl. "You have no idea. If you were the reincarnated Amber, you would know the answer to that question right away."

My heart sank. *Jeez, give me a friggin chance.* Why weren't her words coming to me? The adrenaline rush felt in the pit of my stomach made me nauseous. I needed to do this my way. I took a deep breath and extended my hand to him. "Place your hand in mine."

Julian must have seen something in my expression, because he sat on the coffee table opposite me and reluctantly laid his hand on top of mine, visibly shuddering.

"Christ," he muttered, looking like he was shaking off something.

My body instantly calmed when a chaotic throng of memories flooded my head all at once. Every time I tried to align one, it scattered the rest. I was hoping his touch would help me remember, but not like this. I shook my head, and in my moment of clarity, I cleared my throat and began.

"Ahem. I'll do one better." I placed both of our hands against his muscular chest and stared into his eyes. "We were at our favorite spot along the sandy shores of Windsong Lake. It was the last time we made love to each other. That's when I said '*to the stars and back*' to you."

The tips of my fingers felt Julian's heart thump hard against his rib cage. He closed his eyes tight as if remembering something painful.

"My body was frail, only weeks away from my death." I stopped and studied his expression.

Julian opened his eyes, scrutinizing me as if devouring my words when a lone tear slid down his cheek.

"You told me it felt like you had sand in your butt crack."

Choking back tears, Julian burst out into a strangled laugh. At the blink of an eye, he stood yanking my hand with his and wrapped me in his arms. He squeezed me with every ounce of strength he had.

"It's really you," he cried. "As soon as I saw that birthmark on your back, I knew I couldn't let you go."

I felt his rock hard abs, and strong arms enfold me in his embrace. I snaked my arms around him, burying my face in his chest, inhaling his familiar scent. "Yes, for the umpteenth time, it's really me," I responded, my eyes pricked with tears. *Finally!*

We stayed silent and swayed back and forth, sobbing in each other's arms.

"I'm so sorry. I'm so sorry."

"Sorry for what?"

"Being such a prick. For not believing you."

"I told you I'd be back in eighteen years as Destiny, Julian. Besides, this isn't exactly information that is easily believable. I was just unprepared for your anger."

He released me and disappointment flowed through my body at his loss of contact. "Is that what you meant? Those last words have confounded me for as long as I can remember."

"For eighteen years," I said with a soft exhale.

He stopped and examined me from head to toe. "I haven't been able to get you out of my head since you left my office three weeks ago."

"Really?" I couldn't believe he just said that. He'd felt the same as me.

He nodded. "Your resemblance to Amber drove me crazy."

"It's all new to me too. I knew I'd seen you before. I just didn't realize it was eighteen years ago."

Julian chuckled and started pacing around the room. "So, tell me…how did you get up here? I just want to know if I should have a chat with someone downstairs."

When I explained my investigative sleuth skills to him, he laughed. "When did you say that was?"

"Last Monday night. You arrived after dark." I plunked my body back down on the sofa and watched as his face bolted to me. "I thought you'd seen me when you whipped your head around. You'd done the same thing in the hospital. What was that about?"

Abruptly, he stopped pacing. "Shit, I remember that night!" he bellowed. "I'd always feel the hair stand up on the back of my neck whenever I sensed Amber was near."

"Oh, that explains it."

He turned and looked me in the eyes. "She was extremely close that night."

"Yep, I was. Illegal and all."

"How did you know where I lived?"

I stood and padded over to the window overlooking the towering skyscrapers. "I followed you home." I turned and tried to gauge his expression. It was unreadable. "I was at the hospital collecting some paperwork when I saw you leave."

"I don't know if I should be nervous, angry or grateful."

"I'll take the latter, thank you." I giggled.

"Wow. It may have been eighteen years ago, but there are some sounds I will never forget, and Amber's giggle is one of them." He paused, stepped back and examined me from head to toe. "Is it really you?"

"Yes, I'm Amber, Julian. I have her thoughts, her dreams, and her looks. But above everything else and most importantly, I have her soul," I answered him. "She's here through me. I'm her reincarnated spirit. But don't forget, I am Destiny, too."

He frowned. "I haven't forgotten. I'd love to hear about your parents and siblings."

I pouted, dropping my head to my chest as I moved back to the sofa.

He walked over and sat next to me, draping an arm around my shoulder. "What's wrong?"

"I had a brother, Timmy, who was killed in a car accident."

"I'm so sorry. What happened?" he asked, releasing me. He sat back, faced me and tucked one leg under the other.

"He was home on a break from college and took me out for ice cream. We were hit broadside by a guy running a red light, killing Timmy instantly. I suffered with a gash to my head." Unconsciously, I lifted my hand to my scar.

Julian looked as though he was mulling something over in his head. "When was that?"

Wrapping my hand around the water bottle, I pushed the condensation down, letting it cool my fingers, and then looked up at him. "I was ten at the time, so eight years ago."

His eyes popped as he took a swig of water. "You've got to be kidding me. I remember that night so vividly. I was the neurosurgeon on duty. I had one of those 'hair standing up on the back of my neck' moments. I thought Amber was there watching over you. But...," he paused, "I was treating her...you."

I leaned forward and grabbed his arm. "Do you know what this means, Julian? We connected with each other eight years ago."

He smiled. "Now tell me...what things do you remember?"

"Seeing you triggered my first memory. Then I became obsessed into finding out how I knew you and that led to me figuring out who I was. You dismissed me in your office, but that didn't deter me from my compulsion into digging further." I stopped. "What's so funny?"

"Nothing. I'm just glad you came back after the way I treated you. To think I could've lost you twice with my crude attitude."

"Eh...you were like that eighteen years ago." I snorted.

He playfully narrowed his eyes at me. "Was I?"

"Umm...yeah," I continued. "I didn't know right away that you were someone from my past...obviously. Although, this might explain all the déjà vus I've experienced throughout my life. At times I felt like I was in the body of another person. I didn't remember Robin until I looked her up on one of the social media pages. Then I recognized her face immediately." I shifted my sleeping feet, divest of shoes, to a more comfortable position. "You know…there has to be a trigger."

"And I was your trigger…" His voice trailed off.

"Yes, you were."

"How did you finally work it out?"

I went on to explain from the moment I left his office to where we were now, staring at him, trying to gauge his reaction.

He lowered his head to his chest. "Thank God you wore that halter top."

I laughed. "Do you have your yearbook? If so, look at Amber's page."

Julian stood and disappeared into another room re-emerging minutes later with a book in his hand. I recognized the cover. He sat on the coffee table opposite me and flipped through the first few pages before landing on Amber's tribute page. He looked from her to me and back again.

"Ta-da!" I spread my arms wide, showing off the fact that my hair, makeup, and outfit mirrored hers.

"Well played." He laughed with a deep, throaty sound.

"Tell me about your relationship with her."

"She was the only girl I ever loved," he replied softly. He stood, crossed the room, and retrieved a framed photograph from the second shelf of his beautiful mahogany hutch. He returned and handed the picture to me, resuming his seat on the coffee table.

Glancing at the picture, I slapped my hand over my mouth and then removed it. "Bighorn Mountain! I remember this!" I raised my head and focused on his face. "Earlier in the week I had a vision of myself hiking, and then it quickly faded."

His lip trembled. "Yes," he said softly.

I gulped down a deep breath. "I remember. You saved me. You saved me that day."

Moving to the sofa to face me, Julian spoke with a quaking voice. "I wish I could've saved her…but I didn't."

I reached up and grabbed his face between the palms of my hands, fixating my eyes on his. "But you did, and I'm proof, Julian."

The hint of a smile on his lips took my breath away. God, he was as gorgeous today as he was eighteen years ago.

"You're still handsome. I remember your hair was much longer back then, even though you're more distinguished and seriously beautiful now. I like the shorter hair too, and its darkened down a bit."

"You're just as lovely as I remembered."

"Thank you," I said. "The obituary never mentioned a cause of death."

He tapped lightly on my head. "She had a brain tumor."

I closed my eyes, trying to remember that time. When I re-opened them, I said, "A glioblastoma."

"Yes," he said, looking forlorn.

I trembled, needing to change the conversation in a positive direction. "I don't see a ring on your finger. Were you ever married?"

I braced myself for the answer. What if he was divorced with children?

"No."

"Why?" I asked, sagging into the sofa with relief. He was gorgeous. He must have had women falling all over him.

"Because." He paused, looking like he was weighing something over in his head. "I must have been waiting for you."

Wow. The message those words conjured up in my head had me reeling.

"Where do we go from here? I mean, I'm eighteen years younger than you, Julian."

"What are you asking?"

I shrugged my shoulders, searching for words. "Are we just going to be casual acquaintances or are we going to start up where we left off? Surely our age difference doesn't bode well for you."

The thought of losing Julian again for any reason made me cringe. Could I just be friends? No, I didn't think I could. Though, my parents may object to my relationship with an older man. I shuddered to think of that discussion.

Julian gently took my hands in his. "How would you know what is good for me?"

"I don't, but…,"

"Stop. No more. Don't over think things, Destiny. I'd like to see you again if it's okay with you. If the age difference between us is not an issue, then let's give it a try. Obviously, it's what Amber wanted." He smiled.

Letting the breath out I didn't realize I was holding, a huge smile swept across my face. "I'd love to see you again. I can't stay away. It's like there's a greater presence drawing me to you."

"It's Amber; it's you."

"Yes," I said.

Chapter Nineteen

Night had fallen outside the window of Julian's penthouse. The violet haze of Denver's skyline outlined the landscape of the city. My breath hitched at the ebony skies filled with bright twinkling stars. I stood and stared at the beauty when I felt the swaddle of Julian's arms around me.

I turned and looked into his striking blue eyes. "To the stars and back," I said, and felt him shudder.

He leaned his forehead against mine, crushing me against him. "To the stars and back."

"Julian, I think I'd better go. It's getting late, and my parents have no idea where I am. Honestly, they would freak out if they knew I was here."

His face went pale. "Are we going to have a problem with them? I want to see you again, but not without their approval."

"I'll talk to them tomorrow."

After the best day of my life, the thought of leaving left me empty inside. We'd spent hours reminiscing with each other by thumbing through photo albums and then enjoying his housekeeper's fabulous feast.

"I'd like to take you somewhere tomorrow, okay?"

"All right." I sounded breathy.

As Julian walked me to the door, I lost my balance and stumbled over my own feet, doing a face plant into his chest. He caught me before knocking us both to the floor. I grabbed his muscular arms and righted myself, subtly inhaling his intoxicating scent with a swift, quiet breath.

Looking up into his beautiful eyes, I said, "Cripes, I'm sorry. I'm such a klutz these days." As I spoke, my mind teleported back in time again—to a time when I was Amber. Unable to take our eyes off of each other, there was an awkward stillness between us. "Kiss me."

His lips were on mine with desperation. Our tongues tangled together, devouring each other as if making up for the last eighteen years. I reached up and twisted my fingers in his hair and pulled him tighter against me. This was familiar. I remembered the softness of those full lips.

Suddenly, a chill ran up and down my spine and quickly, I broke the embrace, panting heavily. I stepped back and gulped. "I'm so sorry. I don't know what came over me."

"Don't be sorry. It was how I remembered it."

I GLANCED IN THE REARVIEW MIRROR of my shiny new BMW and watched the towering city lights of Denver slowly disappear. The inky blackness of the night behind me was a sharp contrast to the brightness in my soul. I wasn't quite sure but felt as though I'd found my purpose in life. Was Julian meant to be a part of it? It certainly would explain some of the many bizarre occurrences from times past. But I questioned the uncertainty of our future. Would our age difference be an issue? Not for me.

Somehow, I managed to make it all the way home and to my bedroom without detection by my parents. I climbed into my bed with the intent of sleeping, but my wandering thoughts would not allow for any sort of restful Zs.

SUNDAY MORNING CAME SLOWLY. I climbed into the shower and let the warm flow of water cascade over my tired bones. The headache I felt when I woke up had been soothed by the tepid heat of the spray.

I settled on a pair of blue jean shorts and sleeveless, lace top, and then pulled my hair back into a messy ponytail.

The moment of truth with my parents was at the forefront of my mind as I made my way downstairs for breakfast. A hint of cinnamon filled the air when I walked in the kitchen. My mom stood at the stove stirring something that resembled oatmeal.

I leaned against the counter trying to judge her mood, tapping my fingernails on the smooth surface. "Morning, Mom."

She turned to me and placed a spoon and napkin on the island. "Good morning, Destiny. You were out late."

Drat! I thought I'd made it home unnoticed. Damn her hearing capabilities, I grumbled to myself.

"How was your date?"

And so it began. How much did I reveal? I knew she wouldn't approve of Julian's and my age difference. Although, it wouldn't be the first time I'd tried to withhold pertinent information from her.

I decided to plunge ahead anyway. "How much do you know about reincarnation?"

She placed a bowl of hot cereal in front of me as I moved to sit on the bar stool. "I've never had reason to look into it, why do you ask?" She held my gaze for a moment before her eyes went wide with shock. "Heavens, Destiny, does this boy think he's reincarnated?"

Her response spoke volumes. On the other hand, I had to let her know my vision. After all, this had to be brought out into the open. "No, Mom. I—I think I am."

Her shocked expression switched to a look of horror. "Oh my God, Destiny, what kind of garbage is that boy feeding you? Who is he?" She exhaled in frustration and took a seat beside me.

She was exasperating. "See, you're always judgmental, Mom. I can't talk before you jump to conclusions. Without interrupting, let me explain."

Crossing her arms in front of her, resting them on the island, she told me to go on. The sound of her toe tapping on the hardwood floor put me on edge.

I blew on my spoon, cooling down my oatmeal before placing it in my mouth. I peeked through my eyelashes, trying to interpret her mood. She gave me an evil eye. *Damn.* I looked for the strength to quiet the emotional turmoil within me. "I don't know where to begin. I'm afraid of your reaction."

As I opened my mouth to explain, my dad stepped into the kitchen, walked to the coffee pot and poured himself a cup.

"Good morning, Daddy." I side-stepped the threatening showdown with my mom, letting out the deep breath I was holding.

Even though he had me by five inches, I still had my dad's height. At six foot two and 250 pounds, he was a husky, but gentle man. He sported light brown hair with a touch of gray around the edges and hazel eyes giving him a prominently bold look. He wore a thick mustache and goatee. I always thought he was a very handsome man. And to not disappoint, he wore his signature, tattered jeans and old T-shirt when he sat down beside me.

"Morning, pumpkin. Where were you last night?"

"I went out with a guy I met."

"Did you have a good time?"

"Yes, I had a great time."

Mom chimed in, "Marcus, she thinks she's reincarnated."

My dad's eyes protruded from their sockets as he looked at me. "Whatever makes you think that, pumpkin?"

As I opened my mouth, Mom interrupted again, "It's that boy she saw last night."

"Let her talk, Cynthia."

"Thank you, Daddy."

I was stressed, not to mention the extent of sweat pouring from my forehead.

"Start talking, Destiny," Mom demanded.

I took a deep breath and exhaled. "Okay." I glanced at her. "Do you remember how much I loved to play dress up as a little girl?"

"Yes. That has nothing to do with reincarnation."

"Please, let me talk, Mom, or I'll stop."

"Go on, pumpkin," my dad said. He grabbed the morning newspaper and laid it out on the countertop but kept his attention on me.

"Do you remember whose name I insisted you call me?"

"Of course. I remember your affinity for the name Amber," Mom said.

"Exactly!" I exclaimed, remembering years back with my best

friend, Eileen and me as six-year-olds playing dress-up with my mom's old clothes. We argued over what our names would be. She always scowled every time I wanted to use the name Amber. She'd tell me I was over-using the name in a way a six-year-old could. She insisted I pick something else. I told her Amber was my name and who I was.

God, I'd even known way back then.

"Exactly what, Destiny? All little girls have a fascination with role-playing by calling themselves different names."

"The guy I met today had a girlfriend whose funeral was on the same day I was born. Her name was Amber. And there was something about him that was familiar to me."

My mom shot me a venomous look. "Oh my God, Destiny, how old is this man?" The strained look on her face was apparent, and her math skills were still top-notch.

I huffed out a quick breath. "I knew you'd be irrational."

My dad gave me one of those looks that said: *Don't cross me.* "How old, Destiny?" His tone was gruff.

"Thirty-five," I blurted out.

My mom stood and placed her hands on the countertop. Her stare at me was so heated, it could've boiled water. "Where did you meet this man?" Her voice had escalated to new heights.

"His home," I squeaked.

Her hand went to her mouth. "Oh my Lord, what are you doing in the home of a thirty-five-year-old man? He's twice your age, Destiny. What the hell are you thinking?"

"Obviously this conversation is over!" I screamed. "I'm seeing him again today."

"Over my dead body!" she screeched. "He thinks you're his reincarnated dead girlfriend? Are you listening to yourself? Who is this man?"

"He's a neurosurgeon at Denver Medical."

"Well, good, because it looks like you need your head examined."

I started bawling. "You do this all the time, Mom."

"He's obviously preying on young females, Destiny," she stammered, shaking her head in disbelief.

"Your mom is right, Destiny. It sounds as though this man is taking advantage of you. You need to think this through."

"Oh my God!" My mom's mouth dropped open. "Is he married…with children?"

"No!"

"Are you sure?" she snapped.

I rolled my eyes at her. "Positive," I growled. "Neither one of you let me finish, but now there's no point."

I turned and stampeded out of the kitchen to avoid any further misunderstanding. I crossed the living room and darted upstairs to my bedroom, kicked the door closed, and threw myself onto my bed, sobbing loudly into my pillow. It was worse than I thought. In time, they would eventually understand. Right? They had to.

MY THROAT FELT RAW from crying when I woke to the familiar chirp of my cell phone.

Fishing my phone from my pocket, I glanced at the text on the screen.

Julian: Good afternoon, Destiny.

What should I say? I wanted to see him more than anything. If I was going to have any kind of relationship with him, I needed my parents' approval. He made that clear. That was going to have to wait. I'd never lied to my parents before to this degree, why was I willing to start now? *Because he's the love of your past life, that's why,* I screamed at myself in my head.

Me: Hi, Julian. Where would you like to meet?

Julian: I can pick you up.

Me: I'd better meet you, your place, okay?

Julian: Okay, let's say five.

Me: See you then.

A knock on my door interrupted my wandering thoughts, making me jump. "It's me, honey," Mom said through the closed door.

"Come in!" I yelled, looking at the clock. It was a quarter past noon, and my stomach was rumbling, realizing I'd never eaten breakfast. *That was your own fault for storming out of the kitchen earlier.* I scolded myself.

"Can we talk?" she asked, wandering in. She sat on my bed and caressed the hair away from my face.

"That's what I was trying to do earlier."

"I'm sorry, honey. I realize that. We didn't give you an opportunity to explain yourself, so I'm here to listen to what you have to say."

Somehow, I knew anything I said would be futile and would surely re-hash the same argument. "I'd rather show you."

"Okay, show me then."

"Are you up for a drive?"

She flinched and leaned back. "I'm not going to that man's home if that's what you're hinting at."

"No, of course not. I'd just like to take you somewhere," I told her. I needed to see the house that plagued my dreams. I wasn't sure I'd find it, but at least knew the name of the town, hopefully triggering something in my memory as I got closer.

"Where?" Mom snorted.

"Castle Pines."

"What's in Castle Pines?"

"You'll see."

"Okay, but don't think this will change my mind about all of this nonsense."

I sighed. "Fair enough."

Maybe this would put to rest any doubts I had as well as whatever were hers. I had to go to Castle Pines and, of course, see for myself. In any event, she was receptive to me now. Taking advantage of this rare situation was important to me.

Meeting Julian at five tonight, I figured I had time for a short drive. Plus, I had to find a convincing way of making my parents believe me.

MOM AND I HEADED SOUTH on Route 470 toward Castle Pines in my red BMW. As the valedictorian of my high school class, my parents bought me a car after my graduation. Because of my brother's death, my parents felt a deep-seated need to keep me safe. That meant having my own car. They repeated time and again how I was not to ride with anyone else. I understood their fear and promised to mollify them. It was the least I could do.

We exited the highway and continued south onto Castle Pines Parkway. My heart pounded out of my chest. I immediately recognized my surroundings. I knew I was close but couldn't grasp this feeling. My breathing accelerated while my palms perspired.

"What's wrong, honey?"

"I don't know, Mom. This all looks familiar to me."

"You've obviously been here before, Destiny."

"I know…in my former life."

She gave me a sharp look. "Stop that nonsense."

I ignored her skepticism as a harsh shiver spread down my spine. A familiar street sign stared me in the face. Aspen Court. I slowed down. The rhythmic ticking of my turn signal clacked loudly in my ears with the same intensity as my heartbeat. My breathing grew heavy and intense. It was like I had no power over my hands as they whipped the steering wheel from my grip and made a detour into this residential area. Suddenly, my foot slammed on the brake and jerked us forward with exaggerated force.

"Destiny!" Mom screeched. "Be careful."

"Oh my God, that's it!" I yelped.

"That's what?" she asked, smoothing her hair back into place.

"The house I lived in years ago, the one I see in my dreams. I remember now. Right there." I sounded out of breath as I pointed to a red brick and white vinyl-sided Colonial home on my left. "It looks exactly as I remember."

"That's absurd, Destiny."

"Why do you do that, Mom?"

"Because you're talking gibberish." She scowled.

As the car idled, I stared at the house, wondering how I could convince her of my former life. "The maple tree," I blurted out loud.

"What about it?"

"Our initials are carved into the trunk of that tree along with a heart." I closed my eyes and shook at the memory of taking my last breath in that spot. Julian held me in his arms as I lifted my hand to touch the heart one last time.

The tree stood tall and proud with branches spread wide as if beckoning me to come closer.

Noticing my emboldened look, my mom's expression mirrored mine. Was she questioning her own doubt? "What were the names of the people you *lived* with?" she asked, rolling her eyes.

I scowled at her. "Lyle and Elizabeth Scott," I said firmly, acknowledging her interrogation. "I had a sister, Robin, and my name was Amber."

"That's preposterous."

I ignored her and just stared at the house I lived in all those years ago. I couldn't wrap my head around it. There was no doubt I was the reincarnated Amber.

Before I realized what she was doing, my mom opened the door and hopped out of the car.

My face filled with horror. "What are you doing, Mom?"

"I'm going to put an end to this and find out who lives here."

"No, no, no, you can't just go up to a stranger's house. What are you thinking? And what if they've moved?"

Without another word, she slammed the door shut and headed up the driveway toward the house. I slid down in the driver's seat, barely able to see over the steering wheel. I gave myself just enough of a view to watch her ring the doorbell.

My stomach churned. I felt nauseous. This could never end well.

I peeked up just in time to see a middle-aged woman open the door. That's when I saw her. It was Elizabeth, my mother from my past life as Amber. Oh my God. I swallowed past the lump in my throat. I wanted to jump out of the car and run into her arms and tell her I was here.

I silenced the engine and stared at Elizabeth and my mom chatting as if they were long, lost friends. It drove me crazy that I couldn't make out their conversation. My mom's arms flailed around animatedly, like a mime stuck in a box. What could she possibly be saying? Elizabeth was smiling. I hoped this put to rest any doubts she had because this was so typical of her.

Before long, she made her way back to the car and climbed in. Her face was unreadable.

"Well, I know what you're going to say because I recognized her. That was Elizabeth, right?" I said, standing my ground.

"Yes, it was, but I'm not entirely convinced. You're going to have to give me more proof than that."

I let out a deep sigh. "What do you want me to say?"

"First of all, why didn't you ever mention this to me before?"

"The realization of it all hadn't hit me until I did a little research on the guy I saw yesterday. He's the doctor I mentioned to you a few weeks ago who guided the tour at the hospital."

Her eyes widened. "That's who you met yesterday?"

I nodded and turned, raising an eyebrow. "So, what did you say to her?"

She scowled. "You don't have to worry. I played it cool. I introduced myself, pretending I was looking for a Belinda Scott. She said, no, she was Elizabeth Scott and didn't know any Belinda."

"Very smooth, Mom." The hairs suddenly stood up on the back of my neck when I glanced at the house to the right. "Oh my God!"

"What is it now?"

"That's his house!" I exclaimed.

She turned and followed my line of sight. "Whose house?"

"The doctor. And don't you dare go up to his house now. You've already freaked me out enough for one day."

"What is his name?"

I hesitated a long minute. Did I want to refresh her memory? I considered what she'd do with this information.

"Well...," she prompted.

"Dr. Julian Cahill," I finally muttered. "We lived next door to each other. We were teenage lovers."

Pursing her lips at me, she shook her head in disbelief. "Okay," she said in her condescending way. "Tell me what you know. I'm all ears." She wiggled herself into a more comfortable position in the front seat of the car.

I turned to face her and cleared my throat. "Where do you want me to begin?"

"Start with your earliest memory."

"My memories are very blotchy, although I remember moving to this house from somewhere else. I didn't grow up here but can't remember from where I did." I silently told myself I would ask Julian. "I moved here as a teenager, and we started dating shortly after."

"Okay, how did you die?"

I looked at her oddly. "What a weird question to ask some who is very much alive."

"Well, do you know?" she asked as if failing to see the humor in my response.

I closed my eyes, replaying the events of that awful memory. "I had brain cancer. I—I was seventeen."

Mom audibly inhaled. "So young."

"Yes, I didn't live here for long before I died."

"What else do you remember?" My mom sounded intrigued now or maybe she was just placating me. I couldn't tell which.

I stared at the Cahill house when another memory surfaced in my head. "I remember his parents. Logan and Lisa were their names. I remember people and places more than experiences, although specific events are usually triggered by a touch or vision." *Yes, the touch of a sexy man living in Denver.*

"I have to admit, this is fascinating, Destiny."

"I know, Mom, that's why I have to see him again, please."

"I understand your need to see him. However, Destiny, you are not dating a thirty-five-year-old man."

"I didn't say I was going to date him." I wasn't sure why I lied, but I'd just told a whopper. "But I need to see him at least once more. Please, Mom."

She groaned, pinning her eyes on me. "Fine, see him and tell him goodbye." She shook her head. "But, I want to meet him first. I don't feel comfortable about this at all."

She wanted to meet him? How was I going to negotiate this? What could be the worst-case scenario? I looked her in the eye and spoke.

"Fine, but don't you dare say anything mean to him. Okay?"

"Okay. I just want to know who my daughter is going out with. Is that so wrong?"

"I guess not. I love you, Mommy."

"Love you too. More than you realize, honey."

The implication my mom alluded to was abundantly clear. "I'm so sorry about Timmy. I wish I knew him better before he died."

Her lips trembled. "Me too, honey."

"Tell me about him." I swallowed past the lump in my throat. I knew very little about my brother.

"He was stubborn…just like you." She smiled. "He also had a dry sense of humor that always made us laugh."

"I think I remember him being tall. Was he?"

"Yes, as a matter of fact, he was taller than your dad."

"Did he have a girlfriend?"

"No, not at the time of his death. He never had time for a girlfriend, as his interests were in track and field. At one time he held the high school record for the mile. He won a track scholarship to college and had a promising future."

"Really? You never told me that."

"We removed all his trophies and packed them away after his death. I can show you if you'd like?"

"I'd love that." A part of my brother I never knew about. "I wish he was still alive."

Her eyes misted. "So do I, honey…so do I."

Leaving the town of Castle Pines behind us, we made our way home. It was three in the afternoon, and I had to get ready for my date with Julian.

I shot him a text.

Me: Pick me up at my house. My parents want to meet you. They aren't happy. Be prepared.

Julian: Okay. No problem. Address, please.

No problem? Did he know my parents? I texted him my address, then showered and dressed in cream-colored capris, a simple, black sweater, and white ballet flats. I blew my hair out in soft curls that flowed down my back. After applying a bit of mascara and strawberry-flavored lip gloss, I felt pretty. My curves were in all the right places.

As soon as I entered the foyer at the base of the stairs, my parents greeted me with what? Apprehension?

Mom looked as if she was struggling with her emotions. "You look beautiful, Destiny."

"Thank you."

My dad's eyes never left mine. "Your mom filled me in on your adventure today."

"I'm still your daughter, Daddy. That will never change. Please don't over think this."

"I'm more worried about you, sweetheart," he said, checking the time on his watch.

"As I told Mom, I'll be fine. Really."

"Do you have your phone?" she asked.

"Yes."

Before my parents decided to change their minds, I collected my purse at the same time the doorbell rang. Mom beat me to the door and opened it. I was conscious of the ever-present butterflies in my belly, waiting for my mom to slip up and declare her disapproval of him. Nervous jitters gripped my body. *Take a deep breath, Destiny.*

"Hello, Mrs. Bradshaw. I'm Julian Cahill. Nice to meet you," he said, extending his hand.

My mom took it. "Come in, Julian. I'm Cynthia, Destiny mother."

I greeted him as he stepped through the door. "Hi, again."

His breath hitched when he looked at me. "You look beautiful."

"Thank you." I blushed, overwhelmed with an urge to kiss him when my dad approached us. "Julian, you met my mother. This is my father, Marcus." I stepped aside to let the men shake hands.

"My pleasure, Mr. Bradshaw."

"Julian," my dad replied politely, lowering his brows.

I stood there, squirming uncomfortably, twisting the ring on my pinky finger when my mom spoke up.

"Where are you two going?" she asked.

"I thought I'd take Destiny out to eat," Julian said, radiating a steady confidence, as he innocently grazed his hand down my back and then continued, "I understand your concern, Mr. and Mrs. Bradshaw, but I only hold the utmost respect for your daughter."

"We hope so."

I glanced at him, wide-eyed. "Shall we go?" I asked, trying to diffuse the inane pleasantries.

My mom pursed her lips at me. "Have a nice time," she said.

I gave both parents a quick kiss and headed out the door to Julian's car. I took several deep breaths to calm myself.

"Where are you taking me?"

He smiled, took my hand and escorted me to his car. "It's a surprise."

"Would you like me to drive?" I asked politely.

"No, Destiny, I'm driving. Do you have your own car?"

I pointed to the third bay of the garage.

There was a hint of a smile on his face. "Ah, a BMW 328i. Nice car. Red, no less. It's yours?"

"All mine, ain't she purdy?"

"Yep, that's quite a car for an eighteen-year-old."

"My parents bought it for me for my high school graduation. I was the valedictorian of my class."

Julian froze and mumbled something under his breath. I couldn't make it out, but I thought I heard him say, *I knew you would be.*

"What did you say?"

He shook his head. "So you *were* valedictorian? I was valedictorian of my class as well, but if Amber hadn't died, I'm certain she would have held that position, instead of me."

"Oh, I don't know about that. You were tough to outdo—shit." I grimaced, confused by my words.

We both laughed as Julian opened the door to his sporty little black car.

"Which model is this?" I asked sweetly. I knew it was expensive.

"It's a Mercedes CL65 AMG Coupe. Do you like it?"

"I love it, Julian. It's beautiful. So, apparently you know your...," I paused and snorted through my nose.

"Did you remember something, Destiny?" Julian asked. He seemed to love my moments of pure epiphany.

"Your Camaro. You had a red Camaro, right?" I was ecstatic when my memory connected with my brain.

"Yes, and I still own it. I store it in my parents' garage."

"I remember you teaching me how to drive a stick shift."

He let out a bellowing laugh. "Yes, and I remember cringing, too."

"This is starting to freak me out. I'm remembering a lot about Amber's life, especially when I'm with you. You're definitely a trigger."

"I'm quite enjoying it. I hope you remember the spot I'm taking you to."

With his hand at my lower back, I climbed into his obscenely expensive car and watched him walk around and clamber into the driver's seat. My eyes roamed his flawless, muscular frame. He wore some pleated gray shorts and a white polo shirt, looking as if he hadn't aged a day in the last eighteen years. He'd definitely found the fountain of youth.

He turned the key and the engine roared to life. After backing out of the driveway, I glanced back and caught my parents peeking through the window as we disappeared from view.

"So, what did you do today?" he asked, heading east along the Denver Boulder Turnpike.

"Um, you wouldn't believe me if I told you." I shifted restlessly in the plush leather upholstery. The seat wasn't uncomfortable...I was.

He turned his head to look at me. "Really?"

"Yes."

"Tell me, Destiny," he said, deliberately raising his eyebrows.

"Well, I drove to Castle Pines to show my mom the house. It was exactly as I'd visualized in my dreams."

Julian jerked his head back, and his eyes went wide. "You remembered the house?"

"Yes. I told you I visualize places, but I'm never sure from where. I knew I'd lived in Castle Pines, so I drove there, hoping I'd recognize it. I did. When I saw the street sign for Aspen Court, I knew where I was."

"So, what did you think?"

"Well, my mom didn't believe me, so she rang the Scott's doorbell and waited for Elizabeth to answer, then made up some cockamamie story about how she was looking for a Belinda Scott." I rolled my eyes. "I recognized her, Julian."

His posture suddenly stiffened when his eyes shot to me. "Did she see you?"

"No, I couldn't do that to her. I stayed in the car."

"Good," he said, puffing out a shallow breath. "I'm not sure how she'd react to you showing up at her door."

We both laughed.

He placed his hand on my thigh. The tiny bit of contact shot tingles through me.

"What else did you remember?"

"My first vision was drawn to the maple tree and our initials."

Julian's head darted around. "And I didn't believe you." He grinned. "Ironic you mention that. I checked them a few weeks ago. They're still there."

My voice caught in my throat. "I remember taking my last breath in front of that tree."

"Yes. Hardest day of my life."

"I'm sorry, Julian."

"Don't apologize. Let's start over again. What do you say to that?"

"I'd love that." *But my parents won't.*

"So, I'm assuming you talked to your parents?"

Was he reading my thoughts? "Yeah. Kind of."

I saw worry etched in the lines of his beautiful face. "What are you saying?"

"They think I'm here to tell you goodbye, but I can't. It was the only way I could convince them to let me see you today."

His neck stiffened, as he drew his eyebrows together. "I'm thirty-five years old, Destiny. I'm not going to tiptoe around, trying to hide a relationship with you. You told me you were going to handle it. I assumed you did. Look, if it helps, I could talk to them."

I flinched. "I will straighten it out with them," I told him. My head dropped to my chest with worry at the thought of that conversation.

"Please do. How's school going?"

"Fantastic. I love it," I exclaimed, happy to talk about something else.

"Are you majoring in neurology?"

"Not exactly. I only did the tour to gather as much information as I could. I read through the brochure you gave us, but seeing the workload and years of education, I changed my mind back to my original major…astrophysics," I said, trying to gauge his reaction.

"The stars."

"Yep. I never understood my fascination with the stars until this past week when I was sitting in my astronomy class. Then it dawned on me."

He cocked his head to the side. "I gaze at them all the time."

"That's when our favorite phrase came to me."

"To the stars and back," we said in unison. I giggled.

Julian turned down an aspen-lined street toward a lake with a sign that read: Windsong Lake. Moments later we were pulling into a sparsely filled parking lot where I counted six other cars.

"We're here," he said, bending over and giving me a chaste kiss on the lips.

I looked around. "I think I remember." I felt a soothing warmth in my soul as if sensing a greater power. "Are we getting out of the car?"

"Of course."

He popped the trunk with the pull of a hidden lever on his door and scrambled out of the car. Rounding the rear, he opened my door, and helped me out. After retrieving a blanket and cooler from the trunk, he linked our fingers together—igniting the electricity between us—and headed toward the lake.

An intense awareness encircled my body. "Over there, Julian." I gasped, feeling a familiarity of the surrounding landscape. "Over there is where we shared our first kiss." I pointed to a private area along the rocky shoreline as another out-of-body experience took me by surprise.

"Yes." He donned a gargantuan smile on his face, radiating pure accomplishment.

Moments later, we made our way to our special place. Releasing my hand, he spread the blanket on the sun-warmed sand and gestured for me to sit. We sat side by side and faced the motionless water of the glassy lake. His close proximity sent shivers through my body.

I gazed at the water, remembering times when we'd watch the sun set over the horizon to a beautiful glow of reds and oranges in the darkening sky. It was the most magnificent sight I'd ever seen.

"You're a beautiful sight, Destiny. What are you thinking about?"

"Thank you," I whispered with a shaky, soft voice. "I remember when we used to come here and just sit."

"I never stopped."

A phone rang. Startled, I jumped. In unison, we both hunted for our phones and laughed. We had the same ring tone. I instantly relaxed, happy it wasn't mine. Julian answered his.

"Dr. Cahill...yes...when...okay....give him ten ccs of CPT-11 and Cyclosporine by IV...no, I switched him from Tegretol to Phenobarbital because his white count dropped...yes, call if there are any changes."

Wow, the life of a doctor.

He hung up. "Sorry, hospital."

"You're a neurosurgeon."

"Yes, what's your point, Destiny?"

"I remember making you promise me you'd attain your dream of becoming a doctor—and you did."

"I did it for her. Every goddamn bit of it." His breath hitched.

I arched an eyebrow at him. "Failure was never an option for you."

"It still isn't."

At once, I lunged at him. I knocked him to his back and my mouth was on his with deep passionate kisses. He moaned and kissed me back. Our tongues strained across our lips. With speed and agility, he flipped me to my back without breaking contact and continued clenching his mouth around mine.

My libido surfaced and was beckoning me with titillating pleasure. A rush of adrenaline sped through my body. I felt his excitement against my belly. I wanted him now. But not here... no... not here in the wide open wilderness. Although I remembered the last time I ever made love to Julian was in this spot. But that was my past life. I wasn't about to squander away my dignity at this moment.

"Your lips are soft," he whispered against my mouth.

I fisted my hands in his now shorter hair and pulled him tighter to me. We held each other close, our legs tangled together. I remembered this.

"Oh, Julian," I panted.

He broke our locked lips apart and sighed heavily.

"What are you doing to me, Destiny? Christ, you look like Amber, you kiss like Amber, you walk like Amber, you smile like Amber ..." He trailed off and for a moment looked lost in thought.

"I know. I know." I said as tears pricked my eyes.

As the words spilled from my lips, he was on me again with passion, devouring my mouth with his. He released me, sat up, and fixed his eyes on me. What was he thinking? A tear tumbled down his cheek. I reached up and brushed it away with my index finger as he clutched my hand and gently kissed my knuckles.

"What's the matter?" I asked.

"I'm just thinking how I'm the luckiest man in the world right now. How many people get a second chance with the reincarnated love of their life?"

He took my breath away. "I'm the lucky one, Julian."

He released my hand and tucked a loose strand of hair behind my ear. "I brought food. Would you like some?"

"Yes."

Julian grabbed the cooler and opened it to reveal an assortment of berries in a clear plastic container. Freshly washed strawberries, raspberries, and blueberries, all with stems removed, were skillfully packed. At the bottom of the cooler was a can of whipped topping. Oh the visuals my mind conjured up with that. Julian regarded me with a sly smile. I imagined Carolyn must have put this assortment together.

"Want some?"

"Yes, please." I giggled.

With agile fingers, Julian plucked a strawberry from the plastic tub and topped it with a smidgen of whipped cream. He slowly lifted it to my lips. As I opened my mouth for his tasty treat, he swiped it across my nose, leaving a trail of whipped cream in its path, and popped it into his.

"Hey," I protested.

"Mmm, just what the doctor ordered."

I smiled.

He leaned in and licked the smattered sweet cream from my nose and gave me a chaste kiss.

After grabbing another strawberry from the container, he dipped the tip in the whipped cream, and fed it to me, letting me taste its sweetness. "You have to be quick around here, Destiny."

"You're so adorable."

"I know. I've had twice as long a life to acclimate myself with this look."

I giggled. He hadn't lost his sense of humor. "So, how many others have you brought to this spot?"

He gazed at me as if I'd lost my mind. "None. Why would I do that? This was *our* spot."

Holy jeez. He took my breath away.

Julian cocked his head slightly to the side, regarding me with a bewildered glance. "Listen, I haven't forgotten what you said about your identity as Destiny. I know I tend to come across as thrilled when you remember something from your life as Amber, and I always will, but that doesn't mean I don't want you to have your own uniqueness and personality. I can't wait to create new memories with you." He cupped my cheek in his hand. "You are your own person and I understand that."

I stared into his beautiful blue eyes, dumbfounded by his words…speechless. The thought he'd care so much as to make sure I had my own identity made me choke up. Julian meant the world to me. "Thank you. This is all new to both of us and I'm enjoying it as much as you. One day I'm sure we'll have our own memories. Until then, let's relive a few of the old ones."

From my purse, I retrieved my cell phone, swiped it awake, and pressed the camera app. I needed to capture this moment forever. With a push of a few buttons, I framed us in the phone's viewfinder. "Hey, Julian, look up, babe." He raised his head and leaned it against mine. Our mouths locked wide with gigantic smiles as I pressed the shutter button. "There, our first selfie together."

It was a perfect afternoon, but darkness was approaching as the sun made its final appearance before slipping beneath the horizon.

"I'm not sure if you remember this, but the last time I had sex with Amber was in this exact spot, shortly before she died."

"I did remember," I frowned, feeling the pain of that day. "How could I forget?"

Julian leaned over and cupped my face in his hands and gave me the sweetest of kisses, silently communicating his approval. He then put the lid on the fruit container and placed it in the cooler with the can of whipped topping. "Shall we go?"

As the best day of my life came to a close, I wondered when I'd see him again. "Thank you for a perfect day. This was the best time."

"I hope it's not over, yet. Would you like to go back to my place?"

"Sure, I'd love to." I felt thrilled to my core. For now, life was perfect. Perfect because I was back in Julian's life, again.

Chapter Twenty

Julian's smoky, seductive voice pulled me out of my dreamlike fixation on the city streets below. "Would you like something to eat?"

I gave him a sideways smile. "Well, since you told my parents you were going to feed me, I guess I better not go home hungry."

"Shameless, Miss Bradshaw," he said, his face alight with humor.

"So, what do you have?" I asked as I stood at the wall of windows in his home, transfixed on the purple glow emanating from the tops of the Rocky Mountains. "I could stare at this view all day."

His arms came from behind me, wrapping them around my waist as he breathed in my hair. "You have an intoxicating scent, Destiny."

I leaned my head back against his shoulder. He always said the right thing at the right time. "I've never seen anything so breathtaking before."

"It's the reason I chose this place. I love watching you enjoy it."

I turned around to face him. Slowly and methodically, I lifted my arms and locked my fingers together around the nape of his neck. He lowered his lips to mine and softly kissed me. I deepened the kiss with my tongue, pulling him into me. He mirrored my impassioned gesture.

He quickly released me with a concerned stare. "Will I see you again?"

"Of course, Julian, why would you ask me that?"

"Just a feeling."

"About my parents' assumption that I was here to say goodbye?" I asked.

"Possibly." His jaw tightened, "Christ, Destiny, I don't want to be led on, only to have my heart ripped to shreds, again."

"Julian, believe me, I feel the same way about you."

With worry etched on his face, he asked, "Tell me then, how are you going to handle this with your parents?"

I lost my voice and shrugged. I wasn't sure how I was going to broach the subject with them. "I don't know, but I'll handle it. Please don't worry."

He lowered his head and visibly trembled. "I don't want to lose you. Amber has given me a second chance, and I can't endure that pain, again."

"I know. I saw your pain." I placed my hands on each side of his face and planted a quick kiss on his lips. "Let's enjoy what we have left of the evening."

He held me close and kissed me back. He was right, though. He didn't deserve to be put through all that pain again. How was I going to approach our relationship with my parents? I needed to find a way to show them how much he meant to me. I told myself I'd deal with that issue later.

"Now, I'm starving, and it smells heavenly in here. What are we eating?"

He exhaled heavily and loosened his grip on me, running his fingers up and down my arms, then strolled to the kitchen. He removed a pot from the oven and placed it on the countertop. "Carolyn's note on the outside of the dish says *Red Curry Seafood Bolognese*. Sound good?"

"Sounds mouth-wateringly delicious."

I couldn't help but stare at Julian sauntering around his kitchen. Every muscle in his body flexed and bulged with every movement he made. "You still work out, don't you?"

"Every fucking day, Dest." He eyed me with a sly grin, placing a loaf of garlic bread in the oven.

I shuffled over to the island and sat on one of the bar stools. "This is such a dream kitchen. My mom would love it."

"And you don't?"

"I didn't say that. It's just that my parents' house is too big for my tastes. I feel more comfortable in small, intimate spaces." But it was abundantly clear that Julian loved extravagance.

He pulled some silverware and napkins from a drawer and set them in front of me. "I put in long hours at work. I don't have time to cook. That's why I hired Carolyn."

I winked. "Duly noted."

I nearly fainted when he smiled back at me.

Handing me a dinner plate, he asked what I'd like to drink.

"Sparkling water, please, if you have it."

He grinned. "No cranberry seltzer?"

I shook my head. "Not with seafood, babe."

From the fridge, Julian grabbed a bottled water for me and a beer for himself.

On the floor of his spacious living room, we sat cross-legged at the coffee table and plunged into Carolyn's seafood feast with gusto. He grabbed his clicker, pushed a button, and the television sprang to life in the large mahogany hutch. Hell, the whole room came alive with the sound cocooning my body. My eyes nearly popped out of my head at the sheer size of the TV screen. Proudly, he went on to describe his eighty-inch, 5.1 surround sound, plasma TV, with a verbosity equal to that of men's description of their cars. *Honestly.* I wasn't a huge television watcher but couldn't help being interested in his enthusiasm of it.

Flipping through the channels, he landed on a *Big Bang Theory* episode. "My favorite show."

"Mine too. Another coincidence," I said.

With the murmur of the TV in the background, Julian chatted about events from my former life, filling in the blanks for me when my memory fell short.

"Do you know where I lived during my early childhood?"

"Upstate New York," he said.

My eyes went wide. "That's right. I kept picturing a lot of colorful maple trees and a red brick house."

"Yep. Halfmoon, New York."

From time to time, Julian looked distant and confused. What were his thoughts? How long would he want to see an eighteen-year-old girl? I mean, I was half his age. People would surely not approve. But, he assured me it didn't bother him. Was being his reincarnated dead girlfriend enough? I wouldn't put it past my parents to lock me in my bedroom and throw away the key.

Finally, he turned to me, hesitating before he spoke. "Would you attend a hospital function with me next Saturday night?"

Julian needed a reassurance that we would be okay. "I'd love to. What's the occasion?" I answered quickly.

"Black-tie awards banquet. I'd love it if you could come with me. It's at eight in the evening."

"Okay. I'd love to." I wondered if this was the awards ceremony I'd read about on the Internet. "I'll be at school."

"Good, I'll pick you up there."

My eyes scanned the vastness of his home. It must have cost a fortune. "Your place is beautifully decorated. Did you do this yourself?" Off the main living room was an office-study with floor-to-ceiling windows and wall-to-wall bookshelves—I suspect housing every medical journal known to man.

"Mostly by myself, but I enlisted the help of my mom. Do you like it?"

"It's comfy. If medicine doesn't work out for you, there's always interior decorating." I laughed and shifted myself around to face him, massaging my aching thighs. "Can we move to the sofa? My legs are falling asleep?"

He sprang to his feet, grabbed my hands, and tugged me up with such force, I stumbled, doing a face plant into his chest. I rolled my eyes at his paltry intent, though it gave me an opportunity to breathe him in. His cologne mixed with his musky scent was intensely arousing.

Without hesitation, his mouth was on me, kissing me softly. Our tongues intertwined together, hot and bothered with gentle strokes. I moaned. He pressed his body against mine, and I felt his excitement against my belly. My heart started pounding. I needed to satisfy the ache between my legs.

"Make love to me, Julian, right now. Please."

His eyes widened with desire. With swift, deliberate movements, he cradled me in his arms and carried me to his bedroom. Holding me with one arm, he used the other to roll the comforter and blankets to the floor. After planting a soft kiss on my lips, he placed me on his king-sized bed. He stood, gazing down at me as the worry appeared to drain away from his face.

"Nothing would make me happier, Destiny."

He dimmed the lights of the room. The muted glow of nightfall cast soft shadows around us.

I shuffled up the bed, laying my head on the plush pillows and motioned for him to join me. The bed shifted as he crawled up my body and positioned himself between my legs. His eyes met mine as he slid the palms of his hands up my legs with a soft caress.

"That feels good." I nearly combusted at the gentle brush of his fingertips, scarcely grazing me, igniting me, recognizing the familiarity of his touch.

"Your skin is very soft." His voice was almost a whisper.

My soul drew me to him despite the fact that we'd reconnected the day before. I barely knew him in the present, but my past life overflowed with flooded memories. I wanted this. I couldn't take another minute of his contact without him inside me. "I want you now, Julian. Please."

"I want to take this slow, Destiny."

I sat up, meeting him face to face—my blue eyes to his. Setting the palm of my hand over his heart, I fixed my gaze in his eyes. "I remember this. I want you, heart and soul."

Snaking his arm around my back, he pushed me into the mattress, taking me with his mouth again. My fingers knotted in his hair, pulling him, meeting him with passionate licks.

His enthusiasm harmonized with mine. Through our clothes, I felt a much-needed friction as he pushed against me, feeling it at my clit. I met his rhythmic strokes, grinding into him from underneath. A rush of blood pumped through my veins as my heart pounded against my chest.

He buried his head in my neck and inhaled with heavy panting breaths. "Your perfume is intoxicating." He started invading my mouth again with his tongue. "I need you now."

I felt the heat of my body rise. "I need you, too."

He lifted his head, meeting my eyes. "Have you done this before?"

I flushed beet red. "Yes."

"Are you on birth control?"

"Yes, I'm on the Pill."

He smiled his beautiful all-white-teeth smile. "Good. Would you prefer I use a condom?"

"No. I want to feel all of you."

Hurrying, he popped the button of my shorts with a sudden maneuver. As I lifted my torso, he slipped his fingers in the waistband and ever so slowly, tugged them off—panties and all—trailing his fingers down my legs, making me tremble. My body came alive, tingling at his sensual touch. His caress sent shivers down my spine.

He brushed his hands up my belly, then beneath my sweater and over my breasts…I wasn't wearing a bra. "These are soft."

I moaned and arched my back while he dragged my top off over my head. Along with my shorts, he discarded them in a pile on the plush carpet.

At a desirously slow pace, he removed his shirt and shorts in succession, then tossed them to the floor on top of mine. I stared at his naked body. Firm, rigid muscles lined his torso. His body commanded sex.

His eyes roamed up and down my naked body, regarding me with passion. "Wow, you have an amazing body."

He lay between my legs, resting his weight on his outstretched arms. I reached up and stroked my fingers through the hair on his chest. My breathing quickened. I closed my eyes, fixing them on the visuals of him in my head. It may have been eighteen years later, but it felt as if no time had passed at all.

He lowered himself, resting the weight of his body on mine, our bodies encompassing each other. Slowly, he eased himself inside me. It wouldn't take long before I'd climax all around him. The surface of my skin reached a heightened sense of awareness to him.

"Christ, Destiny. It feels unbelievable." He groaned. He closed his eyes and hissed through clenched teeth. "I can't believe I'm so damn close, already."

"So am I." I'd never been so ready. I'd had sex before, but this was different. I remembered how extraordinary it was with Julian. He remembered as well. I could tell.

Slowly, he started moving. He continued his descent until reaching the end of me. I felt every inch of him, pushing into me with tender, slow, rhythmic strokes. It was heavenly. Gyrating with his hips, he circled into me around and around, driving my body wild.

A groan emerged from his lips, igniting my passion and urgency.

"Julian, please." It was a demand in addition to a plea because I needed to come.

Immediately, he increased his pace. It didn't take long before my legs began to spasm. My eyes rolled upward while my eyelids fluttered. I started moving with him, meeting him thrust for thrust, worshipping his body. I dug my fingers into the bedding under me. Wrapping my legs around his back, I locked my ankles together. I lifted my hands to his back and pulled him into me, needing more friction.

All at once, I exploded as his name left my lips in a declaration of love. "Julian." Yes, I remembered loving this man with all my heart and soul.

I didn't know an orgasm could be this intense. It screamed through every muscle and sinew of my body. I trembled and loosened my boneless legs from around him.

He moved once more and found his own release, groaning deeply.

"Uhh!" He cried out. He buried his head in my neck and kissed me tenderly. "Whatever you're doing to me, please don't stop."

I pressed my lips against his ear and whispered, "I'm doing the same thing I did to you eighteen years ago."

His lips parted slightly. "Well, keep doing it."

I flinched as he pulled out of me. He shifted his body to cuddle closely with mine. We lay like that until we regained our equilibrium.

"It's exactly as I remembered it," he whispered.

I SAT CROSS-LEGGED on Julian's bed while he laid beside me, stretched out, arms behind his head and feet crossed at the ankle. "So, you attained your dream of becoming a neurosurgeon?"

He took a deep breath and let it out slowly. "Yes. And you know the lugubrious part of the story?"

My eyes went wide. "Are you testing my vocabulary skills?" The devilish part of me reared its ugly head as my tongue left my mouth in a most unladylike way. "You mean there's actually a depressing side?"

"Touché, Destiny." We laughed.

"You keep forgetting my intelligence, Julian. If you want a war of words...well then...you're on."

He rolled to his side, resting his head on his arm, his eyes filled with longing. "You're cute when you're showing off."

I playfully pushed his shoulder. "So, tell me why there could possibly be a downside to you being a neurosurgeon."

He fixed his eyes out the window to the distant mountains. "Poor choice of words, I suppose." A melancholy tone suddenly filled the room.

"What is it, Julian?"

"I might've saved her if it was today. All through medical school, I studied everything I could get my hands on about her particular tumor. There have been so many advancements in medicine that I'm convinced I could've saved Amber."

I shifted my body to lay beside him, caressing his face with my hand. "You did save her, Julian. I'm here. And I knew you'd be the best."

He moved so quickly, I didn't have time to react. He was on top of me with rough, eager kisses, pushing me into the mattress once more. His hands wrapped around my head, pulling me to him.

We made passionate love, again.

"EVIDENTLY, YOU'RE A SUCCESSFUL DOCTOR." Lying in Julian's arms, I looked around at the furniture in his bedroom.

"Why do you say that?"

"Jeez, Julian, every room of your place is filled with beautiful, *expensive* pieces."

"Does it bother you?"

"No...I just—," I paused, at a loss for words as I ran my fingers through his hair, combing out the messy sex look.

"I make a comfortable living, Dest."

"I'd say more than comfortable. Look at this place." Other than the Moroccan rug that covered the floor of his childhood bedroom, everything else was new and of exceptional quality.

He tucked a stray hair of mine behind my ear. "Well, you're certainly welcome here anytime you want, babe."

My eyes landed on a portrait of a couple on the wall above the chest of drawers.

"Do you remember them?" he asked noticing the direction of my gaze.

"Are they your parents?"

"Yes. Are you guessing or do you recognize them?"

My head was swimming with a myriad of images passing through it.

He smiled at me. "You look as though you've stumbled upon something," he said. "You get that mystified gleam in your eyes."

"She appeared in your life much later, right?"

He nodded and filled in the rest of the blanks. Most of it came back to me.

"She's still beautiful, Julian," I said. "I remember that Christmas day when she appeared behind us in the living room."

"Yes," he murmured with a long fixed stare at the photo of them embracing each other, smiles a mile wide. "Eventually I'd like you to meet them."

Was all of this happening too fast? I hoped not. "Do they know about me?"

He squinted, as though contemplating his response. "Not that you're back in my life, but I did mention you to them."

Huh? "What do you mean?"

"I told them about seeing a girl on the tour who looked like Amber. That's all they know."

I raised my eyebrows and tightened my lips. "And...?"

"Elizabeth and Lyle Scott were also in the room when your name came up." Tension spilled from him as he pulled his pillow over his face.

My breath left me in a rush. "Amber's parents?"

"Yes," he said, the muffled sound traveling through his pillow.

I rolled to my side, removed the pillow from his face and gave him a quick peck on the cheek. "What happened?"

"Not much because at the time, I hadn't realized who you were. We have to be very careful how we approach them."

"I'm not sure I want to meet them. I mean, I'd love to, but..." I stumbled on my words. "I couldn't bear to bring back any painful memories."

"I don't think you have to worry about that, Destiny. I think they'd cherish seeing you... again."

"Again? For whatever reason, I don't think they'd see it like that. But, I want to be with you when the time comes."

"Oh, believe me, you will."

I twisted my fingers in his chest hair. "So, what did your parents say?"

"Not much."

"Really?" He was lying, I could tell. What did they think? I was intrigued. I suspect the age difference came up in the discussion.

Relief crossed his face when my phone rang. Ah, saved by the bell. Damn. I noticed the time when I punched in my four-digit unlock code. It was nearly one in the morning. Crap, my mom.

"Hello?" I squeaked.

"Where are you, Destiny?" My mom's voice filled with worry and fear.

I winced and noticed Julian watching me like a hawk stalking its prey. "I'm fine, Mom. Since I'm closer to school, I'll just have Julian take me there."

"Absolutely not!" she screamed. "You're to come here. I need to know you're safe. Now, Destiny!" she yelled. Jeez.

"Okay!" I barked back.

Triple crap. She was mad. I hit the "end" button and made short work of my clothes, putting them on at lightning speed. Of course, I did need my car at home.

Julian leered at me, dragging on a pair of shorts and T-shirt. "Trouble on the home front?" His eyes narrowed, and worry outlined his face.

"You could say that." I rolled my eyes.

He eyed me skeptically. "All my instincts tell me to let you go, but I'm incapable of doing that. Fix it with your parents...please." He paused. "My weekly schedule doesn't allow for much of an extracurricular life outside of work, so I may not see you until next weekend. If I can squeeze you into my week...," he paused as if waiting for my reaction, "I'll call, email, or text, okay?"

"Don't forget..." I tapped my head. "I understood the implication right away, babe, no need to explain."

He laughed. "Touché again, Destiny."

Nonetheless, the thought of not seeing him until next weekend made my stomach twitch. Could I last that long? I'd most likely need a week to convince my parents of our relationship. Or maybe I wouldn't tell them. The latter seemed more feasible.

At any rate, not seeing him for any length of time seemed unimaginable. Ultimately, his career was going to take up much of his time, and I needed to get used to that.

IN THE ELEVATOR, we locked our lips together once more, obviously not able to get enough of each other. After all, we needed to catch up on the last eighteen years.

"Incidentally, did you figure out what the code on my touchpad spells out?"

"No. I haven't given it a second thought."

"I just assumed with your advanced sleuth skills that maybe you cracked the code." He smirked.

I narrowed my eyes at him. "There are only numbers on the touchpad."

"Cross reference them on your phone."

I pulled my phone from my purse and studied the letters that corresponded to the numbers of his personal code. It took me about three minutes to figure it out. "Amber!" I yelled. *Wow.* "I should've known. That's sweet, Julian. Does that mean you're changing it to Destiny now?"

"Hmm, what do you think?"

Amber was the reason we were together. "I think you should leave it alone."

He nodded and smiled at me as he opened the door to his Mercedes. I clambered in. He rounded the car, slipped into the driver's seat and eased the car out onto the open highway.

He placed his hand on my thigh and squeezed gently. "I'll see you next Saturday night for the awards dinner. Text or email me, okay?"

"Okay, I'll miss you." Although I wasn't sure I would see him again. The thought terrified me.

Forty-five minutes later, he pulled into the driveway of my parent's house. He bent down and kissed me once more, brushing the pad of his thumb across my lower lip.

"Miss you, too." His voice sounded strained.

Exiting his car, I closed the door, turned and glanced at his face, markedly filled with pain. I needed to reassure him he would see me again. "I'll see you next weekend, I promise."

In the darkness, I watched him drive away—only illuminated by the glow of an intermittent streetlight—until he was out of view.

MY MOM'S EYES WIDENED when she opened her mouth to speak. "Where the hell have you been at this late hour?" she asked, rising from the sofa when I stepped in the door. She'd waited up for me. I knew this meant trouble. Her look was heated, and she only cursed when she was mad, really mad. "Did he hurt you?" She couldn't force any more panic out of her voice if she tried.

The room was dark except for the soft glow of a lamp sitting on an end table between the loveseat and couch. Even though it was on the lowest setting of a three-way bulb, I could still see the fury in her eyes. *Crap*.

"No!" I said emphatically. "Can we discuss this in the morning, Mom?" I tried to remain calm. I felt tired, still reeling from my amazing evening with Julian.

"No, we will discuss this right now," she hissed through clenched teeth. "You do realize you have school tomorrow, right?"

The thought of crossing her made me go pale. "Yes, I haven't forgotten about school tomorrow." I sighed. "I had the best time of my life, Mom. I would be more than happy to discuss it with you in the morning, but not now."

Her face relaxed. "You're okay then?"

"Yes, I'm more than okay. I had a great time."

"Fine, we will discuss it in the morning. You sure you're okay?"

"Yes, I'm sure. I turned and hustled up the stairs, two at a time, to my bedroom before I could be on the receiving end of another one of her verbal lynchings. Frankly, I couldn't deal with arguing right now.

I slipped into my favorite pink satin pajamas, climbed into bed, and drifted off.

I WOKE TIRED BUT HAPPY, despite the tension and fear that was building inside me at the mere thought of a confrontation with my parents. I heard my dad leave for work, but was sure my mom was waiting with bated breath for me to appear downstairs.

My clock read six in the morning. My first class began at eight. I figured I had a good hour before I needed to head out. I started packing everything into my duffel bag in a feeble attempt to delay the inevitable. With my clothes packed, I made my bed and brushed my teeth. As I shoved the last of my toiletries into my bag, my mom appeared out of nowhere. Damn. Why did I come home for the weekend?

"Good morning, Destiny." I flinched and instantly broke out into a cold sweat. "Are you coming down for breakfast?"

"Yes, Mom, I'll be down shortly." I wiped the moisture from my upper lip with the back of my hand.

"You wouldn't be trying to avoid me, would you?"

She was very perceptive.

"No, Mom." I lied. I needed to come up with a foolproof plan before I could discuss my relationship with Julian. "I'm just trying to get organized and ready to go."

"Okay, honey." She used her sweet-as-sugar tactic, knowing I went weak when she pulled out that weapon.

Finally, she left, leaving me devoid of hope. I plopped down on the floor. My head sagged into the palms of my hands. What should I tell her?

I glanced around my room when my eyes landed on my dresser and a photo of my parents and me at my high school graduation from Boulder High School. I stood between my mom and dad, wearing my white cap and gown, and holding my diploma. I'd just given my valedictory address. But, what caught my eye was the guy standing in the background with golden blond hair and eyes the color of the blue sky. With a contemptuous look on his face, his hand was raised and formed the peace symbol behind me. *Thank God two fingers were up.* Three weeks before this, I'd broken up with him. *Jake Fuller, how dare you...You're such an ass.* I suspected he was photo bombing the picture to spite me.

Our relationship was doomed from the start. We weren't exactly compatible with each other, and the sex was mediocre at best. Until now, I wasn't even sure why I dated him. Then the clarity I felt overwhelmed me. My hand went to my mouth. *Wow!* His striking resemblance to Julian must have been why I was attracted to him.

As a young child, visions were always chalked up as fantasy and a vivid imagination. I grabbed the photo and examined it closely, staring at him, and shook my head. It was just one more confirmation of my reincarnation.

Before any more of the morning passed, I decided it was time to face my mom. I headed down the stairs and made my way to the kitchen. "Morning, Mom."

She stood at the island reading the morning newspaper, sipping a cup of coffee.

I dropped my duffel bag on the counter and poured myself a bowl of cereal with milk. I sat on a bar stool at the end of the island and started eating. I could feel her eyes penetrating me like a snake waiting to strike.

Folding the newspaper closed, she asked, "Anything you want to tell me, Destiny?" She lifted her mug to her lips and blew on the rising steam before taking a sip.

She wasted no time beating me to the punch. "What do you want to know?"

"Did you tell him goodbye?"

I took a bite of my cereal. "Why is that so important to you?" My tone was a bit edgier than I'd intended. I had to be careful if I had any intention of seeing him again.

"What are you saying, Destiny?" She started the rhythmic tapping of her fingers on the countertop.

"Yes, Mom, I told him I couldn't see him anymore. Even though it broke my heart, I did it. Are you happy now?" I lied. Jeez.

"It's for the best, honey."

"For who? You?" I scrunched my face and narrowed my eyes at her. I was angry at her halfhearted attempt to persuade me she was right.

Her expression grew tense. "With all due respect, you can't possibly think that dating a thirty-five-year-old man is okay."

I finished breakfast and deposited my bowl in the sink. I rolled my eyes and decided to ignore her. I let out an impatient huff, snagged my bag from the counter and headed for the door.

"I'm eighteen years old. A legal adult," I retorted.

She crossed her arms and gave me a harsh squint. "You still live under my roof and will obey my rules."

"I'm leaving, Mom. Don't forget that I do live at school now."

"Don't push me, Destiny. I am the one footing the bill for your college."

She was right. I wouldn't be where I was if it weren't for my parents. Reluctantly, I hugged and kissed her, then left. I needed to let off steam in the solitude of my car. I hated lying to her, but a bickering debate would have been unavoidable at this point. Plus, the outcome, if I had told her the truth, most likely would have been much worse.

THE FORTY-MINUTE DRIVE back to college was enough to calm my frayed nerves. I arrived at my dorm with just enough time to drop off my duffel bag and say a quick hello to Gabby and Chloe before heading out to my astronomy class.

On the walk across campus, I thought about the terrible nature of what I'd just done. I'd lied to my mother, and now I was going to lie to the man I loved. How the hell was I going to get myself out of this predicament? I rubbed at the heaviness in my chest.

Midway into my day, I found myself unprepared for the pop quiz my physics professor sprang on us. *Damn!* This was not going to bode well for me if my parents found out. After all, I was on a date with Julian instead of studying. I needed to buckle down.

Back at my dorm after a full day of classes, I plopped onto my bed, opened my physics textbook and started working. An hour later, I shot a quick text to Julian, and then it was back to studying.

Me: Can't wait to see you next weekend. I'm back at school. Miss you.

I waited, but there was no response, so, once again, I buried my head inside my textbooks. Julian was probably in surgery. I had to get used to the fact that he was a doctor with a heavy schedule.

THE NIGHT SEEMED TO CREEP UP on me quickly when my eyes began to droop. I noticed the time on my clock: Nine fifteen. I'd spent the entire afternoon and evening doing homework.

As I rose from my bed to find some food, my phone chimed with a text.

Julian: Miss you, too. Did you have a good time with your parents?

I didn't want to discuss my parents with him right now. My stomach churned, and I wasn't sure if it was from hunger or my insides eating away at me for lying. As much as I longed to chat, I needed time to figure out what to do.

Me: Had a nice time. Tired. Will talk tomorrow. Night.

Julian: Night.

THE FOLLOWING WEEK, my school workload increased tenfold. Julian spent long hours at the hospital, sometimes arriving home after midnight. Though not a day went by where we didn't communicate by some form of technology. We chatted about his journey through medical school—the all-nighters he was subjected to for days on end—all because of Amber. As much as it pained me to do, I had to cut a couple of the phone calls short because of homework.

I knew living away from home, would give me more freedom to come and go as I pleased. I could secretively continue to see Julian without my every move being constantly scrutinized and monitored by my parents. For now, that was my plan. Eventually, the truth would come out, but on my terms, not anyone else's.

Not seeing Julian face to face gave me an opportunity to avoid the subject regarding my parents, too. He didn't ask, and I didn't volunteer information, but all of that could change tonight. The awards banquet was in a few hours, and I couldn't wait. I hadn't seen him since last Sunday and longed to hold him again, run my fingers through his hair, and kiss his satiny lips.

As if he could read my mind, my cell phone rang just as I pulled the perfect dress for our evening from my closet.

"Hey, Julian."

"Hi, beautiful, are you looking forward to tonight?"

"More than you know."

"For me too."

We chatted briefly about our clothing choices for the evening. He said he couldn't wait to see me in my finest. I smiled at the gesture.

"You'll need to wait until tonight."

I wanted to reflect femininity and passion, so I'd settled on a knee-length cocktail sheath dress. The navy blue, sequined gown had a revealing slit up the back—not giving too much away. The soft velvet stretch material would hug my figure perfectly which added to the grace and elegance of the dress. Yes, it would be perfect for this evening.

"I've got to check in on a couple of patients at the hospital this afternoon, but I'll pick you up at seven thirty. Be ready."

"Yes, sire," I said with a mocking tone. He never asked if that time was okay with me and I didn't question his authority. It fueled my fire for him.

SITTING ON GABBY'S BED, I watched Chloe sort laundry, while the three of us finally cleared the air from our earlier misunderstanding. All was good between us after I explained how I pulled off my date with Julian.

In the heap of clothes lying on Chloe's bed, I'd noticed a stunning black wrap dress. I snagged it from the pile. "I love this."

"Thanks, Destiny. We look to be about the same size, so anytime you want to borrow it, you're certainly welcome to it."

"Awesome, thanks, girl. Same goes for me." I glanced at the clock on her nightstand. It was nearly six thirty. I told them I had to start getting ready for my date with Julian. "I'll catch up with you two tomorrow."

"Sure thing, would you like help?"

I grinned. "Sounds great. I'll let you know. Thanks for the offer."

I showered methodically, shaving myself to a sleek shine in all the right places. I washed my hair with my vanilla-scented shampoo. I didn't know if Julian liked this fragrance, but I noticed he liked to bury his nose in my hair.

After I finished, I stood still under the spray, letting the warm water soothe the tension I was feeling.

I dragged on a pair of silk stockings and then slipped my dress over my head, letting it fall into place around my hips. Coupled with my black stilettos and shimmering gold clutch, I felt beautiful. I pulled my hair up in a bun, letting strands of ringlets fall around my face, applied some mascara, and was ready for the evening.

I had a feeling I'd be spending the night at Julian's, so I packed a few clothes in my overnight bag for tomorrow.

As I emerged from my bedroom, Chloe's mouth fell open. "Holy shit, Destiny, you look hot. Where'd you say you were going this evening?"

"Out to an awards banquet with my boyfriend." There, I said it—boyfriend. After all, that's what he was, wasn't he?

Gabby interrupted. "I have the perfect necklace and earrings that would look fabulous with that dress!"

Being the fashion guru that she was, I didn't doubt it.

She quickly turned and disappeared into her bedroom and

reappeared a moment later with a beautiful diamond studded gold chain and teardrop earrings. I turned and let her attach the clasp of the necklace around my neck. Looking in the mirror of my vanity, I put the earrings on.

I traced the strand around my neck with my fingers. "This necklace is perfect. Thank you so much! Are you sure you don't mind?"

"Of course not. Go, have an excellent time, Destiny. You look fabulous."

I stared at myself in my bedroom mirror when a knock on the door at seven thirty had me wavering with nerves. Julian was on time.

My head whipped around when I heard Chloe whoop as she opened the door. "Well, hello there, h—handsome," she stuttered. "I'm free tomorrow evening." No-holds-barred, Chloe said it like it was. I liked that.

"Chloe!" Gabby jabbed her in the arm when I appeared in the foyer.

The look on Julian's face was priceless. He was rendered speechless. His face turned beet red with the hint of a smile.

"Julian, these are my suitemates, Chloe and Gabrielle." I waved my arm at them, narrowing my eyes at Chloe. "Girlfriends, this is Dr. Julian Cahill."

Julian extended his hand to both of them. "Pleasure to meet you ladies."

"Likewise," they said in unison, staring at him with wide eyes.

I stood on my toes and whispered in his ear, "You look hot—as usual." He wore a solid black suit with a charcoal button-down and deep blue silk tie. "And you smell good."

"You look stunning," he said.

"Thank you." I blushed. "I had help from my suitemates."

"Would you like a photo? I'd be happy to take one," Chloe asked, trying to downplay her earlier faux pas.

"Ooh, I'd love that." I clapped my hands with pure joy and handed her my phone. Our first formal picture together.

Julian nodded, wrapping his arm around my waist, pulling me close to him as she took the picture.

"Perfect." She said, glancing at the screen.

When she handed the phone back to me, I stared at it, pleased that we were captured in our finest, forever.

I held it up to Julian, and he smiled. "Shall we go?"

"Yes," I said while collecting my clutch and overnight bag.

With his hand on the small of my back, he escorted me out to the car. I wasn't sure but thought I heard my suitemates giggling through the closed door as we left. I rolled my eyes.

Before opening the door to his Mercedes, he cupped my face in his hands, bent over, and gave me a deep, sensual kiss. "I missed you...a lot." He fought for air as he pulled away from me, then took my bag and tossed it into the back seat.

"Jeez, I was busy doing homework all week and didn't have a moment to think about you at all. Sorry, babe." I giggled.

"Liar." He laughed, not knowing how true that really was. I brushed it off, not taking into consideration all the people I'd lied to in the last twenty-four hours.

"Actually, it was the longest week of my life."

"Mine too. What are you doing to me?"

"Let's just go have fun." I smiled sweetly at him.

Chapter Twenty-One

The five-minute drive to the Colorado Convention Center had Julian and me arriving moments before eight.

A forty-foot-high blue bear, pushing its nose and paws against the glass portico in an attempt to peep within the enormous building, greeted us along the walkway.

Once inside, we were escorted to a large ballroom. "Welcome Julian," a cordial gentleman said. "Are you ready for your evening?" They shook hands.

Your evening?

"As much as I can be, Owen. How are you?"

"I'm well. Who is this lovely lady?" He examined me with a questioning glance. "Your niece?"

I felt Julian tense. "Owen, this is Destiny Bradshaw, my date for the evening. Destiny, this is Dr. Owen Saunders, a colleague of mine."

Looking shocked, Dr. Saunders eyed me cautiously. "How lovely to meet you, Destiny."

"Likewise." I begrudgingly extended my hand to him. His dark brown hair flopped into his eyes. He flipped it back with a flick of his head.

Julian took my hand, linking our fingers together. "Shall we?" He gestured with his other hand, leading me into the ballroom.

As we entered, my jaw dropped. Countless tables of eight, covered with white linen tablecloths, encompassed the room. Each was decorated with blue, damask napkins folded and placed on top of milk-white plates. A vibrant, multicolored floral arrangement provided the centerpiece of each table. It was beautiful, but what really caught my eye were the thousands of tiny stars hanging from the ceiling, illuminating the room like a twinkling universe against a dark sky on a cloudless night.

One by one, men and women approached Julian, all introducing themselves, expressing their congratulations, others shaking hands with a pat on the back.

Julian proudly introduced me. The returning gape from friends, coworkers, and colleagues, no doubt, regarded me too young for him. The term gold-digger came to mind. Nothing could be further from the truth, and I rolled my eyes at the mere implicit suggestion.

While engaging in a pleasant conversation with a stocky woman, who looked to be in her sixties, my head whipped around after hearing a vaguely familiar voice.

"Julian Cahill, how the hell are you?" she yelled from a distance instantly pinning her eyes on me at the same time her hand went to her mouth. She stumbled backward.

"Oh my God!" she cried.

"Shelby, how are you? I'd like you to meet my date, Destiny Bradshaw. Destiny, this is Shelby Wyss." He smiled.

She stared with wide, unblinking eyes. "You—you look like someone else. Wow, exactly like her."

"Pleasure to meet you, Shelby," I said casually, extending my hand. I remembered her. Shelby was my best friend in high school, but I promised Julian in the car that I wouldn't reveal myself to anyone I knew. She was still beautiful with her pageboy style haircut and big brown eyes. I noticed a wedding band on her finger.

Shelby placed her hand in mine. "The pleasure is all mine." She abruptly pulled away and stared at me. I knew why, but for now, it would remain my little secret.

"Oh, congrats, Julian," she shook his hand, keeping her eyes on me.

"Thank you. Is Brad here?"

"Yes, he wouldn't miss your night. I'll tell him to say hello."

"Yeah, I haven't seen him in a few years. I'd love to catch up."

She narrowed her eyes at him. "Absolutely, I think we all need to catch up."

They babbled back and forth like a couple of long lost friends. I wanted to reach out and hug her but restrained myself. That day would come.

Shelby left and sat three tables away from ours. For the next few minutes, I noticed she couldn't take her eyes off us. I tried not to stare back, but curiosity got the better of me.

She and Brad must have gotten married after high school. Though, I remembered her last name as something else. Quade, I think…yes, that was it.

Julian bent down and whispered in my ear, "Did you notice her reaction?"

"Umm, yeah, I did."

We took our place at a table near the front of the room, next to the stage. Glimpsing down, I noticed my name printed in embossed silver lettering on a tiny card placed at the top of my plate. I smiled and sat down.

"Would you like a cranberry seltzer?" Julian asked.

"Yes, please."

He moseyed over to the bar while my eyes darted to the flower arrangement on the table. From the center, a small card, attached to an elongated plastic floral pick, read: VIP table. My mind rambled. Were we at the right table? Hmm, Julian—VIP?

Tearing my eyes away from the card, I scanned the room and spotted Julian standing at the bar talking with a deluge of people. While I enjoyed the view, I was also privy to the body beneath that suit.

All manner of people were shaking his hand. Come to think of it; nobody else was receiving that kind of attention this evening—only him. I glanced around the room to confirm my suspicions.

Dammit! Now I wished I'd read some of the articles about this awards banquet online. All I remembered was the link referring to some award he was receiving. It didn't trigger a memory, so I moved on.

He made his way back to our table. "Here you go. One cranberry seltzer for the stunning lady," he said, softly trickling his fingers down my arm. Six other eyes around the table caught his affectionate gesture.

"Thank you." Ignoring his sweet compliment, I stared at him like he had three heads as he took his place in the seat to my left.

"What's the matter?" he finally asked.

"Julian, what is going on here tonight?"

"I told you, an awards banquet."

"Is this only for you?" I tapped my head, reminding him of my intelligence. "Don't play coy with me?"

"Possibly."

Before I could utter another word, the interruption of the emcee's voice boomed over the PA system, startling me. He asked that we all find a seat. I glanced around the room and observed a chaotic scramble. The throng of guests scattered to find an empty seat like a swarm of bees attacking a hive. There had to be close to five hundred in attendance, all dressed in their finest attire. A hush spread throughout the crowd.

"Welcome to the forty-sixth annual American Medical Association Physician's Recognition awards banquet," a short, balding gentleman with thick black glasses announced. Barely able to reach the microphone, he stood at the podium and spoke in a low croaky voice.

Julian leaned over and muttered in my ear, "In other words, the AMAPRA awards." He grinned.

I rolled my eyes. "I was wondering if there was an acronym for all that."

Julian raised his eyebrows, as if to acknowledge my feigned sarcasm. I shrugged my shoulders. There was a smidgeon of a smile on his face.

Mr. Thick Glasses continued, "The AMA is committed to recognizing and honoring those who exemplify medicine's highest values, responsibility to service, community involvement, and leadership in the profession. The Excellence in Medicine Awards honors physicians who go 'beyond the call of duty' to provide patient care, train future physicians, and advance their specific field of medicine." He adjusted his glasses and went on. "This year's award goes to a doctor who exemplifies all of those qualities. He has shown dedication toward his patients and deserves recognition for his achievements. Through trajectory-intervened gene relocation in the nervous system, he has been able to develop life-altering treatments for brain cancer patients diagnosed as terminal cases."

I suddenly recall my conversation with Julian from last weekend. *There have been so many advancements in medicine that I'm convinced I could've saved her.* Was Mr. Thick Glasses talking about Julian?

A shiver ran through me at the thought that I barely knew Julian at all. Here I was, sitting next to a man who I knew as a teenage boy. We were young, innocent, and naïve. We had our whole lives ahead of us. Now, here he was—eighteen years later—twice my age and a successful doctor.

Maybe my parents were right. He was so far out of my league; I couldn't comprehend everything that was happening. No, I must banish those thoughts from my head.

A lady at the next table coughed, forcing me from my reverie, just as Mr. Thick Glasses finished.

"So, put your hands together and join me to welcome this year's Excellence in Medicine Award winner, Dr. Julian Cahill."

"Oh. My. God." I mouthed the words to Julian as he stood and acknowledged the applause with a wave of his arm. He winked at me, turned, and climbed the three steps to the stage. The applause was deafening with hoots and hollers in the mix. He stepped up to the podium, adjusted the microphone, and cleared his throat. From the inner pocket of his suit coat, he pulled a pair of tortoise-shell glasses and slipped them on. *When did he start wearing glasses?* I didn't care because he was sexy as hell in them. From his front pocket, he retrieved a paper which I could only assume was his thank-you speech.

Julian waited for the applause to die down and immediately started in.

"I am deeply honored to have been selected as this year's Physician's Excellence in Medicine winner. I should admit I was a bit stunned when I learned of this accolade, so let me express my gratitude to the AMA. I am very pleased to receive this award.

"Nineteen years ago, I fell in love with a girl. We were teenagers— I won't bore you with the details of my raging teenage hormones..." he hesitated as the crowd chuckled. "But let's just say she was my whole world. As fate would have it, she died less than a year later, at the tender age of seventeen, of a malignant brain tumor." The room went pin-drop silent. He was talking about me. "It was then that I made it my life's mission to lucubrate all I could about that specific type of tumor and find, at least, a better quality of life, or, if you will, an elixir vitae. Moreover, I made her a promise I'd be a successful neurosurgeon, so I dedicate this award to Amber Lynn Scott. She was the driving force behind my motivation. She taught me to believe in myself and be selfless in achieving the goals that will ultimately benefit my patients."

I tried to swallow past the lump in my throat. His words struck such a chord with me. I did know this man—he was the same person I fell in love with eighteen years ago. He was caring, compassionate, loving, sexy—and above all, successful. And he was mine. I was sure he felt the same way about me, too. We loved each other. I felt a sudden peace and reassurance, just as he was finishing his speech.

"In conclusion, I want to express my indebtedness to my parents, who supported me in each and every one of my endeavors. Without them, all my efforts would have been in vain. Thank you, Mom and Dad."

He removed his glasses and placed them in his pocket as the crowd howled with appreciative applause. I leaped to my feet, slapping my hands together in a frantic motion. The surge of emotion felt throughout the room was overwhelming. Julian received a standing ovation.

He made his way back to our table and kissed me chastely on the lips as we both sat down. I placed my hand on his thigh and squeezed, wordlessly expressing my love and devotion. He rested his hand over mind, while six other heads around our table flinched at us with gaping jaws. It didn't seem to faze Julian, but my body heated with a flush that slowly crept up my back and across my cheeks. I shook my head and smiled at Julian's beautiful face. The effect he had on me was one of complete admiration.

"Great speech."

"Thank you. It's easy when the person you're talking about is sitting right here."

I nodded. "Uh huh."

For the following hour we listened to speech after speech from all manner of people from the medical community, while being served a delicious dinner. Herb-crusted swordfish, baked sweet potatoes, and mocha java cakes with a melted chocolate center for dessert—perfect for satisfying my chocolate addiction—was served on a plate in front of me. I ate every last bite.

Eventually, we made our way over to Shelby and Brad's table. Brad gawked when his eyes met mine. "This is Destiny Bradshaw, my girlfriend," Julian introduced me.

Brad stood, extending his hand across the table to me. "Always a pleasure to meet Julian's girlfriends."

I took his proffered hand. "Nice to meet you too, Brad."

Julian rounded the table and gave Brad a quick fist pump. They exchanged hugs. "It's been a while."

I overheard Brad talking under his breath in Julian's ear, "She's a bit young, man."

Julian scowled at him and didn't respond.

Is that what I'd always hear? I'd felt the penetrating eyes of many all night, regarding me as some young trophy girl.

Shelby turned to me and asked, "Do you know who you're dating, Destiny?"

"Yes, why?" I replied hesitantly.

"Well, Julian is one of the most highly respected neurosurgeons in the nation. He's in high demand all over the country. Did you know that?"

I sucked in a deep breath. Why hadn't he told me this? As usual, his humbleness had thrived after all these years. "Yes, I knew that," I lied.

Julian ended his conversation with Brad and was back at my side. I took his hand and linked our fingers together. Those sitting at the table stared, but I didn't care.

"Would you spend the night at my place tonight?" Julian lowered his voice in my ear as we made our way back to our table and sat down.

"Love to. Are we leaving?" Even though I was having a great time, my feet were sore.

"Sure. I can't wait to get you out of that dress."

I gave him a sheepish grin. After all, I wanted that, too.

Julian was chatting with a gentleman to his left as we stood from the table. I tucked my chair in when a woman to my right, with a thick southern accent, grabbed my wrist and seemed to hold it a bit too firm for my liking.

"You're one lucky girl, darlin'. Dr. Cahill is quite a catch," she said, her lips pressing into a white slash.

I sighed. *Here we go with the age thing, again.* One of my many talents was the ability to slip into different dialects at a whim, and this was a perfect time to unleash my ace southern drawl.

I snagged my arm from her grip and said as sweetly as I could muster, "Well, thank ya kindly, ma'am. Ain't you just as sweet as pie for noticin'. Bless your heart and y'all have a nice evenin' now."

She narrowed her eyes at me. We shook hands with the others at the table and moved on toward the door.

"What was that about?" Julian asked.

I forced a thin smile at him. "Just a little friendly banter."

"Sounded more like a scolding to me." He laughed.

I pursed my lips at him. "Maybe. Let's go."

With our fingers linked together, we'd been stopped by a few of his colleagues along the way expressing their congratulations. Nearly out the door of the ballroom, Julian tugged me back.

"Shit!" He rubbed the back of his neck.

I glanced up into his horrified face. "What's wrong?"

"Damn!"

I tried to follow his eyes, but there were too many people meandering in between us, and I couldn't focus on the object of his anguish. "What the hell is it, Julian?"

"It's my parents. Why are they here?"

"So, we talked about this already. Don't you want me to meet them?" Suddenly it was crystal clear—he regarded me as an embarrassment to him. I was too young. He was unable to view me as his girlfriend. This *was* the way it would always be.

"It's not that Destiny…" he faltered. "Shit."

"Then what is it?"

"Lyle and Elizabeth Scott are here with them."

Chapter Twenty-Two

Nausea settled in my gut. "Oh my God, Julian! What do you want me to do?" Part of me felt relieved at the thought that I wasn't embarrassing him. But another part was terrified at what was taking place in front of me.

He grabbed me by the arm and wrenched my body to face him, my front to his. *Well, this is going to look suspicious, don't you think?* I couldn't will my mouth to say the words out loud.

This was the moment I'd dreaded most of all. Or did I? I was positive Lyle and Elizabeth would recognize me, but would their reaction be positive? Why wouldn't it be? I was their daughter, for cripes sake. No, surely they would freak. Maybe I should leave. My head was spinning. I felt sick.

I looked into Julian's eyes. With sweat on his brow, his eyes gave nothing away. He must have been dreading this moment as much as me. I tried to move, but his hand gripped my arm tighter.

I heard distant voices yelling. "Julian." I heard them again, but closer this time. "Julian."

I tried to yank my arm from his grip. "Let me go, Julian." Noticing my scowl, he released me, and I swiftly scooted behind him, my back to his.

"Mom, Dad, Elizabeth, Lyle... uh... you're here."

"Did you think we'd miss this moment? Congratulations, dear. We're so proud." His mom's voice sounded exactly the way I remembered. "We've been trying to catch you all evening."

"Thank you, Mom. Sorry, I've been moving around."

"Yes, congratulations Julian," another familiar voice said.

I recalled that soft voice. The sweet sounds of Amber's mother…my mother…resonated through me. Tears settled in my eyes. I wanted to be anywhere else, but couldn't force my legs to walk away. Although part of me wanted to run into her arms, feeling them around me again. They had to know someone was standing behind him.

"Thank you, Elizabeth." Julian took a deep breath. "Mom, Dad, Lyle, Elizabeth, there is someone I'd like you to meet." Julian hesitated and let out an audible breath. "Do you remember me mentioning a girl named Destiny at my birthday?"

"Yes, why?" Julian's dad, Logan asked.

I heard Julian swallow hard. "Well, she's my date for this evening. I'd like all of you to meet her."

No, no, I couldn't do this. I jutted forward to walk in the opposite direction when Julian's hand yanked my arm.

"Oh, no you don't, Destiny," he said with a commanding voice.

I felt a dizziness in my head when Julian spun me around to meet the face of a woman I'd remembered in my former life…my beautiful mother. Elizabeth Scott. My eyes landed on the scar above her left eye moments before her knees buckled beneath her.

Her hand went to her mouth. "Oh my!" she cried.

Before collapsing to the floor, Elizabeth sank into the arms of the man I instantly recognized as Lyle Scott…my daddy. "Good God!" he inhaled sharply.

A lump developed in my throat while a fresh tear tumbled down my cheek. Elizabeth was still attractive with a touch of gray in her hair skimming her delicate face. She looked stunning in a shimmering, black, sleeveless cocktail dress.

"Oh my God," were the words uttered by the others standing before me, while tending to Elizabeth.

"This is Destiny Bradshaw," Julian revealed shakily.

Lyle stared at me with disbelieving eyes. "You—you look exactly like my daughter who passed away!"

I am your daughter who passed away. I yelled at him in my head.

"Wow, the spitting image of her!" Mr. Cahill exclaimed. "You were right, Julian."

Lisa Cahill looked to Julian for some kind of explanation. When none came, she held out her hand to me. "It's a pleasure to meet you, Destiny," she said, scowling at Julian. He ignored her.

I took her hand. "Nice to meet all of you, too." I exhaled quietly.

"Oh my." Elizabeth's hand flew to her chest. "You sound like her, too."

"Look, we can stand here and ogle Destiny all night, but I have other plans. I'd like to invite you all back to my place. We can talk there." My eyes darted to Julian. He sounded different, more confident. Was it his plan to reveal my identity? Did I want that?

Lyle looked to Elizabeth and asked if she was up for a visit.

"Yes, I'm fine. I'd love to see Julian's home," she said, unable to withdraw her stare from me.

After Logan and Lisa agreed to accompany the rest of us, we headed toward the exit.

I strolled quietly beside Julian, my hand tucked into the bend of his elbow, while the four parents followed closely behind. We inched along in silence, with the weight of eight eyes penetrating our backs.

A breath of the cool night breeze filled my lungs as soon as we hit the outdoor air. I inhaled deeply. Oh, that felt good.

"Are you okay?" Julian asked.

Was I okay? In the last two weeks, I'd discovered I was reincarnated, found out Julian was in high demand around the country and just met my parents from my former life. My head was reeling. "Yes, I guess so."

He looked at me confused and shook his head. There was the hint of a smile on his face. He knew I was anything but.

Before he could open my door, I grabbed his shirt, tugged his lips to mine and kissed him. "Thank you for staying calm."

"I was anything but calm, Destiny."

"You could've fooled me." I shimmied myself into his car, careful that my dress was lying neatly under me.

He rounded the rear and climbed into the driver's seat.

Weaving our way through the bustling parking lot, I started thinking about the next fifteen minutes of my life. A shiver suddenly consumed my body. "Are you going to give away my identity to the parents?"

"I'd like to, but only if you feel comfortable with it."

"Yes. I'm fine with it," I lied.

This was it. My life as I'd known it will change. The thought of having two sets of parents felt exciting but also a bit unnerving. My mind began rambling with anxiety. How should I address Lyle and Elizabeth? Dad? Mom? My scalp prickled.

Over the past week, I'd thought long and hard about exposing myself as the reincarnated Amber. It felt nice being in our own little world with our own little secret. Was I ready to declare my identity? I liked the bubble I lived in for now.

"You sure?"

I let out a deep breath. "Yes, I'm sure."

"Good. Done."

MASSIVE TRAFFIC JAMS made the drive to Julian's place take longer than normal, giving me ample opportunity to broach a touchy subject. One that I wasn't sure I wanted to hear the answer.

"Does it bother you that I'm so much younger than you?" I asked, wondering why he would want a relationship with a girl half his age. With his looks, he could have anyone.

"Hell no!" he yelled making me flinch. "What would give you that idea?"

"Well, the fact that everyone was giving me the evil eye tonight. I just wanted to hear it from you."

He shook his head vigorously. "I don't give a fuck what anyone thinks. Was that not clear? Dest, my concern is that *you'll* leave *me* because I'm too old."

My eyes bugged out of my head. *He's worried I'll leave him?* How could he possibly think that? I silently laughed at our mirrored thoughts.

"Julian, believe me, there's zero chance of that."

PULLING INTO THE UNDERGROUND garage of the penthouse, we approached the four parents exiting their cars and headed toward the elevator.

Julian punched his access code into the touchpad and the doors slid open. We stepped in. It felt as though I was in a slow motion dream sequence when the elevator doors closed and climbed slower than normal. Tears threatened while idle chit chat surrounded me. Lips were moving, but I couldn't make out any of the conversation.

My thoughts were elsewhere—far, far away from my life as Amber. I wasn't Amber; I was Destiny Bradshaw, the same girl I'd been since I was born eighteen years ago. I remembered falling through a dark chasm and choosing my parents in this life. Marcus and Cynthia Bradshaw were my parents.

Lyle and Elizabeth looked older but exactly as I'd remembered them. In a word, I felt overwhelmed. I couldn't pull my eyes from either one of them.

Are they ready for the truth of who I am? Elizabeth nearly fainted when she saw me at the banquet. How will she react when she finds out I'm her daughter?

The jingling sound of Julian's frenzied twirl of his key ring around his finger pulled me out of my daydream. Finally, we arrived at the twenty-seventh floor.

As Julian opened the door to his home, the smell of lemon furniture polish and fresh pine filled the air. I knew Carolyn had been here. I took a deep breath, feeling a calming stillness. Immediately sauntering over to my favorite place in front of the windows, I glanced out at the busy city streets below. Part of me wished I was down there, away from this impending disclosure to the parents, exposing me as the reincarnated Amber.

Julian removed his suit jacket and draped it over one of the bar stools, then made his way to the kitchen. He looked uneasy himself. What was he thinking?

"What would everyone like to drink?" Julian broke the deafening silence.

After retrieving three beers, three bottled waters and a vegetable tray from the fridge, Julian motioned for us to find seats in his spacious living room. He placed the tray of carrots, broccoli, celery, and cherry tomatoes on the coffee table.

My stomach was in knots, and I don't think I'd blinked in three minutes. I was unable to concentrate on anything except Elizabeth and Lyle and what they would learn in the next few minutes.

Both of them snuggled together on the loveseat while Logan and Lisa took seats on the sofa. I moved to the huge overstuffed chair with Julian sitting alongside me. He relaxed his arm around my shoulders, his fingers grazing my skin.

After popping a cherry tomato into his mouth, he started the conversation. "Destiny and I have some information we'd like to share. It's shocking, so we wanted to make sure you were sitting."

The look of horror crossed Lisa's face. "You're not getting married, are you?"

Julian laughed. "No, Mom, nothing like that."

She visibly relaxed.

Jeez, would that be so terrible? Actually, the thought of being Julian's wife scared me, too. I didn't have my parents' approval to date him so that hardly presented a strong case to marry him.

"Are you all ready?"

There were four nodding heads around the room.

"Christ, Julian, get on with it." Logan scoffed.

"Well, when you look at Destiny, who do you see?"

All four heads looked at him as though he had eight. "What do you mean?" Elizabeth asked, fidgeting with her diamond ring.

Logan leaned forward, resting his elbows on his knees. "We're not in the mood for games, Julian. Get on with it."

Jeez, Julian was making them angry. I had to rescue him but didn't feel good about this at all. I had Amber's soul, but I was still Destiny, and that was how Lyle and Elizabeth would see it. Julian himself told me we needed to tread carefully with this and it appeared he was just going to blurt it out. I needed to take control of the situation now. After all, would I believe the reincarnation of my child if I was in their shoes?

Of all the scenarios that passed through my mind the moment I'd revealed myself to Elizabeth and Lyle, this was not what I envisioned. We needed to handle the shock and awe factor with *kid* gloves...and that gave me an idea.

"Wait!" I said emphatically, and everyone's eyes darted to me.

I pushed up from the chair and moved across the floor and knelt down in front of Elizabeth and Lyle. On brave impulse, I reached up and grabbed a hand from each of them, resting them in their laps.

They looked confused, as if to question my forwardness.

I turned to Lyle, took a deep, shaky breath and started talking. "Lyle, do you remember when Amber was nine-years-old and fell off her bike, leaving a deep gash in her knee?"

"Yes," he said hesitantly, eyeing me with narrowed brows, but continued to hold my hand.

"Elizabeth was away on business at the time. Amber told you she was terrified of going to the doctors and begged you to fix her knee without stitches. You told her she'd only need a Band-Aid." I felt his hand tense.

"Yes, I remember."

I looked around the room, my eyes landing on Julian. His eyes widened with the look of complete surprise. He smiled. If I had any chance of making them believe I was Amber, I needed to come up with stories from my childhood…facts unknown to Julian.

I turned back to Lyle. "She sat on the stool in the bathroom while you carefully bandaged her knee," I said softly, looking him in the eye. "You leaned over and whispered in her ear; '*I don't like doctors either.*' Those were comforting words to her."

Lyle jerked backward with an incredulous stare, shaking. "How do you know this?"

"I'm getting to that." I paused as a rush of adrenaline tingled through my body. I willed myself to go on and turned my attention to Elizabeth and squeezed her hand. "Elizabeth, do you remember when Amber was six-years-old and told you she wanted a Cabbage Patch doll?"

She nodded, her eyes filling with tears.

"She insisted she adopt one named Sandra Augustine because the initials were the reverse of hers."

"Oh my. Yes! I remember." Elizabeth slapped her free hand against her cheek while I continued to hold the other. "She was so adamant about it."

"Later you scolded her for engraving hers and Sandra's initials into the baseboard of her bedroom."

Elizabeth gasped loudly. "Yes. Yes. Yes. How could you possibly know that?"

"Because...," I stopped, tears streaming down my face. I tried to swallow past the knot in my throat.

I turned my gaze to Logan and Lisa who were staring at me so intently, it was a miracle I didn't spontaneously burst into flames.

Julian knelt down and crawled over to me. He wrapped me in his arms and whispered in my ear, "You're doing great, Dest. Keep going."

"Because, why," Elizabeth probed me, squeezing my hand. I think she knew what was coming, but needed that minuscule trace of confirmation from me. I hoped and prayed she would believe me. What would I do if they didn't? I never thought about that.

I looked in their eyes, trying to gauge their reaction. "Because...she is me. I'm the reincarnated Amber."

"Oh my God!" Elizabeth's eyes widened.

"I remember you and Lyle as my parents."

She started bawling. "Seriously?"

"Yes, Elizabeth," I cried, wiping a falling tear from my cheek with the back of my hand.

Julian released me when Elizabeth tugged me up into her arms. Raw emotion spilled from us. No words were spoken until she broke the silence. "You're my Amber?"

"Yes," I whispered, then turned to Lyle as a tear fell from his eye.

He engulfed me in his arms and hugged me like his life depended on it. I remembered those strong arms. "Pumpkin," he cried.

"Yes," I said softly when he released me.

There was a tiny look of doubt in Lisa's eyes when my gaze shifted to her and Logan. "Are you kidding me, Julian?" she asked.

His face tightened at her. "Do you doubt her, Mom? She told Lyle and Elizabeth stories I just heard for the first time myself."

"Everything she said was true, Lisa," Elizabeth said. "Everything."

Logan puffed out a breath. "Good Lord."

I felt shredded, and my stomach was in knots. *Take a deep breath, Destiny.* I willed myself to stay upright and persevere. I stood and rubbed the life back into my legs after kneeling for the last fifteen minutes. I returned to the overstuffed chair and sank my body into it. Julian followed and resumed his seat on the chair's arm.

"The memories of my life as Amber are usually triggered by a familiarity with people and places. What solidified it in this case was seeing Julian during the hospital tour. That's where we met…again.

"In the last five years, I've had some pretty strong déjà vus but nothing concrete until seeing Julian. Even then, I wasn't sure why he looked so familiar to me because nothing led me to believe I was reincarnated…until just recently."

I smiled at Elizabeth. "I remember your stories. You told me how you received that scar above your eye. Your brother's homemade helicopter failed," I said, and continued reminiscing. The memories were coming fast and furious as I felt a surge of energy sweep through me. "I remember having a sister named Robin."

"Yes, you do," Lyle said with a shaky voice. "Go on. This is fascinating."

Elizabeth wiped a falling tear from her cheek while Lisa and Logan looked on with bewilderment. I wasn't sure they were on board with the rest of us yet.

"Maybe we can all talk about something else," I suggested.

Julian looked down into my eyes and gently squeezed my shoulder. "Great idea," he added.

"Can you tell me about Robin?" I asked.

"Absolutely." Elizabeth sniffled. "She lives close by in Broomfield. She married three years ago to a man named Liam Spencer, and they have a one-year-old son named Camden. She's a geneticist at Broomfield County Hospital." She stopped and stared at me as if trying to gauge my reaction. "Robin and Amber were very close, the best of friends. She went through a rough time after Amber died. She's well now. I'm sure she would love to meet you, Destiny. Would you be receptive to that?"

"I suppose," I said. "But I don't want to surprise her. I can't take any more of these eureka moments. Could someone please fill her in first?"

"We'd love to. She has a birthday party planned for Camden next weekend. Maybe you could join us for that."

"That would give me an opportunity to catch up with her as well," Julian said.

A thrill ran up and down my spine at the thought of having a sister. "Sounds great. I'll be there with Julian."

My eyes met Lyle's. I remembered being his little girl. It must have been tough for him. We had a close relationship; I recalled that. "How are you? Been to any hockey games lately?"

His breath hitched. "Wow, you remember that? Sadly, I haven't been to any since Amb..." He stopped.

"Since Amber died?" I finished for him. My heart constricted for him. My wonderful daddy. "Maybe we can go again, sometime."

"I'd be happy to take you." He looked overwhelmed. "Wow, I'm astounded by this. Tell us about yourself."

"Julian has told me I was born on the day of Amber's funeral. Odd, right? I'm eighteen and a freshman at the University. I grew up in Boulder and graduated valedictorian of Boulder High School."

"I knew she would be," Julian stated proudly.

I playfully nudged his shoulder. I felt much more relaxed. But, I noticed Lisa and Logan staring at me. Was I being judged? After all, I was a much younger girl dating their older son. They had to be questioning the scruples of that. "How are both of you?" I asked them.

"Stunned about sums it up for me," Lisa replied.

Logan sat reticent and emotionless, eyes glued at me. "I guess I never believed in this sort of stuff—until now. I mean, here you are, in the flesh."

"Yes."

Later, the conversation turned to my parents and their jobs and my life growing up in Colorado. They all hung onto my every word, no doubt, trying to visualize how life as a reincarnated person emerged.

An hour had passed when Logan stood from the sofa. "It's getting late. I think we should head home. We have a bit of a drive ahead of us."

"I think you're right, sweetheart," Lisa said. In short strides, she made her way to Julian and gave him a hug. "Call me, darling. I don't hear from you enough."

"I work long hours, Mom. I'll try."

She then turned to me, giving me the semblance of a brief hug. "We'll see you at the party next weekend, Destiny."

"Absolutely." I paused, trying to read her lukewarm expression. "I recall you coming into Julian's life much later. It meant so much to him. I remember the significant times of my former life, Mrs. Cahill. I understand your reservations about our age difference, me being so much younger than Julian, but…" My lips trembled as fresh tears started falling down my cheeks.

She snagged me into her arms again with intention. "I understand," she said, brushing the back of her fingers down my cheek.

Part of me didn't want them to leave. I was finally enjoying their company.

"It was a thrill, Destiny," Elizabeth said affectionately. We hugged a longer than normal goodbye. "I have my daughter back."

"I've missed your hugs," I said.

"Me too, honey," she wept alongside me.

"Now don't you be a stranger, okay? You're certainly welcome at our house anytime," Lyle added.

"Thank you. I'll keep that in mind and see you both next weekend."

"We'll be there."

Sadly, all four parents left, leaving Julian and me alone again. In my humble opinion, I felt the evening was a success. But, I couldn't handle any more of these jarring moments. In the short time Julian and I'd known each other, my mind and body had been through hell and back. No more, please.

Julian placed the vegetable tray in the fridge while I dropped the empty beer cans and water bottles in the recycling trash. At once, I felt warm arms around my waist.

"You never told me any of those stories."

I turned to him, grazing my hand up his arm. "I had to come up with something that was exclusive to them and me. As soon as I touched their hands, the memories flooded into my head."

"So you had no idea what you were going to say until then?"

"Not really, but I had an idea something would come to me."

He canted his head to the side as emotion filled his face. "Make love to me, Dest."

"I'd love to."

Without delay, Julian carried me to his bedroom in short, smooth strides. His eyes roamed up and down my body after he lowered my feet to the floor.

"I've been thinking of removing this dress all evening." He licked his lips and smiled. "Turn around and let me unzip you."

I felt his hands move down the back of my dress, caressing my skin in its wake. Reaching up to push it off my shoulders, I felt him trace his fingers around my heart birthmark. It was because of that skin defect that we were standing here today. I've thanked God every day since.

As my dress fell to the floor, pooling at my naked feet, Julian removed his button-down shirt in record time. "I never showed this to you." Pointing to his shoulder, he turned his back to me. "I had this done when I was dating her."

I swallowed hard when I turned and caught a glimpse of a heart-shaped tattoo on his back left shoulder with Amber's name running through it. I raised my hand and ran the tips of my fingers across it. "Very nice. I remember." Part of me felt disappointed it was her name instead of mine, but I quickly dismissed it. He was mine now.

"Yep."

"Okay, now hurry up and get the rest of your damn clothes off before I remove them for you." I chuckled.

He laughed. "Bossy, aren't you?"

"Oh, you've seen nothing yet. Now get them off."

Cupping my hand to his cheek, he leaned into it, and I gave him a sweet kiss. I lowered my hands to undo the button of his linen pants and grabbed his zipper, pulling it down. My hands grazed his erection through the material. "You looked so sexy in your suit," I whispered, pushing the pants off his hips and letting them fall to the floor. Then, I slipped my fingers under the waistband of his boxers and tugged them down while his palms rested on my shoulders.

His hands moved to each side of my face. "Only for your eyes."

"Uh huh." I nodded. "Speaking of eyes…when did you start wearing glasses?"

"A couple of years ago. They're for reading only."

"Well, might I add how sexy you looked in them?"

He lifted my chin with his thumbs and bent down and placed his soft lips on mine. "Sexy, eh?"

My tongue coiled together with his. "Yes," I panted. This is what I needed. All the angst of the evening quickly dissipated as my body pushed against his, feeling the release of anxiety evaporate from my body and soul.

I stood there, nearly naked, as he pulled away and moved down to kiss me in the bend of my neck, then lowered his lips to my breasts, leaving me wobbling on my weary legs. His kisses were gentle butterfly touches that made the hair on my arms stand at attention. I closed my eyes and threw my head back, as he left a trail of light kisses all the way down to my belly. He abruptly stopped and pushed away.

"Julian, don't stop, please. You're driving me insane." I opened my eyes and glanced down at his fixation on the right side of my belly. "What's wrong?"

"How did you get this scar?"

"I was born with it."

"Christ!" He gulped.

"What now?"

"Amber was stabbed at school, right here." He pointed at the area of my scar. "Do you remember any of that?"

"Yes, I read the articles about it online and deduced it to be the reason I had this scar."

"Shit." Julian stood and scooped me into his arms. He threw me onto the bed and tore my panties off. He moved between my legs and pushed himself inside me at lightning speed, like he was trying to escape something unpleasant.

I winced.

An agitation seemed to grip him as his hands moved across my sensitized skin. I tried to meet him thrust for thrust, but his mind was elsewhere. His lips delved onto mine again. Desperate kisses overtook him. He needed this, and I decided at that moment to give it to him.

He moved faster. A passion and longing engulfed him. At last, he groaned loudly as he found his release, collapsing on top of me. He nuzzled his face into the curve of my neck and broke down.

I wrapped him in my arms. "Julian." I massaged his back with my hands, trying to bring him back to the now. I placed feather-like kisses on his forehead.

After a while, he lifted his head and gazed down into my eyes, "I'm sorry. I don't know what came over me."

I cupped my hands around his face. "Don't over-think it, let's go to sleep. I'm tired."

"But you didn't get your orgasm."

"It's okay. I just want to cuddle in your arms." He visibly relaxed. I don't think he had any more to give tonight.

Julian pulled out of me and shifted his body, so he laid his front to my back and wrapped me in his arms. He held me tight, as though never wanting to let go as his body continued to convulse.

"I remember that day," he said.

"Shh, I know. I know."

Chapter Twenty-Three

The clock on the nightstand said eight fifteen when I dragged myself out of bed. A phone call from the hospital at two in the morning had disrupted Julian's sleep…and mine. I suspected this was the life of a neurosurgeon. If I had any chance of a future with him, I had to get used to it. I planted my feet on the floor and yawned.

I tiptoed out of the bedroom and headed to the kitchen for coffee and breakfast. I set the coffee pot on brew and began cooking scrambled eggs, toast, and orange juice when my mind drifted to the night before. I smiled thinking about the look on Elizabeth and Lyle's faces when I revealed myself as the reincarnated Amber. Elizabeth's mouth slackened and face paled as if she'd seen a ghost. For all intents and purposes, she had. They'd both accepted me as their daughter in this life. That meant the world to me. Lisa and Logan, however, looked unconvinced. Would that matter to me? Of course, it would. But how could I persuade them?

A shadow in my peripheral vision startled me when I turned to place the eggs on a plate. A shirtless Julian strolled around the corner wearing a pair of loose-fitting boxers knowing this would get my attention. It did. I couldn't help but stare at his finely chiseled torso with a trail of hair that started at his chest and ran down his abdomen hiding beneath his underwear. I sighed. I was privy to what lay shrouded below, too. He sat on one of the bar stools as those big, steely blue eyes smiled back at me.

"You are one hunky-looking doctor."

With a come-hither stare, he eyed me seductively. "Well, why don't you sashay your cute little ass over here so I can press my hunky-looking body into it?"

I fell victim to those baby blue eyes long ago. I knew better. "No fondling the cook."

He stood and rounded the island, grabbing me before I could escape and poked his fingers into my ribs.

I squealed with side-splitting laughter.

"Did you make coffee?" he asked, planting a kiss on my cheek.

"Yes, perhaps your whiffer is defective. Can sire not smell it?"

He tickled me again. "Smart-aleck."

I giggled nonstop at his torture of my body, trying to break free from his arms. "Stop distracting the help." I giggled, trying to push the words from my lips, but failing miserably, breathless from his constant torment of my ribs. I gasped for air. "Stop!"

Julian fingers stilled as he buried his mouth on mine. "I'm spellbound by you, Destiny. What are you doing to me?"

I leaned my head to the side and gave him my sweetest smile. "Back atcha, now eat before your eggs get cold."

He inhaled sharply. "Amber used to say that."

I gave him a puzzled look. "Say what?"

"Back atcha," he replied.

"We are the same person. Did sire not remember that?"

"Enough of that brash tongue of yours." He tickled me again before resuming his seat at the bar.

I circled the island and joined him on one of the bar stools and hungrily devoured my breakfast. I was famished. "Could I suggest something I'd like to do today?"

He raised his fork to his mouth. "After my behavior last night, we can do anything you'd like, Dest."

"Well, I'd like to visit Amber's grave. Are you okay with that?"

His hand stilled mid-air. "Sure…" He hesitated and shoved the forkful of eggs in his mouth.

"Are you positive?"

"Yes."

"Now I want you to stop feeling bad about last night. You had a lot to take in, and it just came to a head in the bedroom. I don't want to hear another word about it…capiche?"

He frowned and raised his eyebrows at me. "Provided you shower with me after breakfast, I promise not to speak of it again."

"With my pleasure. Can I wash you?"

"Only if I can soap up your gorgeous body first," he said, making a *hmm* noise in his throat.

THE CASCADING STREAM of warm water pounded against my back, as if washing away the previous day's turmoil. Julian stepped into the shower behind me. His arms wrapped around my waist, squeezing me into him, feeling his tender kisses on my neck. I turned and pressed my naked body against his and slid my arms around his taut body. I skimmed my hands up and down his backside. This beautiful man didn't have an ounce of fat on his body. We kissed long and hard. What had I done to deserve him? Was being his reincarnated girlfriend going to be enough? That, I didn't know.

He hoisted me up into his arms. "Wrap your legs around me, Dest."

I clasped my fingers around his neck and swung my legs around his waist locking my ankles behind him. He pushed me against the wall of the shower and in one swift move, buried himself inside me. A deep groan left his lips.

Warmth radiated throughout my body, feeling rejuvenated by adrenaline. "I've never had sex standing in the shower before."

"Neither have I."

We made love, finding our climaxes together.

"God, you turn me on."

"I love you, Julian." There, I said it. I loved this beautiful man. I loved him with my heart and soul. He was mine in my former life and I'd be damned if I was going to lose that love again in this life. I didn't care what my parents believed.

He stilled as I tried to gauge his expression. His face looked deep in thought. Did I say the L-word too soon?

"You don't have to say anything back, okay? I just wanted you to know how much you mean to me. I remember how much we loved each other in my former life. If it's possible, I think I love you more in this one."

His lips parted and he leaned forward, resting his head on my shoulder. Then he pushed back, looked me in the eyes and said, "I love you too, Destiny. I didn't think I was capable of loving again."

We both shared a passionate kiss and collapsed to the floor of the shower. The relief we felt left us both drained to our core.

THE GPS ON MY PHONE said it would take us twenty-seven minutes to reach Castle Pines Cemetery.

It wasn't easy to convince Julian to let me drive his car, but with a little persistence, I won the battle of wills. Perhaps, it's a Y-chromosome glitch. I gave him a sideways grin while he reluctantly climbed into the passenger seat of his Mercedes after I assured him he would arrive safely. He scrunched his face back at me. He didn't see the humor in my attempt to woo him. He made me laugh.

"This car is fun," I said, pressing the gas pedal to the floor, testing the speed limit.

"You get a ticket, it's your insurance."

"Yeah, yeah. Duly noted, babe." I pushed my hand in his face, dismissing him.

His eyebrows shot up, making me laugh.

I proceeded south on Interstate 25, heading toward the cemetery where Amber was laid to rest. Placing my hand on his thigh, I gave him a gentle squeeze. "Thank you for doing this for me. I just felt a crushing need to see her gravesite."

"I haven't missed a yearly visit to her grave for the last eighteen years. I never mind doing this. It always gives me a level of peace when things feel out of control...like now with you driving." He shook his head, giving me a smug glance. "Do you know where you're going?"

I nodded and bit my lip. "Of course I know where I'm buried. Plus I have the cemetery address on my GPS, silly."

He shook his head. "What am I going to do with that shameless tongue of yours?"

I laughed.

Tall Aspen trees shaded the winding dirt road leading through the well-kept cemetery. Although I'd never been here in my current life, I recognized where I was.

Exiting the car, Julian took my hand and tightened his grip as we moved closer to the grave. The sound of my loud breathing, coupled with an increased beating of my heart against the peaceful, undisturbed surroundings, had me feeling faint.

"It's over there," I said, pointing to a gravestone about twenty feet away.

Slowly, we shuffled along toward Amber's grave until we stood in front of it. My heart continued to race. We stood silent, just gazing at the engraving in calligraphic lettering on the front. The stone was beautiful, polished and smooth as glass.

I let go of Julian's hand and knelt down in front of the stone, skimming my fingers across her name. *Amber Lynn Scott, Born May 5, 1982, Died August 2, 1999.* A short phrase lay under her name that read: *Our Angel in Heaven.*

I clutched my arms against me and began shaking all over.

"You okay, Dest?"

A chill ran down my spine. "My middle name is Lynn too."

His eyes widened. "Wow, that's incredible."

"Yes, it is."

Tracing each letter of her name with my index finger, I calmed. It was like the transference of her mind, body, and soul to me. How ironic that here I was, feeling a sense of tranquility, yet Amber was gone, departed, and no longer able to breathe another breath. Her gravestone stood there with a tender radiance, ready to last an eternity. It was a symbol so permanent to represent a life taken too early. But would I be here if she hadn't died? Would her memories have evaporated into obscurity? I owed her my life. That much I knew. I know it sounded ridiculous, but somehow her stone steadied me again with an unfaltering sobriety. I closed my eyes and looked to the heavens. "Until we are reunited again, I will make you proud, Amber Lynn Scott."

I stood up and held Julian's hand again. Glancing up at his face, I saw a tear falling down the side of his cheek. I craned my neck up and gently kissed it away with my lips.

"It was beautiful, Julian."

Confusion crossed his features.

"The song you sang...it was beautiful. I saw you playing your guitar and singing for me...err...Amber. You sat right there." I pointed to the spot where I last saw him in an emotional struggle, singing those beautiful lyrics. "It's the last thing I remember from my former life."

He snaked his arms around me and pulled me into him.

Pink and purple lilies surrounded the stone, like the beginning of the rainbow blossomed on this spot. Looking around, I noticed it was the best-kept gravesite in the entire cemetery.

I couldn't stop staring at her plot. "Who keeps this up? It's beautiful."

"I help the Scotts pay the cemetery for perpetual care of her grave to keep it looking like this. It was the least I could do. They plant fresh flowers every spring."

"Thank you. She knows. Believe me, she knows."

Minutes later, we expressed our parting farewells to her and headed back to the car.

"I'm driving," Julian demanded.

I giggled. "Okay."

"RECOGNIZE THIS PLACE, DESTINY?"

We stood on the sidewalk in front of an upscale red brick building with a sign in neon lime green that read: The Nickel Bistro.

"Yep, this is where you brought me on our first date."

A satisfied smile crossed his lips. "I can't get anything by you, can I?"

Yanking the door open, I turned to him. "Are you disappointed that you can't?"

"Never, Dest."

The waitress ushered us to the same booth Julian reserved all those years ago. Except for a new paint scheme, the place was the same as I remembered it—right down to the woodsy aroma. Julian told me

Edmund Nickels had passed away four years before. His son now managed the restaurant.

"I'm sorry you lost a good friend."

"Thank you, babe."

We enjoyed a hearty meal, chatting about my college and his job. And, like his sixteenth birthday, we shared a ceremonial chocolate cupcake with vanilla icing to round out the perfect evening.

"Would you spend the night with me?" he asked.

"My first class is at eight, so if you can wake me at six, then sure."

"I'm usually up by that time."

"Then sure, I'll stay."

When the young waitress placed the check on the table, Julian pulled his wallet from his pants, handed her a hundred dollar bill and told her to keep the change.

"Thank you, sir," she said, batting her lashes at him. I shook my head when an unpleasant high school memory seeped into my brain. Females swooned over him then, too.

I raised my eyebrows, staring in wonder. "That was a hefty tip." Our meal couldn't have been more than fifty bucks.

"Do you have a problem with that?"

"No, I guess not."

"Good. Let's go."

Julian took my hand and linked our fingers together when we stood to leave. The same tingling warmth I felt eighteen years ago when he held my hand was still present today.

Abruptly, he jerked backward, grabbed me and pulled me to his side when an attractive blond woman came charging toward us. With a seething stare, she stopped in front of him, pointed her manicured finger into his chest and began yelling.

"You bastard, Julian!" Her eyes shifted briefly to me then back to him. "You told me she died! You lied to me! Go to hell!"

What? Who was she and why was Julian talking to her about me? What was going on? He had some explaining to do.

She looked to be in her early thirties, beautiful, tall and thin. Had they dated in the past? Of course they had. I didn't need a Ph.D. to figure that out. But how far in the past is what I didn't know.

Julian grabbed her arm. "You're causing a scene, Sarah."

Sarah? Sarah who?

"Stop…now." Julian scolded her through clenched teeth, then turned and handed his keys to me. "Destiny, please go wait for me in the car."

"Okay, babe," I said sweetly, making sure she understood he belonged to me.

"Don't tell me what to do!" she screamed at him.

I took his keys and headed toward the exit. When I turned to look back, I saw her hand make sharp contact with the side of his face. I flinched while several patrons turned to see what the disturbance was about. The audacity of her to show up and behave like that in the middle of a restaurant was appalling.

They started arguing, but I was unable to make out any of the conversation. There was no doubt in my mind she was a woman from his past who meant something to him at one time and vice versa…a woman who looked his age. My heart sank.

Slowly, I dragged my feet to the car, unlocked the door and slithered inside. Rocking slightly, I clutched my arms to my chest wishing I could make myself disappear. I knew this day would come, but, for whatever reason, I didn't think it would happen so quickly— encountering Julian's women. I felt my former life as Amber resurfacing. His past was colliding with his future, and I remained firmly attached on both ends. How long would he want to be with me? The thought made me nauseous.

Five long minutes later, Julian emerged from the restaurant and climbed into the driver's seat. Eyes forward, he stared out the windshield, as if trying to figure out what to say. Another thirty seconds passed before he spoke.

"I'm sorry," he muttered, and started the car, backed out and headed down the highway.

"Why was she there?"

He sighed. "She said she was with friends."

"Are you going to explain to me what happened?"

"Nothing you should concern yourself with," he said, running a hand through his hair.

What? "Julian, she slapped you!" I raised my voice.

"Destiny...," he said firmly. It sounded like a warning. "Look, I think we should spend the night apart, okay? You really don't want to be around me tonight. I'll see you tomorrow."

The voice in my head screamed, *No. No. No. I want to comfort you,* but I was unable to say the words out loud.

And there it was. The rejection. The brush-off. The slap in the face. Call it what you want, but I knew this was it. My body tensed. I wasn't sure if I felt more sad or angry. I didn't like the thoughts going through my head at the moment. He'd just bumped into a woman from his past and didn't want me around. Was he going to meet up with her? *Crap!* I wish I'd heard their conversation. Tears pricked my eyes.

In complete silence, he shook his head, never taking his eyes off the road for the rest of the ride to my college. He pulled into the parking lot outside my dorm and reached for my hand. Before he could touch me, I pulled away and bolted out of the car. Slamming the door shut, I stomped off, boiling mad. I heard him drive away.

It was almost a perfect day, only interrupted by Sarah. I didn't even know the woman but already despised her.

Checking the time, it was eight twenty in the evening. I breathed a sigh of relief when I noticed Gabby and Chloe weren't here. I couldn't imagine explaining my evening to them.

I had homework to finish and wasn't going to let my issues with Julian cause me to fall behind in college. I lugged my backpack onto my bed, pulled out my calculus book and started working.

By ten forty-five, I'd finished my homework, my mood shifting from anger to hopefulness when my phone rang. It was Julian. My emotions were all over the place. Did I want to answer it? Maybe I should let him fume as I'd done for the past two hours. *Dammit!*

"Hi," I said, waiting for him to start the conversation. I was only giving him five seconds of silence, and then I would hang up.

Four and a half seconds later he said, "Hi. I'm sorry, Dest. We need to talk about what happened. Not tonight, but can you meet me at my place tomorrow...let's say six o'clock. I'll treat you to dinner."

I'd calmed. At least he wanted to see me again. But was it to say goodbye? The thought terrified me. "Okay, I'll be there."

"Good. I'll see you tomorrow." He paused for a second. "And Destiny?"

"What?"

"I love you."

"Love you, too."

My whole body sagged with relief. I hoped this meant we were okay.

I STARED AT THE BLINKING CURSOR on my computer screen. On. Off. On. Off. My eyes began to jump. I wanted to do a search on Sarah but didn't know her last name. *Drat!* As hard as I tried to concentrate during my classes today, my thoughts continually drifted to my evening with Julian and what he would tell me about Sarah. No doubt, it would be another obstacle to overcome.

Somehow, the fourth week of school crept up on me. Time was flying by. Academically, I was doing well except for the one pop-quiz by my physics professor. I'd passed it, but by the skin of my teeth. After that blunder, I'd kept myself prepared.

I stood from my desk and fetched a glass of water from the kitchen.

Gabby sat at the table eating a sandwich. "How was the banquet?"

I thought about her question. *Well, I was looked upon as a gold-digger all evening. I met my parents and best friend from my former life. And found out my boyfriend's skills are highly sought after world-wide.*

"Fantastic. Julian was the recipient of a prestigious medical award."

"Cool. Are you seeing him tonight?"

"Absolutely. Can't wait."

"You have it bad, girl."

"I know."

BACK AT THE ZENITH, I arrived at six on the nose. An unsettled look crossed Julian's face when he opened the door.

"C'mon in."

I stepped into his penthouse, greeted by the heavenly smell of beef. I took a deep breath in. "Smells good. What's cooking?"

"Prime rib and baked potatoes made by me." He grinned.

"You cooked?"

"Yes. I wanted to make something special for you." He shrugged his shoulders. "I don't know how it will taste though."

"I'm sure it will be delicious."

"Let's talk first."

"I like that idea," I said, staring at him. He was wearing a pair of blue jeans that fit perfectly in all the right places and a V-neck pullover. Jeez, I felt like fainting right there on the spot. How was I going to have a serious heart-to-heart discussion with him when he looked like that? Maybe that was his plan. I shook my head.

With his hand, Julian motioned toward the sofa. Together we moved across the room and sat. An uncomfortable silence loomed heavily around us.

I raised my brows at him. "So...start talking."

"What do you want to know?"

What did I want to know? I eyed him with wonder. "Well, for starters, who's Sarah?"

He shifted in his seat to face me. "She was the woman I just broke things off with...because of you."

What? Because of me? I lowered my head to my hands and started twisting the ring on my finger.

"What's the matter, Dest?"

"Umm...Were you dating her when I appeared in your life?"

"Somewhat...Yes."

My heart sank. What if another woman—someone closer to his age—came along? Would I be cast aside like Sarah?

"Destiny, look at me."

I raised my head and gazed into his emotion filled eyes.

"I never loved her. She wanted a commitment, but I was unable to give it to her. It wouldn't have mattered if you came into my life or not." He stopped and took my hand in his. "What you have to understand is that after Amber died, I felt so emotionally screwed up, that the likelihood of loving another woman was not in the cards for me." He cupped my cheek with one of his hands and I leaned into it.

"I love you and only you. You are the only woman I've *ever* said those words to."

My heart swelled. The last time he'd said he loved a woman was to me…nineteen years ago? My thoughts traveled back to 1998. It happened just after my stabbing at school and his "player days" confession to me. It was the first time I remember him saying he loved me. I sensed it was hard for him all those years ago, too.

"Why did she think I'd died?"

Julian sat back and snorted. "That was a complete misunderstanding." He went on to explain how she'd seen the photo of Amber on his hutch and the conversation that followed.

"Oh." I sighed as a feeling of relief flooded my body. "Yeah, I can see how she could've been confused by the two of us. When did you end it with her?"

"I told her last night."

Last night? Did he invite her here? The thought made my scalp prickle.

"Was she here?"

"No." He stopped and stared at me. "Is that what's bothering you? Did you think I invited her here last night?"

"Yes," I said, my voice barely audible.

"I'm sorry, Dest." He shook his head and raked his fingers through his hair. "If I can't give you one hundred percent of me, then I don't want to give you anything. And last night was one of those moments."

"Julian, I don't need all of you every second of every day. I just wanted to comfort you. You need to let me do that for you. It was painful for me to see her slap you."

"I probably deserved it. We'd never officially ended the relationship until last night."

There was one more question I needed to ask and was terrified of the answer.

"Did you sleep with her?"

A hint of a smile crossed his lips. "Yes, but it was just sex."

"I'm not sure what you mean by that."

"A man has needs, Dest." He smirked. "Do you honestly believe

I'd been celibate for the last eighteen years?"

I flushed and shook my head. "I guess not."

He cuddled closer to me and wrapped his arms around my shoulders. "Are you okay?"

"I'm good. Thank you for opening up to me, but your prior relationships are your business. You haven't asked me about my former boyfriends. I don't need to know about yours. There are some things that should remain private."

"Dest, it will only be you from now on."

All was okay with us.

"Let's eat. I'm starving."

I SET THE BAR WITH PLATES and silverware and pulled bottled seltzer water from the fridge for both of us while Julian buttered some bread.

I felt piercing eyes on me as I moved around his kitchen. I was quickly learning where he kept things. He seemed to like that.

"What are you thinking about? I can feel your eyes penetrating my back."

"What do you think I'm thinking about?"

"Oh, I can guess...the only thing males ever think about, right?"

A happy laugh left his lips. "Close, but no cigar, babe."

I pranced around in front of him, flaunting my ass close to his reach, but far enough away to keep him from grabbing me.

"What are you doing, Dest?" His voice sounded seductive.

"What do you think I'm doing, Jules?"

"Very amusing." He scrunched his forehead. "Jules?" he said eventually. "Where'd that come from?"

"Well, you keep calling me, Dest, so if we're reducing our names from three syllables to one, then you're going to be Jules."

He looked deep in thought as if he was replaying the name over and over in his head. "Are you talking about the family type or the body ornament?" He gave me his unequivocal all-white-teeth grin.

"You ass." I laughed and slapped him.

"Either way, I like it, Dest."

"Actually, so do I...Jules."

"JEEZ, JULIAN. This is delicious."

"Thank you," he said between bites of the prime rib. "I was nervous about it. But seeing you enjoying yourself, I'm happy it turned out okay."

Seated next to him at the kitchen island, I peeked at him through my lashes. "So you *can* cook?"

"Nope. I called my mom. She was here earlier to help."

I squinted my eyes at him. "You liar. You told me you cooked this."

"I did. I just left my mom's name out of the equation."

"You ass."

I cut another slice of the tenderest steak I'd ever eaten. It was like slicing through butter. I shoved it into my mouth while my stomach growled for more with each delicious bite. "So, how do your parents feel about us dating? Your mom didn't look all that pleased the other night."

Julian looked at me as though I had three heads. "It doesn't matter how my parents feel. I'm not going to stop dating you. They'll come around eventually. It's a non-issue right now, so don't let it bother you."

"But it's important that they like me."

Julian ran his hand down my back. "They love you, Dest."

After we finished eating the fruits of Julian's labor—or should I say...his mom's—we nuzzled together on the sofa in his living room, listening to the classical sounds of Mozart through his entertainment system. The only light in the room came from the windows overlooking the city below, bathing us in the evening glow of the approaching sunset.

"I have something for you." Julian smiled his beautiful smile. "Hold out your hand and close your eyes." When I did, he placed a metal object into the palm of my hand. "Okay, open them."

I gulped. "Julian."

"I want you to have this key to my home. You are welcome,

anytime." He emphasized the last word. It was a simple gesture that showed how much he cared and loved me and only me.

"Thank you, Jules."

I HAD THE TUESDAY morning blues. I sleepily made my way to the shower. I left Julian's place, making it back to my dorm just before midnight.

"Hey, Destiny, how was your evening with that hunky boyfriend of yours?" Chloe appeared in the adjoining suite as I packed my textbooks into my bag.

I yawned. "Great, but I'm paying the price this morning."

"That's what boyfriends are for."

Spending time with Julian was all I wanted to do, but receiving my degree was also important and I wasn't about to squander it away. I was strong and self-sufficient and the thought of being dependent on anyone to pave my way through life made me flinch. Well, except for my parents.

"Earth to Destiny. Whatcha' thinking about?" Chloe interrupted my internal diatribe.

I laughed. "Julian is all I'm ever thinking about."

"You poor thing. I wish I was afflicted with his image, too."

"Well, you can just erase that vision from your brain, cuz he's all mine and I ain't sharing." I chuckled and tucked a loose strand of hair behind my ear. "You want to know the worst part about it?"

"Hell, yes. Fill me in."

I watched as she cleared some dishes off the table and dropped them in the sink. "My parents disapprove of him. If they knew we were together, I'm not sure I'd be standing here talking to you."

"Oh my God, why don't they approve? He seems like a great guy."

"It's a long story, but he's much older than me. He's thirty-five."

Her hand went to her mouth. "Wow, he certainly doesn't look it. I mean, he looks older than you, but not that much older. I guessed he was in his mid-twenties." She stopped short. "What the heck are you doing dating a guy that much older than you? He's twice your age."

I scowled at her. "Okay, you can stop now. You're starting to sound like my mother."

"Well, I guess you have to put yourself in your parents' shoes. Would you approve of him?"

"There's more to the story. One of these days, I'll fill you in, when we have the time, Chloe, but I've got to get moving to my first class."

I wasn't sure when the right time would be to reveal myself to her but promised I would, one day. Julian and I decided to keep our little secret quiet for now.

"I'm all ears, girl," Chloe said.

"Yeah, me too, Destiny!" Gabby yelled from her bedroom.

BY THE END OF CLASSES for the day, my mood had improved significantly. I'd finished my homework and decided to call my parents. Lying on my bed, I dialed my mom. She picked up after the second ring.

"Hi, sweetheart," she answered.

"I just called to hear your voice and let you know everything was okay."

"How are your classes, honey?"

I folded one leg over the other, bouncing my foot in the air. "Great! I love all of my professors. Astronomy is my favorite class."

"That's great. How are you getting along with your suitemates?"

"I love them. It's like we've known each other forever."

"Your dad and I were thinking about coming for parents' weekend. Maybe we could take you out to lunch."

I knew I was going to meet Amber's sister, Robin, with Julian on Saturday. Weekends were the only time I had him to myself. I hated to give one up, but I also missed my parents.

I stood and started pacing in circles. "I'd love that. How about Sunday?"

"I'll jot it down on the calendar."

We chatted about her "empty nest" syndrome, as she called it.

"You sound so sad, Mom."

"I miss you, Destiny."

"I miss you too, but I'll see you next weekend. Tell Daddy I miss him, okay?"

"Sounds good. We'll see you around noon. Love you."

"Love you, too, Mom."

We hung up. I had the best parents.

MY DECISION TO VISIT JULIAN this late in the evening started out as an impulsive one. The clock said nine fifteen. I was up late the night before and paid the price dearly today. Now, here I was ready to do it again. I wanted to be with him every minute of every day. I had it bad, as Gabby noted. I laughed inwardly.

He wasn't home when I arrived at his place. It was only a ten-minute drive from my dorm, anyway.

I let myself in with my new key. I kissed it after opening his door, and dropped it in my pocket.

What if he didn't get home until midnight or later? My only class tomorrow was at one in the afternoon, so maybe I could sleep here. I hoped Julian wouldn't mind.

Maybe I should make him something to eat? Did he eat after he got home? I decided to send him a text.

Me: What is your ETA?

Julian: Why? Where are you?

Me: Your home.

Julian: I'm just finishing up. I'll be there in ten minutes.

Me: Do you want something to eat?

Julian: Sure, surprise me.

Me: Love you.

Julian: Love you too, Dest.

I decided to make him something light, like a salad. I knew he was a health fiend. I could do healthy.

I sauntered across the room to the kitchen, stopping briefly at my favorite spot in front of the living room windows to steal a peek at the busy life below. I scrolled through my phone until landing on the music app. Moments later, the sweet sounds of Adele's voice filled the room.

I opened the fridge and found some pinto beans, corn, red onion, lettuce, and an avocado. I cut up the avocado and onion and placed them on a bed of freshly washed lettuce. I rinsed and drained the corn and beans and sprinkled them on top of the avocado with some olive oil. I spiced it up with some salt, pepper, and cilantro. As I squeezed the juice of a lemon to finish it off, Julian stepped in the door.

"Hmm, smells delicious in here." His words sounded soft and suggestive.

He was wearing his green scrubs and nametag that read: Dr. Julian Cahill, Neurosurgeon. A stethoscope hung loosely around his neck. He looked so delicious and official. I'd never seen this side of him. He was in his ceremonial white doctor's coat when I saw him on the tour. We'd come a long way since then.

In short easy strides, he made his way over to me. His unshaven face was rough and scratchy but equally sexy as he leaned over and gave me a passionate kiss on the lips. He groaned a low seductive sound.

"I just finished your salad. Now sit down and enjoy, Dr. Cahill."

"I'd like a quick shower first. Do I have time?"

"Sure, I'll put the salad in the fridge."

Fifteen minutes later, Julian rounded the bar and took a seat on one of the stools. I placed the plate in front of him, breathing in his clean scent. He was beautifully sexy with damp, disheveled hair.

"How was school today?" he asked, rocking his head back and forth to the music.

I leaned against the counter opposite him so I could stare into his blue eyes.

"Great," I said, waving my arms around enthusiastically. I ended up rambling on and on about my day while Julian sat there watching me, giving me a nod now and then as he dove into his salad. As it turned out, we both had the same physics professor. "He's a bit older now," I told him with a chuckle.

His head tipped slightly to the side. "You're cute when you're excited." He smiled.

"Did you hear a word I just said, or are you just staring?"

"A little of both, Dest. Sometimes I can't believe you're here."

I leaned over the island, resting my crossed arms on the cool surface. "I'm never leaving, this time."

"Good, because I'm never letting you go." He boosted himself up and gave me a chaste kiss on the corner of my mouth.

"Enough about my day. How was yours?"

He rubbed his eyes. "Exhausting."

"You know, when I arrived here tonight, it dawned on me that I had no idea what you normally did when you got home."

"Usually I crash." He hesitated. "But tonight will have a different outcome—I presume."

"Perhaps, maybe the same outcome as last night?"

"Indubitably." He took a bite of his salad, stopping briefly, and relaxed. "This is delicious. I might have to let Carolyn go and hire you on full time."

"Don't even think it. I enjoy cooking occasionally but wouldn't want a full-time job of it."

He took my hand in his and started massaging my fingers. "Can you spend the night?"

"That was my plan. My first class tomorrow isn't until one."

He grinned. "Good."

"I like having a key to your place." I pulled it from my pocket and flashed it in front of him.

"Based on how this evening is shaping up already, I'm quite fond of it, too. I may not let you go."

"I don't want to go. Cripes, Julian. I couldn't stop thinking about you all day."

He stood and placed his empty plate in the sink, turned and tugged me into his arms. "Same here, babe. Same here." He lifted my chin with his thumb and forefinger, then kissed me.

I pulled back and peered into his eyes. "So, describe a typical work day of yours." I wanted to know more about him. Since the majority of his life was his career, I thought this was a good place to start.

"Seriously?"

"Yes, I'd like to know what a day-in-the-life of Dr. Julian Cahill entails."

He took my hand and pulled me to the living room, sat on the sofa and tugged me down in his lap...my back to his front and planted a kiss on my outstretched neck. "Well, I usually start my rounds at the hospital at six in the morning...of course, that's if I'm not called in the middle of the night, which is quite often."

"As I've noticed, but for what reason?"

He looked at me and frowned. "Any number of reasons, Dest. An unexpected head injury—you know, a fall, a car accident."

"Like the time you treated me when I was younger."

"Yeah, but I was already on duty that night."

"Does that happen frequently?"

"It goes in waves." He grinned, undoubtedly recalling something. "I remember a one week stretch a few months ago, when six out of the seven days, I found myself driving to the hospital in the middle of the night."

"When did you find time to sleep?"

"Catnaps. But you learn to function on very little sleep—literally."

I was impressed, this being the Julian I'd known in my previous life...his head always buried in some medical journal. "How many surgeries do you perform each day?"

"Once again, it varies, but I average three a day."

"Wow." I yawned.

"Boring you? Let's talk about something else. I generally don't talk about my work but felt you needed some perspective on what you're getting yourself into."

"I find it very fascinating. I'm just tired. Long day after a late night." I gave him a sideways smile.

Julian scooped me up into his arms and carried me to his bedroom. The room was dark except for the light of the full moon dancing in the sky, filling the area with muted shadows.

He delicately removed my clothes while seducing me with his eyes.

In turn, I removed his.

"You looked so authoritative and doctor—ish in your scrubs."

"I did?"

"Yes." I smiled.

"I'd like to try something different tonight."

"Okay, what do you have in mind?" I asked, raising my eyebrows. My libido was nodding in agreement already.

"I'd like you on top."

"For you, Jules—anything."

When Julian laid his bare, sculpted body down on the bed, I crawled between his legs.

"Straddle me, Dest."

He pulled me forward while I sat astride him. I sat back and felt his erection pressed against me. I was wet and aroused. I wiggled for some friction, circling my hips. He groaned. He was ready too. He told me to lean forward and place my hands on each side of his head while he positioned himself at my opening.

"Sit back now."

I pushed down slowly, until I possessed all of him. He filled me. He was so deep. This was an entirely different feeling. I moaned at the heavenly pleasure spiking through my body. I loved it. I loved him. I couldn't imagine my life without him.

I looked down into his eyes. Half of his face was in shadows, but I could still see the love he felt for me.

He reached up and filled the palms of his hands with my breasts and used the pad of his thumbs to bring the tips of my nipples to attention. I moaned again, louder this time. I started moving while he moved his hands to my hips and helped lift and lower me. He grumbled a sexy sound.

"I feel so dominated with you on top, Dest. It feels good."

My breathing intensified. "Julian, I'm going to come. I don't want to hold it back."

"Go, Destiny."

I began moving quickly and deliberately. I needed this and I think he knew. My legs started trembling as my body bowed to his intrusion. My eyes rolled back into their sockets and I let go. I screamed his name as my orgasm ripped through me like thunder.

"Julian!"

"Keep going. I'm almost there," he pleaded.

I moved with purpose as he groaned loudly, finding his own release seconds later.

I fell onto his chest and buried my nose into his neck leaving a path of licks and kisses. He squirmed beneath me. I couldn't get enough of him.

Moments later, I sat up and gazed into his eyes. "I like being on top."

In the shadows, I saw a smile against his silhouette.

I lifted myself off him and cuddled into his side. "I love you, Julian, more than you know."

"I love you too, Destiny."

Chapter Twenty-Four

At three o'clock the following Saturday, Julian arrived at my dorm for our trip to the city of Broomfield, a thirty-minute drive from the university. I was meeting Robin and her family for little Camden's first birthday party. I couldn't contain my excitement.

With more than a month of school under my wing, I'd learned how to budget my time with school work while fitting Julian in on the side. I managed to spend an overnight with him on three separate days during the past week. He tried to work shorter shifts on those occasions—enough to spend some quality time with me in the evenings—but not without the constant disruption of his ringing phone.

I was also able to do my homework in his peaceful home surroundings, giving me extra incentive to study hard—something that was missing in my dorm with Gabby and Chloe's incessant gossiping, although I contributed as much as them.

"C'mon in, Dr. Good-Looking." Chloe was spewing off at the mouth again. She never held anything back. I admired that, although Julian seemed uncomfortable, looking unsure of how to handle her when his face turned a deep shade of crimson.

"Hey, Chloe." He nodded his chin at her.

I quickly came to his rescue. "Hi there." I tipped my head to the side feasting my eyes on the hunky man standing before me. Wearing blue jeans with a red polo shirt, he looked every bit the sexy man that he was. "Looking good, babe."

Julian beamed looking like he'd just won the lottery. "Back atcha," he said with a smirk, stealing my line.

"Thank you, handsome." I'd decided on a silk camisole that draped loosely on my hips and a pair of straight leg blue jeans. Gabby said my ankle-strap, high-heeled sandals would finish off the look perfectly. Of course she was right.

I let my hair flow loosely down my back, applied a little mascara to my eyelashes and pink gloss to my lips. I was ready to meet my sister from my former life. It had been eight years since my brother died—the only sibling I'd known. I missed when he would take me out to eat…just the two of us. He'd treat me to triple-scoop ice cream desserts. I was never able to finish them, but that didn't matter to him as much as it mattered to my parents. I'd always hear the same words. *There are starving children in third world countries.* It was a wonder I didn't weigh three hundred pounds. My memories of him were sparse, but I did remember that special time. It would be awesome to have a sibling again.

I headed over to my desk and grabbed the wrapped gift for Camden. "This is from both of us," I informed Julian.

"Thank you. You're better at that stuff than I am. What did you buy?"

"I didn't buy him anything. I made him a stuffed teddy bear."

He shook his head, incredulous. "When did you find time to do that?"

"This week, when I wasn't being held captive by you." I batted my eyelashes at him.

"If I'm not mistaken, it was you who came to me."

"Touché."

"Are you all ready?" he asked sweetly.

"Yes—"

"And before you say another word, I'm driving," he interrupted.

I smiled. "Okay, Jules, but you got there safely with me driving last weekend, didn't you?"

"No more discussion. I'm driving."

He made me laugh. If he didn't want to talk about it, we didn't. It was the end of the story.

My excitement showed all morning, bubbling to the surface. I hadn't stopped dancing until I plopped my butt down in Julian's car. Even then, I couldn't hold back my shuffling in the seat.

"Good Lord, Dest. You're like a child on steroids," he said, easing out of the parking lot.

A laugh erupted from deep in my belly. "I'm going to see my sister for the first time. Well, the first time in this life."

He took a left onto the ramp to I-25 toward Broomfield then gripped my hand and moved it to his lap. His thumb caressed my knuckles with innocent circles. "I called Robin this week and filled her in on the whole story. She can't wait to see you."

My shoulders relaxed. "First of all, thank you for that. I don't think my heart can withstand surprising any more people with my identity. Secondly, I can't wait to see her, too. What was her reaction when you told her?" My excitement spiked again.

"She screamed. The kind of screech that makes you pull the phone from your ear." He laughed. "I tried to fill her in as much as I could remember."

"When was the last time you saw her?"

"I haven't seen her in years."

"Why not?"

Julian's face dropped, as if remembering something unpleasant. "She went through severe depression after Amber died and I was flat out with school work. We lost touch. I regret it now. If it weren't for you, I'd still be out of the loop with her." He glanced at me with a smile. "But now all the Scotts are back permanently…because of you." He released my hand and brushed his knuckles down my cheek.

"Yes, Jules." I took his hand and squeezed it in a loving gesture. "Can I ask you something that's been bothering me for a little while?"

"Absolutely, what would you like to know?"

"Well, at the awards dinner last week, Shelby hinted at the fact that you were in high demand across the country. She scowled at me and asked if I knew who I was dating. What was she talking about?"

Julian looked uneasy. He was never someone who bragged about himself, especially the good stuff.

"What did you tell her?"

"I lied, babe. Sometimes I feel as though I don't know you at all.

What did she mean?"

He subtly shook his head. "You really want to know?"

"Yes, and will you stop answering my questions with another question?"

"Fine." He scrunched his face. "My skills as a neurosurgeon are in high demand, Dest. After Amber died, I put every blessed iota of myself into my education. Through study and guidance from my mentor, I taught myself how to surgically remove brain tumors that were formerly thought to be inoperable. In the last year, I've taught the procedure to a few others around the country. So, I'm one of the few doctors able to perform this operation. I can't save everyone, but I can, at least, give them a better quality of life.

"Amber's death shattered me. I didn't want anyone to experience what I went through after she died. I was completely devastated." He stopped and stared straight ahead, no doubt remembering a sad time. "In other words, Dest, I'm good at what I do…Really good." He looked at me as if trying to gauge my reaction.

My mouth dropped open. "I'm speechless, Jules. I had no idea the extent of your expertise." I was awed by him. When was he going to divulge this information to me? *Gah!* He was so humble. That had never changed. I had to accept the fact this was his life, and now it was mine. "I knew you'd be the best. I remember telling you that eighteen years ago. You didn't believe me." This was the Julian I knew.

He smiled. "Yes. You did."

We pulled into Robin and Liam's driveway exactly thirty-two minutes later. After counting the cars in the driveway, it appeared we were the last to arrive. Logan, Lisa, Lyle, and Elizabeth were already here. Warmth spread through my belly at the thought I'd be seeing Elizabeth and Lyle again as well.

Exiting the car, I stared straight ahead at the cute single-story bungalow with detached garage. The exterior siding—a dark brown— reminded me of the color of coffee with a tiny bit of cream. A smattering of toys littered the front yard. You could tell that a young family lived here. Growing up in a big house my whole life, I loved this pint-sized home.

We strolled along a red brick sidewalk, up the stairs, across the dark, wood planks of the porch, and rang the doorbell.

My palms perspired with sweat, and my breathing sped up. Julian pulled me to his side, noticing my trembling body.

"Don't worry, Dest. It'll be okay."

Seconds later the door flew open, and Robin's eyes met mine. She was just as beautiful as I'd remembered her. Her freckles had faded, but the dimples remained when she smiled. And this time she wore the biggest smile I'd ever seen. Her caramel-colored hair was now short and streaked with blond highlights. She looked younger than her thirty-six years but tired around the edges. I suspected the reason being a baby in the house.

Standing beside her was a very handsome man I didn't recognize. He had jet black hair, a full mustache, and wore black rimmed glasses.

Before Julian and I could open our mouths to speak, she barged in. "Oh my God!" she cried, staring long and hard at me. "Everyone was right. You are the spitting image of my sister, Amber." She turned to the man on her right. "This is my husband, Liam."

"Nice to meet you, Liam," Julian and I spoke in unison. We all shook hands.

"This is Destiny Bradshaw. Destiny, this is Robin Spen—"

"Spencer," Robin interrupted, rescuing Julian's stumble on her last name.

Julian didn't need to introduce me. I knew who she was. *She was my sister. My sister. My sister.* I repeated it over and over in my head. I had a sister.

"Liam, this is an old next door neighbor, Julian Cahill and my reincarnated 'sister,' Destiny," she said with air quotes around the word, sister. "Julian's a big-time doctor now."

Her excitement made me laugh, matching mine from this morning.

"Wonderful to meet you, Julian. What is your area of expertise?" Liam asked.

"I'm one of the staff neurosurgeons at Denver Medical," Julian said.

"Whoa, awesome." Liam turned to me. "Destiny, I'm astounded by the similarities between you and Robin's sister, Amber. I never knew her but have seen pictures."

"Well, her sister is right here. What would you like to know?" I asked, laughing.

Liam was a soft spoken man, precisely the type I always thought Robin would end up with—one who wouldn't break her heart.

As Robin's tear-filled eyes finally retreated to their sockets, she waved us into her home. "Come on in, you two." She shook her head and turned her gaze to my man—the man she was determined was going to break my heart a long time ago. He, of course, didn't. "How are you, Julian? You look fantastic." She beamed. "I've heard so much about you from my parents."

"I'm good, and yourself?"

"I'm great." She nodded and visibly swallowed. Her eyes fixed on me. "It's so awesome to meet you, Destiny. I'd received calls from Julian and my parents filling in the blanks for me. I'm glad you insisted I know before you arrived. I don't think I would have survived this being sprung on me." She moved her hand between the two of us. "I was very skeptical at first, but when Mom told me what you remembered, it was hard not to believe it." She shrugged her shoulders. "I'll have to do some research into reincarnation myself."

"Nice to meet you, too," I finally got a word in edgewise. I fought down the lump in my throat, and my lips quivered. Next thing I knew she'd swallowed me up in her arms. I reciprocated the gesture as we both burst into giggles of joy.

She was my sister. I loved and remembered her, "Oh Robin, I've missed you so much." I shook my head as the strange words fell from my lips. "I'm sorry."

"Don't be, Destiny, I L-O-V-E it. Oh my God, my sister is back! We have so much to talk about!" Her face lit up.

"That sounds perfect, Robin."

I beamed at her confidence in calling me her sister. Since I didn't have a sister, I certainly didn't mind at all. In fact, it had a nice ring to it. My sister, Robin. I repeated it over and over in my head until it slid off my tongue like butter. The feeling was different with her, though. I instantly loved her with all my heart. Other than Julian, she was the only other person I felt an overwhelming connection with in this life.

"Come meet your nephew, Camden." She directed me to follow

her as Liam and Julian headed off to the dining room with the moms.

We strolled into Robin's cozy living room. Camden's face hung on every wall. My eyes landed on a framed photo of Robin and Amber, seated on an end table. Her eyes followed mine as she examined it fondly. I could tell it meant a lot to her.

"That's you and me," she said.

I held it in my hands. "I remember this." I brushed my finger across the glass. "Julian took it when the three of us went hiking in the mountains. It was just before I fell." I felt an instantaneous weakness in my legs.

Robin's eyes misted. "Yes, Destiny. It's the last great picture I have of her and me together. She grew very sick after that day."

I set the picture back down, perfectly positioned so that it was visible from anywhere in the room.

A TV hummed quietly in the background where Lyle and Logan were enjoying a football game.

"Hi, Destiny, wonderful to see you again," Lyle said.

"Great to see you again, too." I gave each of the men a quick hug.

A dining room table to our right was filled with snacks, dips, drinks, and a teddy bear birthday cake. *Perfect,* I snickered to myself.

Across the room, a cute little blond boy with big blue eyes sat in a Johnny Jumper, bouncing up and down to his heart's desire. "And this is Camden, the other beautiful man in my life," Robin said, radiating a genuine love.

"Hi, little guy, happy birthday," I spoke in baby-eze. He stilled and gave me his broad, four-toothed smile with the same dimples as his mom. My nephew? I tossed the words around in my head—my nephew. I had a nephew. I liked it.

"We have so much to catch up on, Amber…oh my God, I mean Destiny." Her hand went to her mouth. "I'm sorry."

I laughed out loud. "I don't mind, Robin. After all, we are the same person."

She laughed, too. "Everything about you reminds me of her."

"I'll take that as a compliment then."

"Absolutely."

Eventually, I made my way back toward the kitchen to find Julian and his mom talking alone. I paused outside the entrance when I saw Lisa pointing her finger at him. I caught some of her harsh words.

"I don't care that she might be the reincarnated Amber. What could you possibly be thinking about dating a girl half your age, Julian? She is way too young," she scolded him.

"Enough, Mom." He raised his voice and narrowed his eyes at her, then turned and made his way to the dining room.

My stomach churned and tears pricked my eyes. This was not a conversation I cared to eavesdrop on. Lisa had a point, but I chose to ignore her. How ironic that my parents were feeling the same way. I wiped the errant tears away from my face and headed for the dining room.

Elizabeth stood next to the table, dipping a sliced cucumber into the spinach dip when I rounded the corner.

"It's wonderful to see you again, Destiny." She held out her arms and I walked into them.

"I'm so glad I could make it." I'm not sure why—maybe it was Lisa's stinging words—but I blurted out, "My parents are coming to see me tomorrow. I can't wait. I've missed them."

"That's wonderful," she said.

I hugged her tight, hoping this gesture would make her feel as important as my mom.

I released her and turned, bumping into Lyle. "Excuse me, Lyle, I didn't see you."

"That's okay, pumpkin." His face turned crimson with embarrassment.

"I like it. You can call me pumpkin any time you want. In fact, I remember when you did it often."

His face filled with emotion. I remembered being his little girl. This had to be difficult for him. Without thinking, I wrapped my arms around him and gave him a tight hug. He didn't resist my embrace. Our adoration for each other transcended time. I released him and placed my arm around Julian, pulling him to my side. He was my safe place.

"When were you going to tell me about your parents' visiting tomorrow?" He whispered in my ear. I couldn't gauge the look on his face, but didn't think he was pleased.

"Eventually. It just slipped my mind, Julian. Let's talk about it later, okay?"

He opened his mouth to respond, but Robin's voice resonated throughout the room instead. "Before Camden gets cranky and tired, let's have him open the gifts." Ah, saved by my sister.

We all gathered in the living room. Julian offered me the large chair, but I refused and sat cross-legged on the floor between his feet. Logan and Lisa sat on the sofa while Lyle and Elizabeth brought a couple of chairs from the dining room. Liam stood behind Robin as she plopped onto the floor with Camden in her lap.

I pulled my phone from my pocket and took a picture of her. I had to capture this moment, forever.

Robin looked at me. "Could I have a picture with you, Destiny?" she asked. "I'd like to place it right next to that one." She pointed to the photo of her and Amber.

"I'd be honored," I said. I gave my phone to Julian and scooted over next to her. We draped our arms around each other with Camden in the middle and smiled while Julian snapped a photo of us.

One by one, the gifts were opened. Camden had a new fire engine, building blocks, some new clothes, and a new tricycle. He'd have to wait until he was older for that.

I'm not sure if it was on purpose or just by accident, but Robin opened Julian's and my gift last.

"Look, Camden, this is from your Uncle Julian and Aunt Destiny."

Jeez, she had us married already. Julian squeezed my shoulder affectionately. I had to admit, the thought of marriage with Julian in the future had crossed my mind, though we'd never actually talked about it. Of course, we had an uphill battle of persuading a few of the parents with the idea first. Mine included. I shot a glimpsed toward Lisa. Her face was unreadable.

With Robin's help, Camden removed the paper from the square box. She carefully lifted the lid and pushed the tissue paper to the side. She looked down and drew in a deep breath, bringing her shaky hand to her forehead. "Destiny, this is…" she stammered, "H—how did you know?"

Back in my former life when "we" were younger, Robin had a teddy bear with a missing button for the eye and tattered blue satin bow around its neck. She wouldn't go anywhere without that stuffed animal.

I knew I had some artistic talent and sewed an identical one-eyed stuffed teddy bear with a blue satin bow. "I remembered," I said.

She jumped up, disappeared into her bedroom, and reappeared with that tattered teddy bear. It looked exactly like the one I made. "You remembered this?"

"Yes, Robin."

She held out her arms and I lunged at her, holding her close, never wanting to let go. "Thank you, sis, I love you! I've missed you so much," she said through a voice choked with tears.

"Love you, too."

Lyle and Elizabeth looked on with wide eyes. You could see the love in their hearts.

We let go and I crawled back to Julian. His look was one of wonder and love.

It was a little past seven when we all gathered in the dining room for dessert. Sitting between Robin and Julian at the large, oval pedestal table, I stuffed my face with chocolate cake and vanilla ice cream, engaging in conversation. Camden began fussing shortly thereafter, clearly tired from the day's activities, so Robin excused herself and settled him into bed for the night.

She reemerged minutes later and resumed her seat beside me. She gave me a gentle nudge when she noticed Julian holding my hand under the table. It was almost like we were teenagers again. Actually, I was. She was just acting it.

"I remember your beat-up Honda Civic, Robin. You used to drive us to school," I said as Julian's gaze cut to me.

"Oh my God, you're right. I drove that car for another five years after that." Robin did a double take at some of the things I'd remembered.

I extended my hand to her, palm up. "Put your hand in mine."

She had a quizzical look on her face.

I went on to explain. "Sometimes when I touch the person, I can see buried memories."

When she placed her hand in mine, I trembled and pulled away abruptly. "Don't want to remember that one."

"What?" she asked.

"Nothing," I said.

"Destiny…spill it." She narrowed her eyes at me.

Instantly, I felt light-headed. How could I tell her the number of times, as teenagers, she tried to warn me off Julian with him sitting here next to me?

I made an inappropriate giggling sound, leaned over and whispered in her ear, "Remember how much you disliked Julian at the start of our relationship?"

"Ha ha. Yep. Let's bury that one."

I glanced around the table. Lyle and Elizabeth were taking in every word I said with a smile. Sitting next to Julian, Lisa was scowling at him, and Logan's attention was on a televised soccer match in the other room. Liam seemed genuinely interested but looked skeptical.

"Anything you feel like sharing with the rest of us?" Julian asked.

No. I shook my head.

"Not particularly," Robin chimed in.

"How much did Julian tell you?" I asked.

"He told me little things, like your memory of me, Mom, and Dad. He told me you remembered our house and went there with your mom."

Elizabeth's mouth dropped. "You were at the house, Destiny? You should've stopped in."

"You practically fainted when you saw me at the awards banquet, Elizabeth. Do you honestly think I would have just shown up at your home? You would have had a coronary."

She laughed. "Yes, I suppose you're right, honey."

"Actually, you did meet my mother. She was the woman who pretended she was looking for a Belinda Scott. Her curiosity got the better of her after my insisting you lived there. She needed proof of my former life as Amber."

She leaned back in her chair, cocking her head to the side. "That was your mother?" she asked, letting out a chuckle.

"I'm afraid so."

"I remember her as well, a beautiful woman," she added.

"Yup, that's my mom. It horrified me when she approached you while I sat in the car. I had no idea what she would say."

Robin cleared her throat bringing attention back to her. "Are you two back together?"

"Yes," I said in a squeaky voice.

"What are your parents like?"

I cringed. I didn't want to talk about my parents. It was just a reminder of how many times I'd lied to them in the last two weeks. "They're very protective of me. I had a brother who was killed in a car accident about eight years ago. They wouldn't let me out of their sight for a long time after that. And they're still a bit too overprotective today."

"Oh my God, Destiny, I'm so sorry." She grabbed my hand and squeezed it. "How do they feel about the age difference between you two?"

Instantly, I had Lisa's attention, feeling her eyes focusing on me. I slid down in my chair when my face heated. I couldn't look Robin in the eyes. I didn't know what to say.

"They're hesitant," I said.

Looking at Julian, an unsettled gaze crossed his face. I knew instantly what he was thinking and what our conversation would be about on the drive home.

"How are they handling your revelation of reincarnation?"

"At first, my mom thought it was all my imagination. But after I drove her to the house and pointed out things like the missing pine tree in the side yard and our initials in the Maple tree, I think she started to believe me. But, she may have just been placating me."

Lyle cleared his throat. "That pine tree died a year after Amber died. I had it cut down."

I gave him a somber look. My daddy. He was such a strong man, but he'd softened over the years—a gentle soul now.

Robin looked at me with a blank stare. "Well, I can't imagine little Camden coming to me someday in the future and declaring that he's reincarnated. That would freak me out. It must have been hard for your parents."

I hadn't thought about that. I'd just acted like they should believe and accept it. I'd been so insensitive. "I haven't had much of an opportunity to discuss it with them." I told myself that would change tomorrow. They deserved to understand more than anyone, and I'd been nothing but inconsiderate about it.

Robin ran her hand down my back. "This has been interesting. I've never known any reincarnated people, and now I have a sister, again."

"Yes, we both do," I said. I thought about what that entailed. Would Robin be someone I could confide my darkest secrets? I remembered when we sat on our beds chatting about boys. Many of those conversations were about the issues I'd had with a much younger Julian.

It was nearly eight in the evening when Lisa, Logan, Elizabeth, and Lyle stood from the table.

Lyle approached Robin and wrapped her in his arms. "It's getting late, so we're going to head home, sweetheart."

"Thanks for coming, Dad. I love you."

"Love you, too." Lyle smiled. I watched the two of them embrace each other. They looked so happy. I suspect Robin grew very close to him after I died and vice versa.

"Is there room in there for me?" I blurted out.

"Of course." Robin laughed.

I stepped into their open arms and the three of us nuzzled together, squeezing each other. I didn't want to let go. I don't think they wanted to, either.

I made my rounds saying goodbye to Elizabeth first. I gave her a tight hug. "It was great seeing you again."

"Same here, honey. You stop by anytime."

"Thank you. I will."

I turned to Lisa with outstretched arms. In spite of her earlier stinging words, she embraced me. I silently prayed she would eventually accept my relationship with Julian. She needed time and I was willing to, at the very least, give her that. Releasing her, I crossed the room and hugged Logan. Julian repeated my motions and one by one, they all left.

Robin looked at Julian. "You're not going too, are you?"

"We can stay a little while longer if you'd like," Julian said as he and Liam made their way to the living room to watch TV.

Robin and I cleared the table and put the food away.

"Did Julian ever mention the birthmark on my back?" I asked her.

"Yes. He told me it was because of the birthmark that he knew you were the reincarnated Amber."

While scraping a plate of uneaten cake into the trash, I relayed the whole incident to her, then turned so she could see my back. "Yep. See?" I pulled the strap of my camisole aside to show her my heart-shaped birthmark.

"Wow!" she exclaimed. "That is so fucking amazing!" she screamed as her hand went quickly to her mouth.

"Do you swear like that in front of your son?" I howled with laughter. It felt like we were back in Castle Pines.

"Surprisingly, I don't." She giggled.

I changed the tone of our chat. "I heard what happened to you after Amber died." I remembered seeing her at my funeral. She was utterly distraught. It was shortly after that when my memories abruptly ended and I was born into this life.

"Yes, it was a time in my life I never want to revisit."

"I'm so glad you're well now."

"Thank you, sis." She squeezed my hand in a loving gesture.

We chatted for another hour or so when Julian suggested we head back to his home. I could've stayed and talked all night, but I did have a big day tomorrow.

Robin and I locked our arms around each other, rocking back and forth. We exchanged phone numbers before Julian and I said our goodbyes and left. It was one of the best days of my life. I had a sister. Someone I could confide in. Someone I could shoot the breeze with. I exhaled happily.

JULIAN PULLED ONTO THE HIGHWAY, and turned his eyes to me, placing his hand on my thigh. "It was nice seeing Elizabeth and Lyle again."

"It's always nice seeing my mother...err...Elizabeth." My thoughts were scattered as I stared out the window. I prepared myself for the weight of his holy wrath, but instead, he surprised me with his softer side.

"Is something bothering you, Dest?"

"I don't know. I just wonder if I'm enough of a daughter for Elizabeth. Do I remind her of Amber? Do I fulfill that role?"

"Hey, she realizes you are her reincarnated daughter. If anything, I think she's fearful that she might push you too far. Do you understand what I mean? She loves you more than life itself."

"So, do you think I should call her Mom?"

"She's happy just having you in her life again. I don't think she cares what you call her. You should only do what makes you feel comfortable."

"Thank you, babe. You're always the voice of reason."

"I wouldn't go that far, but that's what I love about you. Just like Amber, you always think about others. Don't ever change, Dest."

"Thank you. You're too sweet. Changing is not on my agenda...ever." I placed my hand on top of his and a short silence filled the car.

"So, tell me about your parents visiting tomorrow, Destiny."

Crap! I thought he'd forgotten about them. Crap. Crap. Crap.

"They want to take me out to lunch."

"You haven't said anything about me coming along."

Where was he going with this? "I think it would be best if you didn't."

Suddenly, Julian was quiet. Was he upset that he may not see me tomorrow or that I hadn't invited him? After all, he had every right to be. The weekends were ours. Although, I couldn't figure out what he was thinking.

"What's the matter? Suddenly you're not speaking?" I asked.

With a pathetic sad face, he asked, "Are you ashamed of me?"

"Oh my God, Julian, nothing could be further from the truth." How could he think that?

He went silent again. I didn't dare ask him what his thoughts were. I shifted in my seat. I felt uncomfortable.

"Do your parents know about us, Destiny?" He sounded angry.

Shit! He was going to be downright furious, and rightly so. Should I lie again? *Dammit!*

"No, they don't," I mumbled.

"Fuck, Destiny. Why the hell haven't you told them about me? I thought you were going to fill them in on our relationship two weeks ago! Why?" he shouted, making me flinch.

"I haven't gotten around to it yet," I said, my voice barely audible.

"What the hell kind of excuse is that?" His anger intensified. "Fuck this." He slammed his fist into the steering wheel, making me jump.

"They disapprove of me seeing you. What do you want me to say?"

"Of course they do. I'm fucking eighteen years older than you. I can't believe I've been so stupid. I thought I made it clear to you two weeks ago that I wasn't going to play games at this point in my goddamned life!" he yelled. "You promised, Destiny." He growled. "Fuck."

"Stop yelling at me!" I screamed back.

"This whole situation is fucked up. I can't believe you haven't told them. I've been under the impression they knew. I knew I should've insisted on talking to them myself weeks ago."

I started to cry. "Stop swearing at me. I'm sorry, Julian. I'm so sorry."

He hesitated, staring ahead without taking his eyes off the road. He didn't look at me. I couldn't read his thoughts but knew I had screwed up.

"I'm sorry for yelling." His brow creased.

"Don't worry. I'll tell them tomorrow," I lied again. Jeez, what was wrong with me? I was lying to the man I loved. I knew any discussion with my parents about Julian would be futile.

"That's what you told me two weeks ago." He sounded angry again. Did he see right through me?

"They will find out tomorrow. Trust me." I couldn't bear to lose Julian and knew my parents would disapprove of him no matter what I said.

"Trust you? I'm having a hard time believing you right now."

My stomach clenched. "You need to give me time to break it to them. Please," I begged him.

"Destiny, you've had weeks. How much time do you need?"

I had no answer. He was right and I didn't want to sour his mood any more than it was. "Speaking of which…I overheard the conversation with your mom in the kitchen."

He flinched, whipping his head around to me.

"She doesn't approve of me any more than my parents approve of you. It works both ways here, Julian."

A few silent minutes passed before I felt him squeeze my thigh with his gentle touch.

"Can you spend the night or do you need to go back to your dorm?" His voice softened.

What? Talk about a Dr. Jekyll and Mr. Hyde. He could turn it on and off at the flick of a switch. "If I leave by ten tomorrow morning, then I can stay at your place tonight."

"Good, I'd like you to stay, then."

JULIAN WATCHED ME like a hawk while performing my nightly routine. His eyes never left me when I removed my clothes. Then he followed me to the bathroom, staring as I washed my face and brushed my teeth. It was like he needed to commit my every move to his memory, as though he'd never see me again.

"What are you doing?" I asked.

"Looking at you. Do you have a problem with that?"

"No, but you're being weird about it." I giggled.

He brushed his teeth alongside me and together, we went to bed and made slow, passionate love—slower than we'd ever done before.

"I love you, Julian. I'll love you until the end of time, babe."

"I love you too, Destiny, more than you could ever know. Don't leave me."

"I promise I won't ever leave you."

He pulled me close to him, nuzzling his body into mine. I shuddered when a feeling of dread came over me before I fell into a deep, disturbed sleep.

Chapter Twenty-Five

The Buckhorn Exchange was a whimsical place, claiming to be Denver's oldest restaurant, where taxidermy wildlife adorned the blood-red walls. Red and white checkerboard tablecloths and wooden chairs filled the room as far as the eye could see. My mom, dad and I were seated quickly. They'd arrived at my dorm for parent's weekend shortly before noon. I was as excited to see them as they were me.

A tall waitress, dressed in the same western-styled uniform and leather apron donned by the rest of the staff, appeared at our table and took our drink order. She sounded hoarse, apologizing for her sore throat.

After we'd rattled off our drink choices, my mom started in. "So, tell us about school." She smiled at me with the same love I'd seen my entire life.

Tracing a square pattern in the tablecloth with my index finger, I started rambling on and on about my daily schedule, walking both parents through my week.

While tapping my foot in time to the raspy vocals of a woman playing an acoustic guitar across the room, the waitress returned with a tray of ice water and two beers, then took our food order.

My mom started nervously fiddling with her napkin. "It sounds like you're having a terrific experience, honey."

Oh, if she only knew the kind of experience I was having. Seeing the love in her eyes, I knew I couldn't bear to change that adoration by telling her I was still seeing Julian.

"I am, Mom. I love it. My astronomy class is amazing. I'll have to take you and dad to the planetarium. I find the stars so intriguing. It's like you're sitting out under the real sky."

When the food arrived at our table shortly thereafter, I thought maybe this was a good time to discuss my reincarnation with them. They were the only parents I'd known up until a week ago.

I dipped my steak sandwich in my soup and took a bite. It was delicious. "I realize I'd never asked how you two felt since I'd discovered my reincarnation."

My mom did an about-face, looking at me as if I had fingers growing out of my ears, but remained silent. Except for the rumble of a passing train interrupting our meal, the silence was deafening.

"Are you having more memories?" Daddy finally asked, ending the lull in conversation.

"All the time—especially when…" I stopped, almost giving away my relationship with Julian. I sagged slightly.

"Especially when…what?" Mom asked.

"Nothing—" I quickly changed direction. "So, what is your impression of it?"

My mom lifted her shoulder in a half shrug. "I guess I find it fascinating. I mean, why us?"

Why them? I wasn't sure what the answer to that question was. Maybe deep down I'd known Timmy would die.

"Because I chose you."

My daddy smiled and patted my hand. "Fill us in on some of your memories."

"First, do you remember the mark on my belly?"

"Yes." My mom responded with a nod of acknowledgment.

"Amber was stabbed in that exact spot. Secondly, she had a heart-shaped birthmark on her back shoulder, just like mine, in the same spot."

My mom narrowed her brows at me. "And you suddenly had an epiphany with all this?"

"Yes, things come to me every day." I couldn't tell them how Julian triggered most of my memories. I peeked through my eyelashes and took another bite of my sandwich. "So how are things in Boulder?"

She blew on the steam rising from her spoonful of soup. "Other than living in a house too large for two people, things are good."

"Well, I'll be home on occasion."

"We know, sweetheart. Don't worry about us." My dad sighed heavily and looked at my mom with a tight smile.

My mom grimaced at him. "So, why didn't you mention any of these instances years ago?"

"I did, but you always chalked them up as fantasies." I raised an eyebrow, giving her a glassy stare. "Remember?"

My dad steepled his long fingers together. "I'm not thoroughly convinced now. Maybe you're a bit psychic and confusing the two."

I sighed and folded my arms across my chest. "I'm not sure what I need to say or do to convince either of you…" I hesitated. I was taking a gamble, but went on, "Dr. Cahill filled in a lot of the blanks for me the last time I saw him." There, that should satisfy their curiosity.

Mom rolled her eyes while my dad subtly shook his head.

Crap! I opened my mouth to criticize but stopped short when a tall gentleman with snow-white hair stopped at our table to ask if we'd enjoyed our meal. His nametag read: Phil Sutton, General Manager.

"Marcus Bradshaw." My dad stood and shook hands with Phil, who must have been well over six feet. "Great meal. A mystical place you have here."

"Thanks, Marcus. Phil Sutton here," he said.

My mom shifted her gaze around the room. "How many stuffed taxidermy do you have in here?"

Phil waved his hands. "At last count, there were five hundred and forty-two."

"Interesting," my dad said and sat back down.

Phil nodded and tapped his knuckles on the table before moving along to the next table. "Enjoy your meals."

"Thanks," we said in unison.

A half hour later, we'd finished eating. My dad paid the check and placed a generous tip on the table.

"I'm glad both of you came to see me. I had a fabulous time."

Mom brushed her hand down my arm. "Same here, darling."

"I can't wait to show you around the campus."

"Well, lead the way, pumpkin," my dad said.

We stood from the table, ready to leave when I looked up and saw a familiar face staring back at me. I wasn't sure where I'd seen him as he approached our table.

"Marcus, how are you?" The man's eyes stayed fixed on me. Where had I seen him before? He shook hands with my dad as he flipped the hair off his face with a flick of his head.

All at once, a cold dread filled my body, suddenly realizing from where I knew him. *No. No.* He could ruin everything for me.

"Hi Owen, it's been a long time. You're a doctor now, right?" My dad smiled. "This is my wife, Cynthia, and daughter, Destiny." He gestured with his hand. "This is Dr. Owen Saunders, an old friend of mine."

"Pleasure, ladies." Dr. Saunders looked at mom and me and then returned his eyes to my dad.

Good, maybe he didn't recognize me. *Oh, please, let that be the case.*

"What brings you to town, Marcus?" He turned his gaze back to me, scrunching his face tight as if trying to remember something. *Please don't remember. Please.* I willed to him in my mind.

I looked down in an attempt to block my face from his prying eyes. Maybe if he couldn't see me, then surely he wouldn't recognize me.

"We've come to visit Destiny at school. She's a freshman at the university."

"Wonderful, Marcus…an excellent school."

My mom extended an outstretched hand. "Pleasure to meet you, Owen. How do you know Marcus?"

"We were old friends from high school."

Abruptly, recognition filled his face, his eyes bugging out of their sockets. "Now I remember where I've seen you, Destiny. It was at the awards banquet. I didn't realize you were dating Dr. Julian Cahill."

No! Suddenly, I felt every bit of blood drain from my face. This couldn't be happening. I couldn't breathe and felt sick. I became mute when my parents turned to me. I wanted to run as far away as I could.

"Who's Jul…" My mom stopped short, her eyes wide—very wide. "Oh no, don't tell me you're still seeing that older man, Destiny."

I think Dr. Saunders realized his blunder for revealing my secret when his face flushed red—and rightly so. He immediately appeared fidgety and nervous.

"We'll have to get together and catch up, Marcus. I've got an appointment at the hospital in fifteen minutes." He lied. I could tell. After all, I was in the throes of a huge one myself.

I could only assume he recognized what he'd done and seemed to be searching for an escape route.

"It was nice seeing all of you."

I narrowed my eyes at him.

"Sure, Owen." My dad stood and shook hands.

My mom reached for his hand as well. "It was a pleasure, Owen."

He turned and disappeared hastily from view, without a second glance.

Attention was back on me. Shit. My legs wobbled as I sank back down in my chair, unable to speak when my mom continued to probe and interrogate me.

To think, I was only short minutes away from leaving the restaurant with a smile on my face. Now, I sat here wanting to cry.

"Destiny, your silence speaks volumes," she hissed.

Suddenly, I wanted to be anywhere but here, receiving the third degree. This could only end badly for me.

Thank God Mom exercised a respectable amount of discretion (certainly more than Sarah) and agreed to discuss it outside the restaurant. I began wondering if I should start avoiding restaurants altogether. Though, it would only delay the inevitable for me.

Mom was angry, her face a beet red. My eyes may have been playing tricks on me, but I thought I saw her ears smolder.

"Why, Destiny?"

All I could think about was how great everything was between Julian and me. That, I feared, was about to change. How could I make her understand how much I loved and cared for him?

I finally found my voice. "I just went to a hospital function with him."

My mom clenched her teeth and lowered her voice. "And the lies continue." She looked to my dad. "Marcus, let's go."

Was I ready for her wrath? How bad could it be? Yes, my dad would be able to tamper the flames radiating from within her.

"Calm down, Mom. You're scaring me."

"Oh, believe me, Destiny. You're right to feel scared. I'm way beyond angry."

We left the restaurant and made our way to the car. I was reluctant to climb in.

My dad's breathing grew heavy and labored. "Get in the goddamn car, Destiny!"

Shit! My dad was usually a quiet, soft-spoken man. Not much riled him unless warranted and then you didn't want to be standing in the path of his wrath, but he looked as angry as my mom. Maybe more. *Double shit!* It was two against one.

I quickly jumped into the back seat. I snuggled up against the door my dad had slammed shut only moments ago and gripped the door handle just in case I had to make a quick getaway.

My parents hurriedly hopped into the front seats, and my dad proceeded to peel out of the parking lot. I didn't have a prayer.

Gazing outside the windows, my shoulders slouched, and my eyes filled with tears. That's when I noticed my dad driving past the exit for my college dorm. "Where are you going, Daddy?"

"Home." My mom fumed with anger.

"Why? I have homework to do and need to get back to my dorm."

Mom scowled, her rage palpable. "Keep your mouth shut, Destiny. We need a private place to discuss this, and your dorm is *not* the place."

I knew it was going to be bad, now. They meant business. *Damn Owen Saunders. Damn him to hell.* On the other hand, why did I lie? I asked myself that question all the way home. Why was I afraid of telling them the truth? Julian asked me the same question. Would this have been a different outcome if I'd been up-front about it from the beginning? For whatever reason, I seriously doubted it.

Forty minutes later, we pulled into our driveway. My dad exited the car, instantly storming into the house. I opened my door slowly and climbed out, my mom standing by, watching my every move. The look on her face reminded me of the time my brother, Timmy, was caught drinking and driving. I truly think she could've killed him. Right now, the look was the same.

My chest tightened, and I started to cry. Tears flowed in a steady stream down my face.

"Save the waterworks, Destiny."

Dragging one foot in front of the other, I made my way inside the house.

My dad paced back and forth in the living room. "Sit your goddamn ass down on the sofa—*now!*"

I jumped at his demanding tone and sat. Tears continued to flow down my cheeks. My parents looked like two wild animals ready to pounce on a tasty meal, and I was their scared kitty-cat. I knew I was going to be dragged through the ringer.

Mom stood before me, sleeves rolled up and hands on her hips. "What are you thinking, Destiny? Do you have any idea how disappointed we are? I don't know if we're more upset you lied or the fact that you're still seeing this older man when we told you to break it off."

"But—"

"Shut your mouth. You will listen to what we have to say before you will be allowed to speak," she interrupted me.

"Jeez. Treat me like a child. That'll make me talk." I couldn't hold my tongue anymore.

I saw it a split second before I felt the burning sting of her palm as it made contact with the side of my face. *Ouch!* I'd never been hit before in my life by either of my parents. I knew at this moment that my relationship with her would never be the same again.

I raised my hand and gently rubbed my cheek, hoping to soothe the sting of the slap.

I wanted to run as far away from here as I could. I wanted to be with Julian. I wanted to run into his arms, but that wasn't going to happen—ever again. That's when it dawned on me…he damn well knew this was going to happen. His incessant need to watch my every move the night before and make slow passionate love to me was all an act of desperation. Oh, why didn't I tell them when Julian asked me?

"Don't you dare hit me again…ever." The fierceness of my words spilled from my mouth before I could control them. "Okay, you want to know about my relationship with Julian?" I didn't know what came over me, but suddenly, I felt brave. Really brave. I took a deep breath and started yelling. "Yes, I've been seeing him for the last two weeks. I love him, and he loves me. We were teenage lovers eighteen years ago in my former life, and I'll be damned if I'm going to lose him again, in this life!"

My mom looked at me with cold, dead eyes. "Don't you take that tone with us, and stop with all that reincarnation garbage! What the hell do you know about loving someone anyway? You're eighteen, for heaven's sake. And furthermore, you are *not* going to see him again—end of story."

My phone chimed with an incoming text. I knew it was Julian based on the ringtone I assigned to him. I pulled it from my pocket and quickly read the message. I had limited time.

Julian: Destiny, where are you? Please tell me you're okay?

A panicked urgency in his words gripped me. I wanted desperately to answer him. The fact that I couldn't was tearing me apart. All I wanted were his arms around me, telling me everything would be okay. How would I go on without him? *Oh Julian, please come and get me. Take me away from this nightmare.*

"Go to your bedroom, Destiny," my dad ordered. "Your mom and I need to discuss a fitting punishment. But before you go, hand over your phone."

"But…"

"Now!"

I exited the message screen before gruffly handing my phone over to him, and then stood and stomped my feet up the stairs to my bedroom, slamming the door. Would I be spending the night here? Would I be allowed to go back to school at all?

How could one person go from being on top of the world one day to the depths of despair the next? I felt broken.

Without my phone, I had nothing. Not being able to talk with Julian, I wouldn't be able to function.

I plopped onto my bed head first and sobbed loud cries into my pillow. My mind drifted to the last two weeks of my life with Julian—learning I was the reincarnated Amber, making love, his awards banquet—and then it dawned on me how I should've stayed out of the public eye. That's where I went wrong.

No, I was not going to hide my relationship with him, but I should have known I'd be spotted by someone my parents knew. I scolded myself.

Who was I kidding? It was the fact that I'd lied. If I'd been upfront about our relationship from the start, perhaps my parents would eventually have come around. My head was reeling.

Moments later, a knock on the door pulled me out of my personal hell. I ignored it. I wanted to be left alone. My mom strutted in anyway and handed me back my phone. "Your phone number has been changed and just so you know, there is a tracking device in there." She stood, hands on her hips, looking down on me lying prone across my bed. "We will be watching you. Apparently, you can't be trusted. We'll know every call you make and receive, so don't think you'll get away with anything."

I could tell she was waiting for my reaction, of which I had nothing to give her. I felt empty, and a strangled sob left my body. I just lay there, completely numb and glared at my phone as if at any moment, it would self-destruct.

I couldn't look at her, either—she was the mother who slapped me across the face. I'm not sure, but I think I hated her at this moment.

"You need to choose between staying with him or us continuing to pay for your college. Your choice. But, we will completely cut you off if you decide on him. It's him or us. Do you understand the rules?"

I stared at her with contempt, sniffling between hiccups. "I, at least, owe him an explanation."

She raised her voice a notch. "Maybe you didn't hear me when I said you were *not* to have any contact with him, again. He'll get the message eventually."

What a horribly cruel thing to say. I didn't dare say the words out loud, for fear of another strike across my face, but certainly thought them. I gave her my full-on scowl instead.

The anger bubbling inside me grew. I heaved my phone across the room. It slammed against my closet door and then skidded across the floor underneath my dresser. It meant nothing to me.

"Fine, you break the phone, and you'll have nothing."

I pressed my trembling hands into fists and hissed at her, "I already have nothing." The thought of giving college up made me ill, but I loved Julian, too. "I'd like to get back to school. I have homework to complete for my classes tomorrow."

"We'll know if he shows up at your dorm as well, just so you know, Destiny."

I never questioned their unexplained intrusion into my life. Since my brother, Timmy's death, I'd learned to live with it. "I have no control over that and chances are, without an explanation from me, he undoubtedly will show up."

"Destiny, you know the rules. Live with them or else."

DROPPING ME OFF AT MY DORM shortly after nine in the evening, my dad glared at me before I exited the car, making my knees go weak. "Bye, Destiny."

I ignored him. Chloe and Gabby greeted me at the door when I wandered in. My tear-filled eyes quickly gave me away.

"Holy shit, Destiny, what the hell is going on? Julian's been here looking for you. He said your phone is no longer in service," Gabby said, rapid firing the events of the day as they unfolded. "Call him."

I started bawling loudly. "My parents found out about him, and I've been forbidden to have any contact whatsoever!"

Chloe held out her arms, and I buried myself in them. "How the hell did they find out?" she asked, caressing my back.

I pushed back and told both of them about the restaurant fiasco. "They reprogrammed my phone with a new number and put a tracking device on it. They'll know if I have any contact with him."

"Jeez." Chloe pulled her phone from her pocket and held it out to me. "Here, call him from mine. They can't trace this."

It was tempting but too dangerous at this point in the game. "I wouldn't put it past them. So, thank you anyway, but I can't take that chance. Not now, anyway."

"So, you're going to cut him off, just like that?"

"I have to. That's what my parents demanded I do."

"Wow, that's cruel and unusual punishment," Gabby interjected.

"Yeah, tell me about it." I let go of Chloe, straightening myself, and dragged my exhausted body into my bedroom. I sat down on my bed and stared at the floor. My eyes lifted to the picture sitting on my desk that Chloe took of Julian and me right before we headed to the awards banquet. Thank God I printed it out before my phone database had been wiped clean.

I held the framed photo in my hands and focused on our faces. We were so happy that night.

Of course, that damned Dr. Saunders was the reason I was in this predicament right now. With tears streaming down my cheeks, I raised the photo to my lips and kissed Julian. I was going to miss that beautiful face. A tear fell on the glass. I wiped it away with my thumb and plopped down face-first into my pillow, hugging the framed photo, and cried myself to sleep.

I SKIPPED MY FIRST CLASS on Monday morning. I wasn't in any frame of mind to attend school. Plus, I hadn't finished any of my homework assignments. In less than twenty-four hours, my life was in shambles.

I stayed in bed all morning. Lunch with my parents the day before was the last meal I'd eaten. I wasn't hungry, either.

Then it registered that I needed to return Julian's key. It would give me an opportunity to leave him a note, too. He deserved that much. I knew he'd be working all day, so I was sure I'd be safe from running into him. I made a rash decision, enlisting the help of Chloe, asking if she'd drive me to his place.

"Absolutely, girl." She grinned with humor, saying she'd love to snoop around a wealthy guy's bachelor pad.

"Thanks, Chloe." I frowned.

Looking like I'd been hit by a Mack truck, I finally got dressed for the day. I went through the motions of brushing my hair and teeth before finding a disguise to hide my face. Chloe let me borrow one of her boyfriend's baseball caps. It was an effort, but I managed to tuck all my hair under the rim of the cap. I applied some heavy makeup to my eyes and signaled I was ready to go, feeling confident I had all my bases covered.

Ten minutes later, we pulled into the underground garage of Julian's building. Relief gushed through me when I didn't see his car and I was pretty sure we weren't followed.

As I punched in the access code to the penthouse elevator, Chloe gasped, "Penthouse! Holy crap!"

I nodded, feeling unemotional. Together, we rode up to the twenty-seventh floor.

She wrapped her arm around me, holding me upright. "Are you okay, Destiny? You're shaking like a leaf."

"I'm so nervous my parents will find out I've been here. They said they'd know my every move, but I left my phone at the dorm, so I hope I'm safe."

"Well, your secret is safe with me."

When the door of the elevator opened, we climbed out. I held the key to Julian's place in my hand. This was it—the only part of him I had left, and I was about to abandon that. Suddenly I broke down again and sobbed softly. "Thank you for coming with me, Chloe."

"Anything for my favorite roomy."

I inserted the key into the lock and opened the door to Julian's home.

Chloe's mouth dropped open. "Holy shit, look at this place. It's huge."

"He's a doctor. What did you expect?" I nudged her.

She laughed. "Since you won't be dating him anymore, could I have him?"

Part of me wanted to scowl at her, but I knew he wasn't mine anymore, so instead, I just giggled softly. I looked around for a sign that he'd been here. A fresh pine scent mixed with stale beer hung in the air. I knew Carolyn had been here in the last couple days.

Five empty beer bottles, sitting on the coffee table, and disheveled sheets on his bed told me he drank himself into a stupor the night before. My poor, beautiful boyfriend. What had I done?

I shuffled my feet to my favorite place in front of the wall of windows of the living room and stared out at the beauty in front of me. I tried to memorize the landscape.

I gave Chloe a tour of the place—part of me wanted to take one final look around myself. This was the last time I would be here.

I promised him I would never leave, yet here I was…saying goodbye forever. Completely wrecked, I placed the key on a hand-written piece of stationary I brought from my dorm, and set it on the kitchen island.

Dear Julian,

My tears are endless as I write this. I am so, so, sorry to say that I can no longer see you. Please don't try to come to me; it will only make things worse for us. Please know that I had to do this. Our times together were the best of my life. I will never forget you. Please promise me you'll be happy. I hope that you can forgive me.

I will always love you with all of my heart.

I'm sorry again.

I love you, forever, Julian.

Love, Destiny

I told the love of my life goodbye, one last time, and then left.

"Goodbye, Julian," I silently whispered to myself. The tears flowed heavily down my face. I wiped them away with the back of my hand as Chloe wrapped her arm around my shoulder. Eventually, we made our way back to the car.

Back at our dorm minutes later, I couldn't stop crying. The pain I felt cut through me to my soul; a mental and physical grief. I tried to do some homework, but the lack of food in my stomach was a shock to my system and depleted my energy, too.

I sank into my bed again and fell asleep through more tears.

I WAS JARRED AWAKE by the sound of pounding on the door. The darkness of my room sent a cold chill through me. I lifted my head and looked at the clock. Eleven at night. I switched on my bedside lamp. Then I heard him.

"Destiny! Destiny! Open the goddamn door!" Julian bellowed.

In my sleepy stupor, I babbled incoherently to myself. *He's here to save me. My man's here to save me.* Then reality jolted me awake like a cold shower. No, no, he mustn't see me. He can't be here. They will know. No, no!

An out-of-breath Gabby appeared in my bedroom. "Destiny, what do you want me to do?"

"Tell him I can't see him." I started bawling again. I couldn't believe I had any tears left.

Gabby turned and scampered away. "She not here, Julian!" she yelled through the door.

"The hell she's not. Open the goddamn door." He pounded again. "Her car's in the parking lot. I know she's in there."

"I can't do that, Julian."

"I need to talk to her. Please open the door." He sounded calmer but still terrified. "Please."

Gabby returned to my room and stood in the doorway. "Destiny, he sounds so desperate. What should I do?"

"I can't see him," I said, sounding more forceful. "My parents will know. Trust me. It's ripping me apart to ignore him, but I just can't."

"Destiny, we can work this out. Please talk to me." Julian stopped as if waiting for a response from me. When none came, he continued to pound on the door. "Destiny, I know you're in there. Please don't do this to me, again." Another long silence.

A confused look crossed Gabby's face. "You did this to him before?"

"It's a long story. I'll explain at another time. Okay?"

"Sure, girl."

I wanted to go to him but feared my parent's threats. I stayed in my room. I knew he needed me and I needed him...more than anything.

"Fuck this, Destiny. This is it. I'm through. Done! I knew I should have let you go!" he shouted. Did he know I heard him?

Oh, please don't give up on us, Julian. There will come a day when I will come back to you. Please, be patient. I was utterly shattered. Damn my parents. Damn Dr. Saunders.

Eventually, silence filled the air for the rest of the night. I knew Julian had left.

MY PHONE RANG the following morning. I prayed it wouldn't be my parents but knew it was. They were the only ones who had my new number. I looked at the screen when I reached for it from my nightstand. I sagged into my mattress. It was my mom.

Barely giving me time to say hello, she started in after I answered. "Do you want to explain to me why you went to his place of residence yesterday? I don't think you understand the severity of your misstep, Destiny."

I clutched my arms to my chest. Shit. How did she know? I broke out into a cold sweat. This was it. I needed to figure out a way to pay for college. There was no doubt in my mind that my parents were going to cut me off.

"You were smart not to let him into your dorm room last night."

Her intrusion into my life was out of control. I had no privacy whatsoever.

I let loose on her. "Do you have someone watching me?" I'd decided to stop lying. "He wasn't home when I dropped his key off, Mother." She was no longer "Mom" to me; she was only the person who gave birth to me. I had another mother who loved me.

"We know. You're lucky," she spat at me.

"Jeez, I don't feel all that lucky with your constant meddling in my life." I'd had enough. "Now, if you're done berating me, I have homework to do." I clenched my hand into a white knuckle fist and slammed it into my mattress. "I haven't seen him nor have I talked to him, so call off the dogs and leave me the hell alone!" I screamed at her but didn't care.

"Destiny, I'm sorry, but you will thank us later. Trust me, darling." Her voice had softened.

I hit the end button on my phone and hung up. I didn't want to hear another word from her telling me how this could be a good thing. She didn't call back, either.

Chapter Twenty-Six

An entire agonizing month had crawled by since I'd left Julian. My parents called me on a weekly basis. I wondered why because I had nothing to say to them. My mother's attempt to wheedle information out of me ended in futility for her. I wanted nothing more to do either one of them. I followed with short one-word answers, in hopes of making the conversation brief. It worked.

Eventually, they stopped hounding me with every move I made, but that didn't change the way I felt about them. I still resented them for my unhappiness. I had no one. Would Julian ever forgive me? Would I ever see him again?

I returned to school but couldn't concentrate. I always felt sad. Julian hadn't come back after that last night, either. I missed him so much.

I cried all the time. Confusion swamped my head with jumbled thoughts, unable to think straight. I had to snap out of this, but how?

My health had declined as well. I was lucky if I ate one meal a day and my head ached all the time.

NOVEMBER CREPT NEAR with cooler temperatures matching my mood, forcing me through the motions of my daily life with no direction. I'd lost fifteen pounds while Chloe and Gabby grew increasingly worried about me. My dorm room looked as if a tornado hit it, surrounded in turmoil, just like me. Clothes were strewn across the floor and hanging from doorknobs.

I went for a long walk around campus trying to clear my head of all my misery and sorrow. I arrived back at my dorm to Chloe and Gabby's inquisition of my whereabouts.

"C'mon, you two, my parents are bad enough. I don't need you two chastising me as well." My voice was edgier than I intended.

"Sorry, Destiny," Chloe snapped back, returning her attention to some homework at the kitchen table. "Can't I be concerned about you?"

"Sorry, my life is hell right now, and I shouldn't be taking it out on both of you."

"Apology accepted," Gabby responded with a half-smile.

THE FOLLOWING MONDAY, I'd finished my classes for the day when it occurred to me. Could Robin shed some light on this? Should I call her? *Yes, call her,* I told myself.

I sat on my bed, pulled my phone from my back pocket and scanned the contact list. To my surprise, her information was still intact. My parents hadn't erased everything. I stuck my tongue out, and snorted dismissively at them, then dialed Robin's number.

"Hello." Her voice sounded like music to my ears.

"Robin?"

"Yes, who's calling?" she asked.

"This is Destiny. Could I come up for a short visit or are you busy?"

There was a long pause. "What do you want?" she snapped, filling the void.

My head drooped, sensing her anger. No doubt she knew exactly what happened. Of course she did. She was a close family friend of the Cahills. Why wouldn't she know?

For a moment, I'd considered hanging up. Tears threatened my eyes. She was the only person I had left to share my feelings, but now I feared her rejection, too. "Please don't hang up, Robin. Just give me a minute to explain my side of the story...please."

She let out a deep breath. "I don't have anything to say to you. I'm not going to beat around the bush, Destiny. I know that you broke

Julian's heart and I'm pretty furious with you. He's devastated. How could you do this to him? The sister I knew would never have done this."

My hands began to tremble and my mouth went dry. I stumbled over my words, trying desperately to organize my scrambled thoughts. "Please," I begged, rubbing my sweaty palms down my pants. "You're the only person I can talk to."

For a moment, silence filled the air. "Fine, I just put Camden down for a nap." She sounded gruff. "Can you come now?"

"Yes." I let out a deep breath. "Thank you. I'll be right there."

THIRTY MINUTES LATER, I found myself ringing the doorbell of Robin's house. She opened the door, greeting me with her scowled expression, filling my head with thoughts of escaping. The smell of baby lotion and a fresh, minty deodorizer filled my nostrils when I stepped through the door.

A dull hollowness suddenly engulfed me. "I need you. I have no one anymore. I'm desperate."

She stood there, examining me with hands on her hips. "Whose fault is that?" she asked brusquely. "Forgive me for saying, but you look horrible, Destiny. How much weight have you lost? Your face is pale and sunk-in and don't even get me started on those dark circles around your eyes."

I couldn't swallow past the ache in the back of my throat and the waterworks began, again. Lately, crying seemed to be the only thing I did well.

"So tell me, what the hell happened?" she asked abruptly, making me jump. Suddenly, my body was hyperaware to noise. Robin motioned for us to move to the living room.

I dragged my listless legs to the comfy cushions of the sofa and plopped my body down. She followed. I filled her in on everything I could think of at that moment from the restaurant and phone fiasco to my parents cutting me off permanently. She tucked one leg under the other and faced me. I mirrored her position. Her eyes never left mine as I talked. It felt so good to unload my emotions on her. It was as though a weight had lifted from my shoulders.

"I love and miss him so much." I sniffed, wiping my nose with the back of my hand. She leaned over and wrapped her arms around me. I buried my face into her shoulder and sobbed big, fat tears. "I think I've lost him forever, Robin."

"That explains why I couldn't reach you. I tried to call, but your number is disconnected." Her body sagged with relief. "He'd contacted me to ask if I'd heard from you. I told her I hadn't. Shortly after, he left the country, taking a sabbatical to get away." She sighed. "I haven't seen him in a few weeks, but right after you left him, he was a wreck."

My burning eyes bugged out of my face. I pushed away from her. "Really? I haven't seen or heard from him since that night he showed up at my dorm. That's probably why." He left the country. My poor devastated Julian. I longed to go to him and heal his broken heart.

She peered into my eyes. "I've heard he's back but don't know where he's staying. I'm guessing he's most likely at his home." She paused, looking as if she was mulling something over. "There's a huge age difference between you two. You should've assumed there'd be issues."

My body went limp. "I know," I whispered.

A whimper from Camden led Robin's attention to the baby monitor. He quieted, and then she returned her focus to me. "I don't know what to tell you, Destiny. All he wanted was to talk, but you wouldn't even give him that." She regarded me cautiously. "Have you tried to work it out with your parents?"

"They won't listen to anything I have to say. They continue to threaten me whenever they can. Anyway, I want nothing to do with them."

"Why don't you go talk to my mom and dad?"

"I'd love to, but my parents seem to know my every move. I'm sure they'll be asking me about this trip to see you."

She closed her eyes and shook her head in disbelief.

Moments later, Camden began crying again. When she stood and left the room, my thoughts drifted to her words. *I'd heard he left the country, taking a sabbatical to get away...he's a wreck.* I did this to him. How could he ever forgive me?

She returned with Camden in her arms a few minutes later.

"You're such a great mom, Robin." I could tell she loved and adored him. It made me think of when Julian met his mom for the first time. She loved him with all her heart.

"Thank you, sis. Would you like to change his diaper?"

"Sure, I did a bit of babysitting when I was in high school."

Robin laid Camden down on the sofa beside me, handed me a diaper and some wipes, and I made short work of his soiled bottom.

"So, where did you come up with the name, Camden?" I asked as I snapped the legs of his pants together.

"Well, I tried to use some letters from Amber's name to come up with a boy's name. That's how I arrived at Camden." She giggled. "He was almost named Camber, but I couldn't do that to him. Liam put his foot down on that one, too."

I laughed. "Very clever."

"Liam won't be home until later. Would you like to stay for dinner?" She eyed me up and down. "You look as though you could use a good meal."

"I saw that, Robin." I rolled my eyes. "I'd love to stay. How can I help?"

"If you could entertain Camden, it would be a huge help."

"In that case, I'd love to get acquainted with my nephew."

Robin stood and disappeared into the kitchen to start preparing dinner while I read Camden a book. I wasn't sure if I'd scrambled the words together when my vision blurred and head began to ache. *What was that about?*

The thought that I had a nephew made my heart swell. Two months before this, I didn't even know I had a sister and now, here I was holding my nephew.

Twenty minutes later, we sat down to a delicious meal of spaghetti and meatballs. It was the first real meal I'd eaten in nearly two months. I was famished.

"So, what are you going to do?" She asked as she buckled Camden into his highchair.

I twirled my fork into the pasta and lifted it to my mouth. "I was hoping you'd offer some ideas. I've exhausted every scenario."

"To be perfectly honest, I would call your parents' bluff."

I nearly choked on my food. "Really? You obviously don't know them as I do. That's out of the question."

She cut up some meatballs onto a plate and placed them on Camden's tray. He dug into his tasty meal with both hands.

She sat down and served herself some pasta and sauce. "Really? Would they cut you off? Think about it. After the death of your brother, you're the only child they have left. Do you honestly believe they'd sever ties with you?"

She had a good point, but I wasn't sure I was brave enough to tempt my own fate, so I decided to change the subject. "This meal is delicious, thank you." I set my fork down and stroked Camden's head. "It's good, isn't it, little guy?"

"Just think about it, sis," she said.

"I will."

Finishing up our meal, we immediately started in on the dishes. Carrying the dirty plates to the sink, I told her how much she meant to me and thanked her for letting me confide in her.

"I'm not sure I was able to help." Her eyes roamed my frame again. "You're too thin, Destiny. You need to eat."

"I haven't been hungry and I've had a headache all week."

Her eyes widened. "Would you like an aspirin?"

I shook my head. "No, I'd better get going. Thank you for listening to me."

"Could you wait until after I put Camden to bed?"

"Sure, let me help. I wiped Camden's face with a wet cloth and lifted him from his highchair. Following Robin toward his bedroom with him resting on my hip, my right leg went numb and I felt dizzy and faint. I screamed for her to catch Camden while I clutched him close to me and collapsed to the floor.

"Oh my God, Destiny." She bent down and lifted him into her arms. Panic filled her eyes as she looked him over. "He's okay. Thank God for the soft surface. What happened?"

"I don't know," I said, my voice trembling in fear. "My leg went numb, and I felt like I was going to faint."

"Shit! I can't go through this again." She held Camden closer.

"You are not going anywhere tonight, except to the hospital."

What? "I'm okay now." I tried to placate her. The dizziness subsided while I sat on the floor. My right leg felt as if it wasn't attached to my body, but I didn't want to worry her any further.

"No, you're not okay. Wait here." Robin placed a screaming Camden in his crib and disappeared to the kitchen. I heard mumbled conversation. Who was she talking to? She must have made a phone call.

She returned a short time later. "You need medical attention, Destiny. I called Julian. He's home and will be here shortly."

What the hell!

"No, I can't see him, Robin," I said adamantly, panicked and dizzy.

Her face filled with dread. "To hell with that. You're sick." She extended her hand to me. "Let me help you to the sofa. I want you to lie down."

Through all the hysteria, Camden continued to wail from his crib. Jeez, what was up with the sudden diagnosis that I was sick? I'd fallen and she'd turned it into a three-ring circus.

Robin kneeled and wrapped her hands under my arms and lifted me. I limped slowly to the couch and sat down. When I looked up into her eyes, they were wet with tears.

"I'm okay, Robin," I tried to reassure her, but deep down I was terrified. What just happened to me?

"I hope that's true, sis."

"Go tend to Camden. He needs you," I insisted.

"Will you be okay?"

"Yes. I'm fine." I lied.

She left the room and soon after, Camden's cries stopped when I heard her coo softly to him.

I dropped my sister's baby. How could I be so irresponsible? Tears pricked my eyes as my head started throbbing again.

I closed my eyes as the doorbell rang.

JULIAN LEANED OVER ME, his eyes meeting mine. I saw such pain and hurt in them.

"Hi," I said, unable to blink. I couldn't believe I was looking into the eyes of the man I loved. "I've missed you so much."

For whatever reason, this was not how I pictured our reunion. I'd envisioned us running toward each other on a sandy beach in slow motion, like one of those cheesy romantic movies. Then, we'd live happily ever after. But this reunion was very different. My instincts told me something was seriously wrong with me, with my future being uncertain.

Julian stayed quiet. Although he still looked as sexy as hell in his tight blue jeans and white T-shirt, but tired, nonetheless. He knelt down beside me and moved a flashlight across my eyes, as if to check the dilation of my pupils. He then pulled out a tongue depressor and pressed firmly on the back of my tongue.

"I'm checking your gag reflex," he said.

I gagged. "Confirmed."

"Do you have any pain in your head?"

"I've been fighting a headache all week."

Julian's eyes bulged as a horrified fear crossed his face. "Damn. Point to the location of the pain."

I placed my index finger on the area above my right ear. "You're scaring me. What's wrong?"

"I'm not making any diagnosis before we do some tests at the hospital."

I let out a panicked scream. "Hospital?"

Robin stood by looking on, as fear filled her face. "Thank you for coming, Julian."

"No problem, Robin. I'm glad you called. I need to get her to the hospital." Julian retrieved his phone from his pocket and dialed a number. "Owen...Julian...yes...I need to schedule an MRI, stat...I don't care how late it is...no...I don't care, find someone...I'll be there in thirty minutes...okay." He hung up.

That was gruff, but I was watching Dr. Julian Cahill in full-on doctor mode, giving me a warm fuzzy. I knew I was in good hands.

"Hi," he finally said, brushing the hair back away from my face. "I've missed you, too."

"I'm going to be in a heap of trouble seeing you. My parents will be cutting me off for good, and I'll have to drop out of college."

"I don't give a shit how your parents feel. I'm taking you to the hospital right now."

"No, Julian. You're not. I'm fine."

"I'm not going to argue with you." He started firing commands at me. "Get your coat, purse, or whatever you came with and get into the damned car."

"Jesus Christ, Julian. What part of I-can't-be-seen-with-you do you not understand?"

He raked his hands through his hair, and then slapped them on the sofa cushion. "I'm not discussing this with you as your boyfriend. I'm a doctor and you're sick. Now get up and walk or I'll carry you. Either way, you're going."

I eyed him with contempt, raising my voice. "Oh, forgive me for misunderstanding. So you're ordering me around because you're my doctor now? Is that what you're saying?"

"Yes, that's what I'm saying."

"Well, just so you know…if I have to fill out a form later on to rate your bedside manner—it sucks." I crossed my arms, scowled, and didn't budge.

There was a hint of a smile on his face. "Suit yourself, babe."

Julian scooped me up from the sofa, cradling me in his arms.

Oh, how I missed these strong, muscular arms. This is where I wanted to be. I felt out of harm's way with him. I succumbed to his power and wrapped my arms around his neck, burying my nose in his hair as he carried me to his waiting Mercedes—his intoxicating scent forever ingrained in my brain.

A tightness settled around his eyes. "You're light as a feather. How much weight have you lost?" He placed me in the front passenger seat after Robin opened the door.

"I don't know!" I snapped. I didn't appreciate him scolding me. I reached for Robin's hand. "Thank you for everything, sis. I'll be back to pick up my car later."

"Don't worry about the damned car, Destiny. Just get to the hospital." She bent down and gave me a hug. "Hope you feel better soon. Bye." Her lip quivered as tears welled in her eyes again.

Julian climbed into the driver's seat and pulled out of Robin's driveway with an intensity I'd never seen before. He flew down I-25 toward Denver at speeds reaching Mach five. At least that's what it felt like.

"How have you been?" I asked hesitantly.

"How do you think I've been? I'm pissed at you. Why, Destiny? Why couldn't you talk to me? You completely cut me off."

My stomach knotted in pain. "I'm sorry. So, so, sorry. My parents were watching my every move. I couldn't. They threatened me. They knew you were at my dorm that night. I think they're following you, too."

With a strained jaw, he ran his hand through his hair and stared straight ahead. "Fuck. I don't need this shit," he mumbled out loud, eyes pinned to the highway. "Well, I suggest you call your parents right now and let them know where you're headed. And I don't give a shit how they react."

"Okay." I broke down and sobbed aloud when I pulled my phone from my purse. I dialed my mom's cell phone.

"Hi." My voice was barely audible.

"Destiny, you sound strange. Are you okay?"

"Mom, I'm on my way to the hospital. I'm sick."

I heard her take a quick breath. "What hospital? What happened?"

"I nearly fainted and collapsed."

"How are you getting there?"

"You mean to tell me you don't know? You don't have your goddamn guards watching me?"

She hesitated. "No, I don't."

"Julian is taking me." There, I said it. Part of me didn't care that she knew, either.

"We'll discuss that later, Destiny. What hospital?"

"Meet me at Denver Medical, Mother. I'll explain there." I hung up and then called Chloe to fill her in on my whereabouts. She said she'd let Gabby know and they'd pray for me.

Just then, a thunderbolt moment struck me. "Oh my God, Julian, do you think I might have the same tumor that Amber had?" Suddenly, the reason for the hospital urgency became crystal clear. This was it; I was going to die—just like Amber. Fear gripped my body, and my hands began to quiver.

"I told you, I'm not making a diagnosis before receiving the test results."

"I'm scared."

"I know. How's school?" Julian calmed and changed the direction of the conversation, I suspected intentionally.

"I'm struggling to keep up. I ache without you, Jules. I don't want to live my life without you. Can't you see that this has been hell for me? I think about you twenty-four hours a day. I can't breathe."

"I know, babe. I know. I've felt the same way."

"Robin said you left the country. Is that true?"

Julian looked at me. "Why does it matter?"

"Everything you do matters to me. It broke my heart when I'd heard you were wrecked."

He looked at me and subtly shook his head. "We could've worked it out together if you'd given me a chance, but you shut me out." He sounded angry and stared at the road again. "If you'd just talked to them when I told you to…" His voice trailed off.

"I didn't know how to do it. You don't know my parents."

"And you didn't give me a chance to discuss it with them, either."

"Well, you'll get your chance soon enough." I knew that meeting wasn't going to go well. He had no idea.

Julian pulled up outside the hospital twenty-five minutes later. Before he climbed out of the car, he turned, grabbed my face, and planted a chaste kiss on my lips and pulled away.

"Can you legally treat me, Jules?" The thought that he may not, terrified me. "No matter what happens from this point on, I'll always love you with all my heart and soul."

"As long as we aren't dating, I don't see a problem. But, please be extremely discreet, Dest." He smiled sadly. Then with agility and swiftness, he cradled me in his arms and carried me through the doors of the emergency room. He placed me onto a waiting gurney surrounded by a team of three other doctors and a woman in green scrubs.

Julian started rapidly firing directions at the team. "I want a complete scan of the right hemisphere."

Right away, Dr. Cahill," the nurse in green scrubs said.

"Stop right there. What in God's name is going on here?" My mom and dad appeared from down the hall.

Julian was in full doctor mode when he approached them. "Mr. and Mrs. Bradshaw, I'm not sure if you remember me. I'm Dr. Julian Cahill." He extended a hand but pulled back when receiving nothing in return. His calm, cool, and collected demeanor amazed me. "Look, I've ordered a complete MRI of the right frontal lobe of Destiny's brain. I suspect an abnormality in her right hemisphere."

What? An abnormality?

My mom scowled at him. "We don't want you anywhere near our daughter, so find me another doctor, immediately."

"As you wish, but she needs medical attention, right now."

Julian remained unflappable. He had the patience of a saint. Obviously, he'd had years of experience dealing with parents like mine. Maybe he was right. Maybe I *should've* let him handle this situation. Surely, he would have eventually won them over with his charm.

"Mom, Dad…Dr. Cahill is the best neurosurgeon around. I want him to be my doctor." As I sat up to dangle my legs from the gurney, the pain in my head intensified. "Ouch, my head is throbbing." I cringed and gingerly lay back down.

"Absolutely not, Destiny," my father chimed in.

"Marcus, Dr. Cahill is the best neurosurgeon we have."

I recognized that voice. When I looked up, approaching us was the man from the restaurant, the man who was the cause of all my pain of the last two months. I glanced at the nametag on his white coat: Dr. Owen Saunders, Chief Administrator. Yes, that was him.

Before my dad could respond, the transport team of three whisked me away down the hall through some doors, leaving my parents, Dr. Saunders, and Julian standing there—glaring at each other.

Chapter Twenty-Seven

I stared at the four walls of my assigned private room following the MRI. I recognized the nurse who helped me get settled into the bed. Maribelle Hayes, RN was the woman who eyed me suspiciously at the awards banquet. Oh yes, I remembered that southern twangy voice. If I'd known I would cross paths with her again, I would have been more fastidious about my tongue lashing. *Crap!*

With wide-set hazel eyes against a pale complexion, she treated me as pleasant as could be. *Whew! Maybe she didn't recognize me.* Her cheeks plumped in her round face when she smiled. When she leaned over me, I got a whiff of the powder-scented deodorant emanating from her armpits and my head started aching again.

"There, how's that, darlin'?" she asked.

"Good, thank you," I said, exaggerating my normal voice.

"Well, if ya' need anythin', you let me know, okay sweetheart?"

"Yes, thank you."

Moments later, my parents walked in the room. I turned away, wanting nothing to do with them.

My dad sat himself down in the chair next to my bed while my mom stood and swept the hair away from my face.

Despite my disrespect, my father took my hand in his and raised it against the prickly stubble of his cheek. "Hey, sweetheart."

Mom's lip trembled. "How are you feeling, honey? You look awfully thin." The look on her face suggested something was very wrong.

I swallowed hard and tightened my knees to my chest. "Am I

going to die?"

My mom's eyes widened. "Stop talking like that. No, you are not going to die. We have a consultation scheduled with Dr. Saunders tomorrow morning. It's late, and you need some rest."

I'd had enough of my parents evading my questions. "What the hell is going on?"

My mom fidgeted as though chills were running up and down her spine. "Nothing, just get some rest, Destiny. We'll talk to Dr. Saunders in the morning."

"Why do you treat me like a child? I'd like to go back to school."

She wiped her shaky hand across her forehead. "They felt it was better if you stayed here for the night. I've asked them to bring in a cot for me. I'll stay with you."

"I don't want to stay here. I want to go back to school. Why do I have to stay here? Answer me." I started rocking back and forth when a feeling of nausea swept over me.

"Just sleep, pumpkin," my dad said soothingly.

"No, stop dodging my questions. Tell me what is wrong." I felt exhausted and started shaking.

Mom hesitated as her head dropped. "The preliminary scan shows a mass in the right hemisphere of your brain. But we won't know for sure until they've done a thorough reading."

I sucked in a sharp breath, feeling all the blood drain from my face. "I'm going to die, just like Amber!"

"No, you're not, honey. Stop thinking like that."

"I don't want Dr. Saunders to treat me. I want Dr. Cahill!" I screamed. "He's the best in the country."

"No, he's not going to be any part of your treatment."

Panic clawed at my throat. "It's my body, my brain, and my decision."

"Look, we will discuss this in the morning. You're getting too worked up when you should be resting."

I clenched my teeth together. "Don't do this, Mother. I want Dr. Cahill to treat me."

I couldn't believe how they continued to stand by their decision to keep Julian out of my life, even though he might be my best chance at survival. What could they possibly be thinking? My anger bubbled to new heights. Before I could mutter another word, my vision blurred and my body began shaking uncontrollably. The last thing I heard was Nurse Hayes' words...

"She's having a seizure."

THE CLOCK ON THE WALL said twelve o'clock when I managed to open my protesting eyelids. The room was dark except for a streak of light coming through the lone window in my room. I looked around and saw my mom sleeping on a cot to my right. There was an IV in the bend of my elbow and patches and wires attached to my head. A rhythmic beep came from a machine over my head as fresh oxygen blew into my nostrils through some tubing wrapped around my ears. What happened to me?

"Mom," I called softly to her, but she didn't move. She was asleep.

Someone stirred in the shadows from a chair across the room. I squinted in the darkness, but could only see a hunched figure with elbows resting on the knees and steepled fingers under the chin. Slowly, they lowered their hands, pushed up from the seat and approached me. A smile plastered over my face when they came into view.

"Hi, handsome," I whispered.

"Hey, how are you feeling?" Julian asked.

"Okay. What happened?"

"You had a seizure. Shh, stay quiet, okay?" His voice was barely audible.

"Okay." I didn't want to wake up Momzilla, and I'd do anything for Julian, even if it meant pushing him away. As he told me in the car...we needed to remain discreet.

In the darkness surrounding us, he bent down and gave me a sweet kiss. I longed for this man with all my heart. My eyes filled with tears. "Am I going to die?"

Julian shook his head and caressed my forehead, brushing the hair away from my face. "Shh, don't cry."

"I can't help it. I'm scared," I said softly.

"Hey, we don't know what it is until we do a biopsy, so relax until that happens."

"I'm afraid, Julian, but I know you'll save me. I know you will." I watched as his face dropped. "I'm serious. You will save me."

"Shh, go back to sleep, and we'll talk about it in the morning."

With no words spoken, we stared into each other's eyes with adoration. I scooted over so he could sit on the bed beside me. He leaned down, gave me another kiss and rested his head over my heart.

"Love you, Jules."

He pushed himself back up and angled his head to the side. "Love you, too, Dest."

I SQUINTED INTO THE SUNLIGHT spilling into my stark white room from the window. Glancing at the empty cot where my mother had slept, her absence left me unsettled. Where was she?

I couldn't help but think if it weren't for my head issue, Julian would not be back in my life. But at what cost to me? If I had the same brain tumor as Amber, would I die? My life paralleled hers in so many ways. Why would God spare me and not her?

But Julian could save *me*, right? He said it himself—*I could've saved her if it was today.* Yes, he would save me. Was Amber intervening here? I looked to the heavens, put my hands together and prayed. "Save me, girl...save me."

A commotion at the door pulled me out of my moment with Amber and God. My mom and dad barged into my room. "Morning, pumpkin," my dad said.

"Stop with all the niceties. It's getting old. I'm still angry at both of you," I said, proud of myself for finally finding the courage to stand up to them.

My mom's face dropped, deeply etched with worry. "Shh, Destiny. Don't get all riled up again, please."

"Then let Dr. Cahill treat me." If I was going to beat this, he needed to be the doctor in charge of my care. I felt it in my soul.

Their expressionless faces remained still. I was going to win this battle; I didn't care what it took.

"Dr. Saunders will be in shortly to discuss what the next step will be," Mom stated matter-of-factly.

My whole body began shaking with anger. I shut my eyes tight and screamed. "No! I don't want him. I want Dr. Cahill!"

"Stop yelling, Destiny. You're going to have another seizure if you don't calm down." My mother was stubborn, but so was I and I wasn't backing down on this.

"Don't you dare tell me to calm down," I hissed at her.

She pinched the bridge of her nose and shook her head. "Dr. Saunders is a highly respected doctor, who can treat you just as well as Dr. Cahill."

"Cynthia, just leave it the hell alone," my dad admonished her.

Surprisingly, my mom closed her mouth, pursing her lips together. I think she was actually sulking. Had she ever been scolded by my dad before? She turned and sat in the chair vacated by Julian only a few hours before while my dad left the room.

A short time later, Julian and Dr. Saunders entered the room followed by my father. My smile stretched across my face. I had high hopes my dad was finally coming around.

"Good morning, Destiny," Dr. Saunders said. "Are you feeling better?"

"I'm feeling fine, but I'd rather talk with Dr. Cahill." I smiled at Julian. He shook his head and gestured to listen to Dr. Saunders. I nodded at him. "Go on, doctor. I'm listening."

I saw my mother scowl at Julian as she stood from the chair and approached my bed. He remained unruffled.

"I guess you've heard that you have a mass in the right hemisphere of your brain."

My breathing labored, and the sound of my heartbeat began thrashing loudly in my ears. The thought of a something growing in my brain scared me to death. "Yes. My mom told me." My voice trembled.

"We'd like to schedule a biopsy at some point today."

"What will that entail?" I asked.

"We need to surgically remove a small portion of the mass and run some tests on it to determine what it is."

"Okay," I said, clutching at the pain in my head. "Who will be doing that?"

"One of us will."

"The only person allowed to treat me is Dr. Cahill."

My mom's voice cracked. "Destiny, please, stop."

I glared at her. "No, you stop. I swear I will get up from this bed right now and leave this hospital under my own free will if any other doctor treats me but Dr. Cahill."

My dad exhaled heavily. "You are as mulish as your mother, Destiny."

Julian interrupted, "Dr. Saunders will be fine to do the biopsy. Okay, Destiny?"

I let out a deep breath. "Okay," I acquiesced, trusting his opinion.

"Then let's get her prepped for surgery." Dr. Saunders said.

I STILL FELT GROGGY from the anesthesia when I opened my eyes. An orange glow from the late afternoon sun filled the sterile room.

I reached up and felt the bandage covering the right side of my head.

"Hey." My mom's soft voice came from the chair across the room. She looked tired, her hair unruly as if she'd slept on it.

"Hi." My voice was raspy and faint.

"How's my little girl?"

"I'm tired. What did the biopsy show?"

My mom stroked my face with the back of her hand. "The tests aren't back yet. Sleep, honey."

"Where's Dr. Cahill?"

"I don't know, sweetheart."

"I want to see him, Mom. Please go find him."

She rolled her eyes. I saw her grimace and let out a subtle humph before she turned and left the room. Was she conceding to my demands because of my condition? I wasn't sure if I should feel honored or fearful. Did she know the truth of my illness? A panic seized me.

Oh please, God, don't let me die.

A moment later, she returned, followed by Julian, my dad, and Dr. Saunders. It figured that she'd bring the whole damn army with her.

While my mom and dad spoke with Dr. Saunders across the room, Julian hovered over me, wearing his blue scrubs, as if he'd just come out of surgery. As always, sex rippled off him. "Are you okay, Dest?"

I cleared my throat and reached for his hand. "I'm better, now that you're here. Are the results of the biopsy in yet?"

"Not yet. They won't be in for another week or two."

"When can I go home?"

"I'd like to keep you here overnight to make sure your seizures are under control. Until then, I'm going to prescribe an AED for you until the results come in."

"What's an AED?" I asked.

"Anti-epileptic drug."

I rolled my eyes. "Why didn't you just say that then?"

"Weren't you the valedictorian of your class?" He smirked.

I raised an eyebrow at him. "Sarcasm doesn't suit you."

He grinned and brushed the hair away from my face. "I've got to check in on some other patients of mine. I'd like you to get some rest."

"Okay. Will you be coming back tomorrow?"

"I'll check in on you before I head home tonight." He ran his knuckles down my cheek then turned and left.

My spirits lifted at his words. I needed this right now at a time when my health hung in the balance. If I died, how would he cope with losing me a second time? The thought made me shiver. He had to save me this time.

In the meantime, I called Chloe and Gabby and filled them in on my status.

"Oh my God!" Gabby exclaimed. "Are you going to be okay?"

I wished I knew the answer to her question. My stomach quivered as I let out a deep sigh. "I hope so. We'll see when the results of the biopsy come back."

"I'll let Chloe know. We'll be praying for you."

"Thanks, girl." They were the only school friends I had. They took care of me during my breakdown without Julian, and I owed them so much.

"Okay, Destiny. Get well, sweetie."

"Thanks." My voice was almost a sob.

I STARED OUT THE WINDOW at the crescent-shaped moon thinking about my parents when Julian strolled into the room. My attitude had softened toward them. I hated to admit it, but I needed them, especially now when my life hung in the balance. Their love never wavered, even in spite of my recent rude behavior. Though, my mom hadn't changed her opinion of Julian. Well, I could be just as tenacious.

I reached out for Julian's hand. "Hey, you're just the face I want to stare at right now."

He sat on the edge of my bed. "Any pain?"

"My head is sore, but nothing I can't handle. Are you done for the day and heading home?"

"I was…unless you'd like me to stay."

I wanted nothing more than for him to stay all night with me, but I knew he'd be back here at the crack of dawn and needed sleep. "You don't have to stay all night, but could you visit for a little while?"

"If you want me to stay all night, I will."

"You'd do that for me?"

"I love you, Destiny. I'd walk over burning coals for you."

As much as I craved him, I knew he should go home. "I can manage to be alone." Though, the thought of it made me break out into a cold sweat. I swore I heard the heart monitor beep an extra beat.

"Don't look at me with those pitiful, sad eyes."

"You do need your sleep. Please go home. Anyway, my mom will be staying with me. I'm in good hands, babe."

"Okay, Dest. I'll see you tomorrow." He turned and headed for the door.

"Wait." I sounded panicky. "I need to say something first." I had to tackle a delicate subject with him. He had to know why I left him. He'd witnessed my mother's wrath head-on, even though he handled it better than I thought.

"What can't wait until tomorrow?" he asked, walking back to my bedside.

I grabbed his hand and pulled him down to sit. "Do you see why I had to break up with you?"

His eyes went wide. "Quite frankly, no Destiny, but why are we discussing this right now?"

"Because we need to talk about it," I stated firmly. "It tore my heart to shreds during the time we were apart, but my parents were tracking me with a device they installed on my phone—I couldn't call or text you. And as you discovered, they changed my phone number."

He tucked a loose strand of hair behind my ear. "We could've worked it out."

"Well, maybe that's what you think, but I'm not sure you know my parents very well."

"I have to admit your mom is pretty adamant about my presence around you." He chuckled.

"Oh, you've seen nothing yet, Julian." I glanced at the clock, hoping it wasn't time for her to reappear.

"I deal with people like her all the time. Just don't shut me out again. Okay?" He pursed his lips at me and winked. "Anyway, her daughter is just like her."

"Hey." I pouted. Was this where I got my pig-headedness? Was I exactly like my mother?

"Just let me handle her."

A sensation of warmth flooded my body. "Okay, I love you so much."

He brushed his fingers up my arms. "Love you too, Dest."

"So, you've seen the MRI, right?" I asked him.

"Yes, why?"

I grabbed his hand and pulled it against me. "Be completely honest with me. What does it look like?"

"Oh no you don't, Miss Bradshaw. I'm not making a diagnosis until the biopsy tests come back.

"Please, Jules…I can take whatever you tell me. Is it bad?"

"Destiny, this is not a conversation I have with my patients before results come back."

I started crying. "I'm scared, babe, really scared." Julian's silence spoke volumes. I knew it was bad. He would tell me if it wasn't.

He bent over and gave me a chaste kiss on the lips. "Shh, don't get yourself all riled up over nothing."

He snuggled up next to me in my bed while I rested my head on his chest. I listened to his heartbeat in perfect rhythm to the beep of my monitor overhead.

A LOUD DISTURBANCE woke me the following morning. Opening my eyes, I noticed my mom's empty cot and heard a commotion outside my room. The distinct sound of my mother's voice rang through the halls. What the hell was she doing now? At once, she burst into the room and stalked over to my bed. A look of guilt crossed her face.

"How are you this morning, honey?"

I sighed. "What is going on, Mom?"

"Nothing you should concern yourself with."

"If you're talking about me, then it concerns me."

She shook her head. "Destiny, please stop getting all worked up over every little thing."

I folded my arms over my chest and scowled at her.

Dr. Saunders entered my room and approached my side. "Hi, Destiny, how is your head feeling?"

Suddenly, it occurred to me what my mother was up to. Once again, she demanded Dr. Saunders take over my care. I glared at her and was pretty sure she read my mind. "I'm ready to go back to school, Doctor," I told him while not taking my piercing eyes off my mom.

"I think we can let you go home." he said.

"Good."

THE HOSPITAL HANDED me my release papers later that morning. As I climbed into my mom's car, it concerned me that I hadn't seen Julian before I left. "Did you say something to Dr. Cahill?"

If there was one thing I knew about my mom, it was her telling expression when she tried to withhold information from me.

"Destiny, please, he's too old for you."

I knew it! "Stop trying to live my life for me!" I screamed at her. "Have I ever given you a reason to question my judgment before?"

She pulled onto Broadway Boulevard, heading toward my dorm. "You're young and deserve someone closer to your age."

"I don't want someone closer to my age. Does it mean anything to you that Julian makes me happy? I love him, Mother. Why can't you understand that?"

"Because."

"Because, why?"

My mom's knuckles turned bright white as she gripped the steering wheel. Staring straight ahead, her eyes never left the road. She looked deep in thought.

"What is it, Mom? What are you not telling me?"

Her eyes glossed over. She reached over and placed her hand on my thigh. "I was in your situation once, and it ended badly." She hastily admitted. "Your dad and I are just trying to protect you."

"I don't need protection. What are you talking about?" I narrowed my eyes at her, urging her to go on.

"I thought the same thing, honey."

I took a deep breath and slowly exhaled trying to calm myself. "Would you please tell me what happened?"

She fell silent as she pulled into the parking lot of my dorm and found an empty spot hidden from the view of peering eyes. She silenced the engine and turned to face me, tucking one leg under the other. Her distressed look suggested she was struggling internally with her thoughts.

"When I was in college, one of my much older professors asked me out." She paused and looked at me with raised eyebrows. "At first, he seemed like a great guy, and I thought he liked me. Then one evening, after a night of drinking, we went back to his house. When he asked me to have sex with him, I told him I wasn't ready for that, yet. Apparently that didn't matter to him when he forced himself on me. I was defenseless." She stopped and dropped her head to her chest. "He raped me, Destiny. I was too young and naïve to know I should never have gotten involved with an older man."

Whoa! I never expected those words to spill from her lips. My mother was always so strong and confident; nothing ruffled her. Instead, she was once a defenseless teenager, fighting off the advances of an older man.

"Oh my God." I couldn't believe what I'd just heard. "Does Daddy know?"

"Yes." She frowned.

"I'm sorry, Mom, but Julian would never hurt me." No wonder she'd been dead set against me seeing him.

"I thought the same thing, Destiny."

"You don't understand. I'm the one who approached him. It wasn't the other way around. He pushed me away at first. I wish I could make you believe he would never do anything like that to me. But at least I have a better understanding of where you're coming from. Thank you for confiding in me."

"I don't know him well enough to judge his character. All I have to go on is my own experiences."

"Can you please try...for me?" I pleaded with her.

She pushed her hair away from her forehead, lined with worry. "I don't know. Please give me time, okay?"

"Oh, Mom, I'm so sorry for my behavior lately. I love you so much." I bent over and pulled her into my arms, and we hugged. All this time, I had no idea why she felt the way she did. She promised to lighten up on me, but somehow, I didn't feel the conviction in her words.

"Don't forget to take your seizure medicine," she reminded me as I kissed her goodbye.

"I won't."

I stepped out of the car and ambled along to my dorm, greeted by the onslaught of hugs from Chloe and Gabby. A get-well sign hung on the wall of the living room suite.

"Aw, thank you. That's very sweet."

Gabby held me at arm's length. "How are you, girl?"

"The results aren't back yet, but I'm trying to stay positive."

Chloe clasped her hands together, fingers to the heavens. "We're going to keep praying for you if that helps."

"Of course it helps." I hugged them both again. "Thank you for always being there for me. Just thank you."

Chapter Twenty-Eight

My cell phone rang. It'd been two weeks since my biopsy. My head still donned a small bandage from the surgery. I glanced at the caller ID and saw a number I didn't recognize. Was it the doctor calling me with the results? Did I want to hear them? My body shook as I answered on the second ring.

"Hello."

"Destiny Bradshaw?"

"Yes."

"Destiny, this is Nurse Tuttle calling from Dr. Saunders office. The results of your biopsy are back. Could you come in for a consultation this morning at the hospital?"

My face turned ashen and the hair on my arms lifted. This was it. Would I live or die? "Yes," I whispered, my voice wavering. "Is it bad?" I asked, huddled against the pillow on my bed.

"You'll have to discuss the results with Dr. Saunders. Can you be here by ten?"

"Yes," I whispered, hung up and immediately called my parents.

FOUR MASSIVE, CONCRETE COLUMNS graced the entrance of the Denver Medical Center, each with an ornate themed engraving on the front. My parents and I walked through the revolving doors into the lobby, my legs ready to give out from under me. I felt nauseous. Once inside, I shuffled along toward the elevators. My dad pressed the button with the arrow pointing up. The door opened immediately, and we stepped in. My parents were uncharacteristically quiet. What were they thinking? Probably the same thing I was. I had an unshakable sense that something was terribly wrong. My mouth went dry, but I couldn't stop swallowing.

The elevator whisked us up to the ninth floor where a nurse, who introduced herself as Jane Tuttle, escorted us into Dr. Saunders' office.

"Please have a seat. The doctors will be right in," she said.

Did she say doctors...plural? Did my parents have a change of heart? *Oh, please let that be the case.* I didn't have any fight left in me. As I said the words in my head, Dr. Saunders entered the office followed by Julian. My body relaxed. I hadn't seen him since my discharge two weeks before. For sure, he was a sight for sore eyes...or should I say...sore head. Though, I couldn't gauge the look on his face.

Dr. Saunders flipped the on-switch of the lightbox, and the images of my brain sprang to life. He sat in the leather chair of his overly large desk while Julian leaned against the edge.

"Hi, Destiny, how are you feeling?" Dr. Saunders asked.

"Scared and terrified."

"Any difficulties managing everyday tasks?"

"Not that I'm aware of. What did the biopsy show?" *Let's get to the punch here, doctor!*

He got up and went to the light box and pointed to a light pear-shaped area on the x-ray. "Destiny, Marcus, Cynthia...right here in the right hemisphere of the brain is a grade I Pilocytic Astrocytoma malignant tumor."

Malignant! This was it. I *was* going to die, just like Amber.

"Oh!" My mom convulsed. She clutched my hand tight like she never wanted to let go. I squeezed her hand back. My dad wrapped his arm around her shoulders, attempting to comfort her.

My stomach roiled. I covered my hand over my mouth to fight back dry heaves and started sobbing quietly.

Dr. Saunders continued, "The positive side is that the tumor is in the earliest stage and is a slow growing tumor, but also in a difficult area of the brain." He moved his finger along what looked like a bumpy spot. "Surgery is the standard treatment but also very dangerous. However, if not surgically removed, it could metastasize and progress to a higher grade, making it more challenging to treat, possibly rendering it inoperable. I would suggest you make a decision about your options in the next day or two."

My head was reeling. I wasn't sure I understood all the medical jargon he was throwing at us but thought I heard him say I had a chance.

"Also, it is imperative that you be diligent about following up with continued medical treatment after the surgery, Destiny."

My mom wept as she held onto my hand.

What did this all mean? Could I be disfigured for life? "Am I going to die?" I asked, wiping a sheen of sweat from my upper lip with the back of my hand.

"Stop talking like that, honey." Mom frowned. "So, will you do the surgery, Dr. Saunders?"

"The only doctor in this hospital capable of handling that surgery is Dr. Cahill, Cynthia. He's the best in the entire country."

"I don't want him anywhere near my daughter."

"Cynthia." My dad quietly scolded her…again.

"Mom!" I yelled. "Either Dr. Cahill does my surgery, or I walk out of here and go home and die. Got it?"

Dr. Saunders anchored his attention on my mom. "Cynthia, Dr. Cahill is the only doctor here equipped to handle this type of surgery. I can't emphasize it enough. Destiny is right, either he does the surgery, or it won't happen. You could go elsewhere, but you won't find the expertise that Dr. Cahill exemplifies. It's your choice."

"You don't leave me many options, do you?"

"You need to put your vendetta aside and think about the life of your daughter right now," Dr. Saunders added bluntly.

She squeezed her eyes shut, and her mouth formed a straight line. "Okay, Dr. Cahill," she spat out.

My dad chimed in, "Dr. Cahill will be fine to do Destiny's surgery."

Julian stood and approached us. I don't know how he did it, but he remained unruffled. "Thank you, Mr. and Mrs. Bradshaw. I promise I will take good care of Destiny." He extended a hand, and this time, they both reciprocated with a firm handshake in return.

Hallelujah! I stood and gave him a tight hug, wrapping my arms around his mid-section. He gently rubbed my back. It felt so good to bury myself into his firm chest. I inhaled deeply. He felt safe. I knew I wasn't being very discreet but didn't care.

BY SEVEN THE FOLLOWING MORNING, the prepping for my surgery was complete. My body felt groggy from the intravenous drugs that flowed through my veins. My mom and dad stood alongside my bed caressing my arm and murmuring reassuring words to me.

"I'll be fine, Mommy and Daddy," I slurred. "Julian's the best in the country."

"We know, honey," Mom said so soft that I barely heard her.

The transport team hoisted me up onto a waiting gurney, and Nurse, Maribelle Hayes adjusted my blankets. "How's that, Destiny?"

"Great, thank you." My words sounded all fuzzy.

Chloe and Gabby joined us in the hall as we headed to the operating room. "We're praying for you, Destiny." The ghostly sounds of Chloe voice resonated in me as she grabbed my hand and squeezed it.

All ready for whatever God had in store for me, the transport team pushed me through some automatic doors. A sign above the doors said: O.R. Once inside, bright lights overhead practically blinded my already blurry eyesight. Even in my pre-surgery haze, I forced my eyes to scan the room and find Julian before I succumbed to sleep. He looked so sexy and official in his blue scrubs with cap and mask.

"Okay, Dest. Are you ready?" he asked.

I think I nodded my head as the anesthesiologist placed a mask over my face, being the last thing I remembered.

"HEY, PUMPKIN," my dad said in a soft voice. His hand caressed my cheek when I opened my eyes. He looked tired and disheveled.

"Hey, Daddy. How did my surgery go?" My voice sounded croaky through an oxygen mask. I noticed the darkness in my room when I struggled to open my eyelids.

"Good. Dr. Cahill was able to remove the entire tumor."

In my head, I thought I smiled but wasn't sure. *I knew he would save me.* "It's late. Please go home and get some rest. I'll be okay," I said, then closed my eyes and drifted again.

SUNLIGHT FILLED MY ROOM when I heard Julian's voice. "Hey, Dest."

I fought to open my rebellious eyes. "Hi, babe." My throat felt raw as I struggled to speak through a raspy voice.

Julian hovered over me running his knuckles down my cheek. "How's my favorite patient?"

I smiled. "I heard you removed my whole tumor."

"I believe I got all of it, yes. You're going to be fine. There was very little nerve damage."

His words washed over me. *You're going to be fine.* "I'm not going to die?"

"Nope, not anytime soon, anyway." He chuckled.

I tried to smile, but failed miserably. "How did it go?"

"Good, babe. You should make a complete recovery," he said, holding my hand against his heart. "I'll discuss more of it with you later when you're more alert."

My eyelids protested. "Why can't I wake up?"

"Just sleep it off, Dest. I'm sure your parents will be here soon, okay?"

I didn't argue. All I wanted to do was sleep, and soon enough, I did.

DARKNESS FILLED MY ROOM again before I was finally able to keep my resistant eyes open. My mom slept on the cot next to me. I squinted, trying to see who was sitting in the chair across the room.

"What time is it?" My voice was barely audible.

Julian approached my bed. "Midnight," he whispered gazing down into my eyes. "You missed the whole day."

His beautiful blue irises tugged at my heart. "I feel like I've missed a couple of them," I said groggily.

"You have. You've been in and out."

"Don't you have anything better to do than to stare at me?"

"Nope. Do you have a problem with that?" He grinned.

"Nope, not at all."

I attempted to lift my non-responsive arm to feel the bandage wrapped around my head. I grimaced. Tubes peeked out from underneath. My head felt sore, though, a good kind of sore. A tube, fed through my nose went to my stomach preventing me from being sick.

Julian handed me a button attached to the IV in my arm. "This is a PCA pump, which means Patient Controlled Analgesia." He grinned.

I rolled my eyes at him.

"You can administer drugs as you need them for the pain. Okay?" Julian caressed my forehead with the back of his hand.

"I don't want to take anything that will make me feel groggy again," I said softly, in hopes I wouldn't wake my mom.

"You should be sleeping right now, anyway. I'll see you in the morning. I just came to check on my best girl."

"Are you leaving?"

"Yes, I've been awake for over twenty-four hours. I need to go home and get some sleep."

"Jeez, Julian, I hope you didn't stay awake on my account."

He smiled, squeezed my hand, bent down and placed a gentle kiss on my lips. "Your lips are so soft."

"I love you, Dr. Cahill. Thank you for being the best neurosurgeon in the world."

"I wouldn't go that far, but you're welcome, Dest."

And there was the humble Julian I knew so well. God, I loved him.

"Love you too, babe." He pressed his lips against my forehead, giving me a delicate kiss, then turned and left.

I FELT PAIN EVERYWHERE. The incision on my head was sore...very sore. I held the button in my hand Julian mentioned to me the night before. Even though I was reluctant to press it, the discomfort was too much. I pushed it.

Moments later, relief flooded my body. Eventually, I would have to fight through any tendency toward pain medication to relieve the throbbing. I refused to depend on drugs to soothe the crushing ache.

I finally had an opportunity to look around. A deluge of beautiful flowers spilled over from pretty vases, while balloons—with get-well messages written on them—swayed back and forth at the base of my bed. A pile of unopened cards covered every available surface of my room. I started reading through a stack of them when a knock on my door made me jump. I glanced up.

"Hey, sis."

"Oh my God, Robin, come in. You're my first visitor since my surgery, except my parents of course...and Julian. But he doesn't count because he's my doctor." I laughed.

Robin came over to my bedside and grabbed my hand. "Oh Destiny, it's so good to see you smiling. How are you feeling?"

"I'm relieved it's over. Everything happened so fast after I left your house that night. Although, I'm sure Julian expedited the process because it was me."

"I heard he was able to remove your entire tumor. That's awesome." She looked down, a hint of sadness filling her face.

"What's wrong?"

"I wish he could've saved Amber."

"Robin, he did save her. She's right here." I held my arms out in a *hug-me-please* gesture. "God gave him a second chance, and he saved me this time."

Robin bent over and gave me a tight bear hug. "You are absolutely right, sis." Tears filled her eyes.

I looked up, my eyes bugging out of my face when Elizabeth and Lyle strolled in.

"Hi, Mom and Dad." Robin gave each of them a quick hug.

Elizabeth looked at me with a genuine love in her eyes. "Hello, sweet girl. How are you? You gave us quite a scare. I can't take any more of my daughters developing brain tumors. Let's have no more of that, please." She smiled as she approached my bed and kissed me on the forehead.

"I promise," I said when my parents walked in and stood by the door. Did they hear Elizabeth call me her daughter? Oh, this could be awkward. "Hi, Mommy and Daddy, come on in. I'd like to introduce you to some special people."

Reluctantly, my parents meandered over to my bed and eyed Elizabeth hesitantly.

"Mom, Dad, this is Elizabeth and Lyle Scott." I was taking a chance but decided to go all in. I swallowed hard and took a deep breath. "And this is my sister, Robin Spencer." I introduced my parents back to everyone.

My mom cautiously offered her hand. "Nice to meet all of you," she said.

I jumped in again. "Elizabeth and Lyle are Amber's and Robin's parents, which, of course, made them my parents in my former life."

Part of me didn't want to hurt my parents' feelings, but deep down, anger and blame still bubbled within me for the past two months of misery they put me through.

My mom narrowed her eyes at me. I reciprocated the gesture back and smiled. I really did love her.

I think this was the first time my mom was speechless. My dad extended a hand to both of them.

Elizabeth picked up on the awkwardness of the moment and chimed in, "It's a pleasure to finally meet Destiny's parents. She speaks so fondly about both of you."

My mom's face lit up like the Times Square ball on New Year's Eve. Suddenly she found her lost voice. "Thank you, Elizabeth. If you remember a woman showing up at your door a couple months back, looking for a Belinda Scott...well, that was me."

"Yes, Destiny did mention that to me. I do remember you, now. Of course, that was before we knew who she was."

They laughed a bit uncomfortably.

I started to relax. This was such a happy moment for me. Both sets of parents interacting with each other, and nobody's killed anyone yet. I think they may have been exchanging notes.

We all ended up sharing stories of my childhood. I found it fascinating listening to Elizabeth talk about me as a young child. Some stuff I remembered, some I didn't.

Before long, Julian's parents entered the room. I felt famous today. It would be my first time seeing them since I left Julian. They questioned our relationship back then. I could only imagine what they thought of me now.

Lisa approached the bed. "Destiny, I heard your surgery went well. Julian has been filling us in on your progress. We were so sorry to hear about your illness." She regarded me carefully. After all, I'd broken their son's heart. I understood their hesitancy toward me.

I held out my arms. "Thanks to Julian, I'm doing well. Thank you for coming to see me. It means a lot to me that you're here." Lisa accepted my outstretched arms and gave me a hug.

I waved my arm at my parents and introduced everyone. They all shared handshakes and greetings. I couldn't believe this good fortune bestowed upon me with all the people I loved gathered around my bed. The only person missing was Julian himself. He was probably busy with his patients. Either that or my mother was throwing her weight around again. He'd stopped in to see me early this morning, but now it was nearly noon. Where was he?

As if he'd read my mind, Julian lumbered into the room wearing his blue scrubs, looking like he just stepped out of surgery. He most likely had. My room was complete with all my favorite people in the world. I felt so loved.

Julian went to his parents. "Mom, Dad, nice to see you." He gave each of them a hug. "Thanks for coming."

I noticed my mother moving her blue eyes to the ceiling for a few silent moments, then sighing. I think she was coming around. As usual, Julian maintained a professional demeanor. He knew how to handle her, and to think I doubted him. Maybe it was me I should've blamed for my suffering.

He turned and approached my bed, while everyone stepped back to give him easier access to me. "Any pain, Destiny?"

I read his unspoken thoughts and placated him. "I'd forgotten that my head was a little sore earlier, Dr. Cahill. All this overwhelming love is better than drugs." I winked at him. He gave me a priceless smirk.

"I'm going to remove some of the tubes from your incision. Would you like privacy?"

"I don't mind all of them staying."

Robin moved forward next to me. "I've got to go pick up Camden from the babysitter, so I'm going to hit the road. It's great to see you doing so well, sis." She bent over and gave me a goodbye hug. "I'll stop in again tomorrow."

With the exception of my parents, everyone else said their goodbyes and followed Robin out the door. This was the best day I'd had in a very long time.

While my parents leaned in, watching intently, Julian explained the procedure. "I'm removing the external ventricular drain or EVD for short. This drains excess fluid from the brain to stop build-up." He paused and very gingerly removed the tubing. "Next, I'll remove the ICP, the intracranial pressure monitor. This measures the pressure inside her head."

I leaned my head toward him. "Ouch, that hurt."

"Sorry, Destiny," he said, removing the pressure monitor.

"When can I get these bandages off?"

"Not for another few days, Dest."

Moments later, I was tube-free but exhausted.

While Julian was finishing up, my dad broached the subject of my surgery, surprising me. "Thank you, Dr. Cahill, for saving my daughter's life. My gratitude goes beyond anything I could ever express. I'd heard things got a bit bizarre in the O.R., but you saw it through. So, thank you again."

"Yes, thank you." My mom chimed in.

"You're very welcome. I'd do it again in a heartbeat if I had to."

What were they referring to? I hated how they continued to keep relevant information from me. I pinned my eyes on them. "What happened during my surgery?"

"Nothing you should concern yourself with, honey," my mom stated, leaning down to kiss my forehead.

I nudged her away. "Please stop treating me like a child. Now, tell me what happened."

Julian made a nodding motion to them. They nodded back.

"Somebody had better start talking."

"Destiny, your dad and I are going to grab something to eat. We'll be back later. Dr. Cahill will discuss whatever questions you have with him." They each gave me a kiss on the cheek and left.

"Start talking, Julian. I don't like being left in the dark."

"Okay." He stopped briefly before continuing, "The tumor was in a more difficult location than we suspected. It took close to sixteen hours to completely detach it. The tedious work took its toll on one of my top colleagues. He collapsed, needing immediate medical attention himself, in the middle of your surgery. So, it was a bit insane in the O.R. that day."

My eyes widened. "Oh my God, is he okay?"

"He's taken a sabbatical, but I believe he'll make a full recovery."

"Then let me say thank you, too."

"What you fail to realize, Destiny, is that I'd cut off my right arm for you."

His endearing words meant the world to me, but at the same time made me laugh. "But then you wouldn't be able to save anyone else, dumb-ass." I couldn't have pushed any more sarcasm into my words if I tried. "I love you, Jules."

"Touché. Love you too, babe." He bent and kissed my lips. "Hey, I've got to continue with my rounds. I'll stop in later. Will you be okay?"

"Absolutely." I gave him my sweetest smile.

"Okay." Julian stood, caressed my arm then disappeared.

Wow, to think that one of the doctors needed attention during my surgery. Julian was my hero.

FIVE DAYS HAD GONE BY since my surgery. I'd been up walking, taking small steps with help from the nurses.

I had another MRI to check for swelling and any residual tumor fragments. All was good.

Today the bandages would be removed. I glanced at the clock. It said one thirty in the afternoon when Julian popped his head in the door. "Ready?" he asked.

"Yes, this thing is itchy. Get it off." I shook my head.

"Well, this is just to check the incision and change the dressing, but I'll have to rewrap it. Sorry, Dest."

Sitting on a stool next to my bed, he gave me a mirror and began removing the bandages, layer by layer, until they were gone. A faint five-inch scab started forming at the site of the incision, and my hair had been shaved down to the scalp. I looked like part of a freak show. I didn't care. I was alive, and the tumor was gone.

"It feels so good to get that bandage off."

WITH THE HELP OF NURSE HAYES, I gingerly scuffed my feet out of the bathroom at the same time Gabby and Chloe walked in.

"Hey, Destiny, do you want a couple of visitors? We can come back another time."

"Please stay. I was just freshening up." They sat in the two chairs surrounding my bed. I missed college, having to take a leave of absence from my studies, but planned to return next semester. "I miss you two."

"We miss you, too," Gabby said. "But, guess what?"

The excitement on her face was infectious. "What?"

"I got a job working in New York City as a model with the Zedra Agency. I start in the spring."

"That's awesome, Gab."

"It's a crazy life, though."

"I can imagine."

Chloe draped her arm over Gabby's shoulder. "I'm going to miss my roomy. What a crazy semester we've had."

I laughed. "Yes. We did. I'm sure we'll talk about it for years to come."

"Incidentally," Gabby turned to me with a sly look, "spill it, girl. You've got all the time in the world, and I'm not leaving until you tell me this big secret you've been keeping. What did Julian mean when he alluded to the fact that you broke up with him once before?"

I puffed out a breath. I knew she'd bring this topic up eventually. I promised to fill them in, and this was as good a time as any to tell my story.

"Well, what I'm about to tell you two will shock you to your core, so here goes." I stumbled, trying to decide where to start. Deciding on the shock value, I began, "Julian and I met and started dating nineteen years ago." I stopped to let them catch up.

Chloe leaned forward and interrupted me with wide eyes. "Wait, I'm confused. How old *are* you, Destiny? You couldn't possibly have started dating Julian before you were born, so what gives?"

"You're right. We were both sixteen at the time. You see, I'm his reincarnated girlfriend, Amber Scott. I was born on the day of her funeral."

Their hands went to their mouths, and Chloe burst out laughing. "Next thing you're going to tell me is you're the Queen of England."

"I'm serious. I can tell you all about my life as Amber."

"Do you actually believe in that crap?" she continued.

I narrowed my eyes at her.

Gabby interrupted, "Are you saying you're the girl in that yearbook picture?"

"Yes, I knew it at the time I showed you, but left that detail out."

"Are you sure?" she asked, needing confirmation.

"Positive." I tugged my hospital gown up to show them the scar on my belly, explaining the full stabbing story.

Chloe cocked her head to the side. "Wait. What are you two talking about?"

Ignoring Chloe, Gabby added, "I've never met a reincarnated person before. So, if you were Amber, then how did she die?"

"You wouldn't believe me if I told you."

"Try us," Chloe interrupted.

"Well,…she died of a brain tumor." As I said the words, they both gasped with shocked stares. "Relax, I know what both of you are thinking, and you don't need to worry. Julian was able to save me this time. I believe this was his mission and calling in life—to save me and give us a second chance at love."

"Wow, so that is what he meant when he said not to leave him again?" Gabby asked.

"Yes, but Amber never broke up with him. She died."

"So, he knows about you?" she continued.

"Yes, of course."

Chloe folded her arms over her stomach. "This is crazy. How did you meet up with him in this life?" she asked, sounding unconvinced.

I filled both of them in on our chance meeting during the hospital tour and spent the next half hour telling them the rest of the story.

Gabby brushed her hand up and down my arm. "They should do a news story about the two of you."

My mouth dropped open. "Good Lord, no way. We're not interested in splashing our lives all over the TV. And we'd appreciate you keeping it to yourselves, too."

From my purse, I pulled out a photograph of Julian and Amber together and gave it to them. Like everyone else who'd seen it, they gulped at the resemblance between Amber and me.

Chloe grabbed my hand and pulled it toward her. "Well, in any case, thanks for the unbelievable story, but we have to get to class. Get well, girl."

I wasn't sure I'd convinced her of my reincarnation, but figured she would need time.

"Thanks for stopping by you two. Come and see me again."

"We will, and it's been great seeing you two, too." Gabby chuckled.

"Very funny. I like that."

Just as they turned to leave, my parents entered the room. We chatted briefly. Exhaustion overwhelmed me and I yawned.

"You must be tired, honey," my mom said. She'd stayed with me every night since I'd been here, but I wanted her to go home.

"I'll be okay," I assured her. "I appreciate all you've done, but please go home and get some sleep, Mom. You look tired."

With a trembling lip, she promised to visit first thing in the morning. I kissed each of them and watched as they walked out. I felt a little sad and lonely but didn't want to convey that to them.

My mood lifted when, as promised, Julian, in his blue scrubs, stopped by much later in the evening and sat on my bed.

"You put in long hours here, don't you?"

He ran a hand through his hair and looked positively exhausted. "Yep, I love my job, Destiny."

"I just hope you don't burn yourself out. You look drained. How many surgeries did you perform today?"

He ran his hand up my legs, softly touching them. "Three, but when I did yours, it was my only surgery of that day."

"Wow, no wonder you needed so much education."

"Get used to it, babe." He grinned. "This is the life of a neurosurgeon."

I changed the subject. "It frightens me that my parents are still not on board with our relationship."

"Stop worrying, Dest. We'll work this out."

I knew my parents better than him, yet he seemed so confident they would eventually accept him. How did he plan on doing that? I knew I couldn't live another day without him in my life. I couldn't go through what I did for the last two months, again.

Julian gave me my nightly kiss goodbye and left. Without a doubt, I knew he'd be back at the crack of dawn.

Chapter Twenty-Nine

A protesting squeal of the wheels on my hospital wheelchair echoed throughout the hallway as my mom pushed me down the long, dimly lit corridor of the Neurology floor, passing empty gurneys and wheelchairs strewn along the walls.

After two long weeks in the care of Dr. Julian Cahill, I was going home, tumor-free. I still wore a bandage on my head, covering my shaved scalp on one side. Maybe this would be a good time to cut my hair. I've wanted a shorter look for a while now, and this was all the incentive I needed. A fresh start.

My emotions were all over the place. Being in the hospital, I had unfettered access to Julian, but now that I'd received my discharge papers, would I see him again?

Moving along, Mom stopped abruptly. Straight ahead, standing beside the front desk was Julian; all decked out in his hospital white-coat with slicked back, unruly, longer hair. God, could he be any more gorgeous?

Mom moved forward when he turned and saw us approaching. She extended her hand to him. "Thank you, Dr. Cahill. Thank you for saving our daughter. How can I ever repay you? If it weren't for you, Destiny might not be here. I know I owe you a heartfelt apology. Marcus and I were wrong about you. Thank you from the bottom of our hearts."

Julian placed his hand in hers. "I was doing my job, Mrs. Bradshaw. I would have done the same for any one of my patients. This just happens to be an extraordinary woman...who I love."

Oh my God! My eyes dropped out of my head. He just told my mom that he loved me?

My mom turned and gazed into my eyes. Her strained look told me she was struggling with her internal dialogue. She squeezed her eyes shut. "Go, Destiny. Go to him. You have your dad's and my blessing to date him. He saved your life. How could we say no? Go to him before I change my mind."

I was out of my wheelchair and leaping into Julian's arms before she could blubber another word. He swung me around and kissed me long and hard. He fucking knew all along. When I pushed away from him, our eyes locked on each other. Tears spilled down both our cheeks. I released him and ran over to my mom and wrapped her in my arms. "Thank you, Mommy. Thank you. I knew you'd like him once you got to know him."

"I just want you to be happy, Destiny."

"I am now. I am now."

"Thank you, Mrs. Bradshaw. I promise to take care of her for the rest of my life," Julian said affectionately, as he reached for her hand.

"I'm going to hold you to that, Dr. Cahill. And please call me Cynthia." Looking defeated, she closed her eyes again and dropped her hands to her sides.

"And please call me Julian."

She smiled as I ran back into the arms of my man...the love of my life. "I love you, Julian Hayward Cahill."

"I love you too, Destiny Lynn Bradshaw."

WITH THE HOLIDAY SEASON approaching, my health had improved as expected. After two radiation treatments—which drained me of my energy—my life was almost back to normal. I attributed that to my hunky boyfriend.

For the most part, I'd spent the last few weeks staying with Julian, all so he could keep a close eye on me until I recovered. I spent the weekends with my parents and had strict orders to remain inactive through this time. My parents agreed this was the best situation since I could receive round-the-clock care from Julian. He'd taken a leave of absence from work until after the New Year.

My hair had grown back enough to cover the incision. I finally had my left side cut to match my shorter right side. I liked the simple, carefree look. I wasn't sure, but thought Julian did, too. He'd repeatedly told me how he didn't care what I looked like as long as I was alive.

We celebrated Thanksgiving at Elizabeth and Lyle's house. It was my first time going back to the home I'd lived in during my former life as Amber. I had much to be thankful for, and right now, my life was perfect. My parents accepted Julian into the family with open arms, and I loved them for that. I'd learned a valuable lesson through all my lying and promised myself to never go that route again. Ever.

With his arm draped over my shoulder, Julian and I stepped through the door of the Scott's home. I closed my eyes in an attempt to recall the memories of when I lived here. My whole body shook. Standing to greet us were Lyle and Elizabeth, Logan and Lisa, Robin and Liam, and my parents, shouting in unison, "Welcome home, Destiny!"

My jaw dropped. *My parents? Here?*

My legs wouldn't move; I was stunned. The love in front of me filled my heart with overflowing joy.

"Did you know about this, Julian?" I narrowed my eyes at him. He gave me a smug look.

My mom and dad had come a long way since that dreadful day they found out about Julian and me. They weren't on board with my reincarnation right away, but when I showed them the yearbook photo of Amber, they gradually started believing.

I swept them into my arms. "I love both of you so much."

"We love you too, honey."

"Come see your old room." Robin pulled me from my mother's embrace and dragged me up the stairs. At the end of the hall, she opened the door to Amber's bedroom and my hand went to my mouth. Nothing had changed, looking as if I'd walked in the door to my past, except for one tiny detail. Millions and millions of stars filled the room, hanging on the walls, ceiling, doors…everywhere. My heart lurched into my mouth. I knew Julian had something to do with this.

"Do you like it?" Robin asked.

"I love it." I sounded breathless.

"What do you think?" Julian sidled up from behind, making me jump.

Giving us a conspiratorial wink, Robin disappeared down the stairs, and I lunged into Julian's arms. "It's perfect, just like you. To the stars and back," I whispered, gazing into his eyes. "When you look to the heavens and see a million stars...think of me."

Julian snaked his arms around my waist and pulled me to him, squeezing me tightly. "A day never went by that I didn't think of you when I stared at the stars."

We held each other close, swaying back and forth.

"Thank you, Jules."

SNOW FELL ON CHRISTMAS EVE creating a beautiful landscape, reminding me of New York winters. Julian and I decided to go out and trounce around through the dimly lit, deserted streets, making snow angels everywhere. In some ways, it felt like we were inside our own private snow globe.

I wrapped my arm around his waist. "This angel is Amber."

"You are my only angel, Dest." Julian bent down and kissed a snowflake off the end of my nose.

"You can really be romantic, sometimes, Jules."

We linked our gloved fingers together, paraded around the block of Julian's home and into the park.

"I'd like to live away from the city, someday—someplace with the peace and stillness of the mountains. How about you, Dest?"

"I'd love that—a cozy little house nestled in the tranquility of the woods. I've lived my entire life in extravagance; I really don't want a big house. In fact, I loved Robin's house. What do you think?"

"Anything for you."

In time, the slight chill in the air overtook us. We returned to Julian's penthouse and warmed our shivering bodies in his jetted bathtub...big enough for four people. I poured each of us a glass of Cabernet Sauvignon and delivered one to Julian, who was already soaking in the tub. I'd convinced him to let me drink alcohol on special occasions. Anyway, it wasn't like I'd never had it before.

I quickly removed my clothes and joined him in the warm water, my back to his front. "It smells like a floral garden in here. What is that pleasant scent?"

"Believe it or not, it's called *Amber Blossom.*"

My eyes widened. "No way. Where did you find that?"

He ran his fingers down my arm. "When you left me, I had to get away and traveled to Italy. I found it in a small shop there."

I knew I'd broken his heart. Even now I regretted my decision to follow my parents' demands. "You know how sorry I am that you had to go through all of that, don't you?"

"Let's not ruin our excellent evening bringing that back up. It's a moot point now."

"Julian, I was nothing without you…completely and achingly broken."

He didn't say another word, effectively ending that conversation.

With a clink, we tapped our glasses together, wishing each other a Merry Christmas and took a sip. The water whirled around our bodies as thick bubbles filled the tub, exposing only our heads.

"I enjoyed snowglobing with you this evening, Jules."

"Snowglobing? Is that even a word?"

"Just made it up." I giggled.

Julian looked as though he was testing the word in his head. "I think I like it," he said, running a trail of kisses along the bend of my neck.

I turned and straddled him, planting a kiss on his lips. "Mmm, so tasty."

"What do you say we move this to the bedroom?" His voice made those words sound so incredibly sensual.

"Yes." I sounded breathy. This would be the first time making love since our devastating breakup and my brain surgery. Up to this point, he'd treated me like a porcelain doll during my recovery. I let him, though. He was my doctor and knew best.

Julian dried me with a towel, gently caressing my skin with his expert hands. He ignited my libido as every surface of my body longed for his touch.

We then moved to his bedroom. He lowered the lights until the room was lit by a dim lamp on the dresser along with the moon casting shadows through the window. A romantic glow surrounded us.

"Make love to me, Julian. I love you so much. I need you, and I know you need me, too."

"You're very perceptive, Dest."

In short minutes, we'd slipped under the blankets of his king-size bed.

"You on top, Dest."

My arousal was thick and strong. Unable to wait a second longer, I positioned his erection at my opening and slid down onto him until he filled me. "Oh God, this feels good. I've missed this so much." I moaned in pleasure.

Julian groaned a deep throaty sound. He placed his hands on my hips and helped as I raised myself up and down again and again. My pulse increased. I exhaled a deep breath, the feeling exquisite.

I stilled and stared down into his eyes. They glistened in the darkness, filled with emotion.

"Don't cry, Jules. Life is perfect now."

"I know. I love you so much, Destiny."

A second later, he rolled me to my back, never losing our precious contact. With Julian's handsome face hovering above, we made slow passionate love all night. I too, loved him with all my heart and soul.

OUR PLANS WERE TO DRIVE south to Julian's parent's house in Castle Pines for the Christmas festivities.

Once up and showered, I'd dressed in a long-sleeve, red velvet cocktail dress, finishing my outfit off with my black knee-high boots. From my jewelry box, I snagged my diamond necklace with matching earrings. Julian wore his black linen pants with a red button-down and black tie. He always told me I'd look good in overalls and a straw hat, well…right back at him. God, he was sexy. While we were apart, he let his hair grow out, too. It wasn't as long as it was when we were teenagers, but longer nonetheless. He slicked it back away from his face. It was messy, just the way I liked it.

"I love your much longer hair, babe."

He combed his fingers through it. "Do you?"

"I love the shorter hair, too. You're so unbelievably sexy no matter how you wear it. Jeez, give a girl a chance. Females ogle you all the time."

"Yours are the only eyes I care about," he cautioned.

"Good."

I finished applying my makeup in the bathroom while Julian waited with my coat in hand. He held it as I slipped my arms through the sleeves. He then draped a scarf around my neck and pulled a hat over my head.

"Let's keep this cerebrum warm. It's cold outside," he smirked.

"It's going to give me hat-hair," I growled.

"I don't care. You're wearing the hat."

"Okay, Mr. Bossy."

He raised his eyebrows at me. "Get used to it. I get what I want."

"With pleasure, Jules." I loved this domineering side of him.

"Ready to go?"

I nodded.

Thirty minutes later, we pulled into the driveway of the Cahill home in Castle Pines. I glanced over at the Scott's house, thinking about our Thanksgiving meal with all the parents. And when Robin hauled me up the stairs to my old bedroom...filled with stars. The old saying that you have the *best-of-both-worlds* was literally true for me because I'd lived two different lives.

Julian opened my door and helped me from the car. I was thankful for my hat and winter coat as the chilly air passed right through me. I shivered and together we ran hand in hand to the front door.

"Merry Christmas, kids. How are you, Destiny?" Lisa said warmly, greeting me with a tight hug and huge smile. She'd finally welcomed me into the Cahill home with open arms. I wasn't sure if she was fully on board with my reincarnation but, no doubt saw how happy I made Julian. To her, that seemed to be far more important than anything. Whether or not anyone believed me was their prerogative, but Julian and I knew the truth, and that was all that truly mattered.

"I'm feeling myself again, Lisa. Thank you and Merry Christmas to you and Logan."

She kissed my cheek, then released me and turned to Julian. "How are you, darling?"

Julian stood behind me bouncing on his toes. "Freezing, Mom."

"Get in here." As Lisa pulled the door wide open, I saw her give him a furtive wink.

What was that about?

We moved down the hallway to the living room greeting Lyle, Elizabeth, Robin, Liam, and my parents. I immediately wrapped my arms around my daddy and mommy and told them how much I loved them.

"Merry Christmas, my sweet girl. We love you, too."

Moments later, we sat down to a mouth-watering meal of filet mignon topped with a red wine demi-glace, roasted red potatoes and a baby spinach vinaigrette prepared by Lisa, Elizabeth, Robin, and my mom. Julian and I brought a bottle of our favorite white wine, a delicious and crisp Chardonnay. I was famished. I had regained all the weight I'd lost during my time away from Julian.

Place cards sat above each plate of the beautifully decorated table. A gold satin tablecloth draped the table set with Christmas china, while an assortment of candles flickered in the center. I sat between Julian and my dad. We chatted about the latest upcoming piece of technology and football. What a combination. We were all Denver Bronco fans and hoped they'd make it to the Superbowl this year. I discovered how much Julian loved sports in the last two months, having to sit and endure hours and hours of football on our Sundays.

At Julian's request, when all was said and done, we moved to the living room and found seats around the Christmas tree. Decorated in white lights with gold and silver themed ornaments, it was exactly as I remembered it in my life as Amber. I sat next to Julian on the sofa. He draped his arm around me, moving his thumb in circles over my shoulder. Julian made sure we experienced new memories, too. This was our life, not Amber's anymore, but I always kept in mind that we were together because of her.

I couldn't help but look around, remembering my many visits to this house when I was Amber.

My eyes shot to the door across the room. "The closet, Julian." In my haste, I blurted the words out too loudly when eight heads turned to look at me. I quickly covered my mouth. *Crap.*

"What?" Julian looked puzzled.

"I remember hiding in that closet." I pointed to the door at the other end of the room, using a quieter voice.

"When was this?" Lisa asked, obviously eavesdropping on our whispered conversation.

Oh crap, again. My face flushed.

Julian scrunched his nose at me. "It's nothing, Mom."

"Destiny is remembering something. What is it, dear?" she prodded. "Please share it with all of us, honey."

I broke out in a cold sweat, whimpering. "Um...it's only something I remembered in my life as Amber."

"Oh, please tell us," Lisa urged me again.

"It's not a very happy memory if I remember it correctly," Julian added.

"C'mon, it was a long time ago. Spill it," Robin insisted.

This was so like her. She was so nosey. I grinned because I loved her.

"Go ahead, Destiny. Tell them what you remember." Julian looked at me with a *you-started-it-now-you-finish-it* look.

I narrowed my eyes at him, hesitating before I began. "Well..." I swallowed hard and gripped my elbows with my hands. "I was hiding in that closet when Logan discovered Julian's tattoo." I rushed through the words, unable to stop rocking back and forth, hoping that no one was listening to me. Unfortunately, all eyes were watching me. "And I heard the discussion or should I say the yelling that followed with—Nancy. And she broke that vase." I pointed to the ceramic piece that still sat on the mantel, amazed at myself for remembering her.

"Wait, who's Nancy?" my mom asked.

"Oh, Cynthia, that's a whole other story." Lisa chuckled.

Logan's face turned a dark shade of red. "I'm surprised that you...err...Amber ever stayed around after that. So you were in the closet that whole time?"

I buried my face in my hands. "Yes, I was standing in there for quite a while, if I recall," I said, peeking through my fingers.

"So, why were you hiding?" Lisa asked.

Holy shit! I couldn't tell them how Logan and Nancy had almost caught Julian and I going at it like a couple of horny bunnies on the floor. "Um…I don't remember."

Laughter broke out. I turned to Julian as he rolled his eyes, showing me his sly grin.

"I say we open the gifts and stop with the storytelling." Julian shifted me onto his lap. His eyes lit up. What did he have up his sleeve?

As everyone looked on with keen excitement, from the pocket of his shirt, Julian pulled out a small box with a red bow. "This is for the girl I love." He flashed his all-white teeth smile and handed the gift to me.

I looked around at the group of anticipated faces. Were they all in on this? I carefully detached the bow from the box and set it aside, then removed the soft turquoise paper to reveal a small white box and lifted the cover. Inside was a black velvet ring box. I eyed Julian skeptically. I ever so slowly raised the spring loaded top to reveal a heart-shaped diamond ring. *That heart-shaped diamond ring.* Once again, my hand went to my mouth with a sharp intake of breath. "Oh my God, Julian. I remember this. You gave it to me on my seventeenth birthday." Tears streamed down my face, sobbing uncontrollably.

Julian hoisted me off his lap and stood up. He put his hands on each side of my face and lifted my chin to meet his eyes. His thumb brushed along my lower lip. It was such a tender and intimate gesture.

"Do you remember our only New Years Eve together?"

"Yes. We spent it at your family's cabin."

"Then you remember my promise to you?"

"Yes," I whispered, my heart pounding in my chest. Knowing what was coming, I began delicately bouncing on my toes in anticipation.

"Then…Destiny Lynn Bradshaw, will you marry—?"

"Yes! Yes! Yes!" I squealed before he could finish. I lunged at him, wrapping my arms around his neck and hugging him with every ounce of strength I could muster at this moment. I loved him so much.

The room erupted in whoops, hollering and loud applause. They *were* all in on this. Julian released me, took my left hand, and slipped the ring onto my finger. He lifted my hand to his lips and tenderly kissed it. With everyone looking on, my mouth met his as we embraced into an innocent kiss.

"You are never leaving me again. Understand?"

"Yes." I sounded breathless. "I love you, Jules."

"Love you, too. You're my...Destiny," he said, joining my hand with his. "But there is one more minor piece of business we need to tend to."

I leaned my head to the side and looked at him, confused. "What's that?"

"Come with me."

Julian fetched our coats, hats, and gloves from the coat closet and we slipped them on. Seconds later he took my gloved hand and dragged me outside.

"Where are we going?"

"You'll see. Come."

Linking our fingers together, he pulled me toward the maple tree.

"I don't know if this will work with it being so biting cold out here, but we need to put your initials into this tree, babe."

My heart swelled. With tears swimming in my eyes, I gazed at the man I loved, the man I was going to marry and spend the rest of my life with. "I don't know what I did to deserve you, Jules, but don't ever change."

He smiled and pulled a jackknife from his pocket. "Where should your initials go?"

I tapped my fingers against my lips, studying the trunk of the tree, thinking back to the day we carved our initials into it. We'd chiseled a heart between them, symbolizing a connection between us.

"I think mine should go inside the heart. What do you think?"

"I think I love that idea."

Moments later, with frozen fingers, Julian etched a 'D,' 'B,' and 'C' inside the heart.

"What's the 'C' for?"

Julian looked at me with his you-can't-be-serious gaze. "Did you forget that your name will be Cahill some day?"

I scrunched my face at him.

He laughed with the kind of sound that made me want to smack him. Apparently reading my mind, he playfully raised his fists, ready to fight.

I quickly turned and jabbed his shoulder.

He chuckled. "You're cute when you scowl."

A giggle erupted from my belly, a loud, energizing sound of pure joy. "You make me so happy."

He gave me a chaste kiss and then retraced the weathered and worn initials of his and Amber's name, restoring them to their original grandeur.

Together, we placed our hands on the heart and felt an electricity flow between us. I stood on my toes and kissed the man I loved with all my heart and soul. He kissed me back.

"You know, Dest...after you died, there were many times when I would have given anything to spend just one more day with you." He cupped my face with his gloved hands, tilted my head up and looked deep into my eyes. "All I wanted was one, never realizing I'd get the rest of my life. What more could a man ask for?"

"Yes. Yes," I whispered.

What lay ahead for me was unknown, but I knew it would include Julian, the love of my life. Past, present, and future.

Epilogue

Five Years Later — August 2022

Julian

Twenty-three years ago, I thought my life ended. I was convinced I'd been dealt a shit hand of cards. For years I wondered if this was what God had in store for me. I'd asked over and over. Then Destiny came into my life, and that moment of lucidity overwhelmed me. It was all meant to happen this way.

I rolled to my side on our bed and fixed my eyes on my sleeping wife. I always found comfort in those moments when I could just stare at her. At times though, I thought it made her feel uneasy. She never said so but would ask why I was ogling her all the time. It was an addiction I didn't have any inclination to cure.

She was my beautiful Destiny, my beautiful wife, and the mother of our beautiful one-year-old daughter. I buried my nose into her hair to breathe in her natural perfume, her scent intoxicating. I didn't have to see her to know she was in close proximity. Her natural fragrance gave her away. It instantly aroused me. How could anyone smell that heavenly? To this day, I still couldn't believe she was all mine.

Destiny and I married on a gorgeous, sunny day along the sandy shores of Windsong Lake, May 5, 2020, Amber's birthday. We felt we owed it to her to celebrate the rest of our lives together and marry on her special day.

My sweet Destiny was the most stunning young bride I'd ever laid eyes on. As she walked down the flower-lined aisle, a beam of light encircled her like an aura. I knew Amber was making her presence known.

Both of our parents had gone all out with decorations. A smattering of yellow roses (Amber and Destiny's favorite color) lined the surrounding waterfront, and seventeen white doves were released to the heavens in memory of Amber at the moment we were pronounced man and wife. Robin was Destiny's Matron of Honor, my dad, my best man, and an almost four-year-old Camden showed off his expertise at being the perfect ring bearer.

I'll never forget the incredulous look that filled Destiny's face when she spotted my fire-engine-red Camaro awaiting our departure. The preparation I did to get the car ready for our wedding day took months. It was the first time I'd driven it in years, as it sat beneath a cover in my parents' garage. But, to see the look on Destiny's face made it all worth it.

We traveled to Italy for our honeymoon and spent two glorious weeks there. While in Rome, we visited the Roman Coliseum and the Pantheon. In the evenings we took boat rides along the Tiber River. Then it was off to the peace and serenity of Lake Como. We stayed in a private villa, staring out at the beautiful, blue waters. The resort had gone all out for our arrival with champagne and roses.

I took Destiny to all the memorable places I'd seen when we were apart five years earlier. At the time I was just going through the motions, unable to appreciate the beauty of the country, but with her by my side, I saw more than I could ever imagine. We had the time of our lives. I knew I would love her until I took my final breath. She was finally mine. I laughed inwardly at the thought that it took two of her lifetimes to get me there.

I often wondered why she wanted to be with me. I was nearly forty years old while she was a young and vibrant twenty-three. Would she always love me the way I loved her?

Destiny's eyes opened, allowing me to see those stunning baby blue irises. Today she shared her birthday with our baby daughter, Lyndsey.

"Hey, good morning, my beautiful husband. Are you staring at me again?" She looked at me with a knowing smile.

I crawled on top of her and planted a kiss on her mouth. "Good morning and happy birthday to my gorgeous wife. Your lips are so soft right now."

"Thank you, Jules. So are yours...like satin."

I pushed my erection against her and moved my hips in a circular motion. She always made me ready for sex. "Would you like your first present?"

"Hmm, what would that be?" She asked as she pushed her pelvis up to meet mine, quickly grasping my thoughts.

"You're very perceptive."

"Um, I'd call it sophic, Jules." She gave me a wicked smile.

"Are you tantalizing me with another war of words?" I asked.

"Maybe, what are you going to do about it?"

I lowered myself to my forearms and planted a tender kiss on her lips.

She shoved her fingers into my hair and pulled me further into her. I felt every bit of her desperation and need.

"Holy hell, you're wearing your red teddy. Are you trying to drive me insane?"

"I thought I'd surprise you. I got up in the middle of the night while you were sleeping and slipped it on."

I threw the blankets off her. "Let me see you." Damn, she was sexy. I reached down and removed her underwear, lifted my hips, and positioned myself at her opening, gently pushing into her. I couldn't wait any longer. Christ, she felt tight. I never tired of making love to her. "You look gorgeous."

She moaned. "Oh, this feels great. A birthday fuck from my sexy husband."

"Call it what you like. I'm going to make you come so hard, Destiny."

Her groans spurred me on. I still had difficulty holding back my orgasms with her. She turned me on so much.

She wrapped her legs around my back and pressed her fingers into my shoulder blades. She locked her ankles together, claiming me as her prisoner. There was no question I was forever hers. Moving at an obnoxiously slow pace, I realized there was no place I'd rather be than buried deep inside my wife. I wanted our lovemaking to last forever.

My arousal gripped me, thick and strong. I'd lost control over any cognizant thought as blood pumped through my veins. I held my torso up with my forearms and flicked my tongue over her soft, plump breasts. I teased her nipples. They hardened and puckered as I pulled on the tips with my teeth. Her body writhed and twisted.

"Julian, you're going to make me come doing that."

"That's the plan." I kissed her again and slowly circled my hips into her.

"Julian, please." Her breath hitched.

That was the cue I needed. I thrust myself into her, slamming hard against her sex and moved with an intensity even I was unable to comprehend. I was going to come so hard. I pounded in again and again until her body started trembling. I knew she was close. She closed her eyes and found her release seconds later. I loved watching her have an orgasm.

"Oh, Julian."

My name on her lips pushed me over the edge as I exploded into her like a canon. "Uhh," I groaned. Sex between us tested the boundaries of euphoria.

OUR PRE-DAWN INTIMACY was perfectly timed this morning when, right on cue, the baby monitor on Destiny's nightstand came to life. Lyndsey's babbling sweet voice bounced off the pine walls of our bedroom.

We had a log home built in the secluded foothills of the Rocky Mountains. Destiny wanted something smaller than what she was accustomed to but also wanted space for our growing family. Because she used to love the view from my penthouse, we designed the front of the house to have the same vista. I caught her staring all the time. To this day, she continues to tell me how much she loves looking at the snow-capped mountains. They would always hold a peaceful place in my heart as well.

"I'll get her. It's your birthday, and you get a day off."

"You're too sweet, Julian, but I don't want a day off from my beautiful daughter, who looks just like her daddy," she said cupping her hand against my cheek. "Do you have to go into the office today?"

"No. Why?"

"Well, your phone was ringing off the hook during the night."

I'd finally opened my own practice in the city which gave me more control over the number of hours worked. I was still in high demand, but without the hospital breathing down my throat.

"It's your birthday. I'm not going anywhere near the office today."

Her shrewd smile lit up the room.

"What?"

"I remember telling you you'd be the best neurosurgeon."

My breath hitched. Yes, she did tell me that and sounded so damn sure of herself in the meantime. I grinned. "I love when you remember those days." I pinched her chin between my thumb and forefinger and tugged her lips to mine.

"Hmm."

CASTLE PINES CEMETERY would always command a spiritual presence each time we'd visited Amber's grave. Instead of our usual August second visit, we decided to make the trek to the cemetery today. We would be in Castle Pines for our birthday celebration at my parent's house. Mine wasn't for another week, but Mom decided she could observe all three of us in one fell swoop. Remembering all those years of dread during this time of year, I now embrace it with open arms. Life was extraordinary.

"Ready to go, Dest?" I lifted Lyndsey in my arms and gave her a kiss on the cheek. She giggled and playfully pushed me away.

"Yes, I'm ready for our big day. But first, I need to say happy birthday to my little girl." She leaned over and kissed the top of Lyndsey's head. "Happy birthday, baby girl."

Without delay, we loaded Lyndsey into her car seat and headed south toward Castle Pines. "I see you're wearing my favorite blue jeans, Dest."

"And your favorite crimson wrap top, as well. Did you notice that?" she asked.

"I probably would have once I finished staring at your world class ass in those jeans."

She playfully slapped me.

"I can't help it. It's one of my favorite body parts."

"I know. Don't forget I'm on the receiving end of those stares." Her eyes roamed my frame. "Might I add how delicious you look in your blue jeans, too? Oh hell, you always look hot in anything. It's hard keeping up with you."

I gave her a sardonic grin. "You're holding your own, babe."

We arrived at the cemetery an hour later. Pulling onto the tree-lined dirt road, I noticed a familiar car parked next to Amber's grave. I pulled up behind the blue BMW and quieted the engine of my Mercedes. "Lyle and Elizabeth are here."

Destiny's peaceful expression gave nothing away, but I think she was genuinely pleased to see them.

I unbuckled Lyndsey's car seat straps and lifted her in my arms. "Grandma and Grandpa are over there, Lyndsey." Her eyes followed my pointing finger. She babbled something unintelligible and held out her arms.

Lyle's eyes lit up at the sight of his grandchild. "Hi kids, it's so nice to see you."

Elizabeth ran a hand down my arm. "Thank you for continuing your visits through the years, Julian."

I bent to kiss her cheek as Lyndsey reached out for her grandma. "If I can be here, I will be. I owe so much to her."

She took Lyndsey from me. "And how's my sweet granddaughter? Happy birthday, Lyndsey Amber Cahill, I don't see you enough. You've grown so much. Grandma loves you." Elizabeth nuzzled Lyndsey's cheek with her face. "And a happy birthday also goes to my wonderful daughter, too. Happy birthday, Destiny."

"Thank you, Elizabeth," Destiny said. "Happy birthday to you, too."

Elizabeth laid a hand over her heart and smiled. "Well, thank you, darling."

They both hugged for long minutes until Lyndsey pushed them apart with a whine. We all chuckled. Elizabeth reluctantly handed the baby to an impatiently waiting Grandpa.

Lyle spoke softly to Lyndsey. "Happy birthday to you...my sweet angel."

Destiny bent down to plant a single red flower in front of Amber's stone, representing the red hearts that donned our backsides. She'd done this for the last five years. This year, she bought a bright red dahlia from the local greenhouse.

Elizabeth, Lyle, and I stood arm in arm, gazing at Amber's grave while my sweet wife transplanted the flower to the left of the beautiful stone. A lump formed in my throat when I tried to swallow. I still felt raw emotions when I came here.

We all stood and chatted a while longer until Lyndsey grew tired and started squirming in Lyle's arms. At that point, we decided it was time to continue the drive to my parent's house.

"We'll follow you," Lyle said as we climbed into the Mercedes.

Minutes later I pulled into the driveway of my childhood home, noticing a handful of unfamiliar cars. "What the hell has my mother done now?"

I knew Destiny's parents would be here along with Robin, Liam, their two boys, Camden, almost six—he would tell us—and his little brother, two-and-a-half-year-old Timothy. Robin named Timmy after Destiny's deceased brother, along with insisting that Destiny and I be his godparents. "Absolutely," we told her.

Destiny craned her neck to inspect the scene. "I recognize my parents and Robin's car, but I can't identify the others."

Lyndsey had fallen asleep in her car seat. We hated those moments when we had to wake her up, but this time was different—she stayed asleep, laying like a limp rag in my arms, her head on my shoulder.

My mother greeted us at the door with a sheepish smile. "It's so wonderful to see my granddaughter again."

I raised my finger to my lips, shushing her. The disappointment that crossed her face made me chuckle. As my parent's only grandchild, they doted on Lyndsey. They hated when she was asleep and couldn't immediately manhandle her.

"Happy birthday, Destiny, and to you too, Julian." She kept her voice low while planting a kiss on my cheek.

My dad appeared. "Give her to me. I have a soft shoulder for her to lean on." Without any protest from me, he swiftly took Lyndsey from me. Destiny and I knew we'd see a small window of opportunity to free ourselves from watching her when extended family was around.

The house was unusually quiet for the sheer number of cars gracing the front yard. We followed my dad down the hall into the living room. As we turned the corner, I caught Destiny as she thrust backward, into my arms.

"Surprise!" A roomful of our family and friends screamed in unison. Lyndsey instantly began crying. Damn. Window of opportunity closed.

"Oh my God!" Destiny turned to me with a smile that stretched across her face.

Standing in the room was Marcus, Cynthia, all the grandparents, Robin, Liam, their boys, high school friends, Brad and Shelby, and a few of my colleagues. But my jaw dropped when my eyes landed on Amber's grandma and grandpa Cashmen. I hadn't seen them since Amber's funeral.

"I thought this was going to be a small affair with only family." I regarded my mother shrewdly. She winked at me. But it was nice to see everyone again.

Destiny left my side and headed straight for her parents, giving each a hug and kiss. I made my rounds, starting with my grandparents. "Grandma and Grandpa Cahill, thanks for being here for our special day."

Grandma smiled. "Oh, Julian, do you think we'd miss this? Anyway, this old coot wants to see her great-granddaughter."

"Happy birthday, boy. How are you? I hope you're not burning the candle at both ends with that job of yours."

"I'm good, Gramps. Besides, if it weren't for that job, my wife wouldn't be here," I said.

"That is true, Julian."

Yes. That *was* true. Right there was the reason I invested so much time to my education…to save the girl I loved. In a way, I felt vindicated for all my efforts, sacrifices, and hard work. This was my life and I wouldn't trade it with anyone.

After a firm handshake, I moved on to Amber's grandparents, meeting grandma Cashmen's gaze.

"Julian, you're all grown-up now. We just had to come and see Destiny for ourselves. The resemblance to Amber is uncanny. We would love it if you'd introduce us."

"Absolutely. I'd be happy to."

On cue, Destiny was at my side, holding out her arms. "You're Grandma and Grandpa Cashmen, right?"

"Oh my, yes," Grandma Cashmen said, her hand fluttering against her chest. "You sure know how to make an old woman cry, dear. How are you, Destiny? We've heard so much about you."

Destiny gave her a brief hug. "I'm having a great time seeing all my favorite people here."

While they embraced each other, I left them to get re-acquainted. Moving across the room, I approached Brad and Shelby.

"What's up?" Brad fist-pumped me. "Happy birthday—forty, eh? Of course, you married a youngin'. That alone should keep you active." He snorted a deep throaty laugh. "So, other than her age and how much she resembles Amber, what's the attraction? Shit, she's half your age, man."

Christ, I hated being judged. I'd decided it was time to fill him in. It'd been long enough keeping this secret from my good friend. "Look at her, Brad. What do you see?"

Destiny was making her rounds, greeting everyone when her eyes met mine. I summoned her with a nod of my chin. She gave me an "in-a-minute" sign with her finger.

Brad's eyebrows lifted slightly. "What do I see in Destiny? Is that what you're asking? I just told you. I see a young Amber look-a-like. What are you getting at?"

In short leisurely strides, Destiny made her way to my side and wrapped her arm around my back. Her touches meant the world to me.

I placed my arm over her shoulders.

"What's up, Jules?" she asked coyly.

"Dest, I think it's time to let our friends in on your identity. Is that okay with you?" Both Brad and Shelby narrowed their eyes with a confused and perplexed stare.

"Yes, please tell us who Destiny is, Julian. I've wanted to know the answer to that question since the awards banquet years ago." I took great pleasure when Shelby pinned her eyes on me.

Destiny's eyes went wide. "Only if it's okay with you. But, shall we make them sweat a little first?"

"Great idea. I knew there was a reason I married you." Her laugh mimicked mine.

Destiny started in immediately, "Hmm, let's see..." She paused, tapping her fingers on her chin. "Shelby, remember back in high school when you came for a sleepover at my house? We sat on my bed discussing our men? Honest-to-God discussing?"

"Huh? I met you at the awards banquet, Destiny. What are you talking about?"

"Au contraire, Shelb...my dear bestie."

I snorted. "Good one Dest, but you never told me this story."

"Oh, for God's sake, Julian, all girls chat about their boyfriends with each other. And you were probably the most talked about guy in the entire high school."

Shelby's puzzled look made us laugh. She narrowed her eyes at us.

I turned to Destiny. "Should we let them off the hook, Mrs. Cahill?"

"I guess so, Mr. Cahill. But first, let me say one more thing, and then you can fill them in," she paused with a frown, "Shelby, those were some of the most beautiful, heartfelt words you said at my funeral. Thank you from the bottom of my heart."

"Huh? What the hell is going on here? Somebody had better start talking," Shelby demanded. She widened her stance and flung her hands to her hips, striking the Jolly-Green-Giant pose.

"That was sweet, Dest, but I think it's time to reveal you. Brad, Shelby—Destiny is the reincarnated Amber."

"I'm sorry. What did you say?" Shelby asked loudly, making a few heads turn in her direction.

Brad interrupted, "Are you drunk, man?"

Destiny took Shelby's hand and pulled it against her chest. "Shelby, you were the only friend I had when I started school." She frowned and looked down. "You were there for me at a time when I needed it. That meant the world to me."

Shelby scowled at us. "Impossible. I don't believe in that shit." She yanked her hand from Destiny's grip, looking pissed. "Julian probably told you to say that."

Destiny reached down to the hem of her shirt and pulled it up, just above her naval. "See this?" She pointed to the scar on the right side of her abdomen. "I was stabbed here, in the halls of Castle Rock…next to my locker, by two very mean girls. Now, do you believe me?" She scowled back at Shelby. "Or that time you came for the sleepover at my house, and I showed you this?" Destiny lowered her shirt off her shoulder to reveal the heart-shaped birthmark. "You remember Amber's, don't you? And all those beautiful bandanas you brought to me when I was sick. Remember?"

Shelby's hand went to her mouth. "What the hell. Yes, I do remember." Her voice was barely audible and her eyes welled-up with tears. "I'm so sorry, Amb…Destiny." She coughed. "Oops. You probably hate that."

"No, I don't because we are the same person. I have Amber's soul, but my own body."

Destiny held out her arms and Shelby walked into them. "I really missed you," Shelby whispered.

"I know. And I meant what I said about your words at my funeral."

Shelby abruptly pushed away, regarding Destiny with a smirk. "Well, if I knew you'd be back, I wouldn't have been so sappy at your funeral."

We all burst out laughing, making heads turn again.

Destiny gave Shelby a playful shove. "Nice, real nice."

"This is amazing. Who else knows this?" Brad asked with a bemused smile.

"Only a few people, so please keep it to yourselves," I softly reprimanded. "We don't want the media to know our business."

Shelby smiled. "I feel honored. Believe me; your secret is safe with us."

While Destiny and Shelby strolled to the kitchen, Brad and I caught up with each other.

"This is insane, man. Is her personality like Amber's as well?"

"Exactly like Amber's," I reassured him. "She's as perfect as Amber was. Maybe more so."

"I remember how devastated you were after Amber's death. And now she's back. What deal did you make with God to deserve this?"

"I don't know, Brad, but I thank Him every day for bringing her back to me."

AS WE SAT DOWN to a catered meal provided by The Nickel Bistro restaurant, I glanced around the room, watching the ebb and flow of conversation, catching Destiny's eye. She was doing the same thing. We smiled at each other. It took more years than I cared to count, but this was the life I'd always dreamed of. I had the love of my life by my side, forever.

I laughed to myself...to think she was alive all those years I'd thought she was gone.

After everyone sang an out-of-tune "Happy Birthday," we sank our teeth into the cake and ice cream.

Lyndsey was covered in cake from head to toe. I couldn't help but snicker at my parents' delight in watching her. They laughed and giggled and talked gibberish right along with her.

"She's so adorable, you two." Grandpa Hayward glowed. "It makes me shudder to think of how I could have completely missed her whole life because of our pig-headedness. I thank God every day for this family."

"I'm thankful too, Gramps."

My mom sidled up next to me, ambushing our conversation. "Me too, dad."

He nodded.

BY LATE AFTERNOON the party wound down to a few friends and family remaining. The warm afternoon sun had given way to a cool westerly breeze as we all moved to the outside patio. Each of us found a lawn chair as we watched Camden and Timothy run around the backyard. Lyndsey was in the arms of my mom as she babbled on and on. My mom babbled back.

"Use words, Mom." I narrowed my eyes at her.

"Oh, Julian." She held up the palm of her hand, dismissing me. "I missed this age with you, so please let me enjoy this."

Yes, she did miss this with me. I'll never forget that Christmas when I saw her for the first time. I lived sixteen years of my life without her. I could give her this. "Okay. You're right."

I scrambled over to grab the empty seat next to my beautiful wife and draped my arms over her shoulders. Attention locked onto Timothy as he kept repeating over and over, "Look, Mommy, I running fast with Camen." We all laughed at his unsuccessful attempt to say his brother's name, though intelligible for two and a half. It was true testament to the ace parenting he received from Robin and Liam.

Robin continually acknowledged his plea to look at him. "I see you running really fast, Timmy."

He ignored her. With confused faces, we all watched as he slowly approached Cynthia and climbed into her lap. She lifted him to straddle her legs. We laughed, and I thought he possibly needed glasses. Then he'd climb down, run around some more, and resume his place, back on her lap, repeating the process over and over. "See, I running real fast."

We all acknowledged his joy at running.

Destiny looked at Robin and Liam with a gleam in her eyes. "My brother, Timmy, was a track star in high school and college. Maybe your Timmy will be a track star, too."

"That would be so cool," Robin added.

LYNDSEY BEGAN FUSSING, so we decided to take the cue and say our goodbyes. Destiny gathered up her toys, bottles and diaper bag and moments later, we were thanking everyone with hugs and kisses.

Out the door with Lyndsey falling asleep on my shoulder, I snagged Destiny's hand and pulled her to the maple tree.

I bent over and planted a kiss on her lips. From my coat pocket, I retrieved a small box and handed it to her. "Happy birthday, Dest."

Her wide eyes shifted from the box to me and back again.

"What's this?"

"Just open it."

With shaky hands, she tore away the wrapping paper and sprang open the cover of the small box. "Julian!" She looked up at me with unshed tears in her eyes. "It's the same ring you gave to Amber…um, gave to me on our last visit to Windsong Lake." She hesitated and grabbed my right hand, pulling it toward her. Lifting it to her lips, she gently kissed the multi-colored ring on my finger. "Did you really think for one second I hadn't noticed this ring you'd been wearing, and the symbolic gesture it holds? I know you promised you'd never take it off. And you didn't. Amber and I love you for that, and now I have one to match it."

I slipped it on her finger and watched as she splayed her hand out to stare at it.

"I love it and will never take it off."

Together, we lifted our hands to the engraved heart and touched it. A groggy Lyndsey leaned over and placed her hand on top of ours and muttered, "Ma ma ma ma." Her first words stunned us silent.

AUGUST 11, 2022, MY FORTIETH BIRTHDAY, and the day Destiny would be finding out if she was in complete remission with no sign of her brain tumor. Being five years out from her cancer, she was scheduled for one final MRI. Trained to watch for any symptoms the tumor had returned, I admit, I was programmed to notice these things. It might've explained my obsession in watching her. Amber slipped through my fingers twenty-three years ago, and I'd be damned if Destiny would follow the same path.

The ironic part of the puzzle was how Amber's brain tumor took her away from me; whereas, Destiny's brought *her* back to me. I recalled my mother's words from all those years ago—*your soul shines the brightest in its darkest hour.* That statement couldn't have been any truer than it was today—Destiny's birth being on the day of Amber's funeral...my brightest and darkest hours. If I'd known this would be my path in life, I wouldn't have believed it. I thanked God every day it was.

Up to this point, Destiny hadn't exhibited any signs or symptoms of a recurrence of the tumor. It would be the best birthday gift I could ever receive if she told me she was cancer-free.

I laid awake once more, watching her sleep so peacefully. With slightly parted lips and soft, shallow breathing, she looked perfect. Her hair had grown out again and fell in soft waves over her face and pillow. Her fingers interlocked together like she was praying. Maybe at some deep level, she was.

Her eyelids fluttered open, and again, revealed those beautiful baby blues.

"Good morning, birthday boy. I have an extraordinary gift for you today," Destiny said with a sheepish grin.

What did she have up her sleeve? "Are you thinking what I'm thinking?" I drummed my fingers up her body.

"What is it that you think I'm thinking?" She smirked.

"Are we going to go around all morning like this or are you going to give me my present?" I climbed on her and pushed my erection against her. Everything about her aroused me. I always craved more.

"Oh no, that's not the present I was thinking about."

"Well, it's the one I want right now."

She giggled that sweet sound. "You want that now?" she asked sweetly, reaching her hand to cup my cheek. "I can't keep up with your sexual demands, Julian. You're like the Energizer Bunny."

"Right now." I pushed her legs apart with mine and made slow, gentle love to her. This was the life I'd always dreamed of with Amber, and in a roundabout way, it was exactly what I had. My sweet Destiny was my dear reincarnated Amber.

Sated and relaxed, Destiny turned on her side to face me, propping her head up with the palm of her hand as she ran her index finger through my chest hair. "Julian, I wish I could lay here all day with you, but I have to get up and get ready for my appointment with the doctor."

"Don't go, Dest. I want to stare at you a little bit longer."

"Babe, your eyes must be getting sore from all the staring you do." She giggled. "You have made me the happiest woman in the world. Can you imagine what our lives would have been like if I hadn't attended the tour that day?"

"And that tour was not supposed to be mine. I agreed to work for Owen that day."

Her eyes protruded from her face. "Oh my God, you never told me that."

"Yup, it's true. He needed the day off, so I swapped one of my conference days with him."

"Well, thank God you did."

"I'm sure Amber had everything to do with our chance meeting that day."

"Yes, I'm quite sure she did. I love you. Now I must get up and get ready. I've got a bit of a headache this morning. I'm going to grab an aspirin before my shower."

Every time she mentioned the word headache, I couldn't contain my dreaded fears. I never wanted to hear those words again, especially with her history.

Destiny gave me a quick kiss on the lips and shuffled her way out of our bed. My attention shifted to her backside when she stood and wiggled her perfectly round ass at me. She took three steps toward the bathroom before collapsing to the floor with a deep groan.

Every bit of blood drained from my face as I leaped out of bed in seconds flat, tending to her.

"Fuck! Not this again!"

She slowly regained her footing, turned, and what I saw next made my jaw drop and eyes go wide. I couldn't believe we would be going through this shit again.

"Gotcha!" She laughed. "Happy Birthday, babe. I had my doctor's appointment two days ago and was given a clean bill of health then. I'm cancer-free. Did I scare you?"

I narrowed my eyes at her as she tucked a strand of hair behind her ear.

"I wanted to wait until today to tell you. This is my special gift to you. There is no sign of the tumor. It's gone." She smiled as she leaned her head to the side, eyes penetrating me, trying to gauge my reaction. Damn, she was adorable. "See, I knew you would save me, Dr. Julian Hayward Cahill. I knew it."

She was beautifully flawless. I could barely contain my excitement but decided two could play at this game and instead, held my reaction back to make her sweat a little.

Her somber look made me chuckle. I couldn't resist giving her a taste of her own medicine, but it was time to let her off the hook. "You little shit. You had me fucking scared to death!" I howled. She was so good at these moments. "You're not going to get away with this."

I quickly lunged at her as she tried to run. She squealed when I grabbed and tossed her on the bed, holding her down with my body. She laughed the sweetest sound I'd ever heard.

"This is the best birthday present I've ever received." As I lowered my lips against hers again, giving her everything I had, my heart burst with unconditional love. I pulled away and stared down into her tear-filled eyes. "Thank you, Destiny."

"I have one more gift for you."

"Another one? What could top the one you just gave me?"

"Well, it's something I'd like to give to you now. But you need to let me up."

I released her, and she scooted across the bed to her nightstand. She opened the top drawer and retrieved a large gift-wrapped box, then handed it to me. She sat cross-legged on the bed with the sweetest of smiles on her face and rested her head on my shoulder. With wide eyes, I stared at the wrapping paper. Tiny red Camaros were glued to white paper—the same paper Amber had wrapped a gift for me all those years ago.

"Destiny, you—you remembered this?" I could barely get the words out. I loved when she remembered her life as Amber, and I think she knew it. It reaffirmed that connection to our past.

"Just open the damn present, Julian. Jeez, get on with it." She gave me a crooked smile and giggled.

"Hold on." I got up from the bed, wandered to our closet and retrieved a box from the top shelf. I asked her to open it and couldn't help but watch her expression as she lifted the cover.

"You saved this paper?"

I'd kept a keepsake box of Amber's life, where I'd stored the wrapping paper she'd made for me. "Of course, and I'm going to put this one in here as well."

I kissed her forehead and carefully peeled the tape away from the paper, trying my damnedest not to rip it. Removing the paper, I folded it neatly and placed it into the keepsake box. After returning the box to the closet, I resumed my seat on the bed and finished opening Destiny's gift. I lifted a cover from the box to reveal a bunch of wadded up tissue paper. Her excitement was palpable, like a child waiting for Christmas morning. I reached in and fished through the paper until I felt a small round tube. I snagged it between my fingers and unrolled it from the tissue paper. My hand froze as my eyes practically fell out of their sockets again.

"Holy Crap, Destiny! You remembered. Shit, you remembered! I love you so much." Inside the box was a roll of multi-colored Life Savers.

"Of course I remembered our first date. This is because you saved me in my past life and now you saved me again in this life, Julian. I will love you until the end of time. Amber will always live on through me for the rest of our lives, so if you can withstand a marriage to the both of us, we're here to love you forever."

"Yes!" I exclaimed. "I'll always love you forever, my dear sweet…" She watched, bemused as I scrunched my face, testing the name over in my head before saying it out loud, "Destamber," I finished with a smirk.

She swiftly lurched into me, knocking us off balance. I fell to my back on the bed, and her mouth was on mine, devouring me with desperation. Her fingers twisted in my hair, pulling me to her. I loved when she took charge.

She sat up, straddling me. "I love that, Jules. You are such a kind, caring, and beautiful man, and you are forever my sweet husband." She placed her hand over her heart. "I love you to the stars and back, with all *my* heart and Amber's soul."

If it were possible, I loved her more now than I ever had and to know I would be sharing the rest of my life with her made me the happiest man in the world. A life I finally had. "To the stars and back, Dest."

I shifted my body to gaze deep into her eyes.

"What's wrong?" she asked confused by my incredulous stare.

"Something has really confounded me."

"What's that?"

"Well, how did Amber know on the day of her death that she would be coming back?"

Destiny traced her finger across my lips and gazed deep into my eyes. "Because I knew you still needed me."

I sucked in a deep, cleansing breath. "Yes, I did."

"I love you, Julian Cahill."

"I love you too, Destiny Cahill. My second chance girl."

I nuzzled her against me, and together, we took a deep, gratifying breath and released it, savoring the moment.

MOMENTS LATER, Destiny bolted upright, "Holy Crap, Julian!"

"What's wrong?"

"It's little Timmy." She sounded all breathy.

"What? You're scaring me, Dest. What about him?"

"Do you remember at the birthday party when he kept climbing into my mom's lap? We all laughed it off. And how he kept saying he was running really fast?"

"Yeah, so…"

"Julian, could Timmy be my reincarnated brother?"

THE END

ABOUT THE AUTHOR

Marcia Whitaker lives in Utah with her husband. They have two grown boys.

Originally from upstate New York, she worked as an engineer in the TV industry for 31 years.

In July-2014, she put pen to paper and started working on "A Second Chance." It had always been a dream of hers to write a book. "I finally did it!" she says.

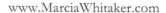

www.MarciaWhitaker.com

Made in the USA
Lexington, KY
30 October 2019